The Thirteen Hallows

THE
Thirteen Hallows

Michael Scott AND
Colette Freedman

A TOM DOHERTY ASSOCIATES BOOK

New York

THE THIRTEEN HALLOWS

A Tor Book
Published by Tom Doherty Associates, LLC
175 Fifth Avenue
New York, NY 10010

www.tor-forge.com

Tor® is a registered trademark of Tom Doherty Associates, LLC.

Library of Congress Cataloging-in-Publication Data

Scott, Michael, 1959–
    The thirteen hallows / Michael Scott and Colette Freedman.—1st ed.
        p. cm.
    "A Tom Doherty Associates book."
    ISBN 978-0-7653-2852-6
  I. Freedman, Colette.   II. Title.
    PR6069.C5953T47 2011
    823'.914—dc22

                                                        2011021618

First Edition: December 2011

0 9 8 7 6 5 4 3 2 1

This is for Sharon & Robert
and
Barry

ACKNOWLEDGMENTS

Colette would like to thank:
 Deb Gallagher for building the foundation.
 Marilee Zdenek for believing.
 Jack Stehlin for encouraging.
 Dippy, Hannah Hope, Moses, David, Zack, and Dylan for their constant support.

Michael and Colette would like to thank:
 Tom Doherty, Bob Gleason, and Whitney Ross at Tor for their support and encouragement.
 Steve Troha at Folio Literary Management for his enthusiasm.
 Jill and Fred . . . for everything.
 Barry Krost and Sarah Baczewski for everything else.
 And, of course, Claudette Sutherland.

Hallows: from the Old English *halga,* meaning "holy" and *hālgian,* meaning "to make holy."

The Thirteen Hallows

*A*fter the battle, all that remained were their memories.

They remembered the world as it was: a new world, a raw world, their world. Where they had been the masters of all creatures. Where the humankind were mere cattle: to be herded, slaughtered, and eaten.

They remembered the taste of the humankind . . . and it was sweet. So sweet.

But their memories were tainted with bitterness: memories of a boy who was not a boy, who had cast them out. Cast them down. Imprisoned them in the Otherworld.

So the demons formulated a plan. It was centuries in preparation, and another century had passed while they waited for the most suitable candidate to carry it out. They were patient, for they did not measure time in human spans and the prize was great indeed. The plan was simple: to bring the Hallows together, to unlock the gate between the worlds.

All they needed was the right agent: a human with a desire for absolute knowledge and prepared to do anything to achieve that end.

And they waited.

SUNDAY, OCTOBER 25

1

A woman died.

She was sixty-six years old, in good health, active, a non-smoker who rarely drank. She had simply gone to sleep and never woken up. Her family and friends mourned, a funeral was arranged, flowers were ordered, a service organized.

Viola Jillian was thrilled.

She had never met the woman, never even known of her existence until she had heard of her death. But she was glad she'd died. Viola was vaguely embarrassed by the emotion but selfish enough not to be *too* embarrassed. After all, the woman's death presented her with an amazing opportunity. And opportunity, as she kept reminding herself, didn't come calling too often, and when it did, you had to grasp it with both hands. This was her opportunity. The buxom brunette with the Elizabeth Taylor eyes had spent the last few weeks in the ensemble cast of Drury Lane's reprisal of *Oliver!* The woman who had died was the lead's mother, and now the producers had informed Viola that she was going to play Nancy the following evening.

The young woman had immediately gone to sympathize with the distraught Nancy, but only after she had shifted her publicist-almost-boyfriend into high gear to ensure that there would be sufficient press in the audience for her debut. This was her chance, and she was determined to make the most of it.

Viola Jillian had always wanted to be a star.

Usually on Sundays, Viola would grab a few drinks with some of the other girls in the cast, but she wanted to be well rested for her proper West End star turn. Viola knew her theater history: Every great star was discovered by accident. And she knew, deep in her selfish heart, that she was a great star. She fantasized that she would be discovered. She had the talent, the looks, and the drive. And she wanted to move beyond the stage and start acting in films. She had already played small parts in the British soap operas *EastEnders* and *Coronation Street*, but she was tired of always playing second fiddle, or even fifth or sixth fiddle, and was afraid that she was becoming typecast. She was nearly twenty-four; she didn't have much time left. Let the others drink all night in the Ku Bar, she was heading home to bed.

It was a spectacular fall night, cloudless and balmy, when she left the bar early, and she decided she'd walk to her nearby Soho flat.

She'd not gone more than two hundred yards when Viola felt the skin on the back of her neck tingle. She'd been a dancer all her life, and every dancer had experienced the same sensation, usually when someone in the audience was focusing on them.

Viola knew that someone was watching her.

At eleven thirty P.M., the London streets were filled with Sunday night carousers. Viola pulled her bag closer to her chest and picked up her pace, walking briskly down Shaftesbury Avenue. There had been a series of violent muggings lately, and she did not plan to fall victim to one of them. Her flat was less than ten minutes away. She kept glancing behind at every corner, but she could see no one, although the tingle at the back of her neck remained. Viola hurried up the less crowded Dean Street and was half running by the time she reached the almost empty Carlisle Place.

It was only when she reached the safety of her building and had closed the door behind her that Viola relaxed. She made a mental note to talk to her shrink about her growing anxiety attacks. For an actress she led a fairly vanilla life, and the chance of someone like her ever getting hurt was practically nil. She laughed at her ridiculous fear as she hummed one of Nancy's signature songs. Standing in the hallway, she checked through the day's mail, throwing away a few overdue bills and keeping a coupon for Anthropologie, which had recently opened on Regent Street. Her mind shifted to far more practical matters as she wondered if she could convince the wardrobe mistress to alter Nancy's red dress in order to show a bit of extra cleavage and accentuate her two best features.

It was when she started up the stairs that she heard the muffled cry in 1C. Mrs. Clay's flat.

Not usually one to get involved in other people's business, especially when the other person was a septuagenarian who constantly complained that Viola made too much noise, she began to climb the stairs. Then there was the faint tinkle of breaking glass. Viola stopped, then turned back down the stairs: Something was wrong.

Standing outside the old woman's door, she pressed her face against the cool wood, closing her eyes and listening. But the only sound she could make out from within was a faint rasping, like the sound of labored breathing.

She knocked quietly, conscious that she did not want to wake the other neighbors. When there was no response, she pressed her finger to the lighted bell. Tchaikovsky's 1812 Overture blared on the other side of the door. For a moment she thought it might be the bell she was hearing before she realized it was probably the classical radio station, the only station Mrs. Clay listened to—usually very early in the morning.

Still no response.

She pressed the bell again and realized that the music sounded unnaturally loud. She'd never heard any sounds from the old woman's flat this late in the evening. Viola suddenly wondered if Mrs. Clay had suffered a heart attack. She looked the picture of health and was extremely spry for her age. "Good country air," she had once told Viola as she chastised her for smoking, a habit she'd picked up at drama school. "When I was a girl, I lived in the country. That kind of air nourishes you for life."

Viola rang the bell again, pressing hard, the tip of her finger white against the plastic button. Perhaps Mrs. Clay could not hear the chimes over the now obnoxiously loud music. When she got no response, Viola fished into her hobo bag and pulled out her key ring. The old woman had given her a key to the apartment "in case of an emergency" months ago.

Sorting through the bundle of keys, she finally found the right one, then shoved it into the lock and pushed open the door. The smells hit her as soon as she stepped into the flat: a sharp metallic odor, harsh and unpleasant, mingling with the stench of feces. Viola recoiled, bile rising, pressing her hand to her mouth as she reached for the light switch. She flicked it up, but nothing happened. Leaving the door open to shed light into the tiny hallway, she walked forward . . . and realized that the carpet beneath her feet was squelching, sodden and sticky with a liquid that was too viscous to be water. What was she standing in? She decided she didn't want to know; whatever it was, it would wash off. She hoped.

"Mrs. Clay . . . Mrs. Clay?" she said, shouting to be heard over the overture. "Beatrice? It's Viola Jillian. Is everything all right?"

There was no reply.

The old woman had probably gone and had a heart attack or something, and now Viola was going to have to go and get an ambulance and probably spend all night in the hospital. She'd look like shit in the morning.

Viola pushed open the door into the sitting room. And stopped. The stench was stronger here, acrid urine stinging her eyes. By the reflected light, she could see that the room had been destroyed. The beautiful music continued to play, a mocking counterpoint to the desecration around it. Every item of furniture lay overturned, the arms of the fireside chairs had been snapped off, the back of the rose floral sofa was broken in two, stuffing hanging in long ribbons from the slashed cushions, drawers pulled from the cabinet, the contents emptied, pictures torn from the walls, frames warped as if they had been twisted. An antique Victorian mirror lay on the floor, radiating spider cracks from a deep indentation in the middle of the glass as if it had been trodden on. Mrs. Clay's extensive collection of glass figurines were now ground into the carpet.

A burglary.

Viola breathed deeply, trying to remain calm. The flat had been burgled. But where was Mrs. Clay? Picking her way through the devastation, glass crunching underfoot, she prayed that the old woman hadn't been here when it happened; yet she knew instinctively that she had. Beatrice Clay rarely left her apartment at night. "Too dangerous," she'd said.

Books scraped as she pushed against the bedroom door, opening it wide enough to slap at the light switch, but again, nothing happened. In the faint glow of the light from the hall, she could see that this room had also been torn apart and that the bed was piled high with dark clothes and blankets.

"Beatrice? It's me, Viola."

The bundle of clothes on the bed shifted and moved, and she heard shallow breathing. Viola darted across the room and saw the top of the old woman's head. Clutching the first blanket, she yanked it back, and it came away in her hand, warm and wet and dripping. The woman in the bed convulsed. The bastards had probably tied her up. Viola was reaching for another blanket when the bedroom door creaked and swung inward, throwing light onto the bed.

Beatrice Clay's throat had been cut, but not before her body had been terribly mutilated. But despite her appalling injuries, she was still alive, mouth and eyes wide in soundless agony, breathing a harsh rattle.

The young woman's scream caught at the back of her throat.

A shadow fell across the bed.

Sick with terror, Viola turned to face the shape that filled the doorway. Light ran off damp naked flesh. She could see that it was a tall, muscular man, but with the light coming from behind him, his features were in shadow. He lifted his left arm, and the light reflected liquid running down the length of the spear he clutched. The man stepped into the room, and she could smell his odor now: the rich meaty muskiness of sweat and copper blood.

"Please . . . ," she whispered.

Black light trembled on the blade of the weapon. "Behold the Spear of the Dolorous Blow." Then, obscenely, he began to conduct the nerve-wracking 1812 Overture with the deadly weapon, and as the overture reached its climactic conclusion, his shoulder shifted and rolled and the light darted toward her.

There was no pain.

Viola felt a sudden coldness beneath her breast, then the warmth that flowed outward to embrace her. Liquid trickled across her stomach. She tried to speak, but she couldn't find the breath to shape the words. She was aware of light in the room now, cold blue and green flames sparking, writhing along the leaf-shaped blade of the spear.

She had been stabbed—dear Jesus, she had been stabbed.

The lines of fire coiling around the shaft of the spear rose to illuminate the flesh of the hand holding the weapon. As Viola fell to her knees, both hands pressed against the gaping wound in her chest, she noticed that the man was disturbingly handsome and tall.

So tall.

Tall, dark, and handsome.

Viola tried to concentrate, wondering if her eyes were playing tricks on her or if the newborn pain was clouding her judgment.

The spear rose, serpents of cold fire splashing onto the head of her attacker, illuminating his face. When she saw his eyes, the woman realized she would not be playing Nancy in tomorrow's performance.

Viola Jillian would never be a star.

MONDAY, OCTOBER 26

2

nother one," Judith Walker said to her cat, Franklin, as she opened a can of tuna. Despite being rescued from behind a garbage can, her tabby was a food critic and snubbed anything other than canned fish. Judith tried to find some solace from her beloved feline, but he was too busy eating.

Another death, and this was the one she had been dreading.

Judith had met Bea Clay seventy years earlier when they were wee little children, and the pair had remained steadfast friends throughout the decades.

Judith had taken the train down to London just last month, where they had met for tea before traipsing around the National Gallery like a couple of giggling teenagers. Theirs was a relationship closer than sisters. They had remained close through the marriages and divorces, children and grandchildren, and indignities of approaching old age. Letters had evolved into e-mails, and they'd kept up a regular correspondence that had brought them closer together than if they had lived next door.

Judith had first met Bea in Wales when they were both children, evacuees together during World War II, and they had formed an instant friendship. Whenever Judith thought of her friend, she remembered a beautiful young girl with jet black eyes and matching hair so thick, it would sparkle and crackle with electricity every time she combed it.

Poor Bea. There had always been so much pain, so much loss, in her life. She had buried three husbands and had outlived her only child. She had a granddaughter living in New York City whom she never saw, and she was lonely.

At seventy-four, most people were lonely.

Bea seemed to always draw the short straw. She had lived through the hungry years and the recession, and then, when property values had spiraled and she'd finally had a chance to make some real money, she'd waited too long to sell her home, gambling that prices would continue to rise. When the next recession had hit hard and prices had tumbled, she'd been forced to move into a tiny flat in a building occupied primarily by students and artists several decades her junior. In her last e-mail, she had been talking about possibly leaving London, cashing in her meager savings and seeing out her days in a nursing home up in the Cotswolds.

Judith had joked that perhaps she would join her. It was getting harder and harder for her to navigate around her cottage with her arthritic hip, and nursing homes were usually on one level. In one of their recent e-mails, they had joked that they would end up being the terrible twosome of the home, causing havoc with their equally stubborn sensibilities. And side by side, they would live out the rest of their days in the peaceful beauty of the north: living an uncomplicated life of reading, playing cards, and basking in a deliciously simplistic tranquillity.

The old woman sat down, suddenly overcome by emotion. "Too late now," Judith Walker lamented to Franklin, who had wandered in from the kitchen and leapt up to stretch out on the windowsill, ignoring her. She smiled grimly: When she died, she would like to come back as a cat and merely sleep and eat all day. Almost reluctantly, Judith picked up the paper and reread the story in *The Guardian*. The bloody death of an old woman, and it rated half a paragraph on the third page.

Pensioner and Good Samaritan Slain

Police in London are investigating the brutal slaying of Beatrice Clay (74) and the neighbor, Viola Jillian (23), who went to her assistance. Police investigators believe that Mrs. Clay, a widow, disturbed late night burglars in her first-floor apartment, who tied her to the bed and gagged her with a pillowcase. Mrs. Clay died of asphyxiation. Police suspect that Ms. Jillian, who lived in the apartment upstairs, heard a noise and came to investigate. In a struggle with one of the burglars, Ms. Jillian was fatally stabbed.

Judith pulled off her glasses and dropped them onto the newspaper. She squeezed the bridge of her nose. What did the report *not* say? What had been intentionally suppressed?

From inside her knitting bag she pulled out a newly sharpened pair of scissors and carefully cut out the story. Later she would add it to the others in the scrapbook. The obituary list was growing.

Bea Clay was the fifth death. The fourth in the last two months. Or at least the fifth that she knew about. If the murder of an elderly woman in London rated less than eight lines, then the death— accidental or otherwise—of a pensioner would probably pass unnoticed by most people.

And Judith had known all of the victims.

Millie had been the first. Ten years ago, Mildred Bailey had died in her home. The invalid, who lived with her nephew in a farmhouse in Wales, was the victim of a terrible accident.

Later, Judith would come to realize that these were no accidents.

Millie had never left Wales. Her parents were killed in the Blitz and she'd been adopted by the Welsh couple who cared for her. Judith remembered Millie, the oldest of the group of children, as extremely practical. At eight years old, she'd taken it on herself to look out for the ragtag group of evacuees, especially the younger children who were no more than four and a half at the time of Operation Pied Piper, when three and a half million children were evacuated to the country in three days. In the early years of World War II, it was believed that German aircraft would bomb all the major cities, and the only way to keep the next generation alive was to evacuate them to the countryside. Four hundred were evacuated to Pwllheli in Wales in the far west of the country, and a small group of thirteen, including Judith, ended up in the mountainous county of Madoc. Twelve of those eventually returned to their homes, but Millie remained. The obituary read that Mildred had somehow fallen out of her wheelchair, tumbled down a flight of stairs, and impaled herself on the steel banister.

Judith had written it off as a horrible event.

Unfortunate. Unexpected. Untimely.

Until the next death.

Judith had never liked Thomas Sexton. Tommy had been a bully as a child. A fat boy with curly red hair and brown piggy eyes, he used to torment the younger children, teasing them incessantly. Tommy had grown up to become an even bigger bully, earning his living as a debt collector in his youth and, after retirement, making a living as a collections agent and moneylender. Two months ago, he had been slain in Brixton in what the police called a gangland killing. The brutality of his murder had excited some press interest: His chest had been opened from throat to crotch, and his heart and lungs had been removed. MODERN RIPPER STALKS LONDON, the headlines read.

Judith hadn't been surprised by Sexton's murder. She had always known that Tommy was going to come to a bad end. She remembered one night when he had been caught shining his flashlight up into the sky as the enemy bombers flew over, trying to attract their attention. One of the grown-ups had caught him and beaten him silly. Later, he boasted to the others that the punishment was worth it; he'd been hoping they would bomb the town because he wanted to see a dead body.

When she had learned of Georgina Rifkin's death in Ipswich three weeks ago, Judith had felt the first icy trickle of fear. The death of two people who knew the secret was a coincidence. The death of three was something more. Officially, Georgie, a retired schoolteacher, had fallen into the path of the National Express. Later, Judith had discovered the online rumor that the old woman had been tied spread-eagled to the train tracks.

Only four days ago, Nina Byrne had died in Edinburgh. The press reported that the retired librarian had accidentally tipped a pan of boiling oil over herself as she cooked in the kitchen of her apartment. Judith knew that Nina never cooked.

And now Bea.

How many more were going to be savagely killed?

Judith Walker knew that they were being systematically slaughtered, and she wondered when it would be her turn.

Judith stood, lifted a sun-faded picture off the mantelpiece, and carried it to the window. Tilting it to the light, she looked at three irregular rows of thirteen smiling faces. It could have been a classroom photo, with the elder children standing in the back and the younger ones kneeling and sitting in the front. The black-and-white photograph had long faded to sepia, and it was difficult to make out any detail in the faces. Mildred, Georgina, and Nina were all standing in the back, asserting their eight-year-old independence with their arms easily slung over one another.

A smirking Tommy was kneeling to Bea's left. Judith was sitting cross-legged beside her; the two girls were wearing identical floral dresses, with their black hair in matching ribboned headbands, hanging in loose ringlets around their shoulders. The small dark girls looked alike enough to be taken for sisters.

Five of those children were now dead.

Walking slowly, leaning heavily on the cane she'd sworn she'd never use, she moved around the small terraced cottage, double-checking that all the windows were locked and the doors were bolted. She wasn't sure how effective a barrier they would prove when *they* came for her, but perhaps it would delay them long enough for her to swallow the prescription tablets she carried with her.

She could go to the police, but who was going to believe the ramblings of a mad old woman who lived alone and was famous for talking to her cat? What was she going to tell them, that five of the children with whom she had been evacuated during the war had been killed and that she was certain she would be one of the next victims?

"Tell us why someone would want to kill you, Mrs. Walker?"

"Because I am one of the Keepers of the Thirteen Hallows of Britain."

Judith paused at the bottom of the stairs, smiling at the thought. It sounded ridiculous even to her. Seventy years ago, she had been equally skeptical.

She climbed slowly, making sure she had a solid grip on the banister, planting the cane firmly before moving onto the next step. She had broken her right hip two years ago in a bad fall.

Seventy years ago; a glorious wartime autumn. Thirteen children had been billeted in the village in the shadow of the Welsh mountains, and in the months that followed they had become a makeshift family. For most of them it was the first time they had ever been away from home, the first time they had been on a farm.

It had been a grand adventure.

When the old man with the long white beard had come to the farm in the summer of 1940, he had been just another curiosity, until he had started telling them his wild and wonderful tales of magic and folklore.

Judith turned the key in the spare bedroom and pushed open the door. Dust motes spiraled in the late afternoon sunshine, and she sneezed uncontrollably in the dry, stale air.

For months the old man had teased them with secrets and fragments of tales, hinting, always hinting, that the children were special and that it was no accident that they, specifically, had come to this place. "Summoned" was the word he'd used.

Judith opened the closet, wrinkling her nose at the pungent smell of mothballs.

For weeks he had called them special, his young knights, his Keepers. But as the summer closed and autumn approached, a new urgency had entered the old man's stories. He began speaking to them individually, telling them special stories, disturbing, frightening stories that were strangely familiar, as if they had always been present in their subconscious and he were merely unlocking them. She still thought about him this time every year when October 31 approached, the ancient Celtic festival of Samhain: All Hallows' Eve.

Judith shivered. She could still remember the story the man had told her. It had created echoes and stirred resonances that had never been stilled. For the last seventy years, her dreams were peppered with fragments of vivid images and startling nightmares that she had used to forge a successful career as a children's writer. Putting the fantastic images down on paper seemed to rob them of a little of their daunting power and, in turn, gave her a little power over them.

Judith Walker reached into the closet and pulled out a Military Bridge overcoat that had once belonged to her brother and had gone out of fashion in the sixties. After hanging the gray coat on the back of the door, she lifted a paper-wrapped bundle from one of the enormous pockets and carried it to the bed, where she slowly, and with great reluctance, unwrapped the parcel.

It took a great deal of imagination to realize that the chunk of red-rusted metal nestled in the yellowed newspaper was the hilt and portion of the blade of a sword. But she had never doubted it. When the old tramp had first pressed it into her hands, he had whispered its true name into her ear. She could still feel his breath, spicy and rancid against her small face. All she had to do was call the sword by its true name to release its power. She hadn't spoken its name in years. . . .

"Dyrnwyn."

Judith Walker looked at the lump of metal in her hands. She repeated the name: "Dyrnwyn, Sword of Rhydderch."

Once, it would have come trembling to life, cold green flames shooting from its hilt, forming the remainder of the Broken Sword.

"Dyrnwyn," Judith called a third time.

Nothing happened. Perhaps there was no magic left in the Hallow anymore. Maybe nothing had ever happened and it had been only in her imagination. The eager dreams of a prepubescent girl mingled with the fading memories of an old woman. She dropped the rusted metal onto the bed and brushed flakes of rust from her lined flesh. The rust had stained her skin the color of blood.

Millie, Tommy, Georgie, Nina, and Bea had also possessed one of the thirteen ancient Hallows. Judith was convinced that they had been tortured and brutally slaughtered for those artifacts. And what about the others she'd lost touch with? How many of them still survived?

Seventy years ago, the old man's last words to each child had been a distinct warning: "Never bring the Hallows together."

No one had ever thought to ask him why.

3

It was so much more than just sex.

They had practiced the ancient ritual until it was perfect. Their damp, naked bodies teasing and arousing each other by any means possible until they would each tremble on the brink of orgasm.

And then stop.

She enjoyed intense pain, while he thrived on hedonistic pleasure, and each knew the exact buttons to push to propel the other to the edge of ecstasy. Then the lithe, athletic young woman, known as Vyvienne, would lie with her toned arms and long legs spread-eagled atop an ancient stone altar stolen from a desecrated church. The man, known as Ahriman, would enter her, male and female becoming one, power flowing together, unstoppable.

They enacted the ancient ritual, generating the most powerful of the magical elements to aid them in their quest, to seek out and find the location of the spirits of the Keepers. And when they discovered them, they went forth to do battle with them.

And destroy them.

Decades ago, it would have been inconceivable to go up against the Keepers of the Thirteen Hallows, but times had radically changed. Now the Keepers were nothing more than tired old senior citizens, untrained and unskilled, most of them blissfully unaware of the treasures they possessed. Although it took much of the sport from the hunt, there was still the kill to be relished. But now with All Hallows' Eve fast approaching, they had recently hired others to help them complete the rest of the butchery.

Nine Hallowed Keepers were dead. Four to go.

Vyvienne watched the man carefully, gauging the tension of his well-defined muscles and the pulsating rhythm of his shallow breathing. Her powerful legs locked around his taut buttocks, keeping him deep inside her but initiating no move that would bring on his orgasm.

That would be disastrous.

In that instant, the moment of power would escape. It would then take them three days of bodily purification—no red meat, no alcohol, no sex—to reach this critical point again.

"The chessboard." She whispered the words into his open mouth.

He swallowed her words. "The chessboard," he repeated, sweat curling down his stubbled cheeks, dripping onto his hairless chest.

They were close now, so close.

Vyvienne closed her eyes and concentrated, every sense heightened, alerted to the possible smells and sounds that would lead them to their treasure. The sensations in her groin were almost too much to bear as she repeated the next object of their quest—"The Chessboard of Gwenddolau"—forcing him to concentrate, to visualize the next Hallowed object.

Ahriman squeezed his dark eyes tightly shut, moisture gathering in the corners like tears, which rolled down his face and splashed onto her belly and heavy breasts. She felt their liquid touch and gasped, and the sudden involuntary ripple of stomach muscles brought him to a shocking, shuddering climax. He cried aloud, passion and anguish inextricably entwined.

Vyvienne stroked his hair. "I'm sorry, I'm so sorry."

When he raised his head, his smile was savage . . . and triumphant. "No need. I saw it. I saw the crystal pieces, the gold-and-silver board. I know exactly where they are."

Vyvienne then drew him deep into her body, hands and muscles locking him in place, in order to satisfy her own desire. She whispered wickedly into his ear, "Then let us do this for pleasure."

TUESDAY, OCTOBER 27

4

Sarah Miller had never done anything extraordinary in her life. At twenty-two, Sarah still had dreams of greatness. They had been instilled in her by her father despite the fact that her overbearing mother had done everything in her power to make sure that those dreams would never reach fruition. The oldest of three children, Sarah had been ushered into a job the day she finished her A levels. "To support your family," Ruth Miller had snarled, guilting her eldest child into an unsatisfying job in the same London bank where her father had worked for thirty years. Rather than pursuing her dream of going to university, she had taken the job and put on the regulation blue blazer and khaki skirt every day for the last four years. It was a dead-end job without prospects, and she realized she would probably be stuck there for the rest of her life. Or laid off in the next round of job cuts. Her father had spent his entire life in the bank as a midlevel clerk. Forced out by compulsory early retirement and unable to spend any length of time in the house with his overbearing wife, he'd taken to gardening. Six weeks after he'd left the job, he was found dead in her mother's prized flower bed. Heart attack, the coroner's report said. Sarah thought her mother was more upset by the flowers he'd destroyed when he'd fallen into them than by her husband's death.

Ruth Miller took full advantage by playing the "poor widow" card. She used every opportunity to remind those around her that she had three children to feed and a mortgage to cover. After exhausting the empathy of neighbors and the sympathy of friends, she began to drink heavily and took in a string of older lovers, all of whom were verbally abusive to Sarah and her little brothers. Eventually, even the lovers left her and Ruth turned her venom on her children. She had never amounted to anything, and she was determined that neither would they. She brought up the boys to be selfish, mistrustful, and fearful. Only Sarah—eight years older than her brothers—escaped the worst of her mother's malign influence. And sometimes, late at night, she wondered if she would ever escape this house, this life. . . .

NICK JACOBS started when his cell phone rang.

"She is coming." The deep, authoritative voice said the three words and then hung up. Jacobs, aka Skinner, looked at the half-eaten scone and the barely touched cup of coffee and knew he wasn't going to get to finish them. Shoving the scone in the pocket of his scuffed leather jacket, he shifted in the metal chair and turned to look at the entrance of the British Library directly across the courtyard. He was wondering how his employer knew so much—he must have a contact inside the library—when the glass doors slid open and a gray-haired older woman appeared, moving slowly and carefully, her cane assisting each painful step. Pushing mirrored Ray-Ban Aviators up onto his recently shaven head, Skinner nudged his companion with his foot.

The hollow-eyed teenager sitting across the table glanced up quickly, then looked down at the pages spread out before him. He pulled out a crisp, high-resolution photograph and spun it toward Skinner. "Looks like her."

"It's her, you idiot," Skinner snapped. He hated working with junkies; you couldn't depend on them, and they didn't give a shit.

"I suppose you're right," mumbled Lawrence McFeely, pushing his scratched Ray-Bans up on his nose. He jerked his chin in the direction of the woman, who was now heading down Ossulston Street. "The report said she'd broken her right hip," McFeely added. "She's favoring that leg."

Skinner rolled his eyes. "Listen to you. You've been watching too much fucking *CSI*." He took a deep breath and felt for the blade in his pocket. "Let's do it, then. Get the car."

McFeely came slowly to his feet, turned, and ambled away. Skinner ground his teeth at his lack of urgency and swore he was going to give the bastard a good kicking when this job was done. He fell into step behind the old woman, matching his pace to hers. She was moving slowly across the red-and-white-tiled square in the front of the modern library building, balancing a heavy Tesco canvas bag on her shoulder, an array of papers peeking through the top. The skinhead glanced back, looking at the glass-and-redbrick building, and wondered what she had been doing in there. The last library he'd stood in had been the school library, when he was ten, when his teacher Mrs. Geisz helped him research a project about stalactites and stalagmites. Much bloody good it had done him; he still didn't know which was which. He remembered her saying that "one held on tight" and the other "might reach the ceiling."

Mrs. Geisz was the first and only adult who had ever been kind to him. Bounced around among several foster homes, Skinner was a text-book case of someone who, following a lifetime of neglect, desperately craved love and attention. At twenty-six, he had only one thing he could boast about: a solid six-pack stomach and freakishly strong muscles, courtesy of working nights at a brewery in Birmingham, where he earned ten quid an hour. To supplement his meager income, he often took on odd jobs here and there. And he wasn't fussy about the nature of the job. That was how his current employer had found him. Skinner had jumped at the chance of earning easy cash with no questions asked. The fact that he got to hurt some people in the process was an added bonus.

Skinner watched as McFeely's tan Volvo cruised by him. It picked up speed as it moved past the old woman and pulled into the nearest available space, a hundred yards ahead of her.

Perfect. Skinner grinned, showing uneven teeth. Just perfect. This was going to be the easiest thousand pounds he'd ever earned.

JUDITH WALKER shifted the heavy bag onto her left shoulder, trying to ease some of the pressure off her sore hip. She hadn't been conscious of time slipping by as she'd sat in the hushed stillness of the library, and now her hip ached abominably and the muscles in her shoulders had locked into a solid bar of pain. And she still had an hour-and-a-half train ride ahead of her.

Researching source material on the Hallows of Britain was like chasing rainbows. An impossible feat. She'd spent a lifetime researching the ancient objects in libraries across England, Scotland, and Wales. She had mountains of notes, scraps of legends and folktales, but no credible evidence. Lately, she'd begun to extend her research online, but now, entering the word *Hallows* in search engines brought up something like four million hits, most of them, as far as she could see, referencing Harry Potter. She found the odd page that listed the Thirteen Hallows; but there was very little about their individual origins.

However, this morning's research had not been a complete waste of time. Later, over a nice cup of tea and some of the raisin scones she had picked up at the market, she would add her latest findings to the hundreds of jigsaw pieces she had collected over the years. Maybe when she looked over the material again, she would find some hint to the true nature of the artifacts and put the puzzle together.

Yet somehow she doubted it.

The Hallows had remained hidden down through the centuries. The very fact that there was so little solid information about them made her suspect that their existence had been expunged from the history books. But how . . . and why?

Now five of the Hallowed Keepers were dead. Five that she knew about. That could not be a coincidence.

But the real question, of course, was what had happened to the artifacts they guarded. She knew that Beatrice had the Pan and the Platter of Rhygenydd. While Judith had carefully hidden her sword over the decades, Bea had displayed her Hallow proudly among the antiques in her sitting room. "Who in their right mind would know its true meaning?" Bea had chuckled. "People only see what they want to see. Tchotchkes collected by a batty old broad."

But someone had known. And they had killed her for them.

A spasm of pain made her stop suddenly. She felt as if there were ground glass in her hip. Leaning against a lamppost outside the Levita House apartment complex, Judith turned to look back down the street, suddenly deciding that she would take a taxi to the train. From bitter experience, she knew that if she pushed on, she'd spend the rest of the day and most of the night in agony with her hip.

Naturally, there wasn't a taxi in sight.

Debating whether to turn back and head down into Euston Road, she was abruptly aware of the shaven-headed man in the dirty jeans bearing down on her. His eyes were hidden behind mirrored sunglasses, but she could tell by his fixed expression that he was coming for her.

The old woman was swinging the bag even before the youth reached for her. It caught him on the side of the head, throwing him off balance and driving him to his knees, sending his sunglasses spinning into the gutter.

Judith screamed, her voice high and raw. And in typical fashion, no one listened. A dozen heads turned in her direction, but no one made any attempt to come to the old woman's aid. Drivers passed, rubbernecking yet not stopping. She turned to run, but there was another youth behind her, blocking her path, his long, greasy blond hair framing a gaunt, hollow-eyed face. He was holding open a car door.

Junkie, she realized as she clutched her bag.

Her bag.

They just wanted to snatch her bag. Ordinarily she would have relinquished its contents; however, its contents were anything but ordinary. She turned back as the shaven-headed youth climbed to his feet, his face fixed in a rigid mask of hate.

She was trapped.

SKINNER WAS humiliated. He was just knocked down by a woman half his weight and three times his age. Plus he'd torn the knee of his favorite Levi's, skinned his hands, and broken his new sunglasses. The bitch would pay. His hand dipped into his pocket and pulled out a flat metal bar. His wrist moved sharply back and forth and the butterfly knife clicked open, the blade appearing from between the handles.

"Stupid fucking mistake," he hissed as he pointed the knife toward her throat, the cold blade jabbing at her leathery skin. The woman hobbled backward, toward the car door.

"Get in," Skinner hissed.

Judith struck out at him again. She knew if she got into the car, she was dead. She opened her mouth to scream again, but the bald youth punched her in the pit of her stomach, doubling her over. The junkie giggled behind her, the sound high-pitched and almost childlike.

A hand wrapped tightly in her hair, close to her scalp, hauling her upright. The pain was shocking. "Get in the car!"

"Hey—stop that! What do you think you're doing?"

Through sparkling tears, Judith caught a glimpse of a redheaded young woman moving toward them. She tried to call out to her, to warn her about the knife, but she was having difficulty drawing breath.

Skinner spun around, bringing up the knife. "Why don't you mind your own f—"

Without breaking stride, the young woman lashed out with the heel of her sensible shoe, catching the skinhead just below the knee-cap. There was a distinct popping sound and Skinner crashed to the ground onto his injured knee, his cry high-pitched and feminine. Judith spun around and caught the edge of the car door, slamming it shut. It closed on the junkie's fingers, tearing skin and snapping bones. His mouth opened and closed, but no sound came out.

Judith scooped up her fallen bag and hobbled toward the young woman, who reached for her hand and pulled her away without a word. They had taken a dozen steps before the junkie started screaming incoherently. Lying on the ground, whimpering in pain, cradling his injured knee, Skinner pulled out his cell phone and hit a speed dial. His employer was not going to be pleased, and that frightened the skinhead even more than his injured leg.

5

"N o police," Judith Walker said firmly as they rounded the corner, distancing themselves from the assailants. Her fingers tightened on the young woman's arm, squeezing painfully. "Please, no police."

"But . . ."

Taking a deep breath, attempting to calm her thundering heart, Judith continued evenly, "It was just a bag snatch . . . or a mugging."

"*Just* a mugging!"

"I'm Judith Walker," the woman said suddenly, stopping and extending her hand, which forced the young woman to turn back, breaking her train of thought. "What's your name?"

The young woman extended her hand. The moment it was enveloped in the older woman's leathery grasp, she became disoriented, a surge of confusing thoughts and odd emotions washing over her. "I . . . I'm Sarah Miller."

"It is very nice to meet you, Sarah Miller. And thanks to you, there's no harm done," Judith continued forcefully, allowing a little authority to seep into her voice. She continued to hold Sarah's hand, using the physical contact to strengthen the link between them. She calmed the edgy young woman's nerves with her gentle touch, while subtly using her skills to envelop her consciousness. It was a talent she hadn't used in more than a decade, but she knew she needed to take control of the situation or the girl would go to the police, and she couldn't afford that. Locking her eyes on the girl's face, she smiled. "Now, I don't know about you, Sarah, but I'd love a cup of coffee."

"Coffee." The young woman nodded absently. "Coffee. Yes, of course."

Judith maneuvered Sarah toward a small Italian café. Three couples deep in conversation occupied all of the tables outside the restaurant. As they approached, Judith concentrated on an American couple in matching J. Crew madras jackets and madras sneakers, who were sitting a little apart from the others, their table partially hidden by a striped umbrella. Drawing strength from the lump of iron in her bag, feeling it heavy and warm in her arms, she willed them to leave. Moments later, the preppy couple stood up, packed up their maps and cameras, dropped a few bills on the table, and walked away without glancing back.

When Judith and Sarah sat down, the older woman immediately ordered two double espressos and some almond cannoli.

Sarah was still too dazed to notice. Somewhere at the back of her mind, she felt as if she had lost something or had missed something. It was as if she were watching a badly edited movie, with frames or sequences missing. She tried to piece together the puzzling events of the last ten minutes. She had just left the bank and was heading to lunch in the café on the first floor of the library when she spotted the skinhead. He was wearing those mirrored shades she detested. Trailing the stink of unwashed flesh, the skinhead had brushed past her, eyes fixed on someone directly ahead of him. Sarah turned and immediately spotted the silver-haired old woman who was his intended target. Even before the skinhead grabbed for her and the woman screamed and swung her bag, Sarah had been moving toward them, drawn by a sudden, uncontrollable, and completely inexplicable urge to help the woman.

The bitter tang of espresso brought her back to the present. Sarah blinked, blue eyes watering, wondering what she was doing here . . . wondering where here was.

"That was a very brave thing you did." Judith wrapped both hands around the thick cup to keep them from trembling and breathed in the rich aroma before sipping delicately. Although her head was bent, she could feel Sarah's eyes on her. "Why did you do it?"

"I just . . . just . . ." The young woman shrugged. "I'm not sure. I've never done anything like this before," she admitted. "But I couldn't just walk away and allow them to assault you, could I?"

"Others walked by or looked away," the old woman said quietly. "I guess that makes you my personal savior," she added with a smile.

Sarah blushed, a tinge of color touching her cheeks, and in that instant she reminded Judith of her brother Peter, standing proud and tall in his green uniform, his cheeks flushed with pride. Although she'd been only a child when she'd last seen her older brother, on the night before he went off to fight in the war, the vivid image of the blushing eighteen-year-old had remained with her. She had never seen him again; Peter had been among the first British casualties of World War II.

"Are you sure you won't let me make a report to the police?" Sarah asked.

"Positive," Judith replied firmly. "It would waste a lot of time—yours, mine, and the police's. I assure you such assaults are not unusual. This is London, these people often target the elderly, considering us easy marks."

"They picked on the wrong woman this time." Sarah grinned.

Judith lifted her bulging bag. "I think this is what they were after. And I'm afraid they would have been sadly disappointed. I'm not hiding the crown jewels in here. Just some books and notes."

"Are you a teacher?" Sarah asked curiously, biting into her cannoli. "You look like a teacher. At least the kind of teacher I would have liked to have," she added shyly.

"I'm a writer."

"What sort of books?"

"Children's books. What were once called fantasies, but are now categorized as urban fantasies. No vampires, though," she added with a quick grin. "I don't do vampires." Judith finished her coffee in one quick swallow, grimacing as she tasted bitter dregs. "Now, I really must go." She stood up quickly, then groaned aloud as a slender needle of agony lanced through her hip and she sank back onto the metal café chair.

"What's wrong? Are you hurt?" Sarah came around the table to kneel by her side. "Did they hurt you?"

Blinking away tears of pain, Judith Walker shook her head. "It's nothing. Honestly. My replacement hip is acting up, nothing more than that. I've been sitting for too long, that's all."

Sarah spotted a black taxi that turned onto the street and automatically raised her arm. "Come on, let me get you to a cab." She hooked an arm beneath the old woman's shoulders and eased her to her feet.

"I'll be fine," Judith hissed.

"I can see that."

Judith wanted to be left alone, wanted nothing more than to go home, climb into a scalding bath, and wash away the skinhead's touch. She could still feel his blunt fingers in her hair, gripping her shoulder, hurting her arm. She dabbed absently at her cheek, where his spittle had stung her flesh. She knew why they'd come for her. She knew what they wanted. She also knew that they would be back. She looked at Sarah again, and for the briefest instant, the bag on the ground beside her leg pulsed a beat of heat.

The young woman's dramatic appearance was an interesting coincidence . . . but Judith Walker didn't believe in coincidence. For her, everything was wrapped up in fate. This woman had rescued her for a reason. She reached out and rested her fingers lightly on the back of Sarah's hand, startling her. "We'll take a taxi to the station. I know there's a train to Bath soon. Then it's only a short walk from the Bath Spa station to my house. You'll come with me, won't you."

The blue-eyed woman nodded.

SARAH MILLER was confused. The events of the last two hours were already sliding and fading in her consciousness, the details blurring like an old dream.

She wasn't entirely sure how she had ended up sitting in the back of a train beside a virtual stranger. Sarah glanced sidelong at the woman. She was . . . sixty? Seventy? It was hard to tell. With her silver hair brushed straight back off her forehead, tied in a tight bun, wisps of stray hairs curling around her delicate ears and onto her high-boned cheeks, she enjoyed an ageless beauty reserved for those people who never worked a day of hard labor.

Sarah wondered why she had come to this stranger's assistance.

Even though she had been taking classes in self-defense—one of her friends told her it was a good place to meet sober men—she'd never actually used any of her training. Weeks earlier, she'd crossed the street to avoid having to walk past five shaven-headed teenagers kicking an Indian boy outside a fish-and-chips shop. Sarah was someone who purposely avoided conflicts.

"Are you okay?" the elderly woman asked suddenly.

Sarah blinked. "Sorry?"

"You were staring at me, but you seemed to be miles away."

"I'm sorry. I was just wondering . . ."

The woman continued to look at her, saying nothing.

"I've never done anything like this before."

"You're a very brave young woman."

Sarah shrugged. "It was nothing."

"Don't denigrate what you did. Few would have had the courage to come to a stranger's assistance. You're an extremely brave woman."

Sarah smiled at the compliment. And they remained content with their own silent thoughts for the rest of the ride.

When the train stopped in Bath Spa station, Judith linked her hand in Sarah's as they walked up Dorchester Street and turned right across the bridge on the river Avon.

"I've never been to Bath before."

"I've lived here most of my life," Judith said.

At the bottom of Lyncombe Hill, she turned right onto St. Mark's Road. "I'm just up here on the left," she said. Pushing open the squealing wrought-iron gate, she immediately noticed that her front door was open. Judith felt the coffee sour in her stomach, knowing instinctively what she was going to find inside. She clenched Sarah's hand, establishing contact once again, meeting and holding her bright eyes. She knew people found it very difficult to refuse something when there was actual physical contact. "You will come in?"

Sarah started to shake her head. "Really, I can't. I must be getting back to the office. My boss is a bit of a prick. Don't want to get fired for taking a four-hour lunch," she said with a smile, but even as she was speaking, she was walking up the path toward the house.

"You must give me your boss's phone number," Judith said softly. "I will call him and commend your actions. People win awards for doing less than you've done."

"That really won't be necessary. . . ."

"I insist," the old woman said firmly.

Sarah found herself nodding. A word of recommendation to old man Hinkle would not do her any harm.

Judith smiled. "Good, then that's settled. Now, let's have some nice tea, and then I promise I'll send you back to work." She had her key in her hand as she approached the door but purposely fumbled with her purse to give the young woman an opportunity to see the open door before her.

"Do you live alone?" Sarah asked suddenly.

"No, I have a cat." Judith had forgotten about Franklin. He had already exhausted six of his nine lives, and she prayed he was all right. As if on cue, the infuriated tabby meowed from behind the bushes where he was hiding. Judith collected him in her arms and calmed him, thrilled that her beloved pet was safe.

"Your front door is open," Sarah said. "Did you lock it this morning?"

"I always lock it," Judith whispered, then added, "Oh no."

"Wait here." Sarah placed Judith's bag of books on the ground and approached the open door carefully. Using her elbow, she pushed it inward. She could not suppress her loud gasp. "I think it's time to call the police."

obert Elliot had always wanted to be an interior designer.

An artistic youth, he would spend hours inside the house coloring at the kitchen table until his father would smack him on the side of the head and yell at him to play football with the other boys. However, Elliot preferred drawing to athletics: sick, dark pictures often involving people being guillotined or animals brutally cut open for dissection. He had a vivid imagination, which was best served confined within the pages of his notebooks. It was safer that way. Yet Elliot's father continued to push him throughout his youth, and the teenager finally snapped on his eighteenth birthday when he made the first of many pictures come alive, bludgeoning his father to death with a cricket bat.

A gifted public prosecutor had managed to commute Elliot's sentence to fifteen years, during which time Elliot continued to draw as well as read voraciously, using the prison library to educate himself. Hardened by his time in prison, Elliot found that jobs for which he was best suited required only two things: an enormous financial incentive and a great deal of violence.

He picked a piece of lint off his chocolate brown Dolce & Gabbana sports jacket as he watched the elderly woman hobbling up the street. Elliot smiled and made a quick call. "She just arrived, sir."

Static crackled on the cell. It was the latest BlackBerry on the market, yet the reception was always fuzzy and when he spoke he could hear his voice echoing back at him. He had no idea where he was phoning. The number was in the United States, but Elliot guessed it was bounced around a dozen satellites before it reached its final destination.

"I'm sorry, sir. What? . . . Oh. No. There's someone with her.

A redhead. Early twenties, I'd venture to guess. She wasn't in any of the lady's pictures."

Robert Elliot listened carefully to the baritone voice on the other end of the phone, abruptly glad of the distance separating him from his employer.

"Presently, I think that would be unwise, sir," he advised cautiously. "The girl's a variable. I don't know how long she's likely to be there. She could be police for all we know."

Static howled and then the line went dead.

Elliot gratefully hit end. He dropped the phone back into his pocket, turned on the engine of his black BMW, and pulled away from the curb. As he cruised slowly past the Walker house, he was unable to resist a smile, imagining the look on the old woman's face when she saw the way he had redesigned her beloved home.

Robert Elliot had always wanted to be an interior designer, and his new employer had finally given him his opportunity.

7

The house had been completely trashed.

Judith clutched Franklin tightly in her arms as she stepped into the hall. There were gaping holes in the floor where the floorboards had been torn up. Anger welled up inside her, burning in the pit of her stomach, flooding her throat, and stinging her soft gray eyes. Holes had been punched in the walls, and all the framed covers of her children's books that had once lined the walls lay crushed and crumpled on the floor.

Judith put the cat down and walked to the end of the hall, stumbling over the shredded Oriental rugs as she tried the door to the sitting room. It would open only halfway. Peering around the corner of the door, she realized that the hideous horsehair sofa she'd always detested was jamming the door. It had been completely gutted, the back slashed open in a big X, wiry hair spilling across the floor, mingling with the feathers from the eight ornate cushions she had embroidered herself. The ebony Edwardian wood cabinet was lying at an angle against the upturned easy chair, drawers and doors hanging open, the dark wood scarred as if it had been cut with a knife.

Hundreds of delicate china teacups she'd spent a lifetime collecting were scattered on the floor, broken into a thousand fragments. All of the photographs had been pulled off the wall, a lifetime of memories torn and stamped to shreds.

"The police are on the way." Sarah reached out to the older woman, but Judith reflexively pulled away. "Is there anything I can do?" she asked lamely.

"Nothing," Judith said as the realization gradually sank in that her life, as she knew it, was now over. "Nothing anyone can do." She put her hand on the banister to steady herself. "I need to look upstairs."

"Do you want me to come with you?"

"No. Thank you. Please just wait for the police."

The worst destruction had been wrought in the bedroom. The bed itself had been slashed to ribbons by a razor-sharp blade. The canary yellow down comforter, in which her late husband used to wrap himself when he watched television, lay in shreds on the floor. She held a sliver of the torn material, trying to smell a fragment of the memory of the man with whom she had shared a lifetime.

And Judith knew that she would be seeing him soon.

Surveying the rest of the room, she noted that nothing had been spared. Every item of clothing had been pulled out of the closet and systematically slashed and torn. The remains of a pair of expensive silk heels she had long ago worn at her nephew's communion were shoved in the overflowing toilet. The smell of acrid urine was almost unbearable. Judith closed the door and leaned her forehead against the cool wood, while tears burned at the backs of her eyes. But she was determined not to cry.

The bedroom she had converted to an office was similarly ruined. The floor was awash with paper, decades of carefully collected and collated notes once neatly filed and cataloged in her cabinet were unceremoniously dumped out, scattered everywhere. Not one of her beloved books remained on the shelf. Paperbacks had been torn in half, every hardback cover was ripped, and some of the older volumes were lacking their leather spines and covers. The original artwork to her children's books was all on the floor, the glass shattered, wooden frames broken, filthy footprints on the delicate watercolors. The twenty-five-year-old Smith Corona typewriter on which she'd written her first book lay crushed, as if someone had jumped on it. Her iMac was completely destroyed, a huge hole in the center of the screen. Stooping, she lifted a random page from the floor at her feet. Page twenty-two of the manuscript of her latest children's book: It was smeared with excrement. Judith allowed the page to flutter to the floor, and the bitter tears finally came. Even if she had the time, it would take her years to sort out the mess. But it didn't matter: Whoever had done this hadn't gotten what they were looking for.

They would be back.

After placing her shoulder bag on the scarred wooden desk, she removed the books and papers she'd been carrying around with her all day. Nestled at the bottom of the bag, still wrapped in its newspapers, was the treasure her assailants had been after.

Dyrnwyn, Sword of Rhydderch.

The old woman smiled bitterly. If only they knew how close they'd been to getting it. Her gnarled fingers closed around the rusted hilt, and she felt a ghost of its power tremble through her arms. She had never harmed anyone in her life, but if she could get her hands on the savages who had done this, who had destroyed a lifetime of work and memories . . .

The metal grew warm and she quickly jerked her hand back; she had forgotten how dangerous such thoughts were in the presence of the artifact.

8

Richard Fenton pulled off the terry towel and slid naked into the water, hissing with pleasure. A perfect eighty-five degrees. A bit too hot for some, but when you reached his age, the blood grew thin and old bones felt the cold. With long, even strokes he swam the length of the swimming pool, turned, and swam back to the deep end again. On a good day he could swim twenty lengths, but he'd had a late night last night, and it had been dawn before he had gone to bed. He hadn't woken until one thirty in the afternoon and was feeling stiff and tired . . . and *old*.

Today, he felt like an old man.

He *was* an old man, he reminded himself grimly, seventy-seven next month, and although he looked at least ten years younger and had a body to match, there were days when he felt every one of his years. Today was one of them. He would try to do ten lengths of the pool and then he'd have Max give him a massage. He had planned to have dinner in the club tonight, but perhaps he'd give it a miss, stay home and relax.

His feet pressed against the teal tiled wall, he pushed off again, his overlong fine white hair streaming out behind him, plastering itself to his skull when he raised his head above the water. Sunlight lanced through the high windows, speckling the water, dappling the tiled floor of the pool, the light bringing the ornate design on the floor to shimmering life. He'd had the architect who'd designed this wing of the house copy the pattern from a Greek vase: stylized human figures copulating in a dozen unusual and improbable positions.

Somewhere deep in the house, a phone rang.

Richard ignored it; Max or Jackie would handle it. He ducked under the water, opening his eyes wide. The water was clean; he would not allow chlorine or any of the other detergents into his pool.

The water was completely recycled twice a day, usually just before he took his morning swim and then again late in the evening. Looking down, he watched the design on the floor tremble and shiver, the figures looking as if they were moving.

The phone was still ringing when he raised his head above the water.

Richard ran his hands through his hair, pulling it back off his face, and turned to the double doors at the opposite end of the room. Where was Max . . . or Jackie, for that matter? They should have answered the phone . . . unless they were otherwise engaged. He suddenly grinned, showing a perfect set of teeth that were too white and too straight to be real. He'd suspected for a while that they were becoming more than colleagues. The old man's smile faded. They could do what they liked on their own time, but he employed them to work.

The phone stopped.

Richard Fenton flipped over and floated on his back, raising his left arm to look at the watch that never left his wrist. Two thirty. It had been his father's watch and his father's before him. It had cost Richard a fortune to have it rendered waterproof, but the money had meant nothing. The watch was a symbol. Every time he looked at it, he was reminded of his father, who'd finished his days coughing up his lungs, the blood black and speckled with coal dust. His grandfather had died down in the pits; "exhaustion," the death certificate said, but everyone knew there had been gas leaking down in the mines. Richard barely remembered his grandfather, though he had vague memories of the funeral.

He remembered his father's funeral vividly.

He recollected standing at the edge of the grave, a clump of earth in his hands, cold and damp and heavy, and swearing that he would never go down into the mines. It was an oath he'd broken only once in his lifetime, and that was when he'd been photographed with a band he'd discovered in the sixties: the Miners. They'd done a publicity shoot in the cages and tunnels, the five teenagers posing wearing miners' helmets, holding the picks and shovels like the musical instruments they never learned to play.

Richard grinned. He hadn't thought about the band for years, a sure sign he was going senile. They'd had two top-twenty hits and seemed destined for great things. The next Beatles, the future Stones, the music press called them. Fenton had sold their contract to one of the big American labels—and walked away with a fortune in his pocket. The boys had complained, of course, and looked for their share, but they had signed a contract, a cast-iron contract, that allowed him to be reimbursed for his expenses. And his expenses had been high, very high. They'd threatened to sue, until he'd pointed out how expensive that would be, adding that they would lose. Eventually, they'd given up; they were convinced they were going to make ten times what he'd stolen from them in the States.

They'd never made another record.

The phone started ringing again, and Richard surged up in the water. Where was Max? What the hell was going on? He struck out for the shallow end of the pool, anger making his strokes ragged and choppy.

Richard Fenton caught the barest glimpse of the object in the air—dark, round—before it hit the pool in an explosion of pink-tinged water behind him.

"Jesus!" Fenton looked up. One of the ornamental hanging plants must have fallen from the rafters. He could have been killed. He turned, treading water, looking for the plant. If he didn't get it out of the pool right now, the soil would clog up the filters.

"Max? . . . Max!"

Where the fuck was the bastard? Controlling his temper, Richard ducked beneath the surface, looking for the plant. He spotted it in the deep end, surrounded by a growing cloud of dark earth, and struck out for it. He was going to make someone pay for the cleanup of the pool, and for new filters, and for the fright it had given him; he could have had a heart attack. He'd sue the gardeners who'd installed the flowers, or the architect, or both. Breaking the surface, he took a deep breath and then ducked back down again. It was only when he swam into the cloud billowing around the plant that he realized it was pink, shot through with thin, ropy black tendrils. As he reached for the thick ball of earth, it rolled over . . . and Richard Fenton found himself looking at the severed head of his manservant, eyes wide and staring, face blank with surprise. The mouth opened, and blood, pale and pink, bubbled upward.

Fenton surged out of the pool, coughing and hacking, heart hammering so violently in his chest that he could actually feel the skin tremble. He coughed up the water he'd ingested, felt his gorge rise, and swallowed. He was trembling so hard that he could barely hold on to the metal ladder as he pulled himself up to the slick, cold tiles. He tried to marshal his thoughts, but his head was spinning, the constriction in his chest was tightening, and black spots were dancing before his eyes. Doubled over, he breathed deeply and then straightened. He swayed as the blood rushed to his head; however, he could think clearly now.

There was a loaded gun in the safe behind his desk, shotguns in the cabinet on the wall, ammunition in the drawer underneath. All he had to do . . .

The water gurgled, bubbles bursting. Fenton turned. Max's head had floated to the surface, bobbing like an obscene buoy.

Richard Fenton had no doubt that whoever had done this to Max had come for him. He'd made too many enemies in his long life, cut too many sharp deals, and on more than one occasion he'd been forced to *take care* of people who got in his way. But that had been a long time ago. He hadn't really been active in many years. . . .

Yet people had long memories.

Richard Fenton padded barefoot to the double doors and peered out into the circular conservatory that connected the main body of the house with the swimming pool. The Spanish tiles were speckled with dark blood. Whoever had killed Max had carried his head out here to throw it into the water . . . which meant that they had watched him . . . which meant that they were still in the house . . . which meant . . .

Maybe he'd forget about the gun. If anyone was waiting for him, they'd be in his study. He could cut across the hall, through the kitchen, and into the garage. The keys were always kept in the cars.

Crouching low, he darted across the tiles and stepped up into the hallway. After the chill of the tiles, the carpet was warm beneath his feet. And moist. He lifted his foot. It came away sticky with gore.

Fenton turned. He clapped both hands to his mouth, trying to keep from crying out, but it was too late. His shriek echoed through the empty house. Jackie dangled upside down by one leg from the curtain rail. Her caramel throat had been cut so deeply that her head dangled too far back, exposing tubes and the hint of bone. Her face was a red mask, her honey hair black and stiff. She was still wearing her Kate Spade glasses.

"Why don't you come into the study, Mr. Fenton?"

Richard whirled around. The door to his study was open. He glanced toward the hall door. Thirty, maybe forty steps away. He was in good condition. He'd make it.

"It was not a request."

Through the door, down the cobblestone drive, and out onto the main road. The nearest house was a hundred yards away, but he'd make it. A naked old man running down the road would certainly attract attention.

The hall door creaked, then opened slowly, shafting afternoon light along the length of the highly polished floor, picking out the dust motes spiraling in the still air. A suited figure stood in the doorway, a long, elongated shadow growing along the floor. Richard frowned, squinting shortsightedly. There was something about the figure . . . something *wrong*.

The figure swayed, then toppled forward. Richard realized then that it had no head. He was looking at the decapitated body of Max.

"Come into the study, Mr. Fenton."

Defeated, Richard Fenton crossed the hall and pushed open the door of his study. He stood in the doorway, arms wrapped around his thin chest, shivering, blinking in the gloom. The curtains had been pulled and the ornate desk lamp turned to face the door, blinding him, leaving the figure sitting behind the desk in shadow. The harsh light made Fenton's eyes water, and he rubbed angrily at the tears on his cheeks. The old man felt the sting in the pit of his chest and for once welcomed it, knowing that it might save him the pain he knew was coming.

"You have something I want, Mr. Fenton." It was a male voice, soft, accentless, precise, controlled.

"There's money in the safe," Richard Fenton said quickly. "Take it." Maybe this was nothing more than extortion, a Young Turk out to make his reputation by ripping him off. He'd give him what he wanted . . . and then hunt him down like a dog.

"I don't want your money," the shadowy figure said, his voice tinged with amusement.

There was movement beside the curtain, and Richard realized that there was a second person in the room. Although the air was rich with meaty blood and the odor from the hide chair and ornate leather bindings, he thought he detected the scent of flowers. But there were no flowering plants in this room. Perfume? A woman?

"We have come for the chessboard." The woman's voice was soft, albeit clipped, the vowels touched with the hint of an indefinable accent.

"I have many chessboards," Fenton began. "I've collected them all my life. Take what you want."

"Oh, but this one is not on display. We've come for the Chessboard of Gwenddolau."

The old man was not surprised. He'd always known that someone, someday, would come for the cursed pieces of crystal or the gold-and-silver board. Indefinably old, it was one of the most beautiful things he possessed, yet he never displayed it with his other antique boards for reasons he could never fully explain.

"We want it," the woman whispered.

Richard Fenton started to shake his head.

A knife snapped open.

"You will tell me, sooner or later," she purred, and Fenton had no time to react as the woman threw the knife and it thudded into the polished wooden floorboards between his bare feet. Looking down, he saw the sliver of polished steel vibrating.

"Why don't you have a seat, Mr. Fenton," she asked politely.

He started to shake his head and then immediately felt white-hot pain in his thigh. Looking down, he saw the hilt of a second wafer-thin metal knife protruding from his flesh, inches from his shriveled groin. Bizarrely, there was no pain, only heat.

"In fact, while we're waiting for you to tell us the exact location of the Chessboard of Gwenddolau, we're going to play a little game of chess. Winner takes all."

The beautiful woman stepped out of the shadows. Fenton tried to focus on her face, which was so ethereally beautiful that she almost didn't look human. Her face was long and narrow, lips full, and eyes slightly slanted. A mane of jet black hair flowed down her back. He tried to make out her eye color, but the reflected light painted them bronze and metallic. She looked young, early twenties, perhaps; however, she had full breasts and the soft, curvy belly and buttocks of an older woman. A light green silk gown stretched tight across her full figure.

Gently, she prodded the injured Fenton into a chair and nodded at her shadow-wrapped companion. He stood, and the old man realized he was tall and broad, like a bodybuilder. As his arm moved into the light, Fenton saw that the man was holding a short stabbing spear in his left hand. The head was wet with black blood.

The Dark Man moved around the room, perusing the cabinets of chessboards, pulling out one of the more ornate boards, a six-hundred-year-old treasure from the Alhambra carved in the Arabic style. He placed it on the small table in front of Fenton before taking up a position standing behind him.

"Play," he commanded.

The exotic-looking woman sat facing the old man. Her smile was feral as she quickly laid out the pieces. With black-painted nails, she gripped the pawn and moved it, her eyes never leaving Fenton's face. He tried to make sense out of what was happening, conscious now of the growing pain in his leg, aware that he was probably going to die in this room. "Your turn," she whispered.

Automatically, he moved a piece.

"Ah, the game begins," the woman whispered. It took her less than a dozen moves to trap Fenton's king, white teeth pressed against her lips, the tip of her tongue protruding between them. "I thought you would be a better opponent. Shame, you could have bought yourself a few more hours."

Her smile was savage. "Checkmate."

9

"I insist," Sarah said firmly.

Judith Walker shook her head slowly but remained silent. She needed this young woman to think that she was making her own decisions.

"I'm afraid I would be an enormous imposition," Judith proffered weakly.

Sitting in the backseat of the police car, Sarah nodded emphatically, convincing herself that this was a good idea. "Where else are you going to go? You can't stay here, not until the place is cleaned up." She smiled wanly. "I'll have to warn you that my mother may be a bit difficult, but we've definitely got the space. Stay the night, and in the morning, I'll contact your nephew and together we'll help you get your place back together."

"Really, I really—"

"Don't be ridiculous," Sarah interrupted, but without the same insistent certainty. What was she doing? She'd met this woman only hours earlier, and now she was offering her a bed for the night. . . . Her mother was going to go ballistic.

Judith heard the sudden indecision in the young woman's voice and touched the hilt of the newspaper-wrapped sword, drawing power from it. She then reached out and squeezed Sarah's hand. "It's an extremely generous offer."

Sarah smiled, her dimples accentuating her understated beauty. "I'll have the police drop us at my house in Crawley."

"You need to phone your office," Judith suggested quietly. "They'll be worried about you. You've been gone all afternoon."

Sarah nodded. There was no sense even trying to go back to work. "I'll tell them I can't make it back by the end of the day," she added, pulling out her phone.

Judith listened as Sarah tried to explain to her puzzled boss why she was taking the rest of the day off. She could hear the man's irritated grumbles across the line, and she watched the girl's exasperated attempts to placate him. In any other circumstance, Judith would have felt guilty about using the power of her will to manipulate Sarah in this way; however, this was a special situation.

She had to protect the sword—at all costs.

LATER, WHILE she was lying in the strange bed, watching the reflection of the streetlights dancing on the ceiling, Judith Walker listened to the vague sounds of voices drifting up from the kitchen below. She recognized Ruth Miller's strident clipped delivery drowning out Sarah's softer protestations and knew she was the subject of the heated quarrel. Judith reached beneath the pillow and touched the paper-wrapped sword, concentrating on Sarah, trying to pour a little strength into her. She felt a strange sorority with this young woman, a kinship, which even after seventy-four years of experiences she didn't quite understand.

The Miller family had welcomed Judith's presence with cool politeness. They lived quiet suburban lives in a quiet suburban neighborhood and obviously resented this bizarre intrusion.

Tea had been a frostily civil affair.

Ruth Miller had engaged Judith in brittle inconsequential conversation, while James, Ruth's latest lover, had barely spoken. Sarah's younger brothers, obviously warned by their mother to be on their best behavior, had nattered in hurried whispers throughout the meal and ignored the stranger at their table. Much to everyone's relief, Judith claimed exhaustion following the events of the day and retired immediately after tea. She had been given the youngest boy's bedroom, a tiny box room decorated with posters of NASCAR drivers, football stars, and a scantily dressed tween rock star whom Judith Walker didn't recognize. In the middle of the floor sat an elaborate train set and a scattering of stuffed animals. She found the contrast between the burgeoning testosterone-driven sexuality of the posters and the plush toys vaguely disturbing; she guessed the boy was no more than ten. Another sign of the times: Innocence was one of the first sacrifices to the modern age.

Sitting up on the bed, Judith unwrapped the sword and ran her fingers down the rusted metal. Holding it by the hilt, she brought the broken blade to her lips and felt the familiar surge of power that tingled through her hands and into her arms.

Old magic, ancient power, rising.

Judith felt the warmth flood through her body. Aches and pains from stiffened joints vanished; tired, worn muscles relaxed; her sight grew sharp and her hearing distinct as her senses expanded. She was young again. Young and vital and . . .

Old magic, ancient power, fading.

The power left as soon as it had arrived, and her newly keen sight swiftly dissolved to an unfocused blur. Her hearing became muted. And the aches and pains returned.

Sighing, she wrapped the sword in a faded cotton nightdress and tucked it beneath her pillow. When she lay back, she could feel the hardness of the old iron against her skull. As a child, she'd slept with it beneath her pillow every night, and the dreams . . . the dreams then had been extraordinary. The sword had been her gateway to portals of imagination, lost worlds, and wondrous and magical adventures. Those dreams had shaped her early imagination and sowed the seeds of her later career. When the book critics lauded her wonderfully detailed imagination and fully realized worlds, they had no idea that she was simply repeating and reporting on the places she'd seen.

As she grew older, Judith had hidden the sword away in her brother's old woolen military jacket that hung at the back of the closet. The dreams then came only sporadically, and she began treating them clinically, divesting them of their chilling powers by converting them into marketable fantasy and adventure books for children. There were times when she almost forgot about the power of the Hallow that had so shaped her life.

Almost, but not quite.

But someone still believed that the Hallows were powerful; someone was prepared to kill in order to acquire the artifacts.

And Sarah, where did she fit into the overall scheme? Was her appearance, her intervention, more than coincidence? Even dormant, the Hallows attracted certain types of people—either those sensitive to the tremulous aura they exuded but unaware of their powers or those who deliberately sought the ancient objects of power still scattered throughout the world. Over the years, she'd encountered her fair share of both. And Sarah . . . Judith was convinced she was the former, but there was more to her. There was a strength to her that even the young woman did not recognize.

The argument downstairs finally ended with a slammed door, then stairs creaked. There was a gentle tap on the door.

"Come in, Sarah," Judith Walker said softly, sitting up in the bed.

Sarah Miller stepped into the room, smiling sheepishly. Her cheeks were red and flushed, and her hands were trembling slightly. "I just came to see how you were," she said quietly.

"I'm fine, thanks to you." Judith patted the bed. "Sit for a moment."

The young woman perched on the edge of the bed, her eyes moving about the familiar room, looking anywhere but at Judith's face.

"I'm afraid I haven't made you very popular with your family."

Sarah shrugged. "I've never been popular with them. But they're fine. They were just a bit surprised, that's all."

"I imagine your mother suspects I'm here for the rest of my life."

Sarah shook her head quickly, though Ruth Miller had indeed suggested that very idea. "Once these people move in, they never leave," she had preached.

"No. Nothing of the sort," Sarah said.

Judith reached out and touched the girl's hands. In that instant, she felt a tinge of regret for what she had done—using the girl to provide her with a secure shelter for the night, a place that couldn't be traced. "What you did today was something you should be proud of," she said, her voice low and insistent. "You acted in the finest traditions of old; you came to the aid of a damsel in distress." She squeezed Sarah's fingers and smiled.

Sarah nodded, suddenly feeling confident and sure about her actions. She *had* been sure she'd done the right thing—they had seemed *right* . . . until her mother had explained the hundred different reasons why she should have left the situation alone. Ruth Miller simply could not comprehend why her daughter hadn't looked away and crossed the street.

"Do you believe in a higher power?" Judith asked suddenly.

Sarah shrugged. "We're Church of England."

"No, I'm not talking about a church. I'm not talking about a god or gods or anything so specific. Do you believe in a Being, a Spirit, a force for Good?"

Uncomfortable with the direction the conversation was taking—

maybe her mother was right; maybe the old woman was mad—
Sarah shrugged again. "I suppose. Why?"

"Because what you did today was *right*. It was good. Do not allow people to belittle what you did."

"Honestly, I'm not sure why I did it," Sarah admitted. "But when I saw them attacking you, something happened to me. I just got so angry. I couldn't walk away. . . ."

Judith smiled, deep wrinkles crinkling along her eyes and mouth. "In my youth, the elderly could walk the streets in safety," she said. "But that was a long time ago." She laid down and closed her eyes, indicating that the conversation was over.

Sarah sat with the old woman until her breathing deepened and slowed to whispered breaths. Suddenly, the young woman was acutely aware of the house around her. She felt odd, as if a sixth sense had been granted to her. She was able to tangibly experience the feelings swirling about her: her mother's radiated anger from the kitchen below, her brothers' dull annoyance, especially little Freddie, who had to give up his room. Sarah smiled grimly, returning to her reality. She'd managed to do it again; she'd managed to alienate them all in one go. It was a gift. Christ! Her mother's words came flooding back: She had it all, and yet she still managed to fuck it up; she was twenty-two, in a good job, with a great future, and earning a good salary.

Sarah Miller's smile turned bitter.

She was twenty-two, in a lousy, dead-end job she hated, and she handed over most of her salary to her mother. She should have gotten a flat when she'd had the chance. But she hadn't taken it, and in the last couple of years she'd begun to think that maybe she never would. She'd watched her friends move away from home, get apartments in the city, find boyfriends and girlfriends, and *live*. Some of them were even married now.

Sarah gently disengaged the old woman's fingers from her hand and stood looking down at the frail, tiny woman in the bed. Today, she'd done something positive, something good . . . and her mother had scolded her like a naughty little girl. Well, maybe she shouldn't have brought Judith Walker home, but she couldn't leave her in that horrible house, and somehow, bringing her here had seemed like the only decision to make.

It had been the right thing to do. A good thing.

Besides, the old woman would be gone in the morning, and everything would return to normal, although she knew it would be a long time before her mother would let her forget about it. She turned away, shaking her head, and quietly opened the door. She had to get out of this house before it sucked all the life out of her.

Judith's eyes snapped open when she heard the door click shut. She listened to Sarah step into the room next to hers, heard the bedsprings creak, the tinny crackle of a television or radio. Even without the sword to enhance her senses, the old woman could feel the girl's unease and discomfort. Sarah was obviously dominated by her mother, which explained how Judith had been able to take control of her so easily. Yet that still didn't explain why the girl had come to her aid in the first place. Her type always walked away . . . but not this time.

That night, Judith dreamed of the girl.

The dreams were dark and violent, and in them, the girl was fighting for her life. . . . The sword was in the dream, too. However, Judith couldn't make out if the girl was using the sword to destroy . . . or if the sword was destroying the girl.

he white king was magnificent. Three inches of solid crystal, incised and carved in marvelously intricate detail, down to the delicate design on the sword blade he held aloft. The queen was a masterpiece, the expression on the face perfect and made all the more human by the mole high on the left cheekbone.

"How old are they?" Vyvienne ran her index finger down the length of the white queen. Richard Fenton's blood had stained the white crystal darkly crimson. The old man had guarded his secret until close to the end. Only in the depths of his absolute agony, when she had stripped the flesh from his chest and back with the tiny flensing knives and then started on his inner thighs, had he revealed the secret of the location of the chessboard he had guarded for most of his life.

The man known as Ahriman stepped across the blood that gathered in the tiles at the edge of the pool, picking his way through gossamer strips of flesh that coiled with the consistency of old paper. He carefully lifted the crystal queen from the woman's long-nailed fingers and dipped it in the pool, cleansing it. "A thousand years, certainly," he said eventually. "And possibly another thousand beyond that." Holding the piece up to the light, he tilted it, admiring the ancient craftsmanship. "The Chessboard of Gwenddolau," he whispered, "each piece based upon a living figure. Each piece imbued with a fragment of the soul of that person." He smiled thinly. "Or so the legend has it."

"And do you believe in legends?" the woman asked, looking at the chess pieces in the velvet padded box.

Slowly, sensuously, he rubbed the queen across her pale face, pressing it between her moist lips, pushing it into her mouth. "*These* are legend."

Vyvienne grabbed the chess piece, feeling its surge of power that charged her mentally and aroused her physically. As she clenched the piece in her palm, she undressed, allowing her spectacular body to reflect in the pool's glass surface. As Ahriman's hands caressed her body and she held the piece, Vyvienne turned her attention to the middle of the pool, where Richard Fenton's frozen expression of sheer terror gaped at her as his body slowly sank to the bottom.

The corpse was barely recognizable as human.

And there it was again.
A disturbance.
A tremble in the ether, a shifting in the perpetual night.
Something ancient had been awakened.
Something powerful.

WEDNESDAY, OCTOBER 28

11

I made you some tea. I wasn't sure how many sugars—"

Sarah Miller stood in the bedroom door, her mouth wide open in surprise.

The room was empty: Judith Walker was gone.

Her brother's bed was neatly made, the bright blue duvet folded down and smoothed flat, the hodgepodge zoo of stuffed animals nestling neatly against the pillows. The only clue that someone had been there was the faintest trace of a floral perfume in the air. Puzzled, Sarah returned to the kitchen, sipping the tepid tea and eating the Walkers biscuit she had commandeered from the bottom shelf of the cupboard where her mother squirreled them away. An impossibly tanned TV anchor was reading the seven o'clock news.

What time had Judith Walker left? And why?

Sarah heard creaking upstairs, her mother's distinctly heavy steps on the floorboards. The walls were so thin, she could trace her mother's path from the bedroom to the bathroom. No wonder Judith had left. Her mother was famous for her shrill voice, and last night she had been in rare form. Naturally Judith had sensed the icy atmosphere. No wonder she'd escaped at the crack of dawn.

After finishing the tea, she spent ten minutes looking for her Coach briefcase before she remembered that she'd left it in the office. Sarah was dreading going in; what was she going to say to Mr. Hinkle? She'd just walked out at lunchtime and not returned. Her mother had taken an almost malicious pleasure in reminding her that she might very well lose her job. Last night she hadn't cared, but this morning . . .

She was pulling the door closed behind her as James meandered down the stairs. Occasionally—very occasionally—they managed to catch the train together. Sarah hated that; a journey into the city with her mother's lover was always vaguely embarrassing. She never knew quite what to say to him, and she knew James wanted nothing more than to be left alone to read the newspaper and enjoy a moment's respite from Ruth Miller's constant haranguing. But he'd not be on the train with her this morning. James was still wearing the obnoxiously loud terry bathrobe that her mother had given him at Christmas. Sarah had seen the empty tequila bottles in the sink and knew that the balding car salesman was going to miss yet another day of work. Sarah grimaced, realizing that once again almost her entire paycheck would have to be handed over to her mother.

As she hurried down the street, Sarah felt a guilty stab of relief that Judith had gone. Despite her frustration with the direction her life was taking, Sarah appreciated order, and Judith had certainly put a minor wrench in her comfortably regimented life. She still couldn't quite fathom what had come over her yesterday. First, she had come to a stranger's aid, and after that . . . things had become a little hazy. Well, it was over now: a brief show of courage in an otherwise cowardly life.

She grinned, wondering if perhaps she had finally shown a spark of the latent potential within her. Perhaps this was the beginning of a new future, one filled with hope and possibility. Yet as she entered the dull gray bank building and headed toward her suffocating cubicle, she guessed that her life was destined to continue along its same staid, dreary path.

Sarah's phone was ringing as she approached her desk.

"Hello?"

"I would like to speak with Sarah Miller." The voice was male, cultured, and colored with the vague hint of an unidentifiable accent.

Sarah frowned. Only her clients had this number, and this voice was unfamiliar. "This is Sarah Miller."

"Sarah Miller of Pine Grove, Crawley?"

"Yes. To whom am I speaking?"

"You bravely came to the assistance of an elderly woman yesterday. A Judith Walker. You then proceeded to her home in Bath—"

"Just who exactly is this?"

"She gave you something rather important that belongs to me. And I would very much like for you to return home now and get it for me, please."

"I don't know what kind of prank you're playing, but this is a business line. Now if you'll excuse me—"

The line popped and crackled, the voice echoing slightly: "My representatives will call to your address at precisely noon. I strongly suggest you be there, with the artifact Walker gave you."

"But she gave me nothing . . . ," she began, but the line clicked and went dead.

The phone immediately rang again.

"Look, Judith Walker didn't give me anything—"

"Sarah, it's Hannah. Seth . . . Mr. Hinkle would like to see you in his office immediately."

"I'll be right there." Sarah took a deep breath: The repercussions of her actions had just begun. Dismissing the peculiar phone call, she hurried down the long corridor to her boss's corner office.

Seth Hinkle would have once been considered attractive. Yet the fifty-year-old had spent so many years in his role as a corporate drone that his creative brain had all but atrophied. Now, in a six-hundred-pound tailored suit that barely concealed his bulging belly, nourished by too many late night pints at the local pub in an attempt to avoid going home to his shrill wife and needy twins, Seth Hinkle stood against the window and prepared to pontificate.

Sarah sat down silently.

"As laudable as I find your recent actions, I must remind you that I am running a business here." Seth postured in a way that the backlight of the morning sun formed a disturbing aura around him.

He'd been practicing this, Sarah realized.

"If you cannot accommodate our rather simple rules, then perhaps it might be better if you were to look for other employment." Mr. Hinkle was unable to meet her eyes. He looked away quickly when they both realized that his eyes were fixed in the center of Sarah's chest. "In normal circumstances, I would be left with no alternative but to dismiss you. However," he continued slowly, mouth twisting as if he'd tasted something sour, "Sir Simon phoned this office not six minutes ago."

Sarah tried to suppress a giggle. With his sibilant speech, Seth Hinkle sounded like a sputtering snake as he mentioned the senior partner's name.

"Are you all right, Miss Miller?"

"Fine, sir, just a bit of a tickle in the back of my throat. You were saying?"

"It seems a Judith Walker contacted Sir Simon this morning. She was *extremely complimentary* about you and your heroics as a selfless Samaritan."

The words were coming more slowly now, the s's stretching out to their maximum potential, and Sarah bit harder on the soft flesh of her inner cheek, keeping her face in an expressionless mask.

"Sir Simon is delighted with your fearless actions yesterday. He feels that it projects the correct image for the bank . . ." After drawing in a deep breath, he finished in a rush, "And asked that I personally convey to you his compliments and good wishes."

"Thank you, sir." Sarah stood up to leave.

Seth Hinkle glanced up sharply. "This woman you *saved* yesterday, had you ever met her before?"

"No, sir."

"Did you by any chance know that she was associated with Sir Simon?"

"No, sir."

Seth Hinkle straightened a row of unsharpened pencils on his immaculate desk. "So you mean to tell me that you came to the assistance of an old woman you had never met before, escorted her to her home two bloody hours away, and when you discovered it had been burgled, you generously brought her back to the privacy of your own house, where she spent the night."

"Yes, sir."

"Are you in the habit of picking up strangers, Ms. Miller?"

"No, sir."

"Well, what made this woman so different?"

"I'm . . . I'm not quite sure, sir."

Hinkle laced his fingers together and slowly moved his gaze from Sarah's breasts to a space above her head. "Do you want to know what I think, Ms. Miller? I think this whole business stinks to high heaven. You are fully aware that your position here is tenuous at best and your work has been lackluster to say the least. You have ignored the recommendations of senior staff. I believe you know that in the upcoming restructuring of this department, there may be no position for you." The older man took a deep breath and ran a hand across his flaking scalp. The once rich chestnut hair was now peppered with premature gray. Hinkle was a bully, and it was common knowledge in the department that he liked nothing better than dressing down a staff member, particularly a female staff member. "I think you somehow knew this woman was connected to Sir Simon and you set it up with her to ingratiate yourself with him."

Sarah was about to protest but decided against it.

"You can go. But I'll be keeping my eye on you."

Sarah bobbed her head and turned away quickly before the older man could see the broad grin across her face. She kept her face impassive as she strolled through the outer office, under the imperious stare of Miss Morgan, Hinkle's niece and secretary. She was smiling as she strolled down the long, echoing corridor. Hinkle looked as if he'd swallowed a lemon as he'd passed on Sir Simon's commendation. The first thing she'd do would be to source Sir Simon's address and write him a personal letter of thanks . . . No, the first thing she'd do would be to contact Judith Walker and thank her for bringing her to the notice of one of the senior partners. She had said something yesterday about contacting her boss, but Sarah had forgotten all about it; obviously Judith hadn't.

The cubicle Sarah shared with another junior account manager was deserted, computers humming softly in the silence.

She Googled Judith Walker.

There were dozens of entries. However, all of them involved her children's books: young adult fantasy adventure stories along the lines of *The Enchanted Mountain* and *The Sorcerer's Cloak*, which had made her quite a popular author. Naturally, her address would not be public. There were too many psychos out there who wanted to own a piece of fame. Perhaps it was one of Judith's fans who had done that to her home. Yet why would anyone be that destructive? She could understand if Judith Walker were a rock star or a famous actress, but she was just an elderly children's book author. Why would someone want to hurt her?

If she really wanted to make the effort, Sarah was sure she could find the address again, although the trip there was vague and confused in her memory. She thought she might be able to find it again . . . but she was not entirely sure. She could always contact Walker's publisher, but they wouldn't be likely to give out her address, nor would the library, where she had done her research the previous day. However, the library would have a copy of the register of electors, a database containing electors' names and addresses, and Judith had said she'd lived in the same house for most of her life. Sarah decided she'd pop into the library during her lunch. The phone interrupted her train of thought.

"Hello?"

"I would like to speak with Sarah Miller, please."

Sarah immediately recognized the same cultured male voice from earlier. "Look, I don't know what kind of joke you're playing, but I have an extremely busy day and I would appreciate it if you wouldn't keep bothering me."

"Oh, Ms. Miller, I assure you I am not playing a joke. And I'm extremely disappointed that you're still at work. As I said earlier, my representatives will be calling on your home at noon. I believe, if you leave your office immediately, you'll still be able to catch them."

"Who are you? What do you want?" Sarah felt the first flickers of panic and found herself agitated by the creepy tone of enjoyment that had entered the man's voice.

"I want what Judith Walker gave you."

"I told you, she didn't give me—"

"Please don't disappoint me, sweetheart." The threat was implicit in the eerie baritone voice.

12

Sarah Miller was sweating heavily as she bolted down the street in her sneakers, relieved that she had left her heels at the office. Squinting against the unforgiving noonday sun, she flagged down a taxi that quickly became enveloped in the standstill city traffic. After she'd sat in the cab on Oxford Street for ten interminable minutes, her frustration overwhelmed her and she abruptly paid the surprised driver, then leapt out of the cab and darted down the street into the Tottenham Court tube.

The endless journey on the tube was insufferable. The train was hot, airless, and stinking with food, stale perfume, and unwashed bodies. Although she was usually timid, she found herself glaring at a Rastafarian musician begging for a few quid and being positively rude to a Korean tourist in an ugly red vest who was trying to ask for directions in broken English. She changed trains at Victoria station and was forced to stand until the train had left the city behind and started out into the suburbs. When she finally got a seat, she pressed her pounding head against the cool glass and watched the countryside slip past. In the back of her mind, she had convinced herself that this was no more than a badly timed practical joke, perhaps even a perverse scheme dreamed up by her boss just to get her fired. And when Hinkle discovered that she'd walked out of the office without telling anyone, she'd certainly get the sack. Yet the voice on the phone had been so calm, so insistent, and so chilling that deep in her heart, Sarah knew this was no joke.

By the time the train pulled into Crawley station, she was in a breathless panic. Hurrying from the station, she was running as soon as she reached the road she'd grown up on. She slowed then, breath coming in great heaving gasps, a wickedly painful stitch in her side, before finally stopping in the shadow of the neighbor's neatly trimmed hedges. She looked at her mother's house. Everything seemed to be in order. All the windows were closed, the gate was locked, and Freddie's bright blue racer was abandoned on the uncut and sunburned lawn.

Sarah glanced up and down the street, but there was nothing out of the ordinary. No strange cars, no strangers loitering. She glanced at her watch; the caller had said that his *representatives* would arrive within the hour, yet that had been nearly forty-five minutes ago. What sort of representatives? Had they come and gone? Were they waiting inside, even now watching her through her mother's ridiculous lace curtains? What exactly did they want? Something Judith Walker had allegedly given her.

Sarah stepped out of the shadows and walked up to the gate. Something wasn't quite right. She knew it was staring her in the face, yet she couldn't see it.

She looked at the neighbors' houses on either side, comparing them with her own. They were identical in style, shape, and size: four-bedroom detached redbrick houses built just after the war with large, generous rooms, high ceilings, and large bay windows.

She reached into her pocket for a handkerchief to wipe the perspiration from her forehead . . . and then realized what was wrong. This year had been the wettest, coldest summer on record, but then, shockingly, surprisingly, the fall had been spectacular, with a high-pressure zone settling over most of the south of England, pushing temperatures into the unseasonably high seventies. All the houses on either side of her mother's home had windows open in an attempt to circulate fresh air through the rooms. Yet the windows in her own home were closed.

They were all closed.

Perhaps James was trying to sweat out his hangover. Or her mother and brothers had gone out. But they wouldn't have left the bike in the garden. . . .

Sarah pushed open the squeaking gate and hurried up the driveway. Walking up to the front door, she was conscious of her own thundering heart, beating hard enough to nauseate her. She realized she was afraid. She tried to convince herself that everything was going to be fine. She was going to put the key in the lock and push the door open, and Martin would come barreling down the hall in his football kit, and then the kitchen door would open and her mother would appear, all grim and disapproving, surprised to find her home so early, and . . .

And Sarah would be relieved.

The key turned easily in the lock, the heavily lacquered door opening silently on well-oiled hinges. She stood blinking on the doorstep, squinting into the dim hall, and she had opened her mouth to call out to her family when the smell hit her with full force. Sarah covered her mouth and nose, trying not to breathe in the mixture of noxious odors, new smells that were completely alien to the usually flower-scented interior of her home. Some smells she recognized: the bitter stench of urine and feces, the sharper tang of vomit. But there were others—dark, meaty, metallic—that she couldn't quite identify.

Sarah stepped into the hall. Liquid bubbled and squelched underfoot, and she jerked her leg back, rubbing it on the white step, smearing thick dark crimson across the alabaster marble.

Frozen in fear, Sarah began to hyperventilate. She tried to calm herself, pretending it was a prank, something her family had cooked up to get her back for inviting a stranger into their home. As she tried to make sense of the smells, she felt something dripping on her in a slow, repetitive rhythm. Something hot and thick. Sarah looked up.

And then the screams began.

13

Sarah was planting flowers for her mother.

She was up way too early on a Saturday morning for a teen-age girl, but she was desperate to please her perpetually irritable mother, so she had volunteered to plant the bulbs. She dug her hands into the warm soil, which felt oddly moist on her small fingers. As she pulled her hands out of the dirt, the brown earth turned bright crimson. She abruptly fell back and noticed that the entire garden was bathed in bloody red flowers now mingled with the dismembered body parts of her dead father. She frantically tried to gather the fragile flowers, piecing together his broken body; yet the petals fell away like ragged strips of skin, revealing pale weeping flesh underneath, blood dribbling from her hands, forming a strange hieroglyphic pattern. . . .

All around her flowers bloomed, each one more hideous than the last, each one bloodred and bone white.

There was blood.

So much blood.

She had never seen so much blood before in her life. . . .

14

M s. Miller? . . . Ms. Miller? . . . Sarah?"
The voice was male. Bright and chirpy. More mature than her brother Martin's voice—*bright hair black with blood*—but younger than James—*blue eyes missing from their sockets.*

Sarah Miller bolted upright with a scream that tore the lining of her throat. She screamed again and again, breathing in uncontrollable gasps, blood pounding in her temples, heart hammering in her chest, tasting metal in her mouth, the same meaty, metallic odor that had permeated the house.

There were voices all around, officious-looking people in white coats, concerned faces, bright lights. Sarah was only vaguely aware of them. There was a sting in the crook of her arm and she looked down to see that one of the white-coated figures had pushed a needle into her arm.

She was unaware of them, conscious only of the dark images, the terrible vision of her mother splayed across the kitchen table, little Freddie broken and butchered on the stairs, Martin hanging from the chandelier in the foyer . . . and James, dear God, what had they done to James? There had been so much blood. So much blood. She had never seen so much blood before in her life.

And then the needle worked its magic and she slept.

THURSDAY, OCTOBER 29

15

ow do you feel?"

The face swam into focus, an earnest young man with a kind smile, who showed a little more than just professional concern.

Sarah's eyes slowly focused as they followed the young man in blue scrubs. As the male nurse moved around the bed, she gradually became aware of her surroundings. She was in a hospital, in a private room. There must have been an accident, but she couldn't recall anything. She didn't seem to be in any pain, and there were no tubes in her, no plaster casts.

Sarah licked her dry, swollen lips. "What happened?" she attempted to say, but it came out in a scratchy whisper.

"You're going to be just fine," the nurse said, not answering her question as he brought her a cup of water with a straw. She drank gratefully while he lifted her left arm and applied a blood pressure cuff. When he had finished taking her temperature and blood pressure, he tilted the back of the bed upward, raising her to a sitting position.

"What happened?"

Still not answering her, he said, "There are some people who want to talk to you. Do you feel like talking to them now?"

Sarah struggled to straighten up, but the nurse gently pushed her back onto the pillows. "How long have I been here?"

"Sixteen hours."

"What happened?" she asked a third time.

The nurse wouldn't meet her eyes. "There was an accident in your home," he said eventually. "Some sort of gas leak, they said. That's all I know," he added quickly, turning away before she could ask any more questions. Sarah stared at the door. A gas leak? She didn't remember a gas leak . . . but then again, she couldn't even remember how she got here. She lifted her hands and touched her face: It was soft and damp. No cuts, no bruises, no marks. Squeezing her eyes shut, she tried to remember . . . but the images that flickered at the edges of her consciousness darted and twisted away, leaving only the impression of dark shadows.

"Ms. Miller?"

Sarah opened her eyes and knew instinctively that the butch young woman with the close-cropped platinum hair standing at the end of the bed was a police officer. Behind her, a craggy-faced older man perched on the window ledge, watching her intently.

The woman indicated the older man. "This is Detective Inspector Fowler and I am Sergeant Heath, London Metropolitan Police—"

"What happened?" Sarah interrupted. Her voice cracked with the effort, and she started coughing.

Sergeant Heath came around the bed to pour her some more water.

"Please. What happened at my house? No one will tell me anything."

"We were hoping you would be able to tell us," Inspector Fowler said abruptly, pushing himself off the window ledge to stand at the end of the bed, big, hard-knuckled hands clutching the metal bed rail. His lips were so thin, they were almost invisible.

"The nurse said there was a gas leak. . . ."

"There was no gas leak," Fowler said firmly.

The sergeant sat on the bed next to Sarah. "What do you remember?" she asked quietly, trying to catch and hold the girl's attention. Yet Sarah was having trouble listening.

"We know you received two phone calls on Wednesday morning," the police sergeant continued. "You left your office immediately after the second call, caught a cab, subsequently ditching it in Oxford Street approximately fifteen minutes later. Then you caught the tube out of Tottenham Court Road, changed in Victoria, and headed home. You were back in Crawley around twelve forty-five—"

"And then," Detective Fowler interrupted sharply, "what happened then?"

Sarah looked at him blankly. It was the same question she had been asking herself. Something had happened. Something terrible. . . .

"Why did you leave the office so quickly?" the sergeant asked, eyes locked on Sarah's face. "Who called you?"

The phone calls. The voice.

Images danced, dark and bloody.

"The phone calls?" Sergeant Heath prodded gently.

"The man. There was a man with a strange voice, and he said . . . he said that I had something belonging to him, and that . . ." Her voice trailed away.

"And what?" Heath murmured. "What did he say?"

"He said that his representatives would call for it at noon."

Heath glanced quickly at Fowler, but the older man was staring fixedly at Sarah Miller's face. The sergeant turned back to Sarah, anxious to keep her talking. "Does this caller have a name?"

"No. I mean, he didn't give me a name but . . . I don't think I asked," Sarah said quickly. She needed to talk and keep talking, because when she stopped, the images, the dark shadows, drew closer. "But he knew . . . he knew my name and my address. He knew my address."

"Have you ever spoken to this man before?"

"No. Never. I didn't recognize his voice. It was so deep and there was some sort of an accent . . . but I'm not sure."

"What do you have belonging to this man?" Fowler asked quickly.

"Nothing."

"So he just picked you at random?"

"No. I don't think so. He said . . . he said the old woman had given me something."

"What old woman?" Heath asked patiently, keeping her face expressionless.

"The woman who stayed the night with us. Judith. Judith Walker. The man on the phone said Judith had given me something that belonged to him and that his representatives would call for it at noon."

"For what?"

"I don't know!" Sarah was starting to get agitated. She was close to something. So close.

"Who was the woman?"

"Judith Walker. I just told you that. Why aren't you listening to me?"

"Why did she stay the night?"

"She was attacked on the street in front of the library. I helped her. And . . . and . . . and when I took her back to her house, it had been burgled, just completely destroyed . . . so I invited her to stay the night at my place. She didn't have anywhere to go . . . and of course my mother freaked out, thinking that she was going to stay and never leave. My mother was horribly rude to her at tea . . . they all were, but especially my mother . . . but when I woke up the following morning, the old woman, Judith Walker, was gone. She made the bed, it was like . . . it was like she was never there." Sarah couldn't stop babbling.

The shadows were closer now.

The words were coming quicker, and she was breathing in great heaving gasps. "And when I got to work, there was this phone call. I thought it was a joke . . . one of the guys from the office . . . and then my boss called me into his office. I thought he was going to fire me for not coming back to work the previous day. . . ."

"Because you were bringing this Judith Walker home?" Sergeant Heath asked.

"Yes, but he told me Sir Simon called to commend me. But when I got back to my desk, there was another call from the same man. The man with the deep voice. He told me to give him what was his . . . but I didn't know what he was talking about. I didn't know what was his . . . Judith Walker hadn't given me anything . . . I swear, she didn't . . . but he wouldn't listen to me. And there was something about him . . . about his voice . . . something about his voice scared me, so I went home, and then, when I got there, when I walked in the door, when I . . . I . . . I . . . I found . . . I found . . . I found . . ."

The darkness washed over her, bringing with it the images—the terrible, terrifying images, of death and bloody destruction.

FOWLER AND Heath stood in the corridor and listened to Sarah Miller's screams fade as the sedatives took effect.

"What do you think?" Victoria Heath asked. She patted her pockets, searching for the cigarettes she'd given up six months ago.

Tony Fowler shook his head. "No one is that good of an actor," he said regretfully. He'd had Sarah Miller pinned as the murderer. In the vast majority of cases of domestic homicides, a member of the family or a close friend usually committed the crime. And from what he'd been able to put together from the reports of relatives and friends of the deceased family, Sarah had always cowered under the thumb—some would have said the heel—of her overbearing mother, who controlled every aspect of her daughter's life. So one day she cracked and butchered her entire family: exorcising twenty-two years of repressed hostility in an orgy of bloodletting.

Her terrible screams had drawn the neighbors, who'd found her paralyzed in the middle of the dining room, standing in a pool of blood, surrounded by the dismembered and butchered bodies of her entire family.

An open-and-shut case, Fowler had thought.

But now, having listened to Miller scream aloud her hurt, he wasn't so sure. And if Miller wasn't guilty . . . well, Tony Fowler didn't even want to consider that. Right now, Miller was their prime suspect, and he was going to proceed along those lines.

The door opened and the exhausted-looking doctor appeared. "I thought I told you not to upset her!" he snapped.

"We didn't," Heath said easily.

"When can we talk to her again?" Fowler demanded.

"You can't. Not right now. I've sedated her. She'll be unconscious for at least eight hours. And I insist you leave her alone. Detectives, she's been through an extremely traumatic experience. I want you to give her some time to recover."

"Well, we can't have everything we want, can we?" Tony Fowler said, turning away. "We'll be back in eight hours." As they walked down the corridor, he pulled out his phone. "Let's see if we can get anything on this Judith Walker. Be interesting if she didn't exist, wouldn't it?"

"Be even more interesting if she did." Victoria Heath smiled.

16

Robert Elliot dialed the number from memory, amused albeit unsurprised to discover that his fingers were trembling slightly. He was frightened, and rightly so. There was no shame in fear, he reflected.

Fear was mankind's most potent imperative, its most valuable tool. Fear had kept primitive man alive; fear of starvation and rival tribes had sent the first migrants out across the world. Fear kept the many from rebelling against the few. It had fueled most of mankind's finest inventions, and it was that same fear that would ultimately prevent humanity from destroying itself.

Elliot had followed the same rules . . . and they had kept him alive.

Robert Elliot was an expert on fear. Small, unprepossessing, and physically weak, he had discovered its value in the playgrounds of his childhood. In the years that followed, he had studied the nature of fear, learned how to inspire it, how to prosper from it. In doing so, he had explored the limits of his own fears and discovered that little frightened him . . . until he received the phone call at dawn on a pristine summer morning from a man who knew too much about him and his dealings. And who had backed up his vague threats by sending him the rotting remains of a troublesome youth Robert Elliot had buried six months earlier.

Static howled on the line. Knowing from experience that no one would talk, Elliot spoke first. "I've found her. She's at Crawley Hospital, suffering from shock. She's been sedated. I'll visit her shortly."

"And the . . . item?"

Sometimes, when he concentrated, Elliot thought he could detect a trace of an accent in the baritone voice. West Country, perhaps? Welsh? Irish? But despite his best efforts, he had been unable to trace his mysterious employer. "It wasn't in the house, and I searched her office last night. Nothing there. However, I'll be sure to ask her . . . personally."

"Do that. Having seen your handiwork, I'm sure she'll understand that we're quite serious, and I'm confident she will cooperate." The connection was broken and Elliot shoved the phone back in his pocket.

Although he'd orchestrated all of the arrangements, Elliot hadn't been in the house on Wednesday morning. He didn't know exactly what had happened when he'd instructed Skinner and the junkie to do his dirty work; however, he had given them explicit instructions.

Elliot had made sure he had a very public alibi for that time: lunch at the Athenaeum with an old friend. He had worn his new houndstooth Armani blazer and given the waiter a memorable tip.

Later, through a source, he'd obtained a copy of the police report and crime scene photographs. He kept a private collection of eight-by-ten photos of all his "jobs." He collected them in a keepsake memory book, whose first page contained a graphic photo of his bludgeoned father taken just moments after the murder.

As he looked at the photos of the butchered Miller family, a part of him couldn't help but wonder if the girl *would* cooperate. Elliot had instructed Skinner to leave a brother or two alive. Killing *all* the family was a mistake; one family member, perhaps two, was all that was needed to make a point.

Now, the girl had nothing left to lose.

In Elliot's experience, people with nothing to lose made dangerous enemies.

17

Judith Walker sat on the park bench, her arms wrapped tightly around the bag on her lap, the weight of the ancient metal heavy on her frail legs. She'd left Crawley on the first train the previous morning and returned to Bath. She'd been sitting on the wooden bench since, petrified to go back to her devastated home. A Frisbee landed by her feet, and Judith smiled at the young man who darted in and quickly picked it up. The park was teeming with children, full of laughter and life, full of hope for their futures. She watched them, mothers and fathers playing with their children, brothers and sisters running, all squalling and screaming around one another.

She'd be joining her brothers soon: her older brother, who had died in the war, and her much younger brother, who was killed in a car accident with his wife several years earlier, leaving her nephew, Owen, an orphan. The boy had grown up in America and was very much an American, right down to the accent. Despite the fact that he had recently moved to London for work, she hadn't seen much of him. She still remembered the mischievous curly-haired toddler who stayed with her on long holidays all those years ago. He would scamper up into her attic, creating a fortress of wooden boxes, and then tuck himself in to read his aunt's books and create his own illustrations in pencil and crayon. But that had been a long time ago.

Focusing on the present, Judith fixed her eyes on the metallic sheet of dirty pond water before her. If she closed her eyes, she could imagine herself reaching into the bag, pulling out the paper-wrapped bundle, and tossing it into the center of the pool. In her dreams, no hand rose out of the water to grasp it, and it sank without a trace.

But it would change nothing.

She'd heard about the tragic Miller family *accident* on the six o'clock news—*gas leak wipes out entire family*—and she'd known for certain that it had been no accident. One of the reasons she had left the house so early the previous morning was to try to minimize any risk to Sarah and her family. But it was too late. A whole family destroyed . . . and for what? A rusted hunk of metal. And people would continue to die as long as this scrap of the sword remained in the world. Far simpler to cast it into the center of the pool and allow it to rot.

Judith reached into the bag and touched the metal through the torn newspaper. Immediately, a warm tingling sensation spread up along her arthritic fingers into her wrist and flowed up her arm. This wasn't just a rusted chunk of metal. This was Dyrnwyn, Sword of Rhydderch, the Sword That Is Broken.

An iron age chunk of metal, a relic of another time.

And one of the Hallows of Britain.

Judith's fingers moved slowly, sensuously, across the rusted metal, no longer feeling the flaking slivers of oxidized iron, the metal now polished smooth beneath her touch, gold wire twisted around a leather-wrapped hilt, a cut chunk of quartz deep-set into the pommel, the blade smooth, deeply grooved, the metal ragged and torn where it had been shattered just above the hilt. When she opened her eyes she saw, for a single instant, the sword as it had been before, before it blurred and shifted to the shapeless chunk of rusted metal it was now.

Someone was prepared to kill to possess this.

At least six of the Hallowed Keepers had been slain. Richard Fenton, arrogant, aggressive, double-dealing Richard, who'd sown the seeds of his fortune on the black market after the war, had been the most recent killing. It had taken place on the same day she'd been attacked. The brief radio report said that he'd been found dead in his pool and mentioned his heart condition.

Six dead—six that she knew about, though no doubt some of the others had been slain also, their deaths disguised to look like accidents and so remain unreported, quiet little obituaries of a forgotten generation tucked neatly into a small square of type on the obit page.

And it seemed that she was the only one who had figured it out.

But why had the Keepers been slain in such brutal fashion? Once upon a time, the Thirteen Hallows, both individually and collectively, had been incredibly powerful, invested with a fragment of

ancient power that linked them to Britain's primeval past. Her research into the Hallows revealed that many of the artifacts had been
blessed in blood and flesh, skin and fluid, in order to heighten their
latent powers—

Judith stopped, her heart suddenly racing as the grim realization
dawned. The Hallows were being *fired*.

Legend had it that there were certain blood rituals that could *fire*
the Hallows, reviving their ancient power, bringing them to life.

The Once Kings knew the grisly rituals; they had used human
flesh and pain to feed the latent power. The Land Wed Rulers had
practiced the old dark magic and had ruled through the powerful
Hallows. With the passage of time and the dispersion of the Hallows, the rituals had been forgotten—though not entirely. There
was evidence that Henry VIII and Brandon, his court magician, and
later his daughter Elizabeth, under the guidance of Dr. John Dee,
had fired their individual Hallows. Henry owned the Chessboard of
Gwenddolau and had sacrificed at least two of his wives to the Hallowed chessmen, bathing the crystal pieces in their blood. Similarly,
Elizabeth had worn the Crimson Cloak, and legend had it that Dee
had possessed the Pan and Platter of Rhygenydd. There were rumors
that Elizabeth had ordered Essex's death—and Mary's, too—to ap-
pease the ancient rituals and consolidate her rule.

The Hallows could be fired only by the blood sacrifice of significant people. Not just any human sacrifice would do; they had to be
people of power. Once, only the blood of kings would have been sufficient to bring the sacred objects to life; now, it was the blood and
skin of the hereditary Keepers, the old men and women who had
protected the artifacts since their childhood.

Judith stood up, her stiff hip immediately protesting as she began
the long walk around the pond, heading back toward the park gate.
She couldn't keep hiding. If the Hallows were being collected, she
needed to warn her old friends. She had to return home. She had to
speak to Brigid and Barbara. She must tell Don. . . .

She needed to warn all the surviving Hallowed Keepers that they
had each been marked for sacrifice.

18

Robert Elliot liked playing doctor. He relished the power of the white coat as he walked unhurriedly down the hospital corridor, head bent, hands thrust deep into his pockets. It was a uniform that carried tremendous power and unquestioned authority.

Elliot stopped at the nurses' station on the fifth floor and thumbed through the pile of manila patient files. The pretty young Indian nurse busily writing her patient reports didn't even glance up.

The small, blank-faced man pulled out one file at random.

"Sarah Miller."

Elliot was abruptly aware of the big, hard-faced man standing in front of the nurses' station and the younger blond woman behind him, and he knew instinctively that they were both police. He shifted his body slightly, turning away from them, and concentrated on a file.

"Where is she?" the man snapped. "We've just been to her room and it's empty. I thought she was still supposed to be under sedation."

Elliot made notes in the file.

The nurse looked up and was about to protest when the woman produced identification, confirming Elliot's suspicions. "Ms. Miller signed herself out two hours ago," the nurse said quickly. "Dr. Castrucci tried to stop her . . . ," she began, but the two police officers had already turned and walked away.

Tucking the chart under his arm, Elliot strode off in the opposite direction.

Where was the girl going to go? As far as Elliot knew, there were no relatives living in England and few friends. Robert Elliot smiled grimly; if he'd been in the girl's shoes, he'd want answers. And only Judith Walker could give her those answers. The small man glanced at his Baume & Mercier watch; if Sarah Miller had gone immediately to Judith Walker's home, she would get there precisely as his associates were finishing their business. And they could kill, literally and figuratively, two birds with one stone.

19

After a while, the pain vanished.

Judith knew that it was possible to feel so much pain that one's entire body becomes completely numb as it realizes it is about to cross the bridge from life to whatever lies beyond.

The faces of the mocking, grinning youths had faded into indistinct, almost abstract masks, the room had dissolved, melting the walls and floors together into swirling patterns of color. She watched the colors for a long time, concentrating on them, knowing that if her attention was to falter, even for a second, her consciousness would drift back into the basement of the violated house, where she was tied to a chair while the cold-eyed youths hurt her, again and again and again.

If she lost focus, she would feel the pain, and she couldn't afford to die. Not yet.

They had come for the sword.

The Broken Sword.

Dyrnwyn, Sword of Rhydderch.

The image of the sword grew in her mind, flowing out of the colors, solidifying into a solid bar of golden light. Judith Walker concentrated on the light, which allowed her to focus on another time, a more innocent age, when thirteen children were drawn together from all across Britain to a village in the shadow of the mountains to fulfill an ancient destiny.

The tiny portion of her psyche locked into the present was aware of the pain's intensity: a searing precipice of agony threatening to break through the images, the stink of burning flesh strong in her nostrils.

Her burning flesh.

Judith focused on the image of the sword. In its shiny blade, she saw the face of the tramp, the battered, one-eyed tramp with the sour, bitter breath who had given each of the chosen children one of the thirteen ancient objects. He had whispered arcane secrets to them, tales of the origin of their especial hallowed object. The tramp's face was just as she remembered it, skin so deeply creased with wrinkles that it seemed scarred, the left half in perpetual shadow from a drooping, broken-brimmed hat, half concealing the triangular patch that covered the left eye. There was a question she wanted to ask him, a question she had wanted to ask him more than seventy years ago. Then, she had wanted to know why she had been chosen to receive the sword . . . now, she wanted to know why she was being tortured . . . why she was suffering so much pain . . . why . . .

SARAH MILLER wandered through the streets in a confused daze. The events of the past few days had condensed and flowed together, whirling into a foggy jigsaw of images, most of which were dark and terrifying, stained with innocent blood.

A concerned doctor had tried to prevent her from leaving the hospital, but Sarah had ignored him as she'd dressed, and just once, when the doctor had touched her, urging her back into bed, Sarah had given the man a look. All of the pain, anguish, and rage that bubbled inside had blazed through her eyes, and in that moment the doctor had backed off.

The young woman's last clear memories were from forty-eight hours earlier, when she had first encountered Judith Walker: two short days that seemed like an entire lifetime. A make-believe world in which she had a life, a family, a future.

That world was gone now, lost forever.

The jigsaw images returned. They were mostly faces: those of her mother and of James, Martin, and Freddie. Little Freddie. She would never be able to wipe that image from her memory: her brother's face, forever frozen in a terrified mask. . . .

Her fault.

Sarah shook her head savagely. No, not her fault: Judith Walker's fault. A frail, silver-haired old woman who had brought death and destruction into her home.

ALTHOUGH ALL the streets in this part of Bath looked identical— rows of postwar houses, bay windows, pocket gardens, metal railings, multicolored FOR SALE signs sprouting in every third garden—Sarah recognized the street the moment she stepped into it.

The voice on the phone had said that Judith Walker had given her something. Sarah knew she hadn't, and her family had been butchered because of it. Judith Walker was the catalyst; she had destroyed Sarah's ordered world. She would have the answers.

The gate squealed as she pushed it open, one end dragging across the path in a short arc. Sarah slowed as she reached the front door and then stopped with her hand on the brass knocker, suddenly wondering what she was going to say. She lifted the lion's head and allowed it to fall. The sound echoed hollowly inside the house. She heard the faintest of scuffling sounds and knocked again, harder this time, the sound resonating in the silent street. Movement rasped and slithered within again.

Sarah pushed open the letter box and called through, "Judith, it's Sarah Miller. I know you're in there."

The smell wafted through the open letter box, a mixture of excrement and stale sweat coupled with the bitter metallic odor of blood. The jigsaw images locked together, and suddenly she was home again, standing in her darkened hallway, smelling the same odors, so alien . . . so terrifying.

"Judith? . . ." Pressing her hand against the door, she pushed. It swung inward silently, and a sudden scream stopped Sarah in her tracks, raising the hackles at the back of her neck. The sound was human, but only barely so, a raw scream of absolute agony, high-pitched and terrible. It was coming from the direction of the stairs. She should turn and run, get the police, get help . . . but almost unconsciously, she stepped forward into the devastated hallway. There was a door under the stairs.

"Judith?"

Sarah stopped with her hand on the handle of the low door and pressed her face against the wood. The smell was stronger here, a mixture of blood and feces and something else . . . the stale, acrid odor of burned meat.

"Judith?" Sarah asked, pushing open the door.

"JUDITH . . ."

The one-eyed man had turned his head; only the slightest sparkle in his single eye provided evidence that he was facing her. Had he called her name?

"Why, Mr. Ambrose, why?" Seventy years and she'd never forgotten his name.

"Judith? . . ."

"Because you are the Keepers of the Hallows. The blood of the blessed flows in your veins, diluted certainly, but there. You are the descendants of those chosen to bear the Hallows and keep the land. Only the bloodline are worthy enough to keep the sacred Hallows."

Had he spoken, or had she imagined the answer, culled it from years of research into the artifacts?

"Judith? . . ."

The voice broke through her consciousness, shattering the images, pulling her back, making her feel the pain.

"DEAR GOD!"

Sarah clapped both hands to her mouth, feeling her stomach heave. The figure tied to the chair in the tiny cellar was barely recognizable as human; in the glow of the single bulb, it looked more like a side of meat from a butcher's window.

"Judith?" Her voice was a rasp, barely audible in the noisome closeness of the cellar. Sarah wondered how long the woman had survived the incredible agony. Shockingly, the woman raised her head, blood-filled eyes turning to the sound. Her torturers had spared her face, making the damage to her body all the more obscene.

"Judith . . ." Sarah reached out to touch her, then drew back her hand, realizing that every movement must be agony.

Incredibly the woman recognized her voice. Judith Walker smiled. "Sarah?" Her voice was a gargled mumble.

"I'll get the police . . . and an ambulance."

"No." She attempted to shake her head and cringed with the effort. "Too late . . . much too late."

"Who did this?" Sarah knelt in the blood and fluids and worked at the thin wire bonds that secured the old woman to the chair. They had obviously been twisted shut with pliers, and in places the wire had sunk deeply into her flesh.

"They came for the sword. . . ." Judith's voice was a thread now, rasping, sobbing.

"The what?" Sarah eased a wire away, blood weeping from the torn skin.

"Dyrnwyn, the Broken Sword. Listen to me. There's a bag in the kitchen upstairs. From Tesco. It's on the table, a shopping bag filled with notes and papers and what looks like a rusted piece of metal." She coughed suddenly, fine blood misting the air. "Take them to my nephew, Owen . . . his address is in the bag." Suddenly her free hand shot out, flailing blindly until it touched Sarah's shoulder, bloody fingers biting deeply into the young woman's flesh. "Promise me this. You must give it into his hands. His and no one else's. Promise me. You must protect the sword. Promise."

"I promise."

"Swear it." Her body was trembling now, shivering wildly. "Swear it."

"I swear it," Sarah said.

"Bring him the bag . . . and tell him I'm sorry. I'm so sorry."

"For what?"

"For what's going to happen."

20

Tony Fowler pounded on the wheel of the car. "I don't believe it. She exists? There really is a Judith Walker?"

Victoria Heath grinned as she replaced the radio. "There is. And she was burgled on Tuesday. Miller was telling the truth. We've got the call logged in at three fifty-five. Officers arrived on the scene at four twenty. They took statements from Judith Walker *and*"—she paused for effect—"a Miss Sarah Miller."

"Miller! What was she doing there?"

Sergeant Heath shrugged. "One of the officers did ask about the relationship and was told by Miss Walker that Sarah Miller was a friend. It seems they went off together in a taxi."

"Find me that taxi."

Victoria Heath grinned. "I'll bet you money that it took them to Miller's home."

Tony Fowler nodded glumly. "Where does this Judith Walker live? We'd better talk to her."

"We're forty-five minutes away . . . tops." Victoria Heath smiled. "If you use the lights."

"Love using the lights." Fowler put the siren on the car and accelerated through the traffic.

SARAH PRESSED her fingers against the side of the old woman's neck. There was no pulse. Judith Walker was finally at peace.

She slowly backed away from the corpse, head pounding, stomach wracked with cramps, acrid bile in her throat. She had to get out of the room. Stopping on the stairs, she turned to look around the tiny cellar again. It was bathed in blood: It speckled the walls, washed across the floor in viscous puddles, even the bare lightbulb dangled a long thread of dark blood. In the last few days, she had seen so much blood. She was twenty-two years old and the only blood she had seen spilled before came from minor cuts and scrapes or the ersatz blood on television and in films. Feeling her stomach rise in revulsion, she turned and fled up the stairs.

Sarah found the canvas shopping bag in the kitchen on the table, where Judith had left it. She lifted it, the weight of the metal making it heavier than she expected. Peeling back the newspaper, she discovered an unremarkable rusted chunk of metal. Was this what Judith had been killed for? Some papers and a piece of rusted metal? It didn't make any sense. Why had she allowed herself to be brutally tortured to death if the item her killers had wanted was just above her head? And for what—a worthless piece of metal?

The crunch of glass made her look up.

There was a face at the back door, the snarling mask of a skinhead—the same skinhead who had attacked Judith on Tuesday—wraparound sunglasses lending his face an insectile appearance. There were three others behind him.

Sarah snatched the bag and ran. Behind her, the thugs kicked the kitchen door off its hinges.

SERGEANT VICTORIA Heath tapped her colleague on the arm. "This one here. Number—" She was pointing toward the house when the front door was flung open with enough force to shatter the glass panes and the wild, disheveled figure of a young woman raced out.

"Miller!" Heath and Fowler said simultaneously.

The young woman was looking over her shoulder as she wrenched open the gate and darted out onto the street, slamming against the police car, which Fowler had swung onto the pavement.

For a single instant, Tony Fowler and Victoria Heath stared at the terrified face of Sarah Miller . . . before she turned and raced off down the road.

Fowler slammed the car into reverse, clipping the car behind him, and took off after Miller, tires screaming and smoking on the road. Victoria snatched up the radio and then stopped, jerking her head back sharply. There was a perfect bloody handprint on the window in front of her.

"Leave her, Tony," she whispered, "we have to go back."

· · ·

IT TOOK her a long time before she realized that she wasn't being followed. She had raced through rows of streets, past women gossiping on doorsteps, through children playing on street corners, down alleys and lanes, across gardens, into side streets, running until her breath was acid in her lungs and her stomach was cramped into a tight ball. Finally, she had pushed through rusted iron gates and slumped on the same warped and scarred wooden bench Judith Walker had used hours earlier. Holding her head in her hands, Sarah attempted to make sense of the last few hours.

Judith Walker was dead, brutally killed for . . . for what?

For the contents of the bag.

She reached into the bag and touched the chunk of iron, and suddenly she remembered the phone call to the office, the coolly insistent voice.

She gave you something rather important that belongs to me.

The mysterious caller's *representatives* had killed her family looking for the artifact, and Judith had died protecting it. The sword, Judith had called it. Sarah peered into the bag. It didn't look like a sword, it looked like something you'd find in the trash. But her family had died for this metal. Judith too.

Sarah ran her fingers along the metal and they came away rust red, bloodred. What made this so special?

And the police . . . What had they been doing there? Looking for her or Judith?

And why had she run?

Sarah knew she should have stayed and spoken to the police, but the skinhead and the others had been waiting and she hadn't been thinking clearly. She should go back and talk to them before they got the wrong impression. Sarah bent her head, her forehead touching the cold metal in the bag on her lap. She should not have run. . . .

"SO THAT'S why she ran," Tony Fowler said tightly, pinching his nose, breathing only through his mouth. He was standing on the stairs, looking down into the cellar, trying not to inhale the noxious odors. The puddle of yellow light shed by the naked bulb highlighted the mutilated body. Victoria Heath stood behind him, a scented handkerchief pressed tightly to her mouth, eyes swimming.

Tony and Victoria backed up the stairs. He closed the cellar door on the terrible scene, took a deep breath, held it, and exhaled sharply, trying to drive out the pervasive stench of death. "She must have come straight here from the hospital."

"Why?" his partner mumbled, swallowing hard.

The detective shrugged. "Who knows? We'll ask her when we catch her. But we were right the first time. Her reaction in the hospital was obviously nothing more than an act. An Oscar-winning performance."

"I believed it," Victoria whispered. "She fooled me."

"She fooled me, too. And now she's on a spree. First her family, and now this poor woman. God knows who's next."

"I honestly didn't think she'd done it," Victoria mused. "She just didn't seem the type."

"Trust me—they never do."

21

hey were coppers," Skinner justified to Elliot as he leaned into the car, feeling the cool rush of the air-conditioning against his sweaty skin. "She ran out the front door, smack into their car. There was nothing we could do."

"How do you know?" the small man asked coldly. They were several blocks from the old woman's house, and Elliot could smell the metallic odor of blood radiating from the skinhead's flesh and clothes and realized that he would have to get his car detailed again. Elliot's sleek BMW hardly blended into the bleak, desolate wasteland of brick and rubble that was being converted into a car park. Behind him, Elliot could see Skinner's three accomplices sitting on the ground, passing a joint back and forth. They were laughing in high-pitched excited squeals. "How do you know they were police?" he repeated.

"They had that look," Skinner said defensively. "I know police."

"Describe them."

"Man and a woman. Big craggy-faced bloke and a blond dyke."

Elliot sighed. The detectives from the hospital; they hadn't wasted any time. "Was Ms. Miller carrying anything when she ran?"

"She had the old lady's bag, which was on the table in the kitch . . ." Skinner stopped, realizing he'd said too much.

Elliot pulled off his Ray-Bans and dropped them on the seat beside him. He hit the power switch on the car window and the glass slid up abruptly, trapping Skinner's head in the opening, the edge of the glass biting deep into the pale flesh just below his protruding Adam's apple. Robert Elliot put his two hands on the wheel and stared straight head, and when he spoke, his voice was remarkably composed. "You spent the entire afternoon *questioning* the woman, and got nothing from her. And the bag was on the table in plain sight the whole time?"

"It was a shopping bag . . . nothing more," Skinner croaked. "For Christ's sake, I can't breathe."

"Then why did Ms. Miller take it?" Elliot glanced sidelong at the sweating skinhead. "The old woman was dead when you left her, wasn't she?"

"Yeah." Skinner attempted to swallow.

"You're positive?" Elliot insisted. "There was no way she could have told the young woman anything?"

"No one could have survived what we did to her. We were about to finish when we heard movement upstairs, so we scampered out the back. I had one of the lads check the front of the house, but there was no car. I was going back in to investigate when I saw the bird who kicked me on Tuesday. She was standing at the kitchen table, going through the shopping bag."

"Ms. Miller."

"Miller. Yeah. When she saw us, she grabbed the bag and ran. We were following her when we saw the police. They took off after her, then suddenly stopped and reversed back up the street. So we got out."

Elliot sighed. His employer was going to be very upset. He pushed the ignition button, starting up the car.

"Hey!" Skinner squealed.

Elliot carefully engaged the clutch and let off the hand brake. The car rolled forward, and Skinner's shouts rose in intensity as he scrambled to keep up. "No, Mr. Elliot, please . . . Mr. Elliot, please!" Skinner's thin fingers tried desperately to grip the slippery glass.

"What would happen if I drove off now?" Elliot mused.

"Mr. Elliot, please. I'm sorry. I'm—"

"I'm not sure which would happen first. Either your neck would snap or you would suffocate," Elliot said calmly. There was a slight sheen of sweat on his high forehead. He licked suddenly dry lips with a small, pointed tongue. "I suppose if I drove fast enough, and took a corner sharply, it might tear your head clear off your shoulders. It'd be quick, but it would make a ferocious mess of the car," he added.

"I'll find her. I'll make her tell us what was in the bag—"

"If I drove slowly, you could probably cling to the window, but your legs would drag on the ground." Elliot allowed the car to drift forward and gunned the engine. "I suppose you would be able to run for a while, a little while, at least . . . but what would happen when you got tired? How long do you think it would take to strip the flesh from your bones?"

"Mr. Elliot, please . . ." Skinner was crying now, knowing the older man was perfectly capable of doing just that.

"I taught you about pain, Skinner, but I haven't taught you everything." He suddenly released the window, and Skinner fell back, hacking, both hands pressed to his throat.

"There are some lessons still left to be learned. Don't make me teach them to you. Find Sarah Miller."

22

Elliot believes the girl may have the sword," Ahriman murmured.

Vyvienne sat up on the bed, candlelight shimmering on her naked flesh, running molten on her raven hair. "Elliot is a fool," she hissed. "And like all fools, he employs fools—weak, drug-addled, ignorant fools. A man is only as strong as the tools he uses. . . . And you are a fool for trusting him," she added with unaccustomed boldness.

Ahriman caught her jaw, squeezing it, fingers digging into the soft flesh beneath her eye. "You forget yourself," he whispered.

The woman tried to form words, but the pressure on her jaw was intense.

"More important, you forget who I am. What I am."

She started to choke and he released her, pushing her away from him. "Elliot suits our needs."

"For the moment," the woman said hoarsely, teeth sharp and white against dark, plump lips. "And when you're done with him—remember, you promised him to me."

"He's yours," Ahriman agreed.

The woman rose from the bed and crossed to the bay window, pushing back the heavy velvet curtains and allowing the waning sunlight to wash the gloom from the wood-paneled bedroom. Against the crimson light, her naked flesh was as waxen as the thick candles that dotted the room, her dark mane draping over her sinewy back. She turned, arms folded beneath her heavy breasts, pushing them up. "What are we going to do about the girl?"

Ahriman threw back the covers and swung his legs from the bed. "Find her."

"And then?" she asked. "The girl is not part of the pattern. Not part of the Family."

"I know that. But who knows what patterns are whirling and shifting now? We've lost Judith Walker without recovering the sword; this is our first setback. But we know—we *think*—the girl has it. So all is not lost."

The woman padded across the room and pressed herself against Ahriman, his chill flesh raising goose bumps on her skin. "Be careful. We know nothing about the girl. We don't know her family, her lineage. We don't know how much the old woman told her."

"Nothing, probably," Ahriman said quickly. "Judith Walker was a manipulator, a user. Ultimately, all the Hallowed Keepers become users; they are unable to resist the lure of the tiny fragment of power they control, the ability to make men and women do their bidding. Judith used the girl, and by doing so brought destruction on the young woman's family. I wonder if the girl realized that?" he asked softly. "Probably." He nodded slowly. "Maybe she went back to the woman for answers. . . ."

"And old Walker must have told the girl something," Vyvienne said quickly, her breath warming the man's naked chest. "Why else would Miller have taken the bag?"

"You're right—as always." The big man wrapped his arms around the woman, pulling her close, drawing the heat from her body, the tingle of energy arousing him. "We will know soon," he promised. "We'll have her."

"Do not be so certain. You have unleashed extraordinary forces by simply bringing the Hallows we already possess into such close proximity. I've sensed the ripples through the Astral, distortions in the fabric of the Otherworld. Only the Gods know what you have disturbed."

The man known as Ahriman laughed. "She is a child, caught in a complex situation she could never comprehend. She is of absolutely no danger to us. Elliot's people will find her soon." His smile turned vicious. "And, if you desire, you can play with her then."

23

In the time after the Last Battle, there was only darkness.

Those who had survived—and there were few enough—cowered in the darkness.

And hungered.

The flesh of the humankind was close enough. Close enough to smell, to taste on the air, but not close enough to touch, not close enough to feast upon.

They had been cast away, cast out, cast down, and sealed into their prison by the Halga, by the boy who was not a boy, who was humankind and more than humankind.

Those who survived did not age, and though they had no concept of time, they were aware that a great number of seasons—tens of hundreds and more besides—had passed by.

But now there was light.

A speck in the darkness.

A tiny bloodred pulse, a heartbeat.

As one, they moved toward the light.

For where there was light, there was food.

And they hungered.

24

Sarah was shocked by what she saw.

Catching a glimpse of her reflection in the dark pond water, she did not recognize the wild-eyed woman who stared back at her. When she had left for work a day earlier, she had carefully applied her MAC foundation, mascara, and nude lip gloss. The makeup was gone now, washed away with tears and sweat. Now, the dots of her unconcealed freckles were connected with dried blood. Her eyes were sunk deep in her head, black smudges etched beneath them, the whole effect startling against the pallor of her skin. Her hair, which had been pulled back into a tight ponytail, now hung loose and wild about her face, sticking out at all angles, and when she ran her hand through it, flakes of dried blood—Judith's blood—spiraled away.

Sarah knew that she should go to the police. When she'd seen the skinhead, seen the evil in his eyes, she knew that he would have no compunction about killing her, so she'd panicked and run for her life. She knew without a shadow of doubt that this was the man who had killed Judith and butchered her family.

She needed to get to the police, to talk to the blond sergeant and the gruff inspector. Yet there was something she had to do first. She needed to keep her promise to Judith, to fulfill a dying woman's last wish.

Seated once again on the park bench, Sarah lifted the bag onto her lap and began to systematically sort through it. She laid out the items on the bench beside her. She pushed aside the newspaper-wrapped iron sword before examining the rest of the contents: a cardboard folder stuffed with sheets of printed paper, a padded manila envelope filled with newspaper clippings, and a bundle of letters tied in a faded purple ribbon. Somewhere in this mess she hoped she'd find Owen's address. Sarah turned over the letters; each bore the return address of Beatrice Clay. The stamps dated as far back as the fifties, and the last letter had been sent only a few months earlier. Judith's wallet was at the bottom of the bag. It contained twenty-two pounds in notes and change and her British Library reading card.

Sarah was getting so cold. Although the last few days had been unseasonably hot, the autumn nights quickly grew chill. Now, as the sun dipped, the early evening air turned crisp, making her wish she had something warmer to wear. She needed to get this to Owen so that she could . . . so that she could what? What was she going to do? Where was she going to go?

She felt the dark stirrings of panic and the scream beginning to bubble at the back of her throat. She had nowhere to go and no one to go to. She was . . . she was . . .

Sarah forced herself to concentrate on the bag. What was Owen's address? What was his last name? She couldn't find anything with an address on it. The old woman had been in great pain; maybe she'd only imagined the address was in the bag. Sarah shook her head. No. Judith had been lucid, terrifyingly so. She knew exactly what she was saying. And Sarah couldn't even begin to imagine the pain she must have been going through as she'd given her the message.

She began to return the items to the bag, quickly rifling through the bundle of letters in case one was addressed to someone called Owen. The typed pages in the folder seemed to be notes for a novel. Judith had been a writer, so perhaps these were research notes. The padded envelope . . . She turned it over. It was addressed to Owen Walker, with an address at a flat in Scarsdale Villas, just off Earls Court Road.

SKINNER DROVE in sullen silence, glad of the mirrored sunglasses that concealed his red eyes, aware that the other three in the van were watching him closely. The red line where the window had cut into his throat was still visible on his flesh. They had all witnessed his humiliation, and he knew that was what Elliot intended. The short, unassuming-looking man enjoyed causing pain: the ultimate passion, he called it. Skinner's knuckles tightened on the steering wheel of the battered Volkswagen van. He didn't blame Elliot; Mr. Elliot was untouchable, and Skinner wasn't afraid to admit that he was terrified of him. Skinner blamed Sarah Miller. She was at the root of his humiliation. And she was going to pay. Elliot wanted Miller alive, but he wasn't too fussy about her condition.

"What now?" Larry McFeely drawled. He twisted in the passenger seat to look at the skinhead.

Skinner swallowed hard, the action painful against his bruised windpipe. "We find Miller," he grunted, his voice harsh and rasping. He swallowed and tried again. "We find Miller and the bag. And we take her to Mr. Elliot."

"The bitch could be anywhere," McFeely muttered.

"She's just out of hospital, she's on foot. She couldn't have gone far. Mr. Elliot suggested that we watch the trains. If she's heading back into the city, she'll take Bath Spa to Paddington."

"She could've taken a bus or a taxi," McFeely suggested, brushing long, greasy hair out of his glassy eyes.

"As far as we know, she's never been to Bath before. She won't know the buses. And she won't go for a taxi in case the cabbie remembers her." Skinner shook his head quickly, parroting everything Elliot had said. "She'll go for the train."

McFeely shrugged, unconvinced. He was wired and jumpy; all he wanted to do now was head back to his flat and crash, do some hash and mellow out. The old woman had died hard, and while McFeely had had no problems killing her, he had found her silence disturbing, almost threatening. He loved listening to the screams, he got off on them . . . but the old woman hadn't screamed. Her cold gray eyes had continued to stare at him even as he'd used the knife on her.

Traffic lights changed to red and Skinner stopped the van, rear brakes squealing loudly. He twisted in the seat to look at the two blank-eyed young men in the back. They were passing a crack pipe back and forth, oblivious to everything else, the memories of their bloody afternoon's work already fading, mingling with the crack cocaine dreams. In an hour, they would have forgotten everything.

Perfect puppets.

Skinner snatched the pipe away, watching as they both reached blindly for it. He dropped the glass pipe on the floor of the van and ground it underfoot. He had nothing but contempt for addicts. It was a waste of a life. No focus. And one thing Skinner had was focus.

"I want you two inside the station watching for Miller. You do remember what she looks like, right?" he demanded.

They looked at him blankly.

"Jesus! You take idiot one with you," he said to McFeely. "I'll babysit idiot two." The light changed to green and he pulled away. "And don't let Miller get past you. Mr. Elliot would be very upset."

"And we wouldn't want that." McFeely bit the inside of his cheek to prevent himself from smiling.

SARAH FOLLOWED the train signs. She walked slowly, head down, clutching the shopping bag to her chest, feeling her heart thump solidly against the hard metal of the sword. She stopped once, popping into a shop as a pair of uniformed bobbies hurried past. Sarah ignored the ambulance and police cruiser that sped down the road, sirens blaring, probably en route to Judith Walker's. . . . She found she didn't want to think of the old woman again, because thinking of her brought back the images of the pitiful creature in the cellar. And suddenly there were tears in her eyes, the world dissolving into rainbow-hued patterns. She blinked them away, feeling the moisture trickle down her cheeks. She glanced up, but no one was looking at her except for a small child who was holding his mother's hand. The boy smiled at her, his missing tooth punctuating his youth and innocence. She envied him. The little boy pointed at her and the mother looked up, caught Sarah's eyes, then quickly turned away, eyes clouded with embarrassment, not wanting to get involved.

Sarah dragged her sleeve across her eyes, suddenly realizing what she must look like: wild-haired, red-eyed, dirty clothing. She was just another lost soul, one of thousands who wandered the streets. Only she was more lost than most.

Through shimmering tears, she spotted the sign for the train station and headed toward it. All she had to do was deliver the bag to Judith's nephew, and it would all be over.

25

Inspector Tony Fowler was mesmerized by the bloody print on the glass. Forensics were swarming all over the crime scene, but he did not need modern technology to tell him that they would find Sarah Miller's prints, hair follicles, and clothing fibers intermingled with the remains of Judith Walker's bloody corpse.

"I've spent my life on the force, and I've never seen anything like it," Fowler admitted shakily. "I've seen the Yorkshire Ripper's handiwork; I was part of a special contingent of officers who went to the States in '74 to observe the aftermath of the Ted Bundy killings firsthand. I've see Chinese choppings and Mafia hits, I've seen the aftermath of a Jamaican posse's handiwork, I've cleaned up after IRA bombers . . . but I've never seen anything like that poor woman. How she must have suffered."

Victoria Heath tipped back the plastic bottle of water and took a long swallow, trying to wash away the foul taste in her mouth. She had been a police officer for only seven years and in that time thought she'd seen everything. She was only a few years older than the Miller girl, yet they were on opposite sides of the law. Of morality. Of humanity. Because whoever did that to Judith Walker was a certified psychopath. "What would motivate someone to do that?" she asked softly. "It's inhuman."

"Exactly," Tony breathed. "Inhuman. After a while the killer stops thinking of their victim as a person. It's no longer a living human being, it's simply an object." The detective reached up to place his hand on the inside of the windscreen, matching the bloody print on the glass. "And once they get a taste for the kill, they can't stop. The killings get more brutal as the killer spirals out of control."

"But Miller seemed so . . . so normal."

Fowler grunted. "So did Ted Bundy. I saw the aftermath of one of his killing sprees. He attacked four sleeping girls at Florida State University: bludgeoned two of them to death with a log of wood, battered another two until they were almost unrecognizable. Within the hour he'd beaten another girl to a pulp in an apartment a couple of blocks away. And yet everyone who knew him said what a really nice guy he was."

"Just like Miller," Victoria muttered.

"Just like Miller," Fowler agreed. "At least this should be a relatively simple case. We've caught her red-handed." He grimaced at the unintentional irony. "This shouldn't have happened," he said quietly, climbing out of the car. "We shouldn't have left her alone in the hospital."

"We weren't to know."

"We should have known," Fowler snapped. "This is our fault. We made a mistake. And it cost this woman her life. But I'll make sure it doesn't happen again," he added grimly.

"That sounds like a threat."

"A promise."

26

Sarah knew that she was not alone.

The air smelled hot, stale, and metallic in the train station . . . the same metallic sweetness of spilled blood. Sarah felt her gorge rise and she swallowed hard, images of wet meat appearing before her eyes, an advertisement for the Tate Gallery on the wall opposite dissolving into patterns of raw flesh.

She'd caught the flicker of movement out of the corner of her eye, and the chill autumnal air carried with it the faint stink of unwashed flesh and warm blood.

How many were there?

She dared not turn to look as she ducked into the shadows.

Next Train Two Minutes.

The train station was almost deserted, fewer than six people waiting on the platform. Sarah walked toward the far end of the platform, distancing herself from possible danger. She glanced back over her shoulder, pretending to check the electronic notice board . . . and spotted the two men as they stepped onto the platform. One wore his hair cropped close to his skull and was dressed in a faded army vest and combat trousers, while the second was wearing nondescript jeans and a Rolling Stones T-shirt. Sarah recognized the young man's hair: She had seen the same mop of matted blond hair the day Judith Walker had been attacked, and again, this morning, among the group at the house. The killers.

Next Train One Minute.

She stepped back into the shadow of an arch and prayed they weren't looking for her . . . but she knew they were.

Train Now Arriving . . .

The train appeared in the distance, clicking over the points. It seemed to take ages to reach the station, and at any moment Sarah expected to feel a hand on her shoulder either pulling her back into danger or pushing her onto the tracks toward death.

She remained motionless, barely breathing, and didn't move as the train clattered into the station and doors hissed open almost directly opposite her. A tiny Malaysian woman stepped off, pulling a huge shopping bag behind her. A few people stepped forward onto the train: A young woman pushed a toddler into the carriage before her, then folded an enormous stroller and lifted it aboard. An elderly woman close to Judith's age hobbled slowly aboard, leaning heavily on a cane. A tired worker in stained coveralls slipped in just behind her.

Stand Clear of the Doors.

At the last moment Sarah darted forward and onto the train, barely squeezing through as the doors hissed shut. She managed a single glance down the platform, but the two young men had vanished. Had they left the station or were they on the train? She flopped into a seat, staring straight ahead, heart thumping, chest heaving, stomach cramping. She was bathed in sour sweat, and when she rubbed her hand across her forehead, it came away greasy and stained. When she caught the grandmother staring at her with an expression of disgust, she immediately stood up and turned her back, staring intently at the map on the wall above the window. She kept glancing back down the train.

Had the two men got on? Were they even now moving toward her?

She turned back to the map, needing to work out the shortest route to Earls Court Road. If she transferred at Paddington onto the District Line, it would go directly to Earls Court. And once she had given the bag to Judith Walker's nephew—she pulled out the envelope and checked the name and address again—she could finally go to the police. She could clear her name and move on with her life. Sinking back into a seat, she sighed. A few hours: It shouldn't take more than a couple of hours.

Then it would all be over and she'd be free.

27

They had spotted her the moment they stepped onto the platform. She'd been skulking in the shadows, head bent, arms wrapped protectively around a bulging shopping bag, hugging it close to her chest.

Next Train Two Minutes.

"Get Skinner," Larry McFeely snapped. He brushed strands of his long hair out of his eyes and eased his glassy-eyed companion toward the stairs. "Get Skinner. Tell him we've found the girl." He saw the girl duck into the shadows and wondered if they'd been seen. Larry chewed on his thumbnail, trying to formulate a plan, regretting the dope he'd smoked earlier. It had mellowed him out, sure, but right now he simply couldn't think straight. Should he tackle Miller now and maybe cause a scene or wait until Skinner arrived? But if he did that, the skinhead would probably claim all the credit for himself.

McFeely was still dithering when the train arrived, and he immediately guessed that the girl was going to hang back in the shadows and then dart aboard at the last moment. There was still no sign of Skinner: Where the fuck had he got to?

Train Now Arriving . . .

McFeely darted onto the train and then hovered in the doorway, watching intently for Miller to make her move.

Stand Clear of the Doors.

He'd been just about to step off the train when the woman appeared out of the shadows, moving fast, and jumped aboard. As the doors hissed shut and the train lurched off, Larry had turned to see Skinner and the others come running into the station. Larry grinned at their expressions, but the smile faded when he realized that he didn't know where the train was going . . . and when he dug into his pockets, he discovered he had exactly one pound and fifty pence on him, hardly enough for a phone call and definitely not enough to get back to his flat. He was now trapped on the train with Miller. Straightening, he looked down the train and a slow smile curled his fleshy lips as an idea formed in his befuddled brain. He was alone on the train with Miller . . . which meant that she was his and the psycho skinhead couldn't attempt to steal his reward.

Pushing his way through the crowd toward the door that connected the carriages, he wondered how much Elliot would pay for the return of the girl.

28

Later, shocked eyewitnesses would describe the incident in almost identical terms.

Martha Hill, who was on her way back into London after a visit with her grandchildren, reported that a blond-haired young man had come through the adjoining cabin doors and approached the wild-haired, dirty-looking young woman who was sitting hunched over, arms wrapped tightly around her chest. The two young people seemed to know each other. Martha Hill had gotten the impression that the blond had called the young woman by name: Sarah. She saw them speaking briefly together.

Jonas Gottlieb was coming off a thirty-six-hour shift and was dozing in his seat when he heard the sliding doors between the compartments open and a young man with long, dirty blond hair stepped through. He'd moved unsteadily through the compartment, even though the train ride was smooth, and Gottlieb guessed that the man was either drunk or stoned. He'd stopped before a young woman, who'd stared at him with red-rimmed, sunken eyes. Jonas Gottlieb dismissed them both as junkies. He had heard the blond-haired youth call the girl's name and watched while they chatted together.

SARAH HAD dozed off. Her brief rest was interrupted by vivid dreams, violent nightmares in which she'd been fighting horrific creatures with a shining sword. . . .

"Miller . . ."

The sound of her name brought her instantly awake, and she looked up at the skinny, blond-haired man with the darting wild eyes. He licked his cracked and scabbed lips and smiled, revealing yellowed teeth.

"Hello, Sarah," he said simply. He turned his hand, displaying the surgical scalpel held flat along the palm. "Mind if we have a quick chat?" he whispered as he sat next to her. "Move and I'll take your eye out." He tilted the knife, allowing it to throw a sliver of metallic light onto Sarah's face. "You won't need your eyes where I'm taking you."

"Leave me alone, please leave me alone," Sarah whispered. Her heart was beating so fast, she could feel her ribs trembling.

"We're getting off at the next stop, and you're going to come along nice and quiet like a good little girl. Now give me the bag—real slow."

Sarah didn't move.

"You deaf?" The junkie grinned. "You know, the granny was stubborn . . . and you saw what we did to her, didn't you?" He bit back a giggle. "Only you're not a bad-looking bird; we might be able to have a bit of fun with you first. Now, give me the fucking bag."

Abruptly, the lump of metal was a solid weight in her lap. Sarah almost imagined she could feel it throb against her belly. A chill seeped through her, a numbing sensation that spread up into her chest, tightened her lungs, and set her heart racing. She reached into the bag, and her hand closed around the rusted pommel, fingers sliding naturally into the ancient well-worn grooves.

"No, I won't," she whispered.

"Oh yes, you will," he hissed.

IN A sworn statement, Martha Hill claimed that the girl had pulled what looked like a hammer from a shopping bag on her lap and struck the blond-haired youth beside her.

Jonas Gottlieb had seen an iron bar, possibly a crowbar.

THE BROKEN Sword came out of the bag in a smooth movement and struck the junkie on the temple. The snap of bone was clearly audible above the clatter of the train. Heat raced the length of Sarah's body, and she felt a sudden surge of strength and red rage. A roaring wind filled her head, fragments of whispered words barely audible.

The youth staggered to his feet, swaying, eyes rolling back in his head, mouth opening and closing spasmodically, though no sound came out. Sarah jumped to her feet, braced herself, and hit him again, catching him low on the face, shattering his left cheekbone, the force of the blow fracturing his skull. A long ribbon of bright blood spurted, dappling the window and ceiling. Although he was almost unconscious on his feet, animal instinct sent the young man staggering back, blindly waving the scalpel in front of him. Sarah followed, the blood-smeared Broken Sword gripped so tightly that her knuckles hurt, rusted metal biting into her hand. She knew what she had to do.

He was turning and falling when the final blow caught him on the back of the neck at the base of his skull, snapping his spine, sending him headfirst into the window. With one last thrust, Sarah brought the sword down on Larry McFeely.

And decapitated him.

HORRIFIED WITNESSES then described how the young woman had calmly pulled the emergency cord, bringing the train to a screeching halt. She had used the manual door levers to open the doors and jump down onto the track. The witnesses estimated that from the moment the blond-haired youth had sat beside the girl and spoken to her to the time she'd leapt off the train was probably less than two minutes.

THE ROARING voices stilled, then stopped, leaving only the silence and the realization: She had killed him.

Sarah licked dry lips, tasting the metallic copper of blood. She'd bitten down hard on them, breaking the skin. She had killed the man without compunction. And what troubled her more than anything else was that she didn't feel more upset. Killing him, she realized, had been the right thing to do.

As she raced down the line, gravel crunching underfoot, Sarah shoved the Broken Sword back into the bag. She didn't notice that although she herself was spattered with crimson, there was no blood on the metal.

29

*B*lood.

Fresh and salt, warm and meat. It had been a long time since it had tasted blood. And the blood is life.

Memories stirred. . . .

Memories of the time when the sorcerer-smiths, following a thousand-year-old tradition, had driven the inanimate lump of gleaming metal into the bodies of a score of slaves. And at the moment of their deaths, in that instant of excruciating pain, there had sprung the spark of consciousness.

It had developed awareness.

Consciousness returned. . . .

The sorcerer-smiths thought they were imbuing the artifact with life; however, they were mistaken. They were merely opening a portal. The first blood sacrifice had sent ripples out into the Otherworld, calling, calling, calling . . . and the invitation was accepted. A presence as old as the universe slipped into the newly crafted object, a presence that hungered. In the time that followed, it had feasted off flesh and blood and souls aplenty. This was a time of Chaos when men ruled by the sword, when justice was bought on the edge of a blade. The consciousness that inhabited the length of blade rejoiced as it fed, and the wielder of the weapon experienced a tiny fragment of that alien joy. And it was addictive.

Centuries passed, and then everything changed. The presence in the sword found itself fettered, bound by something far stronger than its own will.

It was still used as an instrument of death, it still feasted off flesh and souls. Yet it took little sustenance from the killings; that energy was directed elsewhere. Now, it drank the souls of men and women of learning and intelligence; it supped off those who worshipped strange gods in dark lands. Those who wielded the weapon had changed, too: Primitive, gnarled hands had given way to leather and then mail gloves, and the iron gauntlets—cold iron—shielded it from the ecstasy of blood.

And then it had been broken.

THE TWO men fighting in the churned field considered themselves knights on the opposite side of an ancient battle. They were fighting for causes that they themselves did not truly believe in. They fought because they were expected to fight and because they knew no other trade.

Nor did they know that they were fighting with weapons that were claimed by entities older than the race of mankind. While the men hacked and hewed, the metal blades sparking and blunting, another battle, bloodless but far more savage, was being enacted in the place known to humankind as the Otherworld.

And because one sword had been fed with innocent blood—sweet and clean—and the heady elixir of virgins, because the wielder was a despoiler of women, who took pleasure in rape and butchery, he was victorious. Battering his opponent to his knees, his demon-blessed weapon had hewn through the other weapon, shattering it into two pieces.

It had lost consciousness then, allowed itself to sleep. . . .

The same scything blow had taken the head from the kneeling knight. The sword had keened in victory, and the armored knight raised it high in triumph. And later generations would call him Arthur and name the demon sword Excalibur.

And the Broken Sword would be forgotten. But it was called Dyrnwyn.

And now, after centuries of hunger, it had fed.

The Broken Sword had awakened.

30

arah pulled out the envelope and rechecked the address before turning into the side street off Earls Court Road. She stood in the dark, nervously practicing her bizarre introduction. "Mr. Walker, I realize that it's really late and you don't know me, but . . ." She shook her head. No, that would be too weird. She should be friendlier, more personable. "Hi, Owen, your aunt Judith sent me . . ." She nodded quickly, reassuring herself. Yes, she must mention Judith's name to get his attention. . . .

She stopped, becoming aware that a young couple on the opposite side of the road was watching her closely, and she realized that she'd been speaking aloud, head nodding. "I must look like a maniac," she muttered as she reached the complex, looking for Owen Walker's apartment.

Sarah ran her finger down the lighted bells on the cream-painted door. Against the faint hue, the blood wedged into her once perfectly manicured fingernails stood out vividly. All of the bells had names on the white cards beneath them. Two were doctors, the rest went by initials only . . . yet there was no Walker. She dug into the bag and checked the envelope again, then stood back to look up at the number on the door. They matched.

The hall door suddenly opened and a tall Asian woman, wearing a nurse's uniform beneath a light coat, stepped out. The nurse gave a tiny gasp when she saw the figure standing before her.

Sarah attempted a smile. "I'm sorry if I startled you. I have a package for Mr. Owen Walker." She showed the nurse the envelope. "I thought he lived at this address."

"He does. But in the basement fl . . ." The nurse started to speak, then stopped as she looked the young woman up and down. She stepped back into the hall and closed the door slightly, obviously prepared to slam it shut. "He works odd hours. I'm sure he's sleeping, so if you'd like to leave the parcel with me, I'll make certain that he gets it."

"I'm sorry. I have to deliver it into his hands."

"It's no trouble," the nurse said quickly.

"Thanks, but I promised his aunt that I'd give it to him."

"Judith?" The woman's defensive face melted into a semblance of warmth.

"Yes, Judith Walker. She asked me to give this to Owen."

The nurse relaxed a little. "I haven't seen her around for a while. She promised me an autographed book for my son. How is she?"

"Fine," Sarah lied.

"Owen's apartment is just around the corner, down the stairs, can't miss it." She pointed helpfully before adding, "Tell Judith that Rika's still waiting for her book."

"I will," Sarah said grimly, turning away.

There was a single bell on the basement door, which was hidden directly beneath the steps. The faded name on the sliver of white paper stuck to the bell said WALKER. Sarah raked her fingers through her tangled hair and smoothed her stained clothing before pressing the button. It buzzed deep in the flat. Moments later, the chocolate-colored curtains to her right twitched. The windows, she noted, were barred. Through the gap in the net curtains, she thought she could make out a man's face, curly hair, eyes dulled with sleep. Again she held up the letter, showing the address. "I've a parcel for Mr. Owen Walker."

The face disappeared from the window.

Footsteps padded in the hallway, a floorboard creaked, and then she heard the rattle of a chain. The door opened, but only to the extent of the safety chain.

"Are you Owen Walker?"

"Who wants to know?" A man's husky voice.

"I do. I have a package," Sarah said, frustrated by the man's caution.

"Do you know what time it is?"

"Yes."

"A bit late for a delivery."

"I know."

"I'll take that," the man said impatiently.

"Look, I can only give this to Owen Walker, no one else," Sarah said, squinting to make out some details of the figure lurking behind the door. Tall, maybe six feet. "I promised," she added lamely.

"I'm Owen Walker." He spoke with an American accent. Boston, she guessed.

"Can you give me some proof?"

"What?"

"Proof. Can you give me some proof? Mrs. Walker made me promise that I'd give this to her nephew and no one else."

"Judith? Aunt Judith?" The door closed, the chain clattered, and then the door was reopened.

"Aunt Judith gave me this to give to you."

A young man stepped out of the shadows, tousled black hair glistening in the moonlight. He was handsome in a boyish manner and wore a navy blue Yale sweatshirt. Sarah guessed he was only a couple of years older than she was. His eyes narrowed as they took in Sarah's disheveled appearance, her ashen features, and the deep shadows beneath her eyes. He reached out politely to shake her hand.

"I'm Owen. . . ." His grip was strong, the flesh soft and cool beneath her.

"She told me to give you this and say . . . and say . . ." Sarah suddenly stopped, energy draining away, leaving her legs rubbery, icy sweat on her forehead, her tongue thick in her mouth.

"Are you all right?"

She tried to lick her dry lips, but her tongue felt huge and swollen. "I'm fine," she mumbled, reaching out to grip the wall. "Just a little faint. I'm just out of hospital," she muttered. There were bright red spots at the corners of her eyes, exploding like tiny stars. She swayed and would have fallen if Owen hadn't reached out and caught her midcollapse, scooping her up into his arms.

"Hey. Just take it easy. Take it easy." He carried her into the tiny hall, turned to the right into the small sitting room, and eased her gently into a battered fireside chair.

SARAH LOOKED up into Owen's concerned face. She attempted to push herself upright, but he placed a hand on her shoulder and pressed her back onto the chair. "Just take it easy. Glad to see you're back among the living," he said lightly before he disappeared into the kitchen. She heard a tap running, and then Owen reappeared with a glass of water. Sarah sipped it.

"Slowly. Take your time," Owen advised, "or you'll get a stomachache." Folding his arms across his broad chest, he observed her critically. "You fainted, probably from exhaustion. I know it's not polite to say to a lady, but you really don't look that great."

"Thanks," Sarah whispered. She felt completely disoriented, and if she turned her head too quickly, the world shifted and spun.

"You said you were in the hospital. What for?"

Sarah started to shake her head and stopped as the world tilted and swayed. "Observation . . . shock . . . I don't know."

"You don't know why you were in the hospital?" the man asked, incredulous. "Are you on medication?" he asked.

"No. Nothing. I'm not taking drugs," she said, suddenly realizing what he was saying.

"Which hospital were you in?"

"Crawley . . . I think."

"You think?"

Sarah shook her head. "I'm not sure. Everything is a bit . . . The events of the last few days are confused."

"When were you discharged?"

"Today."

"Didn't anyone pick you up?"

"I discharged myself."

Owen crouched down facing Sarah, emerald green eyes searching her face. "I think you should go to the nearest hospital or even back to Crawley and see if they'll readmit you. I could call someone," he added.

"I'm fine," Sarah said quickly. "I just wanted to get the bag to you."

"The bag?" Owen reached over and dragged the heavy Tesco bag toward him, grunting in surprise at the weight. He pulled out the envelope and glanced at it quickly before looking back at Sarah, eyes narrowing. "Where did you get this?"

"I told you: Your aunt gave it to me. She told me—she made me promise—that I'd put it into your hands. And she told me to say . . . she told me to say . . ." Sarah could feel the burning at the back of her throat, the sour acid in her stomach. Her eyes filled with tears, and the room blurred and fragmented. She stood up suddenly, and

Owen came quickly to his feet to help. Holding an arm out in front of her, Sarah backed away in alarm. "She told me to say that she was sorry, so sorry," she said in a rush.

"Sorry?"

Sarah nodded quickly. "So sorry." Then she turned and staggered from the room. Owen watched in astonishment as she rushed out the door, ran past the window, and disappeared into the night.

31

Robert Elliot struck Skinner sharply across the face, the sound echoing in the underground garage. The signet ring on his index finger caught the skinhead on the cheekbone, opening the skin in a wide, deep cut. For an instant, rage sparked behind the skinhead's muddy eyes and his fists clenched. Elliot laughed at the reaction. "Touch me and I'll kill you." Then he deliberately turned his back on the skinhead, leaving him to dab at the wound on his cheek with his sleeve as he walked back to his car.

"It wasn't my fault," Skinner said plaintively. "I wasn't even on the train. Larry was probably out of his head on something. . . ."

Elliot pulled out his car keys and pointed the remote control at the black BMW. The lights flashed and the door locks thumped. "I told *you* to find the girl. I told *you* to bring her back . . . I told *you . . . you . . . you.*"

"I'm sorry, Mr. Elliot, I'll find her."

The small man opened the car and climbed in. "I know you will, because if you don't, then our association will be at an end," Elliot snapped, and pulled the door closed. "And trust me, you don't want me to lose interest in you, do you?" Without waiting for an answer, Elliot slid the window up and the BMW pulled away with hardly a sound.

Skinner waited until the car had vanished before he whispered, "Fuck you." Then he dug his hand into the back pockets of his jeans and went to look for Sarah Miller. "How am I going to find her? I don't even know where to begin." He needed to stay sharp. He was on borrowed time now with Elliot. He'd seen what the older man had done to people he'd lost interest in. And it hadn't been pretty.

. . .

THE GIRL led a charmed life.

Not only had she eluded him again, she had killed one of his people.

Robert Elliot cruised London's streets in the BMW, trying to work out how he was going to tell his mysterious employer that he had failed—yet again—to bring him Sarah Miller.

Elliot knew exactly how McFeely had died. He hadn't slipped and fallen, cutting his throat on broken glass, as Skinner reported. Elliot had used a police connection to get an up-to-date report on McFeely's death. According to eyewitness reports, Miller had decapitated the boy with what had variously been described as an iron bar, a metal bar, or a hammer.

Elliot knew it had been the sword. And he knew that his boss was not going to be happy about that.

He finally made the call from a phone box in New Cavendish Street—one of the few still remaining in London. He'd driven around for thirty minutes, trying to think of a good excuse, finally deciding that honesty was the safest policy.

This time the call was picked up on the first ring. As usual, no one on the other end responded.

"It's me," he said shortly.

"The girl?" demanded the harsh, arrogant voice on the other end of the phone.

"We haven't found her yet—she evaded us on the train. One of my men was with her, but there was some sort of accident; it looks as if Miller killed him."

"Killed him?" The question was left hanging.

Elliot took a deep breath. "I believe she used the sword."

The phone was slammed down so hard, it hurt his ear.

32

ad news?" Vyvienne asked. She slithered up on the bed and knelt behind the naked man, wrapping her arms around his chest, pressing her breasts against his shoulders.

"The sword has tasted blood," Ahriman shouted with a mixture of rage and fear. "Tasted blood . . . but not the blood of its Keeper." Pushing her away, he surged to his feet. He strode across the room, then swung back to face the woman. "Do you know what this means?"

"Another of the Hallows has become active?" she suggested. "But you've been firing the artifacts with the blood and pain of the Keepers. . . ."

"Of the Keepers, yes. But Miller killed with the sword, she allowed it to taste unhallowed blood." Ahriman's voice was thick with emotion, his cultured accent slipping momentarily. He realized he was trembling. "Have you any idea of the implications?"

She shook her head, long dark hair trailing across her eyes.

"The power within the Hallow has been dormant for centuries. The blood of the Hallowed Keepers fires the artifact and simultaneously calms it, leaving it replete with power. But Miller has given it a soul to drink. Now that it is awakened, it will begin to renew itself . . . not only in this world, but in the Otherworld as well. Even now, its energy is probably rippling through the Astral." He stopped suddenly, then leaned forward to cup the young woman's chin, tilting her face up to his. "Could you find it? Could you follow a disturbance in the Astral?"

"Probably . . . ," she said, sounding doubtful.

"Then do it. Do it now!" Fleshy lips curled in a smile. "If you can find it, then we can trace it back to the girl."

The woman smiled lasciviously. "I will need your strength if I'm to go adventuring. . . ."

ELLIOT HAD been driving aimlessly for an hour, the sleek black car moving silently through London's never-sleeping streets. He was frightened: The situation was getting out of control, and maybe it was time for him to get out of the city.

The phone buzzed against his chest. Startled, Elliot tapped the brakes and there was the blare of a car horn behind him. No one had his personal number. It was a cheap pay-as-you-go phone that he used only for outgoing calls. The small rectangular screen showed UNLISTED. It buzzed a dozen times before he finally pressed answer. He recognized the husky voice immediately and felt a trickle of fear. How had this man gotten the number?

"Judith Walker has a nephew, an Owen Walker. The boy lives alone in a flat in Scarsdale Villas. Miller has been there already, she's given him the sword."

Elliot blurted, "But how do you—"

"I know." There was a dry, rasping chuckle. "I know everything, Mr. Elliot. Everything. Remember that."

33

It would seem like an open-and-shut case," Victoria Heath said tiredly, heels clicking as she walked along the tiled morgue floor. It was just after ten and she'd been on her feet for nearly sixteen hours.

"There's a *but* in your voice . . . ," Tony Fowler said.

"I don't believe she had the time. It's almost impossible."

"I agree."

"You do?"

"Sure." Tony Fowler fished in his pockets and produced the coffee-impregnated handkerchief he kept for visits to the morgue. "I think Miller had help. A friend or friends who started the proceedings, as it were."

"And you think this corpse was one of those friends?"

"I'll lay money on it. The witnesses on the train said they knew each other. Maybe this friend was trying to blackmail Miller . . . and Miller killed him."

"But why? None of this makes any sense."

Tony Fowler grinned sourly. "After a while you'll realize that there's a lot of police work that will make very little sense: the killings, the muggings, the rapes, the robberies. Sometimes there's a pattern; however, usually it's just a mess."

Victoria Heath shook her head. "I don't want to believe that."

"When you've been on the force as long as I have," Fowler said, pushing open the heavy swinging doors, "you will."

"THE SUBJECT is a white male, early twenties, twenty-two, twenty-three, six feet in height, a hundred and forty pounds . . . which is underweight for this height," the pathologist added, glancing across at the two police officers. Fowler was staring at the pathologist, deliberately avoiding the naked body on the metal tray; Heath stared fixedly at the headless corpse.

"The subject shows extensive puncture marks along both arms, indicating systematic drug usage—"

"Mac," Fowler said suddenly, "we've both had an incredibly long day. Do we have to stand here while you do the full routine? Just give us the highlights, eh? In layman's terms."

"Sure." Gavin Mackintosh grinned. He reached up and turned off the dangling microphone. The enormous Scotsman proceeded more informally. "What you have here is a wasted junkie. He's been shooting up for two, maybe three years."

He turned the arms, showing the track marks, some healed to black spots, others still scabbed and crusted. "When he ran out of veins on one arm, he moved over to the other. And if you check between his toes, you'll see he tried shooting up there too. He's underweight, as I noted, jaundiced, hepatitis, maybe even HIV positive."

"I don't want his medical history. I want to know how he died."

The Scotsman grinned again. "Someone cut his head off—that's how he died."

"That was the glass in the train window . . . ," Sergeant Heath said tightly.

Mackintosh shook his head. He lifted the young man's broken head off a metal tray on a side table and held it aloft. Victoria Heath felt her stomach flip.

"He was struck three times, here . . . here on the face, and"— Mackintosh turned the head easily, almost like a basketball—"here at the back of the neck. These two blows were struck by a flat, blunt object, the third blow was from an edged weapon. This blow severed his head and drove him forward and into the window. Falling glass severed flesh and tendons on the body, but the youth was already dead by that time. We excavated the wound and discovered slivers and flakes of oxidized metal. Rust to you and me. In my opinion, this young man was killed by a sword. A rusty sword."

"A sword!" Fowler snapped. "None of the witnesses reported seeing a sword."

"They said it was an iron bar," Victoria added.

"A sword *is* an iron bar . . . with an edge," Mackintosh said. "The two blows here were caused by the flat of the sword. The killing stroke was with the edge of the sword. I'll bet my pension that your murder weapon is a rusting sword."

"This is getting too weird," Victoria whispered.

"We haven't even come close to the weird part." Mackintosh moved his hands down the corpse's torso. "Look at our young friend. Can you tell me what's missing? Besides his head, I mean," he added with a grin.

Tony Fowler looked at the body and shook his head.

Victoria Heath swallowed hard and forced herself to look at the body. "Blood," she said finally. "I would have thought there'd be more blood."

"Bravo. There are eight pints of blood in the human body. In a traumatic wound such as this, you would expect to lose quite a lot, until the heart stopped beating and circulation ceased. But there would still be some blood left in the corpse."

"The train carriage looked like an abattoir," Tony observed.

"A little blood goes a long way." Mackintosh jabbed a finger at the corpse on the table. "We estimated he lost about two pints in the carriage. However, our friend here has no blood in his body. None," he mused. "It's as if he's been sucked dry."

34

This time Elliot was taking no chances.

Although his employer hadn't threatened him explicitly, Elliot had *heard* the implicit threat in his voice, understood it, and known that this time he couldn't afford to fail. He still didn't know how the man had gotten his number or how he knew that Miller had given the sword to Judith Walker's nephew. He had the feeling that it was time he started thinking about a holiday, a nice long holiday, far away. Australia was nice at this time of year.

He had driven to Scarsdale Villas in Skinner's van; Elliot wasn't going to risk having someone see his car in the vicinity of what could turn out to be a murder site. He was dressed in army surplus fatigues and cheap sneakers, and he'd pulled on a pair of surgical gloves before he had climbed into the van. Even if anything should go wrong and he was spotted, he had a cast-iron alibi: He was playing Texas hold 'em with his buddies in Chelsea; three solid citizens would vouch for the fact that he won the pot that evening and sprang for a bottle of seventeen-year-old bourbon to celebrate.

Robert Elliot was a man who did not believe in taking chances.

The only people who'd know he was there were his two companions, Skinner and a blank-eyed mulatto youth named Karl, whom Elliot suspected was Skinner's slave or lover or possibly both. If necessary, Elliot would dispose of them both without hesitation: a lover's suicide pact. The police wouldn't even investigate.

"You're in good form, Mr. Elliot," Skinner said, watching the small man's thin lips curl in a smile.

"This should be an amusing evening," he murmured as he glanced along the row of houses, checking the numbers.

This was a quiet street; they would not be able to let the boy scream. "Get in quick, and get him under control," he ordered as they strolled down the street, taking their time, drawing no attention to themselves. "We want the bag Miller gave him and the sword. And then let's see what other information we can get out of him."

"How do you know Miller was here, Mr. Elliot?" Skinner asked quietly.

Robert Elliot grinned. "I have my sources."

35

Owen Walker stood in the doorway, leaning against the jamb, sipping the Earl Grey tea he had just made, looking at the bag the wild-eyed stranger had given him. It was still on the floor where she'd left it. He'd been half tempted to contact the police but dismissed the idea as ridiculous. What was he going to tell them: An exhausted girl brought me a message from my aunt? He had tried phoning Aunt Judith, but the phone had been engaged, which was a little odd given the lateness of the hour. But he knew his aunt often worked through the night. A cursory glance through the contents of the bag revealed that it was filled with manuscript papers and some old letters. Why would his aunt send him a bag of papers? And why didn't she use the regular post? It all felt rather covert. Maybe his aunt was beginning to lose it. She spent her days and nights living in a fantasy world; it was only a matter of time before she lost contact with reality.

Owen put his cup on the table and sank into the battered, balding fireside chair, feeling a vague twinge of guilt. When was the last time he had visited his aunt?

Owen reached for the telephone and hit the redial button. The busy tone cut in immediately. He frowned. On the off chance that he might be phoning the wrong number, he checked it in his Black-Berry, then dialed again. It was still busy.

He glanced at the clock, tapping the phone against his bottom lip. Ten forty-five. He dialed the number again. Still busy, but now he was beginning to think that it was out of order. She had a cell phone, but he knew there was no point in calling it: She rarely turned it on.

Owen looked at the clock again. He'd call her in the morning, and if it was still busy, he'd take the first train to Bath.

He was reaching for his aunt's bag when he heard footsteps on the stairs leading down to his basement flat. A shadow passed his window and then a second and a third.

Owen Walker peered through the curtains. Three men were standing outside his window. A skinhead, a younger man with a tight-cropped haircut, and a short, bulky man. He saw the bulky man reach up to press the doorbell and noted the signet ring on his little finger . . . and then realized that it was indistinct, the pattern blurred, and he recognized the effect: He had watched enough episodes of *Law & Order*. The short man was wearing flesh-colored surgical gloves.

The bell rang.

Owen jerked back from the window, but not before the short man had turned and looked directly at him and smiled. From inside his pocket he pulled out a pair of pliers. The look on his face was terrifying.

Heart thundering, Owen scrambled for his jacket. He had to get his phone.

And all the while the doorbell rang continuously.

ELLIOT KEPT his finger on the bell while Skinner worked on the lock. Most people never expected to be mugged, never thought they'd be attacked in their homes or that they'd be burgled. That sort of thing always happened to someone else, so when it did happen, they were completely unprepared. Right now Mr. Walker was probably rigid with fear. The constant jangling of the bell would set his nerves on edge. Maybe he was looking for a weapon, a kitchen knife or a poker; Elliot hoped so. He always made a point of using their weapons against them.

Skinner grunted with satisfaction as the lock clicked open.

And the three men stepped into the hall.

"I'VE CALLED the police." Owen attempted to slow his ragged breathing and think clearly. His heart was thumping so hard in his chest that his entire body was vibrating. The adrenaline racing through his system made his fingers tremble, and he was having trouble turning on his phone. He punched in 999. He would just have to hold off the intruders until the police arrived. "They're on the way."

He caught the edge of the table and pushed it up against the door, then snatched up a poker from the grate. There was no escape through the back; the basement flat gave onto a tiny walled garden. There was no way out through the barred windows, and he knew the old woman who lived in the flat directly above his was half-deaf, so even if he screamed for help, no one would hear.

There was movement in the hall, floorboards creaking but no other sounds, and he found that even more frightening.

Suddenly the sitting room door moved, banging against the table he'd pushed up against it. Then the door was suddenly flung back, moving the table a couple of feet. Gripping the poker in one hand as he tried to grip the phone in the other, Owen Walker swung it at the window, shattering the glass, slivers nicking his forehead, biting into his cheek. Pressing his mouth to the opening, he started to scream, "Help! . . . I need some help! . . ."

"Hello, emergency services, how may I help you? . . ."

Heart pounding, Owen shrieked into the phone, "There's a break-in. My address is Scarsdale Vil—"

The foul-smelling rubber-gloved hand pressed over his mouth while other hands grabbed his shoulders and dragged him, kicking and struggling, away from the window. The phone dropped to the floor, the back falling off, spilling the battery onto the carpet, ending the call.

"You should not have screamed," the short, bulky man said softly. He brought his face so close to Owen's that his hair brushed his skin. Owen recoiled from the touch, twisting his head away from the minty sweetness on the man's breath. He was shoved into a chair, and two youths—the skinhead and his companion with the close-cropped hair—pressed down on his shoulders, ensuring that he couldn't move.

"No, you should not have screamed," the man repeated. "Nor should you have called the police," he added, grinding his heel into the BlackBerry, destroying it. Standing back, he watched dispassionately as his colleagues tied and gagged Owen. The cloth they jammed into his mouth tore the soft skin on either side of his lips, and the young man kept fighting the urge to throw up. If he did, he could easily choke on his own vomit.

The small, cold-eyed man stooped to lift the poker off the floor. "And what were you going to use this for, eh? To start a fire?" In the reflected streetlights, his lips shone wetly. He licked them suddenly, a quick flickering movement, then leaned forward to wrap iron-hard fingers around Owen's jaw, biting into the flesh of his cheeks. "I'd like to start a fire with a pretty boy like you. I really would. We could have . . . such a good time together." He allowed his hand to trail along the line of Owen's throat, down his chest toward his groin. "But time is a luxury I don't have. So I'll be brief. Tell me what I want to know, and we'll leave you alone. Lie to me, and I'll hurt you. Badly. Do you understand me? . . . Do you?" he suddenly snarled.

Owen nodded. He wasn't sure if his message had gone through to the police. Even if they didn't get his address, they must be able to track his cell phone . . . or they'd have heard the panic in his voice. . . . He had to stall for time . . . he had to—

"A woman called Sarah Miller came to visit you today. What did she give you?" The short man abruptly whisked away the gag. Owen winced as blood oozed from his dry, chapped lips. "If you scream, I'll break your fingers," the man hissed, lifting the pliers, working the jaws inches from Owen's eyes.

"Miller . . . ? I don't . . . ," he began.

The small man started shaking his head. "Don't tell me you don't know. That will upset me. You don't want to see me upset, do you?" Holding Owen's head in both hands, he moved it from side to side to side. "Good. Now, I know she was here. I know she gave you the bag. I want to know what she told you, where she is, and what you did with the bag."

Owen focused on the pain of his torn lips and continued to stare straight into his tormentor's eyes. He knew what bag the small man was talking about: It was on the floor almost directly behind Elliot, where it must have fallen out of the chair. All Owen had to do was lower his head and he'd be looking at it.

"A young woman came around a couple of hours ago," he said quickly. "She had a bag with her. She claimed to have come from my aunt Judith. But when I spoke to my aunt, she said she'd never heard of her."

The small man struck Owen quickly, casually, expertly, the ring on his index finger catching him along the line of the jaw. A purple-red welt appeared immediately. "I told you not to lie to me. You couldn't have spoken to your aunt." The small man's grin was fixed, his forehead greasy with sweat. "Because she's dead. My associates here killed her. Slowly. Oh, so slowly. I believe she died hard."

"Dead? No."

"Oh yes." The skinhead standing behind Owen giggled, the sound wet with phlegm. "Dead. Very dead."

The small man's fingers tightened on Owen's jaw again, forcing his head back. "I want the bag and its contents. I want to know if the girl told you where she was staying."

"I don't know," Owen began.

"I think you do." The small man shoved the gag back into Owen's mouth, caught his earlobe in the jaws of the pliers, and snapped it shut. The pain was incredible. Owen convulsed in the chair, grunting against the gag. "Answer me, or I'll rip your ear off." He eased the gag out of his mouth.

"You can go and fu—"

The small man closed his hands on Owen's throat, fingers along the line of his windpipe, and squeezed. Suddenly Owen couldn't breathe and the screams died in his chest.

"Answer me!" the small man demanded, releasing his grip.

Behind him, one of the youths giggled, the sound high-pitched and feminine.

"I'll tell you, I'll tell you everything I know," Owen gasped, knowing that the police would not arrive in time.

36

The one-eyed tramp huddled in the doorway and watched as the wild-eyed young woman appeared out of the shadows. She started across the street, then stopped, hovering indecisively, before darting back the way she had come and returning to the shadows.

The tramp eased himself to a sitting position, and the paper bag in his lap hit the ground with a solid thump and rolled into the gutter, glass clinking and clunking. The tramp watched it, trying to remember if there had been anything left in the bottle. His memory wasn't that good anymore. A shape loomed out of the shadows and the tramp drew back, but it was only the young woman again. Her foot hit the paper-wrapped bottle, sending it clinking farther into the gutter.

"Who are you—what are you doing here?" the young woman whispered in alarm.

The tramp shook his head quickly, keeping his face down, not meeting her gaze, streetlight washing half his face in yellow light and giving it an unhealthy cast. The thick bandage pasted over his left eye was filthy. "I'm nobody. I was just kipping here. . . ."

"How long have you been here?"

The tramp frowned, trying to make sense of time. "A while," he said eventually, then shook his head quickly. "A good while."

"Did you see some men pass by here a few moments ago?"

The tramp nodded again. He had seen them and instinctively recognized them for what they were, survival instincts honed on the streets driving him back into the safety of the shadows. He squinted his single eye at the wild-eyed young woman. Was she with them? He didn't think so. . . .

"Where did they go?"

The tramp pointed with long filthy fingernails. "Down there . . . down there."

Sarah Miller straightened and looked toward Owen Walker's flat. Something cold and sour settled in the pit of her stomach: She had led the killers directly to Owen.

They were going to kill him, and she would be responsible.

37

Pressed against the cold stone wall, Sarah could hear them torturing him.

One of them was talking. A foul-voiced man, his words bitter, twisted, full of loathing and amusement. And then there was a choking gasp, high-pitched, rasping, followed by the sound of someone giggling.

They were torturing him for the same reason they had killed his aunt. For the bag. For the sword.

She risked a quick glimpse inside through the broken window. One man was blocking her view, close enough to touch, but over his shoulder she could clearly see the skinhead standing in the background. She couldn't see Owen or the man with the foul voice, but she could hear the questions and the blows.

The front door gave to her gentle push.

The sounds were clearer now, Owen's choked sobs, the skinhead's giggling, and the small man's bitter voice.

". . . Sarah Miller."

Shocked, she stopped, hearing her own name mentioned. How did they know her? Unless . . . unless . . . Realization washed over her in an icy wave: These were the same men who had phoned her in her office, the same men who had butchered her family.

Propelled by pure rage, Sarah was moving before she was even conscious of it. It was as if time had slowed to a series of images, frozen snapshots:

. . . the small man turning toward her, pliers in his hand.

. . . one of the youths lunging for her.

. . . the shock of recognition on Owen Walker's face.

And then the small man jabbed her in the chest with the blunt end of the pliers. The pain took her breath away and she crashed to the floor, lungs struggling for breath. She hit a chair and toppled sideways, and the steel-toe-capped boot, which had been coming for her head, struck her shoulder, numbing her entire arm, spinning her around in a half circle on the floor, rolling right over the familiar Tesco bag.

"ALIVE," ELLIOT snapped. "I want her alive." He grinned. Suddenly everything was going to work out. He could trade Miller to his employer and make everything right again. He watched the skinhead strike at Miller again, catching her high on the thigh with his steel-toe-capped boot. The youth was moving in for another savage kick when Miller rolled over, pulling a roll of newspaper from a bag on the floor, scattering loose pages across the room.

The bag.

Elliot raised his arm to point, but by then Miller had come up on one knee, holding the newspaper tightly in both hands. She lunged straight ahead, catching the skinhead in the groin. Even before he saw the newspaper turn red with blood, Elliot knew what it concealed.

THE BROKEN Sword punched through the soft flesh, destroying tissue, muscles, and the delicate inner organs. Blood spurted, sizzling where it soaked into the newspaper, hissing when it touched the metal. Sarah jerked the ancient weapon upward, the rusty edge of the sword—dull and blunt—neatly shredding flesh, eviscerating the youth.

Somewhere the distant call of a hunting horn, somewhere the faintest clash of metal off metal, the song of the sword.

Sarah jerked the sword free. The youth swayed, ashen-faced, eyes wide and shocked, mouth open, both hands pressed against the gaping wound in the pit of his stomach. Stepping forward, still holding the sword in a two-handed grip, the woman brought it down in a short chopping motion, catching him below the line of the jaw. There was surprisingly little blood when the head tumbled away from the body.

The hunters were closer, their horns shrilling, the baying of the hounds louder.

Sarah Miller leapt over the butchered body and raised the sword above her head in both hands. The sword struck the lightbulb, plunging the room into darkness, sparks and tendrils of white fire curling down the blade.

Elliot and Skinner turned and ran, racing out into the night as the light of a police car appeared, bathing both men in blue and white. They vaulted the car and ran down the road, with the car in pursuit.

Through the broken window, Sarah watched the police car take off after the men and she knew they would be back soon. She turned to Owen. "I have to get out of here. Can you take me?" She hauled the confused Owen to his feet.

"You killed him. You killed him," Owen said quietly. "Stabbed him, then cut his head off. You killed a man."

"Two, actually. I'll explain later. We're in tremendous danger."

Owen felt sick to his stomach, and the pain in his head was so intense that he knew if he moved, he was going to throw up. "It's going to be all right. I'll tell the police you did it to rescue me. That's why you came back, isn't it?"

Sarah nodded, feeling her head throb and pound with the movement. "I couldn't leave you to them. I saw what they did to my family . . . and to Judith."

"These men were talking about my aunt saying . . . saying . . ." He suddenly remembered what they had been saying. "They said she was dead," he whispered hoarsely.

Sarah reached out and squeezed Owen's hand. She was trying to breathe through her mouth; the stench in the apartment from the dead body was appalling, a mixture of excrement, urine, and blood. "Your aunt is dead, Owen. These men killed her. They butchered her for the bag with the sword I gave to you. She wouldn't give it to them, wouldn't tell them where it was. She was strong, so strong, right to the very end. She asked me to get the bag and the sword to you, and she told me to tell you that she was sorry."

"Sorry?"

"I think she knew this would bring you nothing but trouble." Sarah looked at him, staring into his eyes. "I think you should take the bag and sword and hide them away somewhere safe. Then I think you should do exactly the same. These people have killed before; they killed my family, they killed your aunt Judith, they were prepared to kill you today. Go away. Hide until these people are in custody. We have to go. Now."

"But why?"

"I don't know," she said tiredly. "It has something to do with the sword."

"What sword?"

She raised the length of metal in her hand. Much of the rust had flaked away, revealing shining metal beneath. "This is Dyrnwyn."

Owen reached out and touched the metal with the tip of his finger. A spark snapped between the two, and he jerked his hand back. "But minutes ago, when you stabbed . . . I could have sworn the sword was whole and complete."

Sarah shook her head. "The sword is broken." She turned her head suddenly, the movement sending the room spinning. "Can you hear anything?"

"Nothing. What is it?"

"I thought . . . I thought I heard horns. Hunting horns."

38

Reaction hit them only when they were well away from the flat, Skinner driving hard, clutching the steering wheel in a white-knuckled grip. Suddenly the skinhead swerved to the side of the road, pushed open the door, leaned his head out, and vomited.

Elliot swallowed hard and turned away, wiping his sleeve across his watering eyes and nose.

Skinner slammed the door. His breath was coming in great heaving gasps, and he pounded the steering wheel. "I'll kill her. I'll fucking kill her." They had evaded the cops, but the skinhead knew he was going to have to ditch his beloved van. He was sure the cops had made it. He turned to Elliot. "Just who the fuck is she? I thought she was a nobody, a nothing. You told me she was a nobody," he said accusingly.

"She is a nobody," Elliot said tiredly.

"This nobody's killed two of my people. She killed Karl!"

"I know. I know. Find a phone box. I need to call someone."

"You've got a cell, use it," Skinner snapped. "This is all your fucking fault," he added.

Elliot's hand closed over Skinner's throat, slender fingers squeezing, long manicured fingernails leaving half-moons in the pale flesh. Before Skinner could react, the small man produced the pliers and closed the ends—gently—around the skinhead's protruding tongue. "Don't you *ever* speak to me like that again!" He squeezed the pliers for emphasis. "Now be a good little boy and do as you're told."

VYVIENNE HAD been in the Astral, the Otherworld, when the skinhead had been killed.

With an ease born of long practice, she interpreted the spots and lines of vibrating colors. She was able to visualize what was happening and pinpoint exactly where they were. The colors screamed out at her: The cobalt blue white of the boy's terror contrasted sharply with the forest green and midnight blue of Elliot and his two henchmen. The woman noted that Elliot's bloodlust was tempered with the yellow of sexual arousal. And then the girl appeared, flooding the other colors with her own: cold white, tinged with red and black. Terror. Anger. Then pain.

And then, suddenly, another color had flooded the Otherworld. Bright yellow light blazed, swallowing all the other colors in a flash of bright energy.

The sword had tasted blood.

Again.

Ancient and incredibly powerful pulsations of gold light trembled through the Astral, sending Vyvienne reeling back. For an instant, she had seen directly into the Incarnate World below. She had seen Sarah Miller lift the broken remnant of the sword and plunge it into the boy.

Vyvienne awoke screaming, hands flailing at the yellow fire that washed over her, the wordless howling as the sword sank into the boy's flesh and devoured his blood and soul.

Ahriman held her protectively, soothing her, allowing her to draw upon a little of his strength. With her head pressed against his chest, he drew up the sheet to cover her naked body so that she would not be able to see the puckered water blisters that were beginning to swell on her flesh.

"What did you see?" he whispered, stroking her temples.

"The Broken Sword. It has killed again. Drunk blood. Energy. Life. Such power . . . ," she muttered sleepily. "Such power."

"Where is it?" Ahriman demanded.

"Such power," Vyvienne mumbled, and fell asleep.

In the bedroom, the phone started ringing.

"SO YOU have failed me again, Mr. Elliot. And lost one of your men too."

"But how . . ." There was no possible way that his employer could know. None. Unless, of course, he had someone watching the house.

"You forget, Mr. Elliot, I know everything there is to know about you. I know what you do, and with whom you do it. I know where you go, whom you see . . . I know everything. Now tell me you have the sword."

Elliot frowned. If his employer knew everything, then how come he didn't know whether or not he had the sword? Or was this a trap, to see how much he would reveal? "I don't have the sword," he admitted. "Miller ripped up one of my men and then attacked us. We barely got out with our lives."

"Is she still in the flat with the American?"

"As far as I know."

"Then go back and get them both. I want them alive. Not necessarily unharmed, but I want them alive. And get me that sword. Don't fail me again, Mr. Elliot, or there will be severe consequences," he added, and hung up.

"WE'VE GOT to go back," he said to Skinner, climbing back into the van.

"No fucking way am I going back!"

Elliot ignored him. From under the seat, he pulled out a length of heavy chain and dropped it in Skinner's lap. Then he pulled out a lump hammer. In the reflected streetlights, his smile was ghastly. "All we have to do is deliver them alive. Condition doesn't really matter."

The skinhead smiled and nodded in understanding. Without a word, he turned the van around.

He was going to enjoy breaking Sarah Miller's kneecaps.

39

Where will you go?"

Owen shook his head. "I don't know."

The couple stood in the shadows, watching for any movement on the quiet road. With the exception of a filthy white-haired tramp huddled in a doorway, the street seemed deserted.

Owen pulled out his car keys and crossed the street to the badly parked seven-year-old Honda Civic. Sarah hurried after him, clutching Judith Walker's bag in one hand, the Broken Sword in the other. Owen had the car running by the time she reached it.

Inside, they breathed a collective sigh of relief.

"Drop me at the nearest police station," Sarah said tiredly.

"Are you sure you won't change your mind?"

"There's no point in running. The longer I run, the more convinced they'll be that I'm guilty." She stopped suddenly. "And I am guilty."

"Self-defense," Owen snapped.

"I'm not sure the police will see it that way."

Sarah looked out the window. So much had happened in the last two days, so many incomprehensible things. She wondered if she'd ever get rid of the stench of death. She felt it permanently affixed to her clothes and embedded in her skin, a noxious mixture of gas and excrement, the metallic odor of blood, and another indefinable smell: the stink of fear.

She had killed a man.

Her second today.

She lifted the rusted lump of metal and turned it over in her red-stained hands. She assumed the staining on her hands was rust; however, she suspected otherwise. There was a part of her, in the deep recesses of her mind, that believed the sword was oozing blood.

"Sarah?"

Dyrnwyn, the Sword That Is Broken.

"Sarah?"

She remembered its weight in her hands, the perfect balance as she thrust it, the sword a natural extension of her arm. In the moment when the sword had sunk into the body and fed on the boy, she had felt . . . *satiated.* She remembered the flush of heat and warmth that flowed through her body.

"Sarah?"

She realized that Owen was talking. "I still think I should come with you to the police. Once I explain the circumstances . . ."

Sarah turned and caught his face in both hands, her fingers leaving red streaks on his olive skin. "Listen to me. The police already suspect me of killing my own family. They know I was in the house with your aunt this afternoon. I'm sure they think I killed her too," she added bitterly. "Now they've got a body on the train and another here. They're going to lock me up forever, and I am not dragging you into this. You don't even know me." There were huge tears in her eyes, and she was finding it hard to breathe.

Owen carefully eased her hands away from his face. He squeezed her fingers until they hurt and the pain registered. "I am coming with you to the police," he said firmly. "They'll believe me."

"How?" she demanded.

"I'll make them. I'll tell them the truth."

"What truth?" She laughed shakily.

They drove in silence for a few minutes. At a light, Owen turned to her, asking in earnest, "Aren't you interested in the men behind this? The men who attacked me tonight—" His voice broke suddenly. "The men who killed my aunt. Aren't you interested in seeing them brought to justice?"

Sarah stared straight ahead, refusing to allow any more tears. "These men killed my entire family. I want to see them rot, I want justice . . . but I know there's nothing I can do. These people have killed and will kill again, and I'm certain they're hunting us now."

"But why?"

Sarah Miller lifted the remains of the sword off her lap. "For this."

"A broken antique?"

Sarah shook her head. "More than that. Much more."

"But what is it?"

"I'm not sure yet," she murmured. Then she shook her head. "It's old . . . no, older than old, it's ancient. And deadly."

40

Skinner leaned across the steering wheel. "There they are. In the red Civic."

"I see them," Elliot muttered. The car was pulling out of Scarsdale Villas onto Earls Court Road. "Damn," he swore softly. "I was hoping to catch them in the house or some quiet backstreet, where their screams wouldn't attract too much attention."

"What do I do?" Skinner asked.

"Fall in behind them. We'll move in at the first opportunity." He lifted the hammer and allowed the heavy head to slap into his cupped palm. *Alive,* his employer had said, *but not necessarily unharmed.*

"I THINK there's a van following us."

Sarah resisted the temptation to look. "How can you tell?"

"We're doing just under thirty. Everyone else on the road is going at least fifty, but the van is keeping pace with us."

"Make a couple of turns. See if they follow us," Sarah suggested. Her fingers closed around the hilt of the sword, drawing strength from the oxidized metal.

Without signaling, Owen immediately turned to the left. The car between them and the van stopped sharply, tires screeching, the stunned driver simultaneously hitting brake and horn. At the bottom of the street, Owen turned right, then right again. At the top of the road, he turned left, back onto Earls Court Road.

"We've lost them," Sarah breathed.

As they pulled back out into traffic, the van slipped in two cars behind them.

"No, we haven't," Owen said.

. . .

"HE'S MADE us!" Skinner snapped.

Elliot nodded. "Pull up next to him. Force them off the road."

"In the middle of the city?"

"Do it." Elliot was gambling that no one would want to get involved. With the cell phone revolution, there had developed a collective apathy that suggested people would get involved only to the extent of tapping in the numbers to call the police. They could boast guiltlessly about doing the right thing, while staying physically uninvolved, safely cocooned in their own cars.

No one would dare take the risk.

Miller had taken the risk, and look what had happened to her.

They'd have a couple minutes before someone phoned the police and a few minutes more before the police actually reached the scene. Plenty of time in which to take care of business. And if any do-gooder wanted to take part, well, Elliot would encourage them to walk away. He tapped the hammer in his hand.

WHITE VANS had disturbed Sarah ever since she saw *The Silence of the Lambs*. One could never trust the driver of a white van whose back contained unseen cargo. As the van pulled up beside them, Sarah wondered if it was now her destiny to be thrown into the back of the van.

To die in the dark.

She caught a glimpse of the profile of the passenger, and then the man turned and looked down into the small car. There was a single moment of recognition before the van door opened and the sharp-faced man leaned out, a hammer raised in his left hand. "Owen!" Sarah shouted.

The hammer smashed into the windscreen, spiderwebbing it, showering the front seats with tiny flecks of glass. Owen screamed, jerking on the wheel and sending the Civic into the heavier van, metal crumpling before the lighter car bounced off. He crashed into it again, showering sparks across Elliot, who was clinging to the door by the seat belt.

"Keep driving. Keep driving!" Sarah shouted as she smashed at the windscreen with the Broken Sword, punching a hole through the frosted window.

The white van smashed into the Civic, and Sarah watched as the older man who'd punched her in the chest with the pliers leaned out to slam the hammer onto the car roof, rupturing the metal. A third blow completely shattered the driver's window, crystalline shards speckling Owen's ashen face.

"Brake," Sarah shouted, "brake!"

Owen slammed on the brakes, and the Civic screamed to a halt. There was a sudden crash as a car ran into the back of the Civic, followed by a lesser crash as another car stopped short. And another crash after that. A domino effect. The van shot past before the driver realized what had happened. It took him twenty yards before he slammed on the brakes, white smoke cascading from the van's tires. Its reversing lights flared white.

Owen spun the wheel, cutting across the road, horns blaring, metal and glass crumpling and shattering, as drivers stood on their brakes, most of them too late.

"You're good," Sarah gasped.

"Far too many hours of Xbox with my nephews." Owen grinned as he shot past the reversing Volkswagen and out onto Kensington High Street.

The white van attempted to follow them. It mounted the pavement, scattering late-night strollers, and bounced back onto the road again.

Twisting in her seat, Sarah watched as the van shot forward, but by the time they turned onto Kensington High Street, she'd lost sight of the van. "Dump the car," Sarah said decisively.

Owen wiped the back of his face with his hand, blood from his nicked cheeks and forehead staining his hand. He could feel glass shards in his face. "Forget it. I'm not leaving this car. I saved for two whole years to buy it."

Sarah caught a flicker of movement behind them. She twisted in the seat to look through the rear window, seeing the van dart through the light traffic behind them. "They're back."

"I can see that."

"Then drive faster," Sarah ordered.

"This is as fast as we can go."

Moments later, the van roared up and slammed into the back of the Civic, crushing the bumper to shards.

Owen grunted, seat belt biting into his chest and stomach, feeling the long muscles at the back of his neck tighten, knowing he'd suffered a mild whiplash. He was gripping the steering wheel so tightly, he could feel his fingernails digging into the flesh of his palms.

Where were the police?

The van struck the car again, sending it careering across the road. The rear bumper struck a lamppost, and as the metal pole buckled, the fluorescent bulb exploded into a shower of sparks.

Owen quickly reversed the car and got back on the road. He drove through a red light with the van in close pursuit. A black Mercedes coming through the green light struck the van just above the rear wheel, the heavy car spinning the van ninety degrees. The middle-aged Mercedes driver looked on in shocked amazement as the van drove away, leaving a litter of broken metal and glass in the middle of the street. He had just enough presence of mind to note the license plate number before he phoned the police from the car.

"THERE IT is!" Skinner pointed.

The Civic was parked at the entrance to Derry Street, lights on, right indicator flashing. Both doors were open.

Elliot leapt from the van even before it had stopped moving. He darted past the car, ducking to glance inside. It was empty.

No Miller.

No bag.

No sword.

Holding the hammer in both hands, he hurried down the narrow street. Skinner drove slowly past. The narrow street opened out into Kensington Square. Skinner stopped and climbed out of the van, the chain dangling from his fist. He waited while Elliot came running up. "They could have gone anywhere," the skinhead mumbled.

Elliot raised the hammer, and for a single moment, Skinner thought he was going to hit him.

"What are we going to do?"

Elliot didn't know. His employer was going to be livid.

"You can tell the boss we did our best. It's not our fault they escaped."

"Then whose fault is it?" Elliot snarled.

The skinhead looked at him blankly. Then he shrugged. "What are you going to tell him?"

"Nothing. Nothing at all." Elliot flung the hammer into the van and climbed in. He had a large sum in used notes in his apartment and a variety of passports. If he left now, he could be far away before his icy-voiced employer even knew what had happened here tonight.

MOVING QUICKLY, huddled together like any late-night lovebirds, Owen and Sarah tried to conceal their terror as they hurried down the steps into Kensington High Street tube station, catching one of the last trains of the evening.

FRIDAY, OCTOBER 30

41

Do we have an ID on the corpse?"

"He was a skinhead. They discovered that . . . when they found his head," Victoria Heath added.

Tony Fowler cut across Earls Court Road without bothering to signal, leaving horns blaring in his wake. He was in a pissy mood. It was seven in the morning, and he and his partner were running on fumes. "When did the call come in?" The bodies were starting to pile up, and there was no sign of Miller.

"Around midnight. There was an incomplete call to 999. The operator didn't get the full details, but caller ID identified the full address. A unit drove by to investigate and gave chase to some men running from the building." Sergeant Heath leaned forward and pointed to the right. "It's down there."

"Halloween isn't until tomorrow and already everyone's gone crazy."

"In all fairness, last night was a busy night," the sergeant continued, glancing down at her notebook. "Chelsea lost two–nil to the Villa, and there were a lot of disappointed fans. Seventeen arrests. Then there was a multiple pileup on Earls Court Road, which effectively closed off this whole section of roadway. It was close to two thirty before the unit returned. They spoke to the complainant, the landlady who lives in the flat above the basement apartment. Turns out she'd been talking to one of her tenants who said she'd encountered a stranger on the steps earlier that evening asking after the man in the flat. Landlady hadn't thought too much of it until she heard the screams. . . ."

"And by then it was too late." Fowler sighed. "When will the public ever fucking learn? Phone us sooner, not later."

"The problem is even when they do phone us, it takes us nearly two and a half hours to get there," Victoria reminded him. "The call came from Owen Walker's cell phone, the graduate student renting the apartment," Victoria added.

"Walker? Any relation to Judith Walker?"

"The boy's American, but we're checking it out. He works for a local consulting firm. Been living here for three years." She squinted, trying to read her own shaky writing. She was on her third cup of coffee and had copied the notes over the air from an officer already at the scene.

"What happened then?"

"When the officers reached the apartment, they found the window in Walker's sitting room broken. They shone a flashlight through the window and saw a pair of legs on the floor. They pushed open the door, and inside they discovered the body of an unidentified male. He'd been disemboweled and decapitated by a sharp weapon. Possibly a sword," she added with a sour smile.

"A sword?"

"A sword."

"I don't fucking believe it," Tony Fowler whispered, easing the car into the curb behind the coroner's car. "Any connection to Miller?"

"Too early to say. Boyfriend, maybe?"

"Was there any sign of the Miller woman?"

"None."

GAVIN MACKINTOSH was peeling off his rubber gloves when the two police officers entered the apartment. The Scotsman's face was drawn, deep shadows under his eyes. "What's wrong with this picture?" he asked.

Tony Fowler stopped beside the corpse, pulling down the zipper on the body bag to look over the chilling wounds. Then he stood and looked around the room. "No blood," he said finally.

The Scotsman nodded. "Under normal circumstances, I'd lay money that our dead friend wasn't killed in this room, that he'd been butchered somewhere else and his body transported here. However, these are not normal circumstances. I don't think there's too much doubt that he fought and died here."

"But where's the blood?" Victoria Heath murmured.

"Exactly!" Mackintosh snapped. "Where's the blood? He's been gutted like a fish and bled out. This place should be swimming in blood. He's had his throat cut while still alive. Blood pumping from the arteries under pressure should have sprayed the walls and ceiling." All heads turned to look up at the ceiling. "So, what's the connection between this guy and the body I looked at earlier?"

"The sword," Tony Fowler said.

"The sword." Mackintosh smiled wanly. "They were both killed with the same weapon."

"The same killer?" Victoria muttered.

"That would be a logical assumption." The Scotsman nodded. "I'm glad I'm not a cop."

THE LANDLADY'S name was Diane Gale, and although she felt sorry for the young man in the basement flat, who seemed to have been kidnapped or murdered—or possibly both—by a homicidal maniac, she was enjoying her fifteen minutes in the spotlight. She was also keeping a tight rein on what she said; after all, surely one of the tabloids would be prepared to pay good money for the story, and she didn't want to give it all away for nothing.

"I've given my statement to the other officers," she said, striking a pose in her colorful kimono when the tired-looking man and the masculine-looking woman appeared at her door, both holding police ID in their hands.

"This will only take a minute, Mrs. Gale," Tony Fowler said easily, ignoring her and stepping into the hall.

"It's Miss, actually," she flirted.

"Miss," Tony corrected himself. "I am Detective Fowler, and this is my partner, Sergeant Heath. First I would like to thank you for your invaluable assistance. If more of the public were like you, our job would be made a lot easier." He managed to make the words sound sincere.

They followed the attractive septuagenarian into a tiny sitting room that was dominated by an enormous piano. On the far wall was a new flat-screen television. Toothy breakfast-time announcers listed the overnight stories and disasters in fifteen-second sound bites. Miss Gale turned off the television as the smiling weather girl appeared.

"Miss Gale, what can you tell us about the young man who lived downstairs?" Tony Fowler said immediately.

"He was an American. Quite lovely. Rather handsome. Frankly, I wish he were twenty years older and I were ten years younger. Shame. Still, he always paid his rent on time."

"Did he have any girlfriends . . . or boyfriends?" Victoria Heath asked quickly.

"Well, of course. He was stunning; there were always young people coming and going. Young people do like to entertain. But there was no one special, if you know what I mean."

"Any of them skinheads?"

She looked shocked. "Absolutely not. There are no skinheads in this establishment."

Heath and Miller looked at each other.

"Did Owen shave his head?"

"He most certainly did not. He had a very nice head of hair."

"What about family?" Victoria asked.

"Just an aunt. His parents are both dead; such a shame. I cooked him a Thanksgiving dinner last year, a real American tradition, and he got rather weepy when talking about them." She took a deep breath. "It seems that—"

"Is his aunt English?" Tony interrupted.

"Yes, yes, of course, she lives—"

"Do you have a name for this aunt?" Victoria interrupted. "We'll need to contact her."

"Of course. She's a big-time children's author, you know. I have every one of her Dark Castle series. Here, I'll show you, they're autographed and everything." Diane Gale reached up to the bookshelf and pulled down a brightly illustrated children's book. She smiled broadly as she opened the book so the two police officers could read the signature. But the smile faded as the officers turned and hurried out of the room.

A UNIFORMED officer stopped the detectives on the steps. "Excuse me, but there's a constable here I think you should talk to."

The detective and sergeant followed the officer across to one of the police cars, where a young, red-faced officer was standing, shifting uneasily from foot to foot. "This is Constable Napier, he's with the local station."

"What can we do for you, Constable?"

"I was on my way to this address to talk to the owner of a red Honda Civic, registration number—"

Fowler raised his hand. "The point?" he snapped.

"The car, registered to a Mr. Owen Walker, was found abandoned at the corner of Kensington High Street and Derry Street. We believe, judging from the damage to the car, that Mr. Walker had been involved in a multiple-car crash. We initially thought he might simply have driven off, but we've established the existence of bloodstains on the upholstery. We think he may have been injured."

Fowler caught the older officer by the shoulder. "Get Mackintosh. Tell him to meet us there. You"—he grabbed the younger constable by the arm—"take us there immediately."

"It's Miller, isn't it?" Sergeant Heath asked.

"Has to be. She probably kidnapped the boy and was driving away in his car when he struggled, the car got out of control, and crashed."

Victoria Heath nodded, but it didn't make sense: Sarah Miller was a petite five feet four, while Owen Walker, according to the description they had, was a six-foot all-American athlete. It made absolutely no sense.

Fowler snapped, "Contact HQ. Tell them to make an addition to Miller's sheet. She should not be approached. Use extreme caution."

"I wonder where Owen Walker is now?" Victoria Heath whispered.

Fowler grunted. "Dead. Or if he's not dead, then she's probably torturing him to death right now."

42

The deliciously aromatic smells of roasting coffee and burning toast awakened him from his troubled dreams. Owen rolled over and struggled to sit up in bed. He brushed hair out of his eyes, groaning aloud as his hand grazed his battered cheek. The entire right side of his face was hot and felt swollen to the touch, and he could feel hard points of glass beneath the skin.

So it hadn't been a dream.

The wild car ride had chased him through his dreams, only now the cold-eyed man with the hammer hadn't pounded the windscreen and bashed on the roof; he had been striking him directly with the hammer, the blows cracking bones and breaking skin.

Owen barely remembered the tube ride to Notting Hill Gate. He'd made the journey slumped up against Sarah, numbed by the events of the evening, his bruised face nestled against her shoulder to hide the cuts. He'd taken Sarah to the flat of a friend in Notting Hill, just off Portobello Road. Joyce was one of a string of women he was dating. She was away for the week and had given Owen a set of keys so that he could feed her cats.

A shadow loomed in the door, and his heart lurched as he remembered the shadowy figures of the previous night.

Sarah tapped on the door with her foot before stepping into the room. She'd recently showered, and her long red hair was plastered close to her skull; her eyes, which had seemed so dead and lifeless the previous day, were now brighter. The pink towel clung to her shapely body, and Owen averted his eyes in embarrassment. She sat on the edge of the bed and waited until he had straightened the pillows and pulled the sheet up over his groin before placing a tray on his knees.

"I haven't had breakfast in bed for a long time." He attempted to smile, but it pulled the skin on his face. With his hands wrapped around a mug of coffee, he sipped slowly, feeling the scalding liquid burn his tongue. He sighed and sank back onto the pillow.

"How do you feel?" Sarah asked.

"How do I look like I feel?"

She grinned quickly, her face suddenly girlish. "Like shit."

"Exactly how I feel."

She leaned forward to examine the tender flesh on his cheek. "I cleaned it as best I could," she said, "but there may be some glass still in there."

Owen shook his head. "I don't remember you doing that." He suddenly lifted the covers and looked under them. He was naked. A blush washed up his cheeks and was instantly mirrored on Sarah's face.

"There was glass all over your clothes . . . ," she began. And then she smiled shyly. "And after everything that had happened last night, I was in no state to do anything, not even look."

Owen nodded. "I didn't get a chance to thank you last night. . . ."

"You can thank me by eating your breakfast. Don't make a girl eat alone. It's rude."

Sarah chewed on a corner of toast and looked at the man, seeing him properly for the first time. She recognized his aunt in his features, the same determination in his green eyes, the strong jaw.

"Who owns the flat?" she asked cautiously, noting the tasteful feminine decor, aware that the silence was lengthening between them.

"A . . . friend," he said, unsure why he wanted to hide the fact that he had slept with Joyce several times. "She's in my statistics class, and she's away for the week." An ancient gray tomcat hopped onto the bed, eyes fixed on the milk jug. "I promised to feed Romulus and Remus. What can I say, I'm a softy for animals."

"I love cats," she murmured, and then sneezed. "Though they don't love me."

Owen tipped a little milk into the saucer and placed it on the bed. Instantly, a second cat, a slender tabby, jumped up. Both cats squatted down to lap at the milk. "Do you think we'll be safe here?" he asked, not looking at her, gently stroking a cat.

"I don't know," she said. "It depends how organized these people are. Maybe they'll get around to checking out your friends. But you've probably got a few days."

"Are you still going to the police?"

"I am."

"Then I'm still coming with you."

Sarah started to shake her head.

"It's not up for discussion," Owen said firmly. He finished his coffee. "I want to grab a shower and try and clean up my face first."

Sarah picked up the tray and carried it back into the tiny kitchen. There was a small picture taped to the refrigerator. It showed Owen and a beautiful Asian woman standing before the London Eye. Their arms were flung around each other in a way that was far from platonic.

"I wish I was this close to all of my friends," Sarah muttered to Romulus, who had followed her, hoping to get more food. She turned on the tiny television in the kitchen. After watching the news for several minutes, she relaxed a little, realizing that there had been no mention of the man she'd killed. There had been pictures of the pileup on Kensington High Street, half a dozen cars scattered across the road, the reporter's face washed blue and red in the lights of the emergency vehicles. Although there had been several serious injuries, no one had been killed.

When she finished doing the dishes, she heard Owen climb out of bed and pad into the bathroom. Moments later, the shower turned on.

Sarah wandered back into the sitting room and sank into an overstuffed easy chair. She reached into the bag at her feet and lifted out the Broken Sword.

Hunting horns. Faint and distant.

Calling.

Sarah blinked. For an instant the sword had been whole, a shining sliver of silver metal, and then the sunlight had run liquid down it, blinding her, making her eyes water. When she'd been able to see again, the sword was nothing more than a rusted bar. Someone had killed to possess this chunk of metal. Judith Walker had died in appalling agony to protect its secret. Maybe there was solid gold beneath the rust, a modern-day Maltese falcon. She picked at the rust with her thumbnail, bloodred slivers of oxidized iron tumbling to her lap, but no shining metal shone through.

And yet the sword was special.

Last night when she had plunged it into the skinhead, she had felt . . . What had she felt? For a brief moment, she had felt strong, powerful, her terror had faded and she felt . . . *alive*. And earlier, when she'd struck the youth on the train, she'd reacted instinctively, bringing up the metal bar to crack him across the side of his head. In the moment when the youth had smashed into the window, Sarah had felt . . . What had she felt? How could she explain the sensation? Regret . . . horror . . . fear . . .

No, she had felt *content*.

Cradling the sword in her arms, Sarah Miller lay back in the chair and closed her eyes; the only sound in the apartment was the distant hissing of the shower in the bathroom. It sounded like rain.

Just like rain. . . .

43

*I*t's raining."

"It's always raining in this cursed country."

"What a godforsaken place."

A shadow fell across them. "No place is forsaken by God."

Both men turned away and bent to their tasks as the raven-haired boy passed. They refused to meet his cold, empty eyes, and both surreptitiously touched amulets and talismans stitched inside their clothing. The boy looked back over his shoulder, lips curled in a wry smile, as if he knew what they were doing.

The gray-haired, white-bearded man standing in the prow placed his arm on his nephew's shoulder and pointed toward the distant line of the white cliffs. "We'll be there before the night falls."

Rain hissed across the waves, thrumming against the leather sail, spattering off the wooden deck. "Are we far from home, Uncle?"

"Far indeed, Yeshu'a. We'll make landfall on the beach below the cliffs."

The boy rested his elbows on the rail and leaned forward, staring curiously toward the approaching land. "Uncle, the sailors think we've come perilously close to the edge of the world, and the Egyptian is predicting that if we were to sail a day farther west, we will fall off the edge."

"The Egyptian, despite his learning, is a fool. If we were to sail a day west and north, we would encounter another land, a wondrous green land, peopled by savage warlike tribes. It is a land rich in gold, and its people are skilled in working the soft metal."

"Will we travel there, Uncle?"

"Not this time." The older man pulled his woolen hood over his head as the wind shifted, driving the sleeting rain into his face.

"We will trade for tin, spend ten days replenishing our supplies, and then return home."

The boy, Yeshu'a, turned his face to the rain, closing his eyes and opening his mouth to catch the icy water. "It tastes of cold soil and bitter herbs," he said without opening his eyes. Then he turned his head and his dark eyes opened and fixed on his uncle. "What will you trade for the tin?"

"So many questions! Well, not the usual trade goods. These people are artisans and craftsmen; they only appreciate the interesting and the unusual." He gestured toward the center of the squat-bellied ship, where an assortment of items lay covered beneath an oiled leather tarpaulin. "One of the reasons they will trade with me, when they refuse to do business with others, is because I always bring them something unusual. Sometimes I think they are like children, desiring only the newest toys."

He stopped suddenly, realizing that he was alone. The boy had wandered away, moving sure-footedly down the length of the ship toward the covered goods. The Master Mariner shook his head and turned back toward the land. Yeshu'a was his grandniece's child, a strange boy who had been an oddity from the moment of his birth. He looked and acted far beyond his young years, preferring the company of adults to children; however, for some reason his very presence made many adults nervous. He was given to wandering off by himself for days at a time, and although he had reached the age where he should have been beginning to learn a trade, he showed no interest in any of the crafts.

Josea was hoping that this trip to the edge of the world would pique the boy's interest. If it did, then he would take him on as his apprentice, teach him the ways of the sea, and show him the wonders of the world: the lands of the Yellow Folk of the far east, the hairy demon breeds of the mountains, men with hair the color of fire, skin the color of chalk. It would be enough to capture any man's imagination.

It had captured Josea's imagination when he was a boy.

Josea's father, Joshua, had first taken him to sea when he too was a child. It had been a short journey, north and west to the countless isles of the Greek Sea. Joshua had shown him the cities beneath the waves, perfect streets, paved roads, grand houses, glittering palaces,

*and ornate statues. He regaled him with tales of the lost civiliza-
tion that had once thrived there, and he gave him a dagger, plucked
by a diver from one of the houses beneath the waves. He told him
there were other civilizations, other races, other mysteries and treasures to be found.*

*Josea still carried the knife, an extraordinary creation of banded
metal and copper wire, long bladed and ornate, incised with a spiraling pattern that he had not encountered again until he had come
to the Tin Lands. When this trip was complete, he would take the
boy to the Greek Sea. Together they would explore the many islands, search for treasures in the golden sands . . . and maybe Josea
would be able to convince the boy to follow him.*

*Josea turned to look at the white cliffs again. They were nearer
now, and already fires were burning on the clifftops, warning of
the approaching ship. This was a hard life, but not a bad life, and
no harder than that of the craftsman, the farmer, or the shepherd.
Glancing over his shoulder, he watched his nephew examining the
trade goods, then turned back to the approaching cliffs. All he had to
do was direct the boy's curiosity.*

*Yeshu'a's long fingers moved over the leather-wrapped bundles.
Closing his mind to the countless thoughts and emotions buffeting
him, concentrating on the endless hiss of the sea to clear his head,
he picked up a package and undid the leather cord that bound it.
Color blazed against the gray morning air. Yeshu'a smiled his rare
and wondrous smile. It was a cloak, a cloak woven of deep crimson
feathers, the pattern and patina of the feathers marvelously placed
and shaped to give the faintest impression of an ornate design on
the back of the cloak.*

*On impulse, the boy pulled it onto his shoulders, enveloping him-
self in its deliciously delicate feathers. And then his smile faded and
his lips twisted in a bitter grimace. A wave of terror rose up to en-
gulf him. He was trapped in a net, struggling helplessly, bones snapping in a desperate effort to pull free . . . and was surrounded by
countless thousands of birds. Red-feathered birds, squawking,
screeching in terror. And creeping through the bushes were dark-
skinned men with painted faces and spears in their hands.*

The boy pulled off the cloak and tossed it onto the deck.

"Yeshu'a!"

The boy turned, eyes blank and expressionless. His uncle was glaring at him. "Pick that up, and wrap it before the seawater destroys it. It cost me a fortune."

Yeshu'a reluctantly touched the cloak again and wrapped the leather sheet around it. He had the briefest glimpse of the struggling birds, but he savagely blanked the thoughts from his mind. As he searched through the items, his slender fingers touched cold metal.

When he unwrapped the leather covering, he discovered the sword. He touched it, and heat flowed along the length of his arm. . . .

44

Sarah Miller awoke with a start, convinced that she had just stood on the boat with the boy and his uncle. She had been holding a three-foot shining broad-bladed sword, the hilt wrapped in rich red leather, the blade etched and incised with spirals and intricate knotwork. But when she looked at her hands, she was almost disappointed to find she was holding only a rusted chunk of metal. Lifting her hands, she discovered that some of the rust had come off and coated her sweating flesh in red dye, the color of fresh blood.

Sarah looked up to find Owen standing in front of her, wreathed in steam. His damp hair was already curling up, and his broad naked chest was glistening with water beads. His muscular torso was wrapped in a thick peach towel. "I thought I heard you cry out."

"I dozed off. There was a dream," she began, and stopped, realizing Owen was staring at her bloody hands.

"You should go and wash them," he said gently. "People might get the wrong impression."

She looked at her stained hands and smiled grimly. "I'm pretty sure they already have."

45

Robert Elliot had been preparing for a day like this for a very long time.

There was money salted away in a dozen accounts in as many names in banks all across the world. He held legitimate passports in four nationalities. He was prepared for what he needed to do.

He was prepared to disappear.

The small man pulled the leather suitcase out of the closet and tossed it onto the bed. It was kept permanently packed.

He had no illusions that his employer would come looking for him. Nor had he any illusions about the man's capabilities. Although Elliot and his employees had accounted for five of the deaths of the elderly men and women, he suspected there were others that the voice on the phone had taken care of personally. Only last week he'd read something in the paper about a rich codger found dead in his pool. "Died in agony," the report read. Elliot knew that was his employer's signature: Right from the beginning he had been very particular that the old people had to suffer.

The first call had come in two months earlier at three o'clock in the morning. Elliot was just getting in from one of the West End clubs when the phone had rung. The answering machine had clicked on, and the voice had spoken. "Pick up the phone, Mr. Elliot, I know you're there. You're wearing your charcoal gray Armani suit, a blue silk shirt, midnight blue tie, and matching handkerchief, Dubarry loafers, black silk socks . . ."

He'd picked up the phone, knowing that it was trouble, knowing that he was in trouble: He was being watched. "There is an envelope in the top drawer of your desk. Open it and then we will talk." The caller hung up.

Robert Elliot had felt the first touch of fear.

His apartment should have been impregnable: The caller was demonstrating his power, his access to Elliot's life. The envelope had contained a single sheet of paper bearing the name and address of a man living in Brixton. Thomas Sexton. Elliot had never heard of him.

The phone rang again, and the caller explained that Sexton had an artifact, an antique whetstone: a flat, circular stone with a round hole in the middle. The caller wanted that stone. And Elliot was to kill Thomas Sexton in a particularly bloody manner. The caller was very specific—the man's chest had to be opened, heart and lungs removed, and then the stone was to be placed into the bloody cavity and left there until it was completely coated in blood. Elliot had hung up without saying a word and unplugged the phone from the wall.

The first post brought a parcel. When he'd cut through the packaging and the plastic bag within, Elliot recoiled from the noxious stench that filled the room: It was the left arm, complete with the black scorpion tattoo, of a young man he'd been forced to dispose of three months earlier. Eight-by-ten high-resolution glossy photographs accompanied the parcel, showing Elliot digging the grave in the New Forest, tossing the naked body in, and covering it up again, then returning to his car.

The photos were all time-stamped.

Two hours later, a courier had brought Elliot an envelope containing a single sheet of paper. It listed all of his accounts with their current balances.

A million pounds had just been deposited in his savings account.

When the phone rang in the early hours of the morning, he knew he had little choice but to obey the caller. He'd taken out his frustration on Thomas Sexton. The man had died hard.

Elliot realized that he'd always known a day like this would come—a day when he would fail and his employer would turn on him. He still didn't know how Miller and the boy had eluded him. What mattered was that he had lost them both.

He had lost the sword.

Opening the wall safe, Robert Elliot pulled out his passports and sorted through them quickly. He shoved the two English and American passports into his briefcase and pushed the wine-colored Irish passport into his pocket. Today he was Rónán Eagan, computer salesman. He would not need a passport to fly to the Irish Republic, and once there he could fly anywhere in the world. Elliot glanced at his watch: an hour to Heathrow, then another hour to Dublin. He could be in Ireland before noon, in the States before nightfall.

And then he'd be safe.

46

Skinner finished the last of the can, crumpled it in his fist, and tossed it into the corner. Squeezing his eyes shut, he willed himself to weep, but he had no tears to cry. Yet he could feel the emotion bubbling inside him, acrid and bitter. Then slowly, almost imperceptibly, he curled up on the filthy mattress in the fetal position, turning his face to the flaking wall, and thought of Karl. He could still see Miller bursting into the room, Karl landing one or two good ones on her, then the briefest glimpse of the rusty metal in the woman's hands. And then the sound, that awful sickening, crunching sound of the sword sinking into flesh. For an instant—the briefest of instants—he'd imagined he'd seen a gleaming metal sword in Miller's hands. And as Karl had tumbled and fallen, she'd hit him again, and then Skinner truly had seen the sword blaze whole and complete in the moment it took Karl's head from his shoulders.

The skinhead swallowed bile.

Karl . . . dear, dead Karl; he'd loved that boy, truly loved him. They'd had some great times together. But Skinner couldn't remember the times. All he could see now was his lover falling to the ground, his head spinning slowly away in the opposite direction. He would not even be able to claim the body.

Wrapping his arms tightly around himself, Skinner ground his teeth together. This was all Elliot's fault, and Miller's, especially that bitch Sarah Miller. And by Christ, they were both going to pay.

On the ground beside the filthy mattress, his cell phone started buzzing, vibrating against the bare boards.

Skinner ignored it, and it stopped.

Then started again.

He snatched it up and looked at the screen—unlisted number. It was probably Elliot. For a moment he thought about not answering, but that might bring the psychopath around to his flat, and he didn't want that. His fingers stabbed the buttons hard enough to break them. "What!"

"You are Nick Jacobs, but you are commonly called Skinner, so that is how I will address you." The voice was deep and commanding.

"Who the fuck is this?"

"I am Robert Elliot's employer. His former employer."

Skinner straightened. "You're the guy he keeps phoning?"

"I am." There was a long silence broken only by the line clicking and snapping. "Tell me, Skinner, what happened tonight?"

"Miller and the bloke got away. Karl was killed," he added bitterly.

"And you were close to Karl?"

"I was. It was Elliot's fault. We should never have gone in there in the first place. We should have snatched the bitch on the streets."

"I would agree. It is Elliot's fault Karl is dead. You should exact your revenge."

Skinner sat up straight. "I will."

"Did you know that Mr. Elliot is planning to flee the country?"

"When?"

"Within the hour. If you're going to catch him, you will have to be quick."

"I don't have his address. He never told me."

"Mr. Elliot was a very cautious man." There was a pause, then the voice asked, "Would you like his address?"

"Yes sir, I would."

"Good. Very good, Skinner. I believe we're going to get on quite well. Need I remind you that you're now working for me?"

"Yes, sir."

"After I've given you the address, and your instructions, I'll give you a phone number. You may reach me there at any time."

"Yes, sir."

"And Skinner . . ."

"Yes, sir?"

"Tell him that running was a mistake. Make him suffer."

"Oh, you can count on that," Skinner said grimly.

47

obert Elliot strode across the underground parking lot, heels tapping on the ground. He whistled a song from *Wicked*. He couldn't wait to see it on Broadway. Elliot felt that most American musicals were diluted by the time they reached the West End, and he wanted to see proper American boys dancing and singing in their tight costumes. Perhaps he would reinvent himself next as a producer and personally audition young talent who wanted to make their mark on the Great White Way. Yes. He would set up a small office on Broadway and seduce potential clients. Men only.

Elliot smiled as he approached his car, imagining his future. Enveloped in his dreams, he barely noticed that the air was heavy with gas and carbon monoxide fumes. Since he wasn't planning to return, he'd drive the BMW to the airport. He hated having to leave the car, but he'd buy himself another in America. A Hummer. Black.

The smell of gasoline was stronger at this end of the garage, strong enough to make his eyes water. He used the remote control to open the car doors from a distance. He walked up to the car, pulled open the door, and slid into the leather seats.

"Fuck!"

The interior of the car was reeking of gas fumes. And then Elliot was aware that moisture was soaking into his trousers and back. He touched the passenger's seat . . . and put his hand in a puddle of liquid. He didn't have to bring his hand to his face to realize that it was gasoline.

A shape moved alongside the car, and then the passenger window exploded inward, shards of glass raining around Elliot, tangling in his hair, nicking his cheeks. "Skinner?" he whispered.

"Your former employer told me to tell you that running was a mistake." Skinner's broken yellow teeth gleamed in the sulfurous flare of a long kitchen match.

And then the match was falling, slowly, slowly, slowly, onto the leather seat.

"IT IS happening." On the other side of the country, the naked woman spread-eagled on the silken sheets grunted in ecstasy when the car erupted into flames. Elliot's agony was a vague and distant discomfort, nothing more. If she heightened her consciousness, she could experience Elliot's pain. "He burns. He is in excruciating pain."

On the Otherworld Astral plane, she looked down over the burning car, watching the writhing figure within. Waves of color—the man's terror and torment—spiraled up like smoke. She absorbed the colors, drinking the emotions.

"Remember, do not allow him to die quickly, chain his spirit to his body as long as possible. Let him suffer."

"He is suffering."

"Good. Now show him this."

Vyvienne opened her eyes and looked at the man standing at the end of the bed, wrapped in a red cloak woven of birds' feathers. He stretched his arms wide, spreading the cloak. "Let him see me."

THROUGH SHIMMERING waves of raw anguish, Robert Elliot saw the towering man-bird in the crimson cloak appear before him. He opened his mouth to scream and vomited flames onto the bubbling glass. The windscreen melted, a hole appearing, curling outward. The pain was too great, and he closed his eyes moments before he lost them.

His last impression was the smell of burning meat, and by then there was no pain.

48

Gavin Mackintosh smelled something rotten.

Handsome, charismatic, and witty with the soft Scottish accent made sexy and acceptable by Sean Connery, he was a regular on late night television talk shows and radio phone-ins. In the twelve years he had been a pathologist, he had collected a wealth of amusing and anecdotal stories about his job. Invariably, someone would ask him what he liked least about his unique occupation, and he'd always respond, "The smells." It always got a laugh, but it was actually true. The mixture of decomposing flesh and decaying gases from a particularly ripe corpse was indescribable. However, if the truth be told, after the first year on the job he barely registered the smells. It was as if his olfactory sense closed down once he stepped into the building.

But Mackintosh was smelling something rotten now.

Mac had been leaving for an early luncheon appointment with a charming magazine editor when he'd caught the faintest hint of a suspect odor. Something bitter and sweet, like rotten fruit, sticky with juice and flies. He'd wandered back down the tiled corridors, head thrown back, broad nostrils flaring. He'd worked in this building for so long now that he knew it intimately, its peculiarities, its smells, and the rattling doors and shaky windows that gave the building its haunted reputation. There was mildew in one of the basements, dry rot in another corner of the building, but here . . . here there should have been only the sharpness of disinfectant, perhaps the faintest sweetness of decomposition or the touch of metallic blood.

Mackintosh threw his briefcase and coat onto the desk in the outer office and pushed through two sets of double doors into the morgue. He brought up the lights. Everyone was out to lunch and the building was almost completely quiet; only the distant hum of the air-conditioning disturbed the stagnant silence. The smell was stronger here.

He recognized it now: It was the stench of advanced decomposition. That state of decay when rotting flesh turned the consistency of soap and sloughed off brittle bones. But there was nothing in that state here . . . unless something had come in and he hadn't been informed.

Mac wandered down the numbered freezers, nostrils flaring, identifying the corpses by odor before he read the tag on the door.

Raw, bloody meat: road-traffic accident.

Rancid seaweed and salt: drowning.

Burned meat and petrol: a car suicide that had just come in. The victim had doused his car in gasoline, locked himself in, then set it alight.

As he continued through the room, Mac blinked, eyes suddenly watering.

Unknown Male 44. Unknown Male 45.

The headless young men struck down by the sword-wielding maniac. Neither had been positively identified. Mac pulled open the drawer of Number 44, the youth from the train, and recoiled, pinching his nostrils shut. The smell was appalling. The meaty, fruiting smell of advanced decay. And yet it shouldn't be . . . He tugged back the sheet . . . and then the hardened pathologist spun away and vomited.

The body was a mass of wriggling white worms. Much of the flesh was missing, and the bones were already beginning to show the characteristic yellow white of age. What flesh remained was black and leathery.

Squeezing his watering eyes shut, Mackintosh pushed the drawer closed and pulled out Number 45, the headless body from the flat off of Earls Court Road. The smell here was even more intense, and the sheet, which covered the body, was lying almost flat on the metal tray, only the curve of the skull and the jut of the ribs indenting the sheet. The white sheet was stained yellow and black, and tendrils of sticky liquid dripped onto the tiled floor. Mac staggered back and stumbled out of the morgue.

The bodies, only hours old, looked as if they had been dead for years.

49

"It's a letter, from Aunt Judith."

Tears magnified Owen's bright green eyes as he held up a flimsy sheet of paper that was covered with tiny script.

Sarah sank to the floor facing Owen. Romulus immediately climbed onto her legs, and Sarah's fingers started moving over his sleek fur.

"Did you read it?" Owen asked, almost accusingly.

She shook her head. "I went through the bag to get your address. That's all. I didn't read anything."

Owen took a deep breath and began to read slowly, struggling to decipher the crabbed, often hurried writing.

My dearest Owen,

If you are reading this, then there is a good chance that I'm dead. You must not grieve for me, my boy. Everything dies, but only so that it may be reborn. I pray that this note is accompanied by the sword. It may look like nothing more than a piece of rusty metal, but I must ask you to treat it with all the reverence of a holy relic. The sword is Dyrnwyn, the Broken Sword. It is older than the land, and forms part of the Hallows, thirteen sacred objects that are the Sovereignty of the Land of Britain. When I was a child I was entrusted with the sword and I became one of the thirteen Hallowed Keepers.

I now pass this Keepership on to you.

This is not a task I do lightly, but you are of my bloodline. Guard the sword well, and in time you will be able to wield a fragment of its terrible power.

Owen looked up, eyes burning. He suddenly crumpled the page and tossed it to one side. He looked away, forcing himself not to cry.

Sarah leaned over and retrieved the letter without a word. She unfolded it.

"I knew she was mentally ill," Owen said, sobbing, "but she wouldn't let anyone help her. She lived alone; she wouldn't let me put her in a home. A couple of years ago she fell and had to have a hip replaced. She was incapacitated for two days before someone eventually found her. Two days! She'd written children's books that had won all sorts of awards. But in the last few years, her books had become wilder . . . darker." Owen nodded toward the page in Sarah's hands. "She was obviously slipping further and further into her fantasy world."

"The men who flayed her alive, who abused and killed her, were no fantasy," Sarah said quietly. "The men who broke into your apartment were no fantasy."

Owen stopped and stared at her. "Are you saying you believe her?"

"The men who killed my family were no fantasy." Sarah bent her head and smoothed the crumpled page flat, then turned it over to read the writing on the back of the page.

> *I have spent most of my life researching the Hallows, their forms, identities, and powers. Much of what I have learned or conjectured is contained in these notebooks. How I came to be a Keeper is also contained in the smaller, separate notebook.*
>
> *It is my diary.*
>
> *In the last few months my work has taken on an additional urgency. I have learned that the Keepers of the Hallows are being killed; horribly, cruelly, systematically killed. There are—were—thirteen of us; I am unsure how many survive now, and only the Lord knows how many will still be living by the time you read this. I have listed the names and the last addresses I had for them. I am convinced that the Keepers are being killed for their Hallows.*
>
> *That someone is collecting the Hallows.*
>
> *My dearest Owen, this must never happen. The Hallows must never be brought together.*

Never.

I am sorry, truly sorry, that this burden has been passed on to you. From father to son, mother to daughter, the Hallows have been handed down through the generations, though if the lines die out, then a Guardian is reputed to come to redistribute them to new Keepers. You are my nearest relative. You are all I have.

Do not fail me.

"It's not signed," Sarah said. She looked over at Owen. "Well?" she asked.

"'Well'? What does 'well' mean? Ancient artifacts. Keepers of the Hallows? It's like something out of one of her novels."

Sarah lifted the padded envelope off the floor and shook everything onto the worn mauve carpet between them. There was a notebook, faded and tattered, with "Judith Walker" scrawled in large childish script on the brown cover, a small gilt-edged address book, and a fat scrapbook. A piece of paper curled from the edge of the scrapbook.

Pensioner and Good Samaritan Slain

Police in London are investigating the brutal slaying of Beatrice Clay (74) and the neighbor, Viola Jillian (23), who went to her assistance. Police investigators believe that Mrs. Clay, a widow, disturbed late night burglars in her first-floor apartment, who tied her to the bed and gagged her with a pillowcase. Mrs. Clay died of asphyxiation. Police suspect that Ms. Jillian, who lived in the apartment upstairs, heard a noise and came to investigate. In a struggle with one of the burglars, Ms. Jillian was fatally stabbed.

Sarah opened the book to push the cutting back inside. The pages were covered with neat extracts clipped from newspapers with wavy-edged scissors.

Pensioner Hit by Train

A coroner has returned a verdict of accidental death on Miss Georgina Rifkin (78), with an address at the Stella Maris Nursing Home in Ipswich. Miss Rifkin was struck by the six-thirty Intercity. The coroner dismissed as "malicious" press reports that she had been tied to the track.

Gangland Slaying

Police fears of an upsurge in gangland crimes were repeated today as criminal mastermind Thomas Sexton (76) was slain in one of the bloodiest gang murders Brixton has ever seen. Sexton, whose links with organized crime were well-known to the police, was killed in what a police spokesman described as a "particularly brutal manner." This reporter has learned that Sexton was disemboweled with a knife or sharp sword.

Sarah closed the book with a snap. She picked up the diary and turned it over in her hands before opening it. On the inside front cover was a list of names. Some of them leapt up at her: Bea . . . Georgie . . . Tommy . . .

She closed the diary, then picked up the small address book and flipped it open. Thumbing through the pages, she saw that most of the book was empty, little more than a dozen names in the flimsy pages, all of them written in a splotchy fountain pen ink that had faded to purple. Bea Clay . . . Georgie Rifkin . . . Tommy Sexton . . .

"You should look at this," she said, her voice sounding thick and numb.

"I don't want to."

"Look at it!" she suddenly snapped, shoving the scrapbook into his face. "Look at it." She could feel the rage bubbling inside her now, a burning, trembling rage. "Look at these names, here and here and here. And now look at your aunt's diary. And now the address book. Here. And here. And here."

The anger subsided as quickly as it had begun, leaving her drained and exhausted. "Don't you see, Owen? Judith knew all of these people. And they're all dead." Crouched on the floor, she reached across and cupped Owen's face in her hands. "If she wasn't dreaming, or fantasizing or raving . . . what then, Owen? What then?"

Owen Walker looked into her eyes. "She was crazy."

Sarah stared at him, saying nothing.

"She was crazy," Owen insisted, trying to convince himself. His eyes fell on the papers on the floor. "She was crazy," he whispered, yet much of the conviction had gone from his voice. Then he picked up his aunt's diary, opened it at random, and began to read aloud.

Monday.

The tramp Ambrose returned to the village today. Bea and I saw him hiding in the woods. We know he saw us, but he would not come out. He stayed in the trees, staring at us with his one eye. Everyone says he's harmless, but I'm not so sure. He scares me, and Bea told me she was frightened of him, too. Bea also said that she'd been dreaming the strangest dreams about him; I wonder if I should tell her that I was dreaming about him, too?

Tuesday.

Dreamt about Ambrose again last night. The strangest dreams, only this time all the others were in the dreams, too. We were in the middle of the forest. Ambrose was the only one who was properly dressed, he was wearing some sort of long gown.

We gathered in a semicircle around Ambrose, who was standing next to an enormous tree stump. On the stump were loads of strange objects. Cups, plates, knives, a chessboard, a beautiful red cloak. One by one we walked up to Ambrose and he gave us each one of the beautiful objects. I was last, and there was only a piece of rusty metal left. The others had gotten better things: He gave Georgie the pretty red coat, Sophie got a spear, and Donnie got a knife. Even Bea got something pretty. I didn't want to take the rusty metal, it was ugly, but Ambrose insisted, and he leaned so close that I could see the burst veins in his single eye.

"This is the most precious of my treasures, guard it well."

Owen closed the book with a snap. Sarah was turning the sword over in her hands, absently stroking the broken blade with the backs of her fingers.

"Go on," she said softly.

Owen shook his head. "I don't want to. It seems . . . too personal." He reached for the scrapbook and silently read through the catalog of death and suffering. When he was finished he looked across at Sarah, who had picked up the diary and was reading the large, rounded, childish script.

"My aunt knew all these people?" he said.

"From childhood." She tapped the diary pages with the sword. "Listen to this. They were all evacuated together. Thirteen children from all parts of the south of England. They were billeted on a farm in Wales, where they met an old one-eyed tramp called Ambrose. Ambrose gave them all the objects known as the Hallows. This is from close to the end of the diary."

It happened. It was almost exactly like my dream, I thought it might have been a dream. But now I know it really happened. But I'm still not sure when I stopped dreaming and everything started to become real.

I dreamt I woke up in the middle of the night and climbed out of bed, and slipped out into the night. Some of the others were already there, and the rest were coming from where they were staying in the village. When the thirteen of us had all gathered, Mr. Ambrose appeared. He didn't say anything, and we followed him into the heart of the woods. Sometimes I thought I was an old, old woman, wearing ragged clothing, then I was a short man shivering in the cold, then I was a knight on horseback, then a lady wearing a fabulous gown, then an old man with hands twisted by arthritis. There were more, but the dreams slipped past, too quick to follow. Finally I was just myself, but my pink nightdress had disappeared and I was naked, and so were the other boys and girls, but none of us minded. Even though it was October, we didn't feel the chill in the air. We gathered around Mr. Ambrose in a half circle, and he called us forward one by one to take the little objects he gave us. I was last, only this time I didn't refuse the sword. Mr. Ambrose seemed surprised. "I thought you would not want this!"

"This is Dyrnwyn, the Broken Sword," I said, and lifted up the object.

Mr. Ambrose seemed pleased. "Truly, you are a Keeper of the Hallows. The blood of the ancients flows in your veins, diluted certainly, but it is there. You and these others are all descended from the first Keepers of the Hallows, and only you thirteen are worthy enough to keep the sacred Hallowed objects."

Then he whispered the special words in my ear and told me that whenever I was in trouble, I was to hold the sword in both hands and call it thrice by its name, Dyrnwyn.

I asked him what thrice meant and he said three times.

Sarah closed the book, laid it on the floor, and lifted the sword in both hands. "Dyrnwyn," she said strongly.

"Sarah . . . what are you doing?"

"Dyrnwyn."

"Sarah!" Owen's voice was high with alarm.

"Dyrnwyn!"

No sound broke through the long silence that followed.

50

Beyond the physical world exist realms of experience undreamed of by the vast majority of mankind. These are the Ghost Worlds, sometimes known as the Astral plane or simply the Astral.

Scores of religions and beliefs accept that the human spirit, the soul, travels to the Astral while the physical body sleeps and renews itself. These faiths also agree that the spirits of the newly dead linger in the Astral before they take the final journey into the Light.

Powerful emotions in the living world, the Incarnate World, echo into the Astral, tiny pulses of color in the gray landscape. Words of power, either prayers or curses, once fired with emotion, can penetrate the Astral. Places of special worship, holy shrines, and revered artifacts leave their mark in the Astral.

And as in all worlds, predators hunt in the Ghost Worlds.

"DYRNWYN . . . DYRNWYN . . . Dyrnwyn . . ."

A solid cone of light burst through the shifting pattern of clouds, lancing into the upper reaches of the Ghost World. Higher and higher it soared, slicing through realms accessible only to a rare few. The sleeping spirits of humankind roamed the lower levels, while more highly developed souls had access to the middle levels. Only those who had dedicated their lives to the acquisition of arcane knowledge could enter the highest levels.

The gray landscape lit up as the beacon throbbed in the nothingness, washing away the shadows, muting the lights of human emotions and dreams that speckled the gray Astral.

And then the cone took shape, streamers of light flowing, giving the creation form and substance, angles forming, lines appearing, the beam of light tapering from the lowest levels, rising to a slender point high in the Astral.

The image of a sword formed.

It pulsed and throbbed in the Ghost World for less than a hand-ful of heartbeats, and then it winked out of existence. The gray-ness, darker now, slipped back, leaving the pastel lights of human consciousness flecking the Astral.

But the sudden burst of power had attracted the attention of those within and without the Astral. Such power—raw, naked, un-controllable power—had not been witnessed in a score of genera-tions, and those who once tapped the power, twisting and shaping it to their own ends, those whom people called great or good or evil, had not walked the world for nearly two thousand years.

The curious gathered, hunters and hunted. Lights and spots of fire, bright primary colors, solid dark pigments, mirrored whites, reflective blacks, raced across the Astral landscape toward the last location of the sword.

In the Incarnate World, those with the power to see and travel in the Astral recoiled from the blinding, deafening power, while those who were sensitive but untrained awoke from terrifying nightmares.

"DYRNWYN . . . DYRNWYN . . . Dyrnwyn . . ."

And on a shabby London backstreet, an old man heard the words and awoke.

51

"Dyrnwyn . . . Dyrnwyn . . . Dyrnwyn . . ."

Vyvienne's cold gray eyes snapped open. She was leaning against an ancient stone wall, staring out toward the distant Welsh mountains. It was raining in the distance, heavy clouds banked to the horizon, slanting sunlight lending the scene a quality that was almost pretty. But the icy wind robbed the autumnal day of all its charm.

She felt the pulse of raw power as the words echoed clarion-like across the Astral. The sword was being awakened, and the ripples of energy bubbled beneath the surface of the gray landscape, exploding in a wash of blinding power.

She had always been psychic. A seer. An oracle.

Vyvienne had lived a lifetime in her twenty-one years.

Born into a family of modern-day witches, she had always known she was special, different from the mundane little boys and girls whose egos were wrapped up in material needs. She was not satisfied with mere corporeal pleasures. She wanted more. And when she concentrated, Vyvienne could visit the Astral plane, the Otherworld.

Vyvienne was aware that the majority of humankind did not understand the universe beyond its limited experience. They grabbed onto the tangible realities of grass and trees and oceans and sky.

Because the Astral realm is accessible to only a rare few. Vyvienne was one of those people. For her, it was as real as the physical world.

VYVIENNE TURNED and hurried back toward the house, blinking hard. She focused on her surroundings—the chill of the autumn air, the crisp leaves underfoot, the hint of woodsmoke—anything to keep her mind off the images crowding at the edges of her consciousness. She desperately wanted to examine those images, but she needed to be someplace protected and secure. Because when you look into the Otherworld . . . sometimes it looks into you.

By the time Vyvienne was ten, she had walked the myriad lower levels of the Astral; when she gave up her virginity at the age of thirteen to Ahriman Saurin, her skills had been honed by techniques and rituals centuries old. Enhancing her natural skills with the ancient power of sex, Ahriman had encouraged Vyvienne to seek out the artifacts, to read their sleeping signatures in the Astral, and to trace them to their source. And when she'd been handfasted to Ahriman at the age of sixteen, together they had embarked upon the Great Work: to recover the Thirteen Hallows. It had taken him five years to train her properly, though once she recognized the initial Astral shape of the first object they were seeking, the rest came quickly. Once they had the first Hallow, the rest followed. Men and women died, but humankind was born to die, and at least they died with purpose; they had given their blood to fire the ancient objects.

Now only a handful of Hallows were unaccounted for.

And one of those was the Sword of Dyrnwyn.

VYVIENNE FOUND Ahriman in the darkened drawing room, sitting in the carved wooden seat, staring out across the village toward the mountains. He was naked save for the red cloak, the Hallow known as the Crimson Coat. His black eyes were flat and expressionless as he turned to look at her. "What happened?"

"She's called the sword by name. She fired it." Vyvienne took a deep, shuddering breath. "It has appeared in the Astral."

Ahriman stood and spread his arms, gathering the trembling woman into them.

"Such power! You've never felt such power," she whispered.

"A fragment of what we will eventually control."

"But we cannot proceed without the sword. . . ."

He slapped her quickly, huge hands cracking her head from side to side. Her body reacted to his cruel touch, craving more.

"That is for me to decide," he reminded her. Holding her at arm's length, he began to unbutton her coat. "Prepare yourself: It is time to seek out the next Hallowed object."

"Are you sure—"

He slapped her again. "Do not question me. Ever. Remember who I am. *What* I am."

52

Victoria Heath smiled at the handkerchief. "Didn't think you were squeamish."

Detective Tony Fowler walked away from the burned-out wreckage of the car, a dirty handkerchief pressed to his mouth. The underground garage was still thick with smoke, and Fowler's face was smudged, black spots covering the starched white collar of his shirt.

"I'm not. But the smell of petrol makes me throw up. No need to ask what happened here," he added. "Someone doused the car and tossed a match inside." He looked sharply at the sergeant and started smiling. "I've a feeling you're about to make an old man very happy."

Sergeant Heath nodded. "We got a usable set of fingerprints off the car. The piece of burnt meat is Robert Elliot, aka Roger Easton, Richard Edgerton, Ron Edwards, and about a dozen different names. Small-time pimp, dealer, fixer, and fence. Owner of a couple of bondage clubs, two peep joints, and a porno cinema. Occasionally, he imported a little coke, some heroin. He served time when he was a teenager for bludgeoning his father to death. We've been keeping tabs on him on and off over the past couple of years, waiting for the right moment to take him."

"Someone's already taken him," Tony Fowler said grimly.

"Mr. Elliot swung both ways and liked his sex with a little pain. In general he preferred boys. A lad called Nick Jacobs, commonly referred to as Skinner, possibly because he sported a skinhead haircut, was a long-term boyfriend. Skinner in turn was involved with another skinhead youth called Karl Lang."

Fowler stopped. The name was familiar.

"Mr. Lang was the headless body we took out of Owen Walker's apartment this morning."

Fowler stared at her, dumbfounded.

Victoria's smile broadened. "It gets better. Elliot supplied dope to a Lawrence McFeely."

"McFeely was the body in the train," Fowler said.

"The same."

"Jesus Christ—what's going on here?"

"And just so as I make your day complete," Victoria Heath added, "Mac said the two bodies, Lang and McFeely, have melted."

"Melted?"

"Advanced state of putrefaction, he said was the technical term. Melted was what he meant."

"Sarah Miller is the key, you know that."

The woman nodded. "What about Owen Walker? Is he dead?"

Tony Fowler shook his head. "I'm inclined to think not. Miller likes to leave her bodies lying around. I think if he were dead, Mr. Walker would have already turned up. Did you get me the list of his friends?"

"Mostly people from his university," the sergeant said, passing across the single sheet of paper. "I talked to all of them, except this woman here, who's away for a few days."

"Does Owen know her?" Fowler asked sharply.

"Intimately, according to his friends. Apparently they've dated off and on, though he's a bit of a playboy, from what I've heard. Not one for strings and attachments. No one special in his life." She stopped suddenly. "You don't think . . ."

"It's a straw. It's all I've got to clutch at."

53

yrnwyn . . . Dyrnwyn . . . Dyrnwyn . . ."

Feeling utterly foolish, Sarah lowered the sword.

She thought she could still hear the echoes of her voice ringing in the flat, and her arm was trembling from the effort of holding the sword high, even though it didn't weigh much.

Owen was staring at her solemnly, green eyes wide, before he suddenly smiled. "You look like an idiot."

"Thanks." She smiled. "I feel like an idiot."

"What did you expect, thunder and lightning?" He chuckled.

"Yes. No. Maybe." She giggled at how silly she must look before adding sheepishly, "It just seemed like the right thing to do."

The hunting horns were louder, sharper, clearer.

"I think we should warn the people on this list," she said abruptly. She tapped the address book with the sword, flakes of rust rattling onto the page. "Let's assume that there is some truth in what your aunt says. . . ."

"Said," Owen corrected her.

"Said," Sarah echoed. "It has to be more than coincidence that some of the names on this list have turned up dead."

"They were old people," Owen reminded her. "Old people die."

"They were in their seventies. That's not old, not anymore. Plus, they didn't die of natural causes," she said, spreading out the scrapbook, diary, and address book on the floor. "All of the articles Judith cut out pointed to unusual deaths. Unnatural." She tapped each in turn with the sword. "Judith Walker spent some time during the war with these people. They were all entrusted with these Thirteen Hallows, whatever they are. Now someone is killing each of the Hallowed Keepers to gain possession of the artifacts." She glanced up at Owen. "Agreed?"

"It certainly looks that way," he muttered. He rubbed his hand across the back of the diary, rust flakes smearing like blood on the dusty surface. "But why were they killed so brutally?"

"I don't know." She tapped the address book with the broken end of the sword. "I wonder how many of these people are still alive?"

Owen reached for the phone and lifted it off the small coffee table. He picked up the address book and opened it to the first name. "There's only one way to find out."

NINETY MINUTES and twenty-two phone calls later, Owen replaced the phone and looked into Sarah's troubled face. "Including Aunt Judith, eight are dead and four are missing. By missing, I mean I can't trace them, and no one knows where they've gone. The only lady on the list I actually got to speak to lives not too far from here."

Sarah stood up immediately. "We need to go there."

Owen looked up. "And what?"

"We'll tell her what we know."

"You're crazy!"

"If she's a Keeper of the Hallows, then we aren't telling her anything she doesn't know. If she's not, then she'll probably think we're nothing more than disturbed kids."

Owen looked at the white-faced young woman. "You believe all this, don't you."

She took a deep breath before answering. "I don't want to . . . but yes, I do. Don't you?"

"I'm not sure." He smiled at her. "Are we in danger?"

Sarah returned his smile, abruptly conscious of the sudden flutter in the pit of her stomach. She licked suddenly dry lips. "I think we're in terrible danger."

Owen's smile broadened. "You didn't have to tell me the truth."

SARAH WAS pulling on a pair of borrowed jeans when Owen burst into the bedroom. The look on his face stilled her protest. "The police have just pulled up in front of the building."

Brushing past Owen, Sarah headed for the window. "Where?" she demanded, looking down.

"The blue car; it's an unmarked cop car."

Sarah peered closely as the inhabitants emerged from the car: a butch blonde and a craggy-faced man. "Shit. It's them."

"You know them?" he asked, surprised.

"They're the two officers who interviewed me at the hospital. They turned up again outside your aunt's house. We've got to get out of here. Now."

Sarah turned back to the room and began stuffing Judith Walker's papers back into the bag. When she picked up the sword, rust flaked off it, revealing a hint of metal beneath. With no time to examine it, she shoved it into the bag.

Owen cracked open the door and stepped out onto the narrow landing. Voices echoed up from below, and he heard his friend's name mentioned and a man's voice asking for the number of the flat. "We're trapped," he hissed. "There's no way past."

Sarah pushed him out onto the landing. "Upstairs," she whispered. "Quickly."

They hurried to the end of the corridor and then crouched on the stairs leading to the third floor, praying none of the doors on the next floor would open.

Soft footsteps hurried up the stairs, and the officers stopped outside the flat. Sarah put her mouth close to Owen's ear, her lips moist against his flesh. "He's Detective Fowler, and the woman is Sergeant Heath."

They watched as the man produced a key and carefully inserted it into the lock. Then, holding the key in both hands, he turned it with infinite care, ensuring that it made no sound. The detective then eased open the door, and the couple stepped inside.

"Now!" Sarah whispered. Holding Owen's hand, she pulled him down the stairs and they crept past the door. They could hear voices from inside, the woman speaking. "The bed's been slept in, and there are two sets of dishes drying. The teapot's still warm."

"Let's go. They can't have gone far."

Sarah's eyes widened in alarm as she looked around desperately . . . and then Owen pulled the door shut and turned the key, leaving it in the lock. By the time they reached the hall door, the police officers were pounding on the door.

"What now?" Owen demanded as they rounded the corner. "We'll have every policeman in the country after us. They'll definitely think we're guilty."

"Not the royal we. Just me. I am guilty. After me, you're just an innocent victim." Sarah shook her head. "I don't know what to do.

Let me think. I just have to think for a second." She reached into the bag to adjust the sword, which was protruding over the top. A tiny spark of static electricity leapt from the metal to her fingertips.

And suddenly she felt confident.

Straightening, she pointed down the road. "First we'll buy a change of clothes for both of us. I'm sure the cops in the flat saw us from the window, so they'll know how we're dressed." She ran her fingers through her long, tangled red hair. "And I'll get a haircut. Then we'll go to Brigid Davis. We have to warn her."

"Let's just hope we're not too late," Owen muttered.

54

Someone—*something*—had awoken him.

The initial stirring was always the hardest part, the moment when the memories returned, flooding into him as if a dam had broken and a stream of fragmented histories rushed furiously into his psyche. Rising, he nudged the empty paper-wrapped wine bottle at his feet and then shuffled away from his latest refuge near Earls Court.

He tried to remember who he was. His name . . . his identity.

He was . . . Names whirled through his head, and he stopped suddenly in the middle of the busy street, trying to focus on the letters, attempting to work them into a shape and pattern, to make a word. But the words wouldn't come, and he wandered on, moving aimlessly, content to allow his instincts to control his actions, the same instincts that had propelled him into so much trouble . . . and usually out of it again. He had spent several lifetimes relying on the same instincts.

Shifting focus, he looked around him, trying to determine where he was. The buildings were strange, identical, and characterless.

And the people: They were so diverse.

He looked at the faces of the nameless people whirling by him, seeming to move so quickly. So many races, white to black and all shades in between, so many costumes and dresses. All speaking in different tongues. English, French, German, Spanish, Chinese, and Polish.

The tramp looked down at his own body, grimacing when he discovered that he was dressed in foul rags: the overlarge shoes on his feet held together with duct tape, a frayed cord around his waist holding up a pair of dirty trousers. He rubbed his hand against his face. It tangled in his coarse white whiskers.

Dear Gods, how had he ended up like this?

He wandered on, stopping to stare at himself in a dress-shop window. The well-dressed mannequins inside seemed to mock him as he slowly raised and lowered his arms, ensuring that the filthy image he was seeing was, in truth, himself. He was a vagabond, a degenerate, and the patch over his left eye gave him an evil appearance.

He was . . .

It was so close.

He had almost grasped on to his name. Almost. He also knew instinctively that the knowledge would bring pain. And his aged and tired body recoiled from pain; there had been so much suffering in his life. So many deaths. . . .

Deaths.

There had been a death.

Was it a death that had awoken him?

Images flickered at the periphery of his vision, and then with appalling swiftness the people and places around him faded, becoming insubstantial, the landscape evaporated into gray, speckled with tiny winking lights.

And he saw the demons gathering.

Shadow shapes with crimson eyes and snarling beastlike faces. They were gathering, all moving toward the same focal point, in the Otherworld. He blinked, and the images faded, leaving him back on the busy street, shaken and trembling. He never doubted that the beasts were real.

Something had called him . . . something powerful, something ancient.

Digging into his voluminous pockets he pulled out a small flask and took a healthy swig. The fiery liquor brushed past his cracked lips and raced down his throat, burning all the way to his stomach but cleansing the sourness from his mouth. He shuddered, pulled the bottle away from his lips, and screwed the cap back on. The world faded again, and now he was watching letters tumbling, falling, making shapes and sounds and words. Some of them he understood.

Ambrose.

That was his name. Ambrose. And with the name came the memories of who he was.

Of who he had been.

55

In his time, Skinner had tried both male and female lovers and always seemed to end up with a male. It had taken him a long time to admit that he was gay; it was a difficult and confusing process. So when he discovered that he was attracted to women also, he became hopelessly confused.

Then he met Robert Elliot. Elliot too was attracted to men and women, but Elliot had liked his sex spiced with pain and domination. So the small man had taken the impressionable sixteen-year-old youth and shaped him, first introducing him to the shadowy world of bondage, then teaching him to enjoy the heightened sensations that pain brought and the infinite pleasure of inflicting pain. And Skinner, in turn, had gone on to teach others, become master to their slave, just as he had been slave to Elliot, the master. But Elliot was gone now. And for the first time in his life, since he had run away from a brutal father and an uncaring mother and come to London, Skinner was free.

He stood before the burning car and watched the small man twist and writhe in agony, mouth open, leaking smoke, eyes running molten down his face, blue flames licking from his ears. He still couldn't understand why Elliot hadn't simply opened the door and jumped out. If he had, Skinner would have been ready for him. The voice on the phone had told him that there were to be no marks on the body, no visible injuries. Elliot had taught him how to do that, how and where to strike and inflict pain but leave no mark. He had brought along a nylon stocking filled with sand; a blow to the temple would render Elliot unconscious, and the fire would burn away the bruised flesh. But in the end, he hadn't needed to use the cosh. And watching Elliot burn had aroused him.

Now he lay on the stained mattress and watched the woman

moving in the bathroom, the flash of naked skin in the light arousing him again.

He couldn't remember how or where he'd picked her up. He had the vague idea that he'd gone to one of the clubs afterward, drinking to take the taste of petrol and the stench of overdone pork and burned rubber from his mouth. He didn't remember coming back to the flat—though that wasn't too unusual. Pushing up on the mattress, he laced his fingers behind the back of his head and watched the bathroom door, wondering if the woman was any good, wondering if he'd remembered to take precautions, realizing that if he'd been too drunk to remember where he'd picked her up, he'd been too drunk to remember to wear anything.

The woman stepped out of the bathroom and flicked off the light before he had a chance to see her clearly. It took his eyes a few moments to adjust to the gloom. The curtains were long rectangles of light; obviously it was late in the morning, but this morning he was his own boss, in charge of his own destiny. He had nowhere to go, no errands to run, nothing to do. Except the woman, he thought, leering.

The woman moved around to stand before the curtains, a naked silhouette against the light, turning slowly, allowing him to see her profile. She tilted her head back, and long hair cascaded down her back to the small of her spine.

Skinner grinned. He knew now why he'd chosen this woman: long hair. He had always been attracted to men and women with long hair. Sometimes, when he thought of his mother, he remembered that she'd had long hair; he couldn't remember her face anymore, but he remembered the hair.

Crouching low, the woman moved slowly, sensuously, across the floor, then dropped to her knees at the foot of the mattress and crawled toward him. Grinning, he threw back the single sheet to greet her. Pressing her ample breasts against his feet, she slithered up him. He was reaching for her when she reared up, pressing her breasts against his face, her nipples against his lips.

And his cell phone rang.

And Skinner woke up.

He was sitting up on the mattress, his naked back against the flaking wall, arms behind his head, elbows aching, pins and needles tingling in his forearms. Moving his arms was agony; he must have fallen asleep in this position. When he allowed his arms to drop into his lap, sensation flooded back, setting his muscles trembling and cramping. The pain was incredible . . . and enjoyable.

The phone continued to ring.

The insistent ringing was setting his teeth on edge, beginning to pulse in time with the headache that was gathering behind his eyes. He snatched the phone off the floor, hearing the static howl of a long-distance call. "Yes?"

"Were you enjoying the dream, Mr. Jacobs?"

Skinner stared at the phone, recognizing the voice. Elliot's employer, the man who had given him Elliot's address. "The dream?" he said dumbly.

"Yes. She is a particularly accomplished lover. You will enjoy her in the flesh, Skinner, I promise you. And her hair—like silk. She can arouse a man in a hundred ways, she can give you such pleasure. Unimagined pleasure."

There was a long pause, while Skinner tried to make sense out of what he was hearing. Was the man suggesting that he knew what Skinner had been dreaming about?

"You should know, Skinner, that there is very little I do not know about you. The late unlamented Mr. Elliot also knew this, but he chose to ignore it. There is nothing you can do, nowhere you can go, to escape me. And do you know why, Skinner? Because you must sleep, and while you sleep you dream, and no one can run from their dreams." There was another pause and then a rasping chuckle. "Now why don't you wake up—"

The phone rang.

And Skinner woke up.

He was sitting up on the mattress, his naked back against the flaking wall, arms behind his head, elbows aching, pins and needles tingling in his forearms. Suddenly nauseated, confused, his heart hammering madly, he snatched the cell phone off the floor. Static howled on the line.

"So you see, Skinner," the male voice said, continuing the conversation he had begun in the dream, "I don't want you making the same mistakes that Mr. Elliot did. You cannot hide from me. Obey me however, and I will reward you well. Now, here's what I want you to do. . . ."

56

Vyvienne opened her eyes and smiled at the Dark Man. "The poor boy is dreadfully confused. He's still looking at the phone, wondering if this is a dream also, waiting to wake up." The smile faded. "Why are you using him?"

"He is a useful tool. And he knows Elliot's methods, he knows what we require, he's done this work before . . . it does not *disturb* him. But when we're finished you can have him. He's young, strong, and has learned to enjoy pain. You could toy with him for a long time."

Vyvienne sat up on the bed and started twisting her thick hair into a simple braid. She stretched like a cat, extending her sinewy limbs. "You should know that the Astral is in turmoil," she said matter-of-factly to Ahriman. "When Miller called the sword by name, she unleashed dark shadows. I have felt peculiar . . . echoes."

"Are we in any danger here?"

"Not yet. But with so many of the Hallows collected around us, I'm sure even a tiny leakage of their power must be trickling through to the Astral. Sooner or later someone—or *something*—will come to investigate."

"They will come too late," he said confidently.

"Are you sure?" she began.

Ahriman suddenly leaned forward and cupped the woman's small throat in his large hands. "Do not doubt me now. . . ."

Vyvienne choked. "I don't—"

"We already have ten of the Hallows. We know Miller has the eleventh, and the woman Brigid Davis has the twelfth. We'll have the location of the thirteenth within the day. But," he added with unusual caution, "now that the sword has been awakened, do we want it? Can we control it? Do we really need it?"

MICHAEL SCOTT AND COLETTE FREEDMAN

Vyvienne tried to shake her head, but the hand clutching her neck squeezed tightly. "I . . . I . . . I think," she managed to whisper, "we need them all."

"Miller has tainted the sword. She has fed it unsanctified blood," he snapped. "And with Judith Walker dead, we cannot fire it clean again." He spun away in disgust and stood before the arched windows, arms folded, staring out toward the mountains.

Rubbing her bruised throat, Vyvienne pulled out a picture of Owen Walker from the manila folder on the bedside table. It had been taken at a Christmas party the previous year, and the boy's cheeks were flushed, his forehead gleaming with sweat. Vyvienne spent a moment examining the young man's strong, masculine features. She placed the picture of Sarah Miller, which Elliot had stolen from her home, next to Walker's picture. They made a good-looking couple. Miller's blue eyes contrasted with her alabaster skin, and her ordinary face was made remarkably striking by her strong cheekbones and beautiful red hair.

"What if . . ." An idea slowly formed in Vyvienne's mind. She smiled as she formulated her thoughts. "What if Miller were to slay the Keeper?"

Ahriman turned to look at her.

"Miller is now with Judith Walker's nearest blood relative," Vyvienne suggested softly, allowing Ahriman to put the pieces together as she approached him seductively, standing behind him, wrapping her arms around his torso, pressing the palms of her hands against his chest. She could feel the strong beat of his heart beneath her fingers.

"Miller is the sword wielder now. Yet she doesn't know it. She has no idea of the forces she has unleashed. But if she were to slay the Hallowed Keeper . . ."

Her master smiled, following her train of thought. "An unsanctified sword wielder slaying a Hallowed Keeper," he said softly. "That would make the sword powerful."

"Exceedingly powerful."

"Do it!"

The woman spread her arms lasciviously. "I will need energy. You must feed me your power."

Ahriman undid her long silk cloak, allowing it to drop to the ground. He then watched his beautiful young wife return to the bed and open herself up. At times like this, he experienced a tiny trickle of concern at the power the woman had over him. But it wouldn't always be that way.

Soon it would be time for the final sacrifice.

57

I've been expecting you."

The tiny woman opened the door wider and stepped back. Sarah and Owen looked at each other blankly. They had rehearsed their opening conversation with Brigid Davis, trying to devise a gambit that would get them past the door without the old woman calling the police. But the door had been opened on the first ring, the woman smiling as if she knew them.

Brigid Davis lived in one of the faceless tower blocks that had been built on the fringes of London in the sixties and early seventies. The young couple had spent the better part of an hour wandering around the enormous complex, trying to track down the old woman, but all of the spray-painted blocks had names—Victory House, Trafalgar House, Agincourt House—and Judith Walker had not recorded the name of Brigid's building in her address book. Most of the letter boxes in the sour-smelling hallways were hanging open, and Owen suspected that the few closed boxes had been glued shut.

No one seemed to know the old woman, nor did they know the address. Even if they did, they certainly were unlikely to give it to the buzz-cut youth with the bright green eyes and bruised face or the elfin red-haired young woman with the sloppy pixie haircut and intense stare.

Sarah and Owen had been on the verge of quitting when they had spoken to an aged West Indian man who had directed them to an apartment on the eighth floor of Waterloo House. "An architect with a sense of humor," Sarah muttered as they climbed the eight floors to the top of the building. "Probably never came back to look at the building he designed."

Apartment 8A was just to the left of the stairs. The young

couple rang the bell and leaned on the rusted railing, catching their breath, when the door opened and the tiny woman appeared.

"I've been expecting you," Brigid Davis repeated, closing the door behind them, then ramming home two bolts and sliding a heavy chain into place. Catching hold of the couple's arms, linking them both, she maneuvered them down the narrow hallway and into the small sitting room.

"Please sit, sit. Don't look so surprised." She smiled at their shocked expressions as she eased them into the overstuffed settee. She perched opposite them on a scarred rocking chair. When she sat back into it, her feet didn't quite touch the ground, making her look even more childlike.

In her youth, Brigid Davis must have been spectacularly beautiful, Sarah decided. Although she knew she was Judith Walker's contemporary and therefore into her seventies, her skin was mostly unlined, almost translucent in its clarity. Her sparkling blue eyes were wide-set, and her teeth were strong and white. Yellow white hair was pulled straight back off her face, knotted into a long rope that hung along her spine. She was dressed in a simple black dress. The only jewelry she wore was a large turquoise necklace and a matching turquoise ring.

"Mrs. Davis . . . ," Owen began.

"Miss," the old woman corrected gently. "You are Owen Walker, dear Judith's nephew. I was so sad to learn of her death."

"You know?" Owen was surprised.

Brigid nodded.

"I didn't realize it had been on the news."

"Maybe it has and maybe it hasn't," the old woman said in a disturbingly singsong manner before excitedly grabbing Sarah by the hands. "And you are Sarah Miller. The police seem very eager to interview you," she added with a wry smile.

"A misunderstanding . . . ," Sarah began.

The old woman raised a hand, silencing her. "You needn't make explanations to me." Folding her hands in her lap, she concentrated on them for a few moments, and when she looked up again, her wide eyes were further magnified by unshed tears. "You were coming here to warn me about the deaths of the other Keepers. I've known about those deaths for a while now."

"You have!" Owen cried. "Why didn't you tell the police?"

"I'm not sure the police would consider my sources reliable," Brigid said softly.

"What are your sources?" Sarah asked.

"Tea?"

Owen and Sarah looked at her. "I beg your pardon?"

"Tea?" she asked again. "Would you like some tea? Of course you would," she said, standing. "I'll make us some tea, I have Darjeeling and chamomile; complete opposites and yet each quite delicious in its own right. It feels more like a Darjeeling kind of day, don't you think? First tea, then talk." She skipped into the kitchen, and moments later water thundered into a kettle.

"Is she mad?" Sarah whispered.

"I think she's completely bonkers, is what I think."

"I'm not mad or bonkers," Brigid said, popping her head around the door, "though I can understand how you would think so."

Sarah opened her mouth to reply, but Owen pressed his hands to her lips, silencing her. He stood and crossed to a small table below the window where a dozen framed photographs were laid out. Most were of Brigid: in a fuchsia ball dress, a maroon graduation robe, a teal bridesmaid's dress. Others showed her surrounded by small children. One picture, older than all the rest, was at the back. It was a faded sepia photograph of a group of children.

"The Hallowed Keepers," Brigid said, returning with a laden tray. Owen stood to take it from her, and she smiled her gratitude. "Your aunt is there, second from the left, middle row. Your aunt and Bea are wearing the matching dresses and headbands, I'm sitting two down from them, next to little Billy Everett. Gabriel was behind me and he kept pulling my frock. I wore such a pretty emerald green dress that day. Almost the color of your eyes." Without pausing for breath, she added, "Why did you do that to your hair? It is not a good look for you."

Owen uncomfortably ran his fingers across his buzzed skull. It was supposed to be a disguise; however, it seemed only to make him look like a thug.

Changing the conversation, Owen pointed to the tiny blond girl who seemed so much smaller than the others. "Is this you? My aunt has the same picture in her sitting room. You haven't changed much."

"It's sweet of you to say so. That photograph was taken seventy years ago. The last time we were all together. We all got one. A copy of the photograph, that is." She lifted the photograph from Owen's hands and tilted it toward the light.

"Now there are only three of us left alive. Myself, Barbara Bennett, and Don Close. We'll be dead soon. Ashes to ashes, dust to dust," she added matter-of-factly as she poured the tea.

"Barbara and Don . . . they're Hallowed Keepers, too?" Owen asked.

"They are. Donnie's the one in the middle row with the freckles, in between Sophie and Barbara." She glanced sidelong at Owen and Sarah. "He has him, you see? He has Don . . . I think he has Barbie, but it gets cloudy sometimes." She squeezed her eyes shut and concentrated. "Maybe he has Barbie. He definitely has Don. Yes, both of them I think. He has them."

"Who has them?" Sarah asked.

"The Dark Man. And every hour he tortures Don to get him to reveal the location of his Hallow. He hasn't yet, but he will. It's only a matter of time before he tells him. They always tell him. Sugar?" The old woman smiled again, holding out the sugar dish to Owen, and this time he realized that she really was quite mad, quietly and dangerously mad.

"Are you saying that two people are being held prisoner?" Owen asked cautiously, unsure if he had heard correctly.

"Yes." Brigid Davis sat down and dropped two sugar cubes into her tea, then took a large bite of her biscuit.

"Why haven't you told the police?"

"And what am I to tell them?" Brigid asked, looking into his bright eyes. "A man and a woman are being held prisoner, I neither know where they are nor do I know who has them. I simply *know*. What do you think the police will do about that?"

"You obviously know a lot more about what's going on than we do. What can you tell us?" Owen prodded.

Brigid smiled brilliantly. "Enough to terrify you. Enough to convince you that I really am truly quietly and dangerously mad." She smiled again, her eyes locking on his face.

"Lady, if you know something that could help us, tell us," Sarah snapped. "Right now, the police are convinced that I've killed two men, butchered my entire family, and probably kidnapped Owen.

I'm locked in some sort of living nightmare and you're playing word games!"

"Milk?"

"Oh, for Christ's sake!"

"Language!" Brigid snapped. "Thou shalt not take the name of the Lord thy God in vain."

"I'm sorry," she mumbled. "I didn't mean to offend. . . ."

"You didn't offend . . . it is simply that there is a power in names, and it is foolish to call upon them unnecessarily."

She waited until they were both sipping the scalding tea before she spoke. "It is difficult to know where to begin, and we have so little time left. I could begin seventy years ago, when thirteen children were drawn from all parts of this island to the tiny village of Madoc, almost in sight of the Welsh border. I could begin four hundred years ago, when the first Elizabeth ruled England, or I could begin five hundred years before that, when history and mythology met . . . or I could begin nearly two thousand years ago, when the Hallows were first brought to the land that would one day be called England."

"Yeshu'a," Sarah breathed.

Brigid gasped and her teacup dropped, shattering on the floor. "What do you know of Yeshu'a?"

"I dreamed . . ."

"Yeshu'a was a big man, blond, blue eyes," Brigid suggested quietly.

Sarah shook her head. "No, I dreamed of a boy, dark-haired, dark-eyed . . ."

Brigid Davis smiled thinly. "Aye, that's him. So you did dream of the boy." She suddenly reached out. "Give me your hand."

Glancing sidelong at Owen, Sarah put down the cup and stretched out her hand. The old woman caught her, fingernails digging into her flesh. "Who are you?" she whispered.

"I'm Sar . . ." The grip tightened painfully on her hand, silencing her.

"Who are you, really?" The old woman's smiled turned feral. "Don't tell me who you are . . . tell me who you *were*."

The sound of a hunting horn, hounds bellowing . . .

The boy Yeshu'a turning, looking at her, dark eyes lost in shadow, thin lips twisted in a smile . . .

An old man turning, looking at her, half his face washed in the light of a setting sun, the other half in shadow . . .

A powerful warrior, mail-clad, turning, looking at her, blood on her face, a broken sword in her hand . . .

Judith Walker's face, bloody and broken.

. . . the small man with the evil eyes.

. . . the skinhead with the leering smile.

Owen's face.

Brigid's.

"SO . . . ," THE old woman murmured, releasing her hands.

Sarah blinked, the images fading. "What was that? What's happening?" She felt sick to her stomach, a dull headache throbbed behind her eyes, and there was a sour taste in her mouth. Owen reached over and squeezed her arm, and she could actually feel the warmth flowing from his touch, moving through her body, easing across her chest, and settling into her stomach.

She exhaled explosively, realizing that she had been holding her breath. When she brought the teacup to her lips again, her hands were trembling so badly that she could barely hold it.

Owen broke the long silence that followed. He looked earnestly at Brigid. "Why don't you begin with the Hallows," he said.

58

owler kicked in the thin door on his first attempt.

"He's not here," the detective muttered, quickly scanning the squalid apartment. The hallway behind them was already filling with police.

"How do you know?" Victoria asked, padding silently beside him, a long flashlight held tightly in both hands.

"What would you do if someone kicked in your door?"

"Make a run for it . . . or flush the evidence down the loo."

"And what do you hear?"

"Nothing."

Nick Jacobs—aka Skinner—lived in the top-floor apartment over an adult cinema on the fringes of Soho. Amid the clutter of scattered clothes, fast-food cartons, and crumpled beer cans, the flat-screen high-definition stereo television and matching stereo were starkly out of place. Alongside the filthy mattress that Skinner obviously slept on, an impressive sound system had been set up, the massive speakers facing inward toward the bed.

"I'll bet he liked to play them loud," Detective Fowler muttered before he turned to the four officers spread out around the room. "Take this place apart. Bag everything. And if you find anything interesting . . ." He left the sentence unfinished.

Victoria Heath wandered around the apartment. They had just come from Elliot's sumptuous apartment in Bayswater, and the contrast between the two was startling. Elliot had everything. The apartment was exquisitely decorated and was spotlessly clean, with everything meticulously in place. Yet his lover lived in a pigsty. The only thing they both had in common were matching expensive sound and television systems.

She wondered where Skinner was. Had Miller killed him? And

how had Miller, who had never been in trouble with the law before, gotten involved with this unlikely crowd? They had no evidence that Sarah Miller even knew these people, yet two days ago she had butchered her entire family and had then been involved in the deaths of at least another two people and kidnapped Owen Walker. There was a chance that the American was still alive, but for how much longer? She was stepping away from the filthy mattress when she spotted a scrawl of numbers and names written on the floorboards. Most were faded, but one address stood out. It had been scribbled in black ink, obliterating some of the other names and numbers. She tilted her head to read it. "Brigid Davis, apartment 8A, Waterloo House, Hounslow." When she ran her finger across the writing, the ink smeared beneath her fingers.

"Tony! I think we've got something."

59

Skinner eased the stolen Nissan to the curb and turned off the ignition. Draping both hands across the steering wheel, he stared at the blocks of flats, mirrored shades reflecting the gray towers.

The voice on the phone had given him precise instructions, and there had been the unspoken threat if he failed.

But he wasn't going to fail.

From under the seat he pulled out the double-barreled shotgun, the sawed-off barrels only a few inches in length. He had used it only once before, when he'd been sent out to frighten a client who owed Elliot money. Skinner had been told to fire a shot into the ground to frighten him. Unused to the shotgun and the spread of the pellets, he had fired too close to the petrified man and had blown off most of his foot. Skinner's lips twisted in a sour smile as he remembered. The client had paid up; Elliot had made the collection at the poor guy's hospital bed.

The skinhead shook his head and pushed his glasses up onto his forehead. When he thought back on his association with Elliot, he realized that he must have been insane. He did all of Elliot's dirty work, and all he got in return were small crumbs and enormous grief. Well, this was his golden ticket: He was working in the big leagues now, and although his new employer was more than just a bit terrifying, there would be a bigger payoff. Perhaps in a year, two at the most, he could really be someone, with money in his pocket, a car, an apartment, and his own minions to do *his* dirty work. He nodded sharply, the sunglasses sliding onto his nose; that's what he wanted.

In a year or two, he would be someone.

Waterloo House, eight floors up. The woman's name was Brigid

Davis. When he had secured her, he was to make a telephone call—the number was written on the back of his hand—and he would receive further instructions.

Tucking the shotgun under his long coat, he climbed out of the car and walked toward the tower. He was whistling a song from *Wicked*; he loved that show.

60

"There is so much I cannot tell you," Brigid Davis said quietly, "simply because I don't know. And because we're running out of time," she added quickly, watching the expression on Sarah's face. "Let me speak, and then you can ask your questions."

Owen squeezed Sarah's arm, stilling her protests. "Let her speak," he echoed softly.

Brigid Davis took a deep breath, then turned her head to look through the window, across the London skyline, toward the west. "Seventy-something years ago, at the start of the war, it was feared that the Germans would bomb the cities. Children were evacuated out of the major cities and sent to towns and villages in the country. Even today, I'm not sure how we were picked, or who chose our specific destinations. I ended up in a Welsh village called Madoc, just on the border. Including me, there were thirteen children shipped to the tiny village, five boys and eight girls. Everyone was around my age, give or take a few years, and we came from all different parts of the country. It was the first time away from home for most of us, and we thought it was a grand adventure."

The old woman smiled, blinking quickly. "It was a lovely time, and I can say now with complete honesty that it was one of the happiest times of my life. The village was beautiful, the people were kind, the weather that year was glorious, I had new friends . . . and we had a secret. That was the autumn we were given the Hallows."

She nodded toward the bag at Sarah's feet. "You've got Judith's sword with you. I can feel it. The Sword of . . ." She quieted and added respectfully, "Well, let's just call it the sword, shall we? There is a magic in names."

Almost unconsciously, Sarah reached into the bag and pulled out the newspaper-wrapped sword. More of the rust had fallen off, hints of metal amid the oxidization, the sword shape a little more distinct.

Brigid stretched out her hand toward the sword, then drew her fingers back as if they had been burned. "Has it fed?"

Sarah looked at her blankly.

"Has it tasted blood?" Brigid demanded.

"I used it to kill two men."

The old woman's breath escaped in a long hiss, and her face registered panic. The fingers of her left hand moved in a complicated pattern that ended with the hand closed tightly into a fist, index and little fingers extended, thumb crossed over the folded fingers.

"You were telling us about the Hallows," Owen said quickly. "In the village of Madoc, during the war . . . you were given the Hallows."

Brigid's eyes slowly lost their glassy look. "Yes. Yes, we were given the Hallows. Because we children were all strangers to the town, we tended to stick together. In normal circumstances, we would never have mixed. We were from all different classes and backgrounds, and in those days that simply did not happen. Some of us had never even been to the countryside before. We were there about three weeks when we learned about Madoc's famous haunted cave. Naturally, we all wandered out to explore it.

"And that's where we met Ambrose.

"Ambrose was a tramp, and he'd been coming to the village for as long as anyone could remember. He would sharpen knives, mend pots and pans, help out on the farms, and tell fortunes in the evening. During the summer and early autumn, he lived in the cave in the forest on the edge of the town. Over the years, he had added wooden shelves and a makeshift bed of sorts, and the local children would dare each other to creep in and lie on the bed.

"All the children loved him. I suppose we all wanted to be like him. This was a different age, remember, when tramps were looked upon as noble. Gentlemen of the Road, we called them. They had a dignity that you don't often see in modern-day vagrants."

Brigid Davis fell silent, remembering the one-eyed tramp. When she spoke again, her voice was soft, distant.

"I think we all realized the moment we set eyes on him that we had known him before. Impossible, of course. But we knew him. And he knew us. He called each of us by name, oldest to youngest. First Millie and all the way down to Judith. He knew all of our ages, he even knew where we were from. It should have been terrifying, but even now, seventy years later, I can remember that he felt so . . . safe." Brigid took a deep, shuddering breath. "In the weeks that followed, we got to know him so well that we began to dream about him. Odd, curious dreams in which he would be sitting surrounded by mirrors and talking, endlessly talking. Yet his words were strange and garbled.

"They were wild and disturbing dreams.

"It was only when we discovered that the others were also experiencing the same dream that we started to suspect that something very strange was happening.

"We took to gathering outside his cave in the late afternoons. Golden afternoons, with the sun slanting in through the trees, and the air still and heavy, rich with forest smells. It is something I have never forgotten . . . though nowadays the woods terrify me," she added with a smile. "I don't remember the last time I've been in a wood.

"Ambrose started telling us stories, rich, magical tales of legend and folklore. He was a remarkable storyteller: It was almost as if he had been there. And then he told us about the Hallows. The Thirteen Treasures of Britain. A week later he produced the artifacts themselves." Brigid fell silent.

"What happened?" Owen asked softly.

The old woman smiled. "I'm not sure. That day remains confused in my memory, though so many of the others have remained vividly clear. I do recall that the day was heavy with thunder, the air electric. It had rained the previous day, torrential rain that turned the forest tracks to muddy ruts, making them impassable, and we were confined to our various homes. That night, it clouded over early, and those were the days before television, so we were sent to bed—"

"You keep saying we," Sarah interrupted. "Who is we?"

"All of us." Brigid smiled. "Me, Millie, Georgie, Judith, Barbara, Richie, Gabe, Nina, Bea, Sophie, Donny, Billy, Tommy . . . all of us. I'm telling you what happened to me, but it was happening to the other twelve children at the same time. We were all dreaming the same dreams, thinking the same thoughts."

"What happened?" Owen asked.

"We awoke about midnight. We all felt compelled to go to Ambrose." Brigid laughed shakily. "What a sight we must have been:

thirteen naked children moving through the empty streets and back lanes, down the muddy forest tracks.

"Ambrose was waiting for us. He was wearing a long gray gown, belted around the middle with a white knotted cord, and he had a thick hood thrown over his head. He was standing before a moss-covered tree stump, which was piled high with dozens of strange objects. One by one we stepped forward, oldest to youngest . . . and he would reach around, without looking, and press one or another of the items into our hands, and whisper its name into our ears. Then we would step back and the next person would come forward. . . ."

Owen stared at the old woman, suddenly remembering an entry he'd read from Judith's diary:

We were in the middle of the forest . . . gathered in a semicircle around Ambrose . . . On the stump were loads of strange objects. Cups, plates, knives, a chessboard, a beautiful red cloak. One by one we walked up to Ambrose and he gave us each one of the beautiful objects. . . .

He realized that Brigid was staring at him. "What's wrong, my dear?" she asked.

Owen shook his head. "My aunt described the events you're talking about, but she wrote that it was a dream."

"At first it was a dream: every night for ten days, the same dream, the same sequence of events, and Ambrose would whisper the same words. On the eleventh night it came true, and by that time, of course, we were word perfect in the ritual." She gave a gentle shrug. "I think the dreams were sent by Ambrose to prepare us for what was to come."

"It wasn't a dream?" Sarah asked.

Brigid pointed to the sword in her hand, then reached into her pocket and pulled out a small curved hunting horn of old yellowed ivory, capped with wrought gold and inlaid with intricate patterns in stone.

"This is the Horn of . . . B-R-A-N," she spelled out. "I dare not say its name. And no, it wasn't a dream." Holding the horn in a white-knuckled grip, she took a deep, sobbing breath. "When it came my turn, I stepped up to the one-eyed old man and he pressed this into my hand. And when he said its name I knew—I suddenly knew—everything about this object . . . and indeed about all of the other Hallows. I knew what they were, where they came from, and, more important, their function.

"I'm not sure how the others reacted to their gifts. It was something we never spoke about. I got the impression that some of the others simply didn't believe—or didn't want to believe—what Ambrose had told them. When the war ended, we all went our separate ways, and we were all, in minor ways, successful. Professionally. Personally. Both. Those of us who believed in the Hallows, who instinctively understood their power, were a bit more successful than the others. But that had little to do with us; that was the residual power of the Hallows working through us."

"Did the group ever meet again?" Owen asked.

"A few of us kept in touch, but Ambrose was insistent that all the Hallows must never be brought together again."

"Why?" Sarah asked. She thought she could feel the sword becoming warm in her grip, and she knew instinctively that it was the proximity of the Horn of Bran.

Brigid's smile was icy. "Too dangerous. There are thirteen Hallows. Individually, they are powerful. Together, they are devastating. They must never be brought together."

"This Ambrose had brought them together," Sarah said quickly.

"Ambrose was the Guardian of the Hallows, he could control them."

Owen leaned forward, hands locked tightly together. "You said you knew the function of the Hallows. What was it?"

Brigid's smile was cold, distant. "I'm not sure I should tell you."

"Why not?" Sarah demanded.

"When Ambrose gave me the Hallow, he opened my mind to the ancient mysteries. I came from a deeply religious background, and what I learned that night shocked me to the core, making me doubt everything I had learned from childhood. I have spent my entire life in pursuit of religious knowledge, looking for answers, and despite my wonderful gift, I realized that the more I learned, the more I discovered that I did not know." Her smile twisted. "I know that in the last few years, your aunt also delved into the area of arcane lore and folklore, seeking answers in the past to the same questions which have troubled me all my life."

Owen shook his head. "You're not making sense."

"Tell us what the Hallows do," Sarah insisted.

"They are wards, protections, powerful barriers. They were put in place to contain . . ." She stopped and sighed. "I cannot. It is far too dangerous. You are unprotected. Even the knowledge renders you vulnerable."

"Tell me," Sarah insisted. Brigid shook her head, and Sarah experienced a sudden snap of irrational anger. She surged to her feet, the sword clutched before her, towering over the tiny woman, who was now rocking back and forth in the chair. "Tell me!"

"Sarah!"

She suddenly stopped, her breathing ragged, heart hammering, aware that Owen was shouting at her, pulling at her arm.

Brigid reached out and touched her hand, and Sarah felt the sudden red rage flow away, leaving her weak and trembling. Shaken, she sank back into the chair, cheeks flushed with shame at her outburst.

"You see the danger of the Hallows?" the old woman asked. "You are not a woman prone to anger . . . and yet see what it did to you. If you continue to hold on to the sword, in another few days it will control you . . . and the paradox is that you will enjoy it. That is what happened to some of the Hallowed Keepers. They began to enjoy the power . . . and the power corrupted them."

"I'm not a Hallowed Keeper," Sarah said sullenly.

"No," Brigid agreed, "but you are much more, I think."

"Besides, the sword belongs to Owen." Sarah smiled. "Judith asked me to pass it on."

"Then give it to him," Brigid suggested.

Sarah turned to the young man sitting beside her, abruptly alarmed by the idea of giving away the rusted piece of metal. She tried to raise her right hand, the hand holding the sword, but she found she couldn't lift it. A vise closed around her chest, squeezing the air from her lungs, acid burning in her stomach.

"You see?" The old woman smiled. "You see the hold it has on you?"

Sarah slumped back into the chair, bathed in sweat. "What can I do?"

"Nothing. Absolutely nothing."

61

Skinner climbed the stairs slowly, heart hammering, lungs burning. He was so out of shape, and the elevator hadn't been working. He had never liked elevators; it wasn't that he was claustrophobic, but he remembered a story he'd read as a teenager, about a man who gets into an elevator, presses down . . . and it carries him straight to hell, and all the floors he passes are highlights in his life. He'd been ten years old when he read that story, and it had awakened him night after night screaming in terror . . . and then his father would come in, reeking of sour drink, with the leather belt in his hand. . . .

As the skinhead climbed the stairs slowly, he decided that living in a place like this must be a living hell. Identical apartments, identical lives, no jobs, little money, identical grim futures.

At least he had a future.

Technically, he was unemployed. He collected his unemployment benefits every week, but Elliot had always made sure he had more than enough in his pocket. Skinner's grin faded. With Elliot gone, who was going to run the clubs, the cinema; who was going to pay him? His new employer had said that he would be well rewarded, but he hadn't mentioned money.

On the way over here, he'd had to fill up the stolen Nissan with gas. Usually Elliot would pick up the tab for that, but this time it had come out of his own pocket. He had twenty-two pounds in cash at the moment, but what was he going to do when that ran out? The next time he spoke with his new boss, he'd make a point of asking him.

Skinner rested on the eighth floor, breathing heavily, leaning against the greasy wall. His heart was tripping madly, and he had the feeling that he was going to throw up. Breathing in great gulps of air tainted with the smells of sour urine and cabbage, he tried to work out where he was going to put his hands on some cash. Elliot must have had money stashed away, but he had no idea where. He wondered if the old woman kept any cash in her flat. Old people didn't trust banks; they always kept their savings with them. And then he wondered how much his employers would pay him for this hunting horn they wanted. If they wanted it that badly, then they would pay. Handsomely.

62

Brigid Davis stood before the window and stared out across the London skyline. "Individually, the Hallows appear throughout English history in one guise or another, usually as the property of kings and queens, or those closest to them. They are linked with all the great figures of legend, and they turn up, directly or indirectly, at all of history's great tipping points. Their last known appearance was during the dark days of the war." She paused for effect. "And I believe that they've taken on a power of their own, using and shaping the Keepers to their own ends."

Owen smiled tentatively. "You make it sound as if they are alive."

"The artifacts *are* sentient," she said. "I believe they form a symbiotic relationship with the Keeper. They become rather like an addictive drug; you cannot bear to be parted from them." She smiled at Sarah. "As you've discovered."

"But I'm not the Keeper," she said desperately.

"But you've fed the sword. You are linked to it. Since you've come in here, you've not let it out of your hands."

Sarah looked at the sword in her rust-stained hands. She hadn't realized she'd still been holding it.

"Someone is collecting the Hallows," Brigid continued, turning back to the window. "Sometimes, at the very edge of sleep, I think I see him: a tall, dark man, powerfully built. And occasionally there is an image of a young woman, beautiful, deadly, her black hair blowing around her like a cape. . . . I've always had visions, and although these are fairly clear, I'm not sure if these are real visions or just a dream. I'm inclined to think that they are shadows of real people. I don't know who these people are or why they are collecting the Hallows, but they're dangerous. They are firing the energies of the collected Hallows, bringing them to magical life by bathing them in the blood and pain of the Keepers; then channeling the dark emotional energy into the individual Hallows."

"But why?" Owen asked. "Surely you have some idea?"

Brigid nodded. "Yes, I have thought of a reason . . . possibly the only reason someone would want—*need*—all of the Hallows. But it is so abominable that it's almost incomprehensible."

"Tell us," Sarah said softly.

"Why don't *you* tell us?" Brigid suggested.

"Me!"

"The sword is at the heart of the legend." The old woman's voice dropped to a whisper. "Look at it, feel it, listen to it . . . listen to it, Sarah."

Sarah attempted a smile—the old woman was mad—but the sword was suddenly a leaden weight, and she had to grip it in both hands. Her whole body shuddered, the vibration working down through her arms into her small wrists. The sword jerked in her hands, flakes of rust sliding off, revealing more of the sword-shape beneath, and she was suddenly able to see what it must have looked like when it was whole and complete.

Sarah closed her eyes . . .

63

. . . and she began to see.

Mist swirled, moisture beading on the metal, and then the crea-tures appeared, jaws gaping, talons flashing, yellow eyes blazing in the drab light. The boy Yeshu'a lifted the sword and pointed it at the creatures.

"What are they?" The boy's voice was calm.

Josea placed a hand on his nephew's shoulder, taking comfort from the young man's curious calm. "Demonkind," he said simply. "The local people call them Fomor."

Yeshu'a watched the creatures swarm on the beach, angular, mis-shapen figures moving through the early morning fog. They were taller than men, but green gray and scaled like the crocodile from the Dark Southlands, with the same long, tooth-filled jaws. Unlike the blank-eyed crocodile, these creatures had eyes that burned with cold intelligence. They had fallen upon the merchants and mariners waiting on the beach, butchering them in sight of the approaching ships, killing some instantly, playing with others until their screams became too terrible and the sailors pressed wax into their ears. Then the Demonkind had feasted, and the stink of butchered meat tainted the salt fresh air.

Now they gathered on the beach, moving restlessly to and fro, waiting for the boats to land.

Yeshu'a allowed his consciousness to soar, to travel across the waves and hover over the beach, before slowly—tentatively—settling into the mind of one of the creatures . . . only to spin away, revolted by the brief images. "Demonkind." The boy shuddered as his con-sciousness returned to his body on the boat. "Spawn of the Night Hag and the Shining Ones, the Fallen Spirits."

"They hold this land in thrall," Josea said quietly, forcing himself to keep his hand on his nephew's shoulder, willing himself to say the words calmly, quietly, even though he knew that no boy—no ordinary boy—should know about the origins of the demon breed.

But Yeshu'a was no ordinary boy.

"When the First of Men spurned the Night Hag," Josea said, "and cast her out into the Wilderness, she mated with the Fallen One, who had also been cast from the Garden. In time, she brought forth the race known as demons."

When Josea looked down at the young boy, he had a glimpse of the stern face of the man the boy would become . . . and found that it frightened him. "They ruled the world until the coming of man," Josea continued, "and then they were forced out, into the mountains and the marshes and the barren places."

"But not always," Yeshu'a said.

"No," Josea agreed. "Not always. Sometimes they remained, or bred with the humans and created other abominations, eaters of flesh, drinkers of blood. Werewolves. Vampires. Over the centuries they have been pushed out of all civilized lands, and that is why they have ended up here, at the edge of the world. This is their domain, this is the realm of Demonkind."

The boy nodded. "But this is an island; in time they will squeeze the life out of it, and perish."

Josea squeezed his nephew's arm. "There are people here, good people. Are we simply to abandon them to the Demonkind? And what happens when the Demonkind find a way to leave this island and strike out across the mainland into the lands around the Middle Sea? They are powerful enough to do so."

Yeshu'a nodded. "Of course, Uncle. What would you have me do?" he asked simply.

"Can we destroy the beasts?"

Sarah.

"We can kill those who exist in this world," Yeshu'a said simply. "But they will return again and again unless we can seal the door to their realm."

"How?" the Master Mariner demanded.

The boy turned to look at him. "Why do you care, Uncle?" he asked. "These islanders are nothing to you, neither blood kin nor bonded."

"If we do not stop these creatures now, then sooner or later, when they are stronger, much stronger, they will come south, and destroy everything I have spent my life building. And the Lord my God told me to love my neighbor as one of my own."

Sarah.

"And yet there is much that your Lord tells you that will contradict what you have just said," the boy said quickly.

Josea nodded but remained silent. He knew better than to argue points of philosophy or religion with the boy. Once, when he was younger, the boy had gone missing. He had eventually been found arguing points of philosophy and scripture with the Elders in the Temple.

Yeshua's eyes turned flat and cold. "Every creature must be destroyed. None must be allowed to remain alive. Then we must trace them to their lair and close the door between the worlds. We must seal the portal between our world and the Otherworld."

"Sarah!"

. . . and the apartment swam back into focus as Sarah opened her eyes and found she was looking into the cavernous barrels of a shotgun.

64

Sex.

This was the oldest of all the magics, the simplest and the most powerful. When male and female joined together in the ultimate union, the energies generated could be shaped, focused, and controlled.

Vyvienne was the vessel, the conduit. Ahriman would feed her his energy. Vyvienne sat astride him, moving in a gentle rhythm while his lips and tongue and fingers worked expertly at her body, arousing her coldly, deliberately, and without passion. When he saw the flush creep across her breasts, felt the hardness of her nipples beneath the palms of his hands, he knew she was close. He then closed his eyes and concentrated on the ancient formula of words that would focus his power. Sarah Miller's face appeared before him, sharp and clear, and for an instant it was not Vyvienne atop him, but Miller.

Vyvienne's fingers bit into his shoulders, the signal that it was time.

The woman opened her eyes. The photograph of Miller had been taped above the bed, and she was looking directly at it. Pressing both hands against the wall, supporting herself on rigid arms, she stared into the face and imagined it was Miller beneath her. She felt her orgasm building deep in the pit of her stomach, felt it trembling in Ahriman's legs and stomach muscles. Vyvienne focused on the images flickering behind her eyes . . .

. . . *Miller and Owen naked in a nondescript beige room, making love, she moving atop the boy, her hands caressing his torso, sliding up along his throat, across his face. The boy transformed, his face and body twisting into that of a red demon. Sarah's scream was soundless as she reared up, the Broken Sword clutched in both hands, truncated blade pointing downward . . . and the sword was falling, the broken blade biting into the red demon's throat, blood spurting upward, hissing where it touched the metal blade, splashing onto her body, coating her in red, and her orgasm flooded through her as he twisted and writhed in death. . . .*

Ahriman grunted as Vyvienne's own orgasm shuddered through her. They clutched each other, trembling together until the spasms passed. When they were quiet again, her master ran his large hands through her hair. "Well?" he whispered.

"It is done," she murmured. "The seed has been planted. Tonight, Sarah Miller will see Owen as a red demon and kill him with the sword," she said, and fell asleep, still locked around his body.

65

Skinner rested the shotgun on the bridge of Sarah's nose, the rough-cut metal harsh and rasping. "Nice to see you again, luv."

Sarah blinked at him, confused, lost. Where had the skinhead come from? She tried to turn her head to look at Owen and Brigid, but the weight of the gun on her face made movement impossible. Fragments of her dreams whirled and spun, and images of the demons' snarling faces settled into the skinhead, the two becoming one.

Skinner thumbed back the hammers on the shotgun, the noise bringing her back to the present. "I should blow your fucking head off right now!" he hissed. "You killed Karl."

"What do you want?" Owen demanded loudly.

Skinner turned, and the weight of the gun lifted from Sarah's face as he pointed the short-barreled weapon at the boy. "You shut the fuck up. I haven't come for you this time." His twisted smile turned into a leer. "You're just the icing on the cake."

"What do you want?" Brigid repeated Owen's question.

"Shut up." Skinner backed into the center of the room, holding the shotgun close to his chest, observing the trio, suddenly unsure. Getting into the apartment had been childishly easy. He had simply knocked on the door, and when the old woman had called out, "Who is it?" he had replied, "Parcel for Brigid Davis." When she had opened the door, he had put the shotgun into her face and walked into the apartment. Discovering Walker and Miller had been a pleasant bonus. The American had been shocked to see him, but Miller had been staring straight ahead, mumbling softly, filthy hands wrapped around a dirty piece of metal. Skinner had seen that blank-eyed, loose-lipped look before; he hadn't realized Miller was a junkie.

His new employer would be duly impressed with this haul. He

fished the cell phone out of his pocket and checked a scrawl of numbers on the back of his left hand before carefully dialing. It rang nine times before it was picked up, the line clicking and popping.

"Hello?" Skinner said.

There was silence at the other end of the line.

"It's me, Ski—"

"I know who it is," the voice snapped.

"I've got the old woman . . ." He paused, savoring the moment. "And a little bonus. Mil—"

"No names!" the voice growled.

"The male and female you were looking for earlier are here also."

There was a long silence. "You have done very well, Mr. Jacobs, very well. I am extraordinarily pleased." There was another pause. "Would you be able to take the three of them from the apartment without being seen? Answer truthfully. This is no time for arrogance."

Skinner turned to look at the trio sitting on the couch facing him. An old woman, an injured male, and a drugged female. "It would be possible," he said cautiously. "Possibly a bit later, under the cover of darkness. I could bring in some help."

"No help. You must do this yourself or not at all. Be realistic. Could you manage the three of them?"

"Probably not," Skinner admitted.

"Could you manage the old woman and the young man?"

"Yes," he said confidently.

"Then take care of the other. Bring the man and the old woman back to your apartment. You will receive further instructions there. The old woman has a hunting horn, the man has a broken sword. It is imperative that they bring along both objects." There was a click and the line went dead before he could ask any more questions.

Skinner pushed the phone back into his pocket. "Seems only you two are needed," he said, looking from Brigid to Owen. He pointed the shotgun at Sarah. "You're . . . superfluous."

Sarah looked at him blankly. The youth's features were still wavering, caught between their human face and the demon skull. She turned her head slightly and began to mumble incoherently as the walls of the apartment shifted, dissolved, white cliffs gleaming in the distance: She could smell the tart salt of the sea.

"What the fuck is she on!" Skinner snapped.

Owen shook his head. "Nothing."

"Tell her to shut the fuck up."

"She won't listen. She's . . . not well. Hasn't been since the death of her family."

The skinhead's thin lips curled. He nodded slowly. "I remember them," he whispered. "We took them before your aunt. I enjoyed her mother. I'd never done it with an older broad before. . . . Of course, I tried it again with your aunt," he added.

Sarah's scream tore her throat as she suddenly lunged for the skinhead's eyes. Her attack caught him off guard, and he hesitated a moment too long. And then she was on top of him, nails raking his face, tearing the skin off his cheeks, pulling at the corner of his eye. Twisting, he swung the shotgun around and hit her in the stomach with the stock, the force of the blow dropping her to her knees. Towering above her, he gripped the shotgun in both hands, prepared to bring the stock down on her shoulder.

The sound rendered him motionless.

It vibrated up through the floor, thrummed through the air, solid, insistent, and terrible. There was such pain in the sound, raw, endless despair overlain with unendurable agony. The sound went on and on, a terrible, terrifying clarion call.

Pressing both hands to his ears, he staggered away from the crouching girl and then realized that the old woman was holding a curious object to her lips. It was shaped like a ram's horn, yellowed with age, one end encircled with a golden band. For a moment he didn't know what it was, until he saw her cheeks swell and then heard the sound increase. With a tremendous effort he lifted the gun.

He had to stop that deafening noise.

The pain behind his eyes was excruciating, and Skinner felt as if his head were about to explode. Pointing the gun at the old woman, his finger curled around the triggers.

Sarah was looking at the skinhead when Brigid blew the hunting horn. She heard a distant, almost ethereal sound, high and thin and sweet. But then she saw the look of agony on the youth's face and realized that he was hearing something far different. Then she saw him change. His features turned bestial and serpentine, head elongating, mouth filling with teeth. Tiny nubs of horns formed on his skull, and his eyes turned yellow, the pupils a flat horizontal line.

She was looking at a demon.

The skinhead howled in agony. He fired the shotgun, both barrels blazing.

And in the smoking silence that followed, Sarah Miller surged upward and rammed the Broken Sword into the center of his chest.

66

Ambrose stopped in the middle of the street, the sound of a hunting horn ringing in his ears, memories whirling, echoes and images dancing before his eyes. And then he almost doubled over as the agony lanced into his chest. He squeezed his eyes shut, tears of pain trickling down his lined cheeks. Fire burned through him, moving down to his stomach in a ragged tear, as if a blade were slicing through his flesh. He pressed both hands to his stomach and for an instant imagined he could feel the warm wetness of the wound, the gaping hole where his flesh had been torn. When he opened his eyes, he could actually *see* the ghostly image of the sword protruding from his stomach, the ragged wound cut from his chest to his navel.

Dyrnwyn.

The sword was Dyrnwyn, once the Sword of Rhydderch, now the Broken Sword.

Echoes of the hunting horn.

The horn was Bran.

And he was Ambrose.

And with the name came more memories, and with the memories came more pain.

67

"Shots fired in the vicinity of Waterloo House, Hounslow. All cars in the vicinity . . ."

Victoria Heath glanced at Tony Fowler as she leaned over to raise the volume. The senior detective's face was set in a rigid mask, and he refused even to acknowledge the radio report.

"All cars in the vicinity . . ."

Sergeant Heath lifted the radio. "Mobile Four responding."

"Location, Mobile Four?"

The sergeant took a deep breath. "Directly outside Waterloo House."

"Say again, Mobile Four."

"You heard me the first time."

OWEN CRADLED the dying woman's head in his lap. Brigid Davis had taken the full force of both barrels in the chest and stomach, shredding most of the flesh, glints of bloody bone peeping through the seeping wounds. A smattering of pellets had bitten into the soft flesh of her neck and face. Owen examined the wounds and knew there was nothing that could be done for the woman. By rights she should be dead; only her will and determination kept her spirit clinging to her body. Her eyes flickered, then bubbles of frothing blood formed on her lips. "Is he dead?"

"Yes," Owen said softly. Against his will, he turned his head to see Sarah still standing motionless over Skinner's eviscerated corpse. Thick ropes of blood dripped from the Broken Sword, adding to its length and giving it the appearance of wholeness. "Yes, he's dead," he whispered. "Sarah killed him."

Brigid's ice-cold hands found his, pressing the ancient hunting horn, the yellow ivory now splashed with her blood, into them. "Into your hands I command it," she breathed.

Owen bent his head as he brought it close to the old woman's face.

"Madoc," Brigid whispered. "Madoc. That's where it started. That's where it must end. You must go to Madoc."

GASPING, SHUDDERING, Vyvienne reared upright, pulling herself off Ahriman's damp body. "What is it?" he hissed.

"The Horn of Bran has sounded." Closing her eyes, tilting her head to one side, she listened, but all she could hear now were the faintest echoes of the hunting horn.

Ahriman sat up, his broad back to the wall, and watched the woman carefully. "Can you find Skinner?" Placing both hands on her naked shoulders, he poured strength into her. "Find Skinner. Quickly."

Vyvienne's eyes rolled back in her head . . .

. . . AND SHE opened them again in the Astral.

She had walked this shifting, shadowy landscape since she was a child, not knowing then that her talent was remarkable and unusual. She had learned early on how to interpret the colors that danced in the grayness. She recognized the places from the world below that sent dark echoes into the Astral: ancient sites, old battlefields, and certain graves, which were capable of catching and holding a spirit, like an insect against flypaper.

She knew Skinner's color and shape, the abstract criteria by which she identified him in the Astral world. He was a petty soul, dark maroon saturated with anger, bitterness, and resentment. Willing herself to his spirit, she rose over the landscape and then fell toward the countless pinpricks of light that were London.

The sounds of the horn were audible now, faint trembling echoes of the magical sound that had only recently soared across the grayness. Vyvienne found herself tracking the receding sounds, tracing them to their source.

In the dream state, she dropped into the apartment. . . .

SARAH STOOD over the body of the demon. In death, the creature seemed diminished, its scales softer now, the sulfurous yellow of its eyes lighter, its savage rows of teeth retreating into its mouth. Its features melted, twisted, altered subtly, and became almost—but not quite—human. And then Sarah felt a sour bitter wind across her sweat-damp face. A heartbeat later she smelled it, tasted it on her tongue . . . and then another demon, a female demon, stepped into the room, materializing out of thin air.

And with a great howl, Sarah charged at it.

OWEN WATCHED in horror as Sarah cut at the empty air, the Broken Sword slashing a picture from the wall, the metal leaving a long groove in the embossed wallpaper.

"Talk to her," Brigid mumbled as she let go of her last breath of life, "call her by name, bring her back before the sword subsumes her."

"Sarah," Owen whispered. "Sarah . . ."

VYVIENNE JERKED awake with a shriek, her eyes wild and staring, heart hammering wildly. She scrambled off Ahriman and raced into the bathroom, where she leaned over the toilet, expecting at any moment to be sick, stomach lurching, bile flooding her mouth. When nothing happened, she straightened and turned to lean on the sink and stare into the mirror, shocked at her exhausted appearance.

She was only twenty-one; today, however, she looked twice that.

Ahriman filled the doorway. "What happened?" he asked softly, his Welsh accent, which he took great pains to hide, obvious now.

"Skinner is dead, his soul fed to the sword. The sword wielder killed him . . . and she saw me." She turned to look at him. "She *saw* me, struck out at me! How is that possible?" she asked. "I've looked at her aura; she is nothing special. And yet she wields the sword. . . ." She shook her head at the paradox.

"Skinner dead. And Brigid Davis?"

"Dead or dying. Skinner had shot her." She had briefly glimpsed the undulating gray-black envelope around the woman's head as her spirit prepared to leave her body.

"The horn?"

"In the boy's hands."

The Dark Man swore, using an oath that was five thousand years old. He took a deep breath, trying to master his rage. "So they now have the sword *and* the horn."

He was unable to hide the tremor in his voice.

68

"Oh Christ!"

Victoria Heath stopped in the doorway, pulled out her radio, and called for an ambulance, although she knew the old woman lying on the floor was beyond help.

Tony Fowler moved quickly through the flat, ensuring that it was empty before he returned to Skinner's corpse. He nudged it with his foot, though he knew that the skinhead could not possibly have survived the massive wound to his chest and stomach. "Miller's handiwork again. Though I can't say this one causes me too much grief."

"What happened here?" the sergeant asked. She was kneeling in front of the old woman, her fingers searching desperately for a pulse.

Tony glanced from Skinner to Brigid Davis. "Looks as if Miller shot the old woman, and then cut up Skinner."

"Why?"

"Who knows?" he breathed tiredly.

"Skinner could have shot the woman," she suggested.

"He could have, ballistics will let us know. But it's unlikely. I'd lay money that Skinner had never met her before today."

"Then what was he doing here?"

"How do I know?"

"How do you know it was Miller; how do we know she was even here?" she asked.

Fowler bit back a sharp retort. "How many maniacs do we have running around London cutting people open with a sword?" he asked mildly.

Victoria Heath nodded. "Then where is she now? These bodies are minutes old. And where's Walker?"

"Your guess is as good as mine."

"Do you think he's still alive?"

"If we haven't found his body, then I'm guessing he is. Though I'm not so sure that's a good thing." He turned to look out the window. The London skyline in the west was deepening toward twilight, lights appearing in some of the shaded tower blocks. Clouds boiled on the horizon, made darker and more ominous by the setting sun behind them. "She's going to kill him, sooner or later, she's going to use the sword on him," he said without turning around, and Victoria wasn't sure if he was talking to her or not. "All we can do is wait."

"Maybe we can find some connection between this woman and Judith Walker that could give us some clue. . . ."

Fowler turned to look at the sergeant and she fell silent. "Do it. If we have a serial killer on our hands, I want the pattern established yesterday."

He looked back outside, wondering where Miller would strike next.

69

Today was . . . today was Friday, the thirtieth of October.

Was it only two days ago her family had been butchered?

So much had happened in that short space of time that she could no longer distinguish the reality from the fantasy.

On a casual, almost unconscious level, she was aware that she was sitting on a tube platform with Owen holding tightly to her arm, fingers strong against her flesh. She was also keenly aware of the bag on her lap, the weight of the sword in it.

Sarah's last clear thoughts and images were from when she stood before her home on Wednesday afternoon, then pushing open the door and stepping into the darkness. After that, everything dissolved into a terrible unending dream.

"Sarah?"

She turned her head to look at the young man sitting beside her. Was he real or another dream? Was he likely to turn into a demon, was he—

"Sarah?"

He looked real, forehead shining with sweat, a strong clenched jaw, a bandage on his cheek, his full bottom lip bruised where he had bitten into it. She lifted a hand and squeezed his forearm; it felt real enough, the material of his flannel shirt rough beneath her fingers. And he smelled real: a mixture of sweat, fear, and the faintest hint of blood and gunpowder.

"Sarah?" There were tears in his eyes now, magnifying them into enormous green orbs.

"Are you real?" she asked, her voice sounding childlike, lost and distant.

"Oh, Sarah . . . does this feel real?" His fingers dug into her flesh, squeezing as hard as he could. "Does this feel real?" He pinched the soft web of flesh between her thumb and forefinger. "And does this feel real?" He leaned forward and kissed her gently on the lips.

A train thundered into the station, stale air billowing around them, disgorging passengers in a noisy frenzy. Neither Sarah nor Owen moved. When the train pulled out of the station a few moments later, there was a brief lull when the platform was empty and silent.

Finally, pulling her lips from his, she sighed. "Yes, it feels real."

There were tears on her face now, though she was unaware of them. "I thought it was a dream. I hoped it was a dream, a nightmare I was going to wake up from . . . but I'm never going to wake from this, am I?"

Owen stared at her, saying nothing.

"I was hoping I was in the hospital," she said with a shaky laugh. She frowned. "I *was* in the hospital . . . I think, or was that a dream, too?"

"You were in the hospital."

She nodded. "I kept hoping I was going to wake up and I'd find my family standing around the bed. But I won't." She reached into the bag and touched the cold metal. "And it's because of this sword." Warmth seeped into her, tingling up from where her fingers rested on the rusted metal, doubts and fears dissolving in that moment.

"What do you want to do, Sarah?"

Lying atop Owen in a nondescript beige room, the sword held high in her hands . . .

The metal beneath her questing fingers felt soft and fleshlike. "I was going to give myself up to the police, remember?" She glanced sidelong at the young man. "Should I do that now? It would end all of this madness."

Owen looked away, staring deep into the tunnel, knowing how he would answer, knowing that Sarah knew it, too. "I'm not sure it would," he said quietly. "The madness would continue . . . more elderly men and women would die for these ancient objects."

"But at least the police would know what's happening," Sarah protested. "I could tell them."

"What would you tell them?"

"Everything. About the Hallows and the dreams and—" She stopped suddenly, realizing the futility of what she was saying.

"The police think you did it," Owen reminded her. "And the

only way for you to clear your name is to solve the mystery. For us to solve the mystery. Avenge your family. Avenge my aunt."

The sword vibrated softly beneath Sarah's touch. She was about to say that she couldn't get involved. The old Sarah would have shied away. But now she was a part of it and had been from the moment she met Judith Walker. And lately she had begun to think that her involvement predated even that. She was beginning to suspect that the dreams were more than just dreams, that they were hints and clues to the Hallows' true meaning. The small face of the cold-eyed boy Yeshu'a swam into view. "I suppose I should have walked away from your aunt when she was being attacked," she said. "Maybe if I had, then my family would still be alive," she added, unable to keep the bitterness from her voice.

"But you didn't walk away," Owen said firmly. "You were there when she needed you, and then later, you were at the house, which enabled her to give you the sword, and we were at Brigid Davis's flat when the skinhead turned up."

"Coincidence," she said shakily.

"I don't believe in coincidence. That's something I did inherit from my aunt. She once wrote a sentence in a book she gave me that has stuck with me ever since. *'There is a season for all things.'* And she's right. There is no such thing as coincidence. Everything happens in its own time. There's a reason we're here together. There's a reason we were meant to meet. My aunt gave you the sword to give to me. . . ." He grinned suddenly. "Not that I've had a chance to hold it."

He could feel the weight of the Horn of Bran beneath his coat, the metal rim cold against the flesh of his belly. "Maybe I wasn't meant to have the sword. Maybe it was yours all along. Maybe I was meant to keep another Hallow."

Sarah started to shake her head, but Owen pushed on.

"I think we owe it to your family, to my aunt, and to people like Brigid who died to protect these Hallows to find out what's going on. We have to try and stop it. Maybe that way we can clear your name."

She nodded tiredly. "I know." She took a deep, shuddering breath. "What do we do?"

"We should get a good night's sleep, and then we should go to Madoc, the village where it all started. . . ." He stopped, seeing the surprised expression on her face. "What's wrong?"

Sarah raised her arm and pointed straight ahead.

Owen turned his head, expecting to see someone standing next to them. But the platform was empty. "What . . . ," he started to say, and then he saw it. Plastered to the wall on the opposite side of the tracks was an enormous orange poster, the black letters spiky and archaic, a bronze border of twisting spirals and curls. It was advertising The First International All Hallows' Eve Celtic Festival of Arts and Culture . . . in Madoc, Wales.

"Coincidence," Sarah whispered.

"Oh, sure."

The festival was the following day, on Halloween.

70

Ahriman had always known that Don Close was going to be the difficult one.

A professional soldier, sometime mercenary, and criminal who had served time for armed robbery. In prison, he was known as a hard man, respected by prisoners and guards alike. Close was not a typical senior citizen. Ahriman had suspected all along that torture would not be enough and that they needed to find the right tool to break him.

WHEN HE'D first woken up in the dungeon, naked and chained to a weeping, foul-smelling wall, Don Close had immediately planned his escape. The last time he had been in a similar situation, it had been in a cell in Biafra in that grubby war where foreign mercenaries received little pity and no mercy. He'd killed four guards without remorse, knowing that if he failed, he would face torture and a firing squad. Those killings and all the others he had committed, first for his queen and country, later as a paid mercenary, and finally as a security consultant, had all been necessary. The British Army had trained him well, and he could kill without compunction, without taking any pleasure from it.

But killing the pair who had kidnapped and tortured him would be a special pleasure. The thought had comforted him in those first few days when the man and woman had done little other than humiliate and abuse him, depriving him of food and water, leaving him to stand in his own waste. He thought he could take anything they did to him; he'd once spent a year in a Chinese prison, where he was tortured on an almost daily basis, until Her Majesty's Government had negotiated for his release.

On the morning of the fourth day, the dark-featured man had

quietly entered the dungeon and, even before Don had come fully awake, had shattered his two big toes with a hammer and then walked away without a word. Don had screamed his throat bloody.

Later, much later, when the pain had abated, Don had realized that any plans of escaping had been effectively wiped away; any movement with a broken toe would be painful and, with his feet pulped to bloody ruin, now impossible. He was also forced to face the chilling fact that he was a seventy-seven-year-old man in poor health and not the robust thirty-year-old military specialist he had been when the Chinese had worked on him.

The question was always the same: "Where is the Hallow?"

Denying that he even knew what they were talking about was pointless. The couple obviously knew that one of the ancient Hallows had been given into his sacred keeping some seventy years earlier. He hadn't begged for mercy, hadn't even spoken to the couple, though this had driven them to a frenzy and they had taken out their frustrations on his frail body with clubs and canes.

But they hadn't killed him.

And he knew instinctively that as long as they did not have the location of the Hallow, they would not kill him. Even now, with his emaciated body covered in cuts and lacerations, he held out some hope. Surely someone in the street on the outskirts of Cardiff would notice him missing and report it to the police. Deep in his heart, he knew it was a forlorn hope; old Mr. Braithwaite who lived three doors away had been dead in his kitchen for the best part of a week before his body had been found.

Late at night, when the rats grew bolder and he could hear them skittering in the straw and occasionally feel their furry bodies brush against his ankles, Don Close knew that he was standing in his grave. All he could do now was to deny his torturers the location of the Hallow for as long as possible.

The Knife of the Horseman.

He would try to take the secret of its location with him to the grave.

THEY HAD taken him prisoner with surprising ease.

He had answered a knock on the door late in the evening to find a man and woman, well dressed, carrying briefcases, standing on the doorstep. The woman had stepped forward, smiled, consulted a clipboard, and said, "Are you Don Close?"

He'd nodded before realizing his mistake, old instincts coming too late. The man had raised a gun and pointed it directly at his face. Then the couple had stepped into the hallway without another word. Neither had spoken again, and they'd ignored all of his questions. When he had threatened to shout, the man had beaten him into semiconsciousness with the butt of the pistol.

He'd awoken sometime later in the back of a car as it bumped across a bad country road. He'd managed to sit up and look out before the woman slapped him hard across the face, knocking him back down onto the seat. Lying with his face against the warm leather, he'd puzzled over the images he'd glimpsed: purple mountains, the distant lights of a village, and a road sign in a foreign language. The lettering was English, almost familiar. Eastern European, perhaps, but there had been no accents on any of the letters. Besides, he knew he should recognize the letters. They were *almost* familiar. He was convinced then that someone from his checkered past had caught up with him; many of his old enemies had long memories.

When he'd awoken sometime later, he knew that he'd been looking at a sign in Welsh. He hadn't been in Wales for . . . for a very long time. And in that instant, he'd caught a glimmer of the reason he'd been snatched. When the car had eventually stopped, a foul-smelling bag had been pulled over his head and he'd been dragged across a gravel drive, down stone steps, and into a chill room. His clothing had been torn and cut from his body, and then he'd been struck unconscious. When he'd awoken, he'd been chained to the wall by his wrists and ankles and there was a thick collar around his neck.

For three days they'd left him alone.

The real torture had begun on the fourth day.

The day after they'd broken his toes, they'd asked him about the Hallow. Maybe they had expected a quick answer; maybe they'd thought that the starvation, humiliation, and pain would have weakened him to such a state that he would blurt out the secret without a second thought. They had been wrong, but he suspected that they weren't entirely unsurprised, nor were they displeased. It gave them a reason—if reason they needed—to hurt him. They would do it slowly and take great pleasure from his suffering. During a life spent in military service, he had come to recognize and despise the type: the pain lovers.

Closing his eyes, he prayed to a God he'd long thought he'd forgotten. But Don Close did not pray for a release from the pain or even a quick death. He wanted a single moment of freedom to take his revenge on the couple.

THE DOOR creaked open, but he resisted the temptation to turn his head and look. He would not give them the satisfaction.

Don caught the hint of perfume—bitter, acrid—before the young woman with the raven hair stepped around him, a pitying smile on her full lips, though her eyes remained cold and unfeeling. "I am so sorry," she said quietly.

"For what?" he demanded. He tried to put as much authority as he could muster into his voice, but all that came out was a hoarse croak.

"For all this." She smiled.

"I notice it didn't stop you laying into me."

"I had to. Ahriman would kill me if I didn't."

Don filed the man's name away in case he ever got a chance to use it. He knew the scam. This was the honeypot. The couple were playing the good cop, bad cop routine; when he'd served in the Military Police in Berlin, it was a ploy he'd often used himself. He'd play the bad cop while his partner, Marty Arden—poor dead Marty—would play the good cop. He knew the script almost by heart. Next she'd be telling him she wanted to help.

"I'd really like to help you."

She'd tell him she was terrified of Ahriman.

"My husband . . . Ahriman has a temper. He . . . frightens me."

Of course, she had no control over him.

"You don't understand, I've no control over him. He's like an animal."

But if he gave her the location of the Hallow, she'd be able to help.

"If you tell me where the Hallow is, I can help you escape, I promise."

"I don't . . . I don't know what you're talking about," he mumbled through cracked lips.

"Oh, Donnie," the woman whispered, using his childhood nickname and sounding almost genuinely upset. "He knows you have the

Hallow. He already possesses nine. And he's about to get the horn and the sword. The only two outstanding Hallows are the Knife of the Horseman and the Halter of Clyno Eiddyn. You have one, and Barbara Bennett has the other." She smiled as he started at the name. "You remember Barbie, don't you? She was such a pretty girl . . . she always wore her blond hair tied back in two braids. You two were inseparable that summer . . . a couple of little lovebirds. And guess what: Barb is here, too . . . in the next cell, in fact."

Close was unsure if the woman was lying or not.

"I'll try to keep Ahriman from working on her, but I don't know how long I can keep him away. And he's worse with the women, much worse. He tortures them . . . in unique ways." The woman let the word settle as huge tears sparkled in her eyes.

If he hadn't known the scam, Don might almost have believed her.

"He's killed all of the others," she went on. "Sexton and Rifkin, Byrne and Clay, and all the others. He has their Hallows. He's obsessed with them. He's determined to own them all. If you give yours up, then he won't start on Barbara for a while. And I can help you escape. I can help you both escape."

"How do I know you have Barbara here?" he whispered.

The young woman with the stone gray eyes raised her head and smiled. "Listen."

A bloodcurdling scream echoed off the stones, and then a woman began sobbing, the sound piteous and heartbreaking.

And Don Close wept then, not for himself but for the woman who had been his first love.

AHRIMAN PRESSED play.

A CD reproduced perfect sound. Barbara Bennett screamed again and again, replaying screams she had uttered just before she had given them the location of the Halter of Clyno Eiddyn.

Before she had died a month earlier.

"QUICKLY," THE woman insisted, "give me something so that I can make him stop it. I have to tell him something."

Close looked at her. It was only a knife, nothing more than an ancient sickle-shaped knife, the point snapped off, the edges dulled and rounded. He hadn't looked at the Hallow in more than a decade.

The scream that echoed down the corridor died to a dull sobbing.

Was it worth dying for, worth listening to Barbara—little Barbie, with her sweet smile and bright blue eyes, exactly the color of the autumnal sky—being tortured by this evil man? He should have married the girl; maybe his life would have been different. It certainly would have been much better. Last he'd heard, she married an accountant in Halifax.

Barbara screamed again, and now Don heard a dry, rasping chuckle.

"Tell me," the woman said urgently. "Tell me. Make him stop."

Ambrose had said never to reveal the locations of the Hallows. Even now, all these years later, Don could feel the old man's moist breath on his cheek.

Individually they are powerful; together they are devastating. Once, they made this land; together they can unmake it.

Did he believe it? There was a time when he would have said no, but he had fought in some of the most dangerous corners of the world, he had watched African witch doctors, Chinese magicians, and South American shamans work their various spells. He had once fought alongside an enormous Zulu, the bravest man he had ever seen, fearless in battle, who had taken scores of minor wounds without complaint, but who had curled up and died without a mark because he had been cursed with juju.

"Don . . . ? Tell me. Quickly!"

Raising his head, he looked at the woman, watching her sparkling eyes, seeing her lick her lips in anticipation. "You say he has the others?"

The woman visibly relaxed.

"Nine of the others. And the other two he will have before the night is out."

Swear this to me, Don Close. Swear that you will never reveal the location of the Hallow to any who might demand it. Swear to protect it with your life.

Don Close had done much in his life that he was not proud of; he had lied, cheated, stolen, and killed when it was necessary. He had made many enemies, few friends, but all—friend and foe alike—respected him. And they all knew that one thing held true: Don's word was law.

"Tell me," the woman demanded as the screams started again.

He smiled. "I'll see you in Hell first."

She struck him hard across the face, snapping his head against the stone wall, the iron collar biting deeply into his skin, and then she laughed. "You'll tell me first . . . and then we'll see about Hell."

71

The enormous Hotel Thistle in Bryanston Street was suitably anonymous. Because of its central location, the hotel was used to handling hundreds of foreigners a day, mostly tourists, and the Indian woman behind the desk didn't even look up as she filled in the registration form for Mr. Walker, who spoke in an American accent and rented a standard double room for the night.

Sarah was waiting just outside the hotel's double doors as Owen picked up his plastic key card and walked toward the lifts. She quickly entered the hotel and fell into step beside him. Not looking at each other, they traveled in the crammed elevator to the sixth floor, listening to an obese midwesterner drawl to her children about how lucky they were to get to see *Oliver!* that night. Her tweens rolled their eyes as they ignored her and concentrated on the phones in their hands.

When the elevator doors opened, Sarah and Owen stepped out and walked in opposite directions. When the elevator doors closed, Sarah turned and hurried after Owen, who had stopped outside a room at the end of the corridor.

"We should have taken a boardinghouse," Sarah muttered, glancing nervously down the long hall, watching as Owen slid the electronic card into the lock.

"So when the police broadcast our descriptions on the news, the landlady can phone us in? I don't think so." Owen stepped inside and looked around the hotel room. "No, this is good. Here, at least we're invisible."

Sarah crossed to the window and pushed back curtains to look down onto Portman Street. Her stomach rumbled and she couldn't remember the last time she had eaten properly. "Can we order room service?" she asked.

Owen shook his head. "No, we'll go and get something on Oxford Street. Let's do nothing that makes us stand out."

Sarah nodded. It was good advice. She looked at herself in the mirror. Her appearance no longer shocked her, but she was still amazed that she had deteriorated so quickly. The shadows beneath her eyes seemed permanent, and her poorly chopped locks were almost comical. "God, I look a fright. I need a bath. A long, hot bath."

"I think you look beautiful." Owen smiled shyly.

Sarah sank onto the bed beside him, placing the bag with the sword on the ground between her feet. From her jeans pocket she pulled out a leaflet advertising The First International All Hallows' Eve Celtic Festival of Arts and Culture.

"I picked this up at the concierge desk."

Owen leaned against her shoulder to read it. "It doesn't tell us anything new," he said. "And I've never heard of any of these bands," he added, looking at the names of the obscure groups. "Most of them seem to have been named after Celtic islands, Aran, Skellig, Rockall, Orkney . . . and what's this writing here?" He was pointing to script that bordered the page.

"Looks like Scots Gaelic. Welsh?"

He turned the sheet of paper, trying to make out the words. "Maybe it's some sort of greeting. See . . . the festival is being held on All Hallows' Eve . . . Saturday, the thirty-first of October. Tomorrow."

"You know what Alice would have said?" Sarah asked.

Owen looked at her blankly. "Alice?"

"Alice in Wonderland. She would have said—"

"Curiouser and curiouser," Owen finished.

"Yes," Sarah said lamely. "Lots of coincidences here, you'll notice."

"Maybe they're not coincidences," he insisted.

"That's what I was afraid of. But what about free will?"

Owen nodded toward the bag on the ground. "And what about the sword and everything that it represents? What has that got to do with free will?"

"Nothing. Absolutely nothing," Sarah whispered.

72

Sarah Miller had never really had a boyfriend before; her mother had seen to that. Previous attempts at lovemaking had been confined to hasty fondling in the back of a car. It was unromantic, uncomfortable, and forgettable.

She had lost her virginity six months earlier to a fellow bank employee. It was an awkward event after a drunken evening, and afterward they had both regretted it and barely spoken.

Sarah smiled as she turned toward the man lying beside her. After he had brought in dinner from a small restaurant on Oxford Street, they had wolfed down the food and collapsed on the bed, dead to the world. She hadn't anticipated anything happening; in fact, it was the furthest thing from her mind. They had only a few hours to rest before heading to Madoc, and she had planned on using them to sleep. Yet something inside her stirred.

A need. A desire to connect. To feel safe.

Sarah had been around so much pain and death that she knew she wanted to feel the warmth of a human body, to experience a little of life and some pleasure. She surprised herself by instigating it, boldly straddling the dozing man and undoing his shirt. He'd come awake with a start, and for an instant she'd thought he was going to push her off his body. But then he'd reached for her and drawn her close.

As they'd made love, Sarah displayed a passion she had never felt before. It felt wicked, exciting, forbidden.

Eventually, they had fallen asleep in each other's arms, spooning together as if they had been a couple all their lives rather than a pair of strangers who had met only the previous evening.

A few hours later, when she'd awakened, she'd held him close, her face against his back. And in that moment, she'd felt safe.

Sarah gently extracted herself from the sleeping man and headed for the bathroom. She'd bathed before while Owen was getting dinner, but she wanted to wash again. She felt as if the grime and pain of the past few days had soaked into her pores.

Gathering her clothes, Sarah wrapped the sword in a towel and carried it with her to the bathroom. She felt more comfortable, even more confident, with it by her side.

In a little over an hour, they would set out for Madoc. Convoys of buses were leaving Marble Arch every hour, and Owen had already booked tickets on the midnight bus when he'd gone down to Oxford Street. Depending on traffic, they would get to the Welsh village by dawn . . . though once they got there, she wasn't sure what was going to happen.

She drew a bath for herself and tilted in some of the hotel bath salts. The air filled with an indefinable citrus odor. Easing her aching body into the warm water, she reached out to take the sword in her hands and lift it into the bath with her. It felt warm when she cradled it between her small breasts, and she imagined she felt it throb, beating like a heart. Closing her eyes for a moment, she breathed in the warm, scented water.

And a chill, salt-scented wind swept over her body.

73

The boy Yeshu'a watched impassively as the Demonkind gnawed on the right hand of one of the merchants it had slain. With every bite, the merchant's fat fingers wriggled, giving it an appearance of ghastly life. There were at least a hundred of the creatures on the beach. Most of them were feasting off the fallen, though some were simply standing at the water's edge, continuing to stare intently at the boat.

Waiting.

And although the boy had made a deliberate effort to blank out their thoughts, wave upon wave of their dark, violent emotions washed over him, until their thoughts became his thoughts. The Demonkind wanted the boat, but not exclusively for food. They desired transport and a crew to bring them south, to the center of the known world, to lands of teeming peoples, warm lands, rich lands, unlike these cold northern isles. The boy shuddered, imagining the creatures free in the cities of Italy or Egypt.

All that was chaining them to the island was the barrier of salt water.

"Legend has it that the Fomor came from the dark north, the Lands of Ice." Josea stood behind his nephew, watching him intently, aware that a cold energy was shimmering in the air above the boy's dark skin. The salt air tasted bitter.

"They are not of this world," the boy said firmly. "They belong to a place beyond the ken of most of humankind; the demon realms, the abode of spirits and raw elemental forces. But a doorway was opened, a portal from the Otherworld. Blood sacrifices called them, and these abominations have walked through into this world."

"They grow more dangerous and more numerous every year. I've heard reports of them attempting to build boats."

*Yeshu'a suddenly turned his head, dark eyes flashing danger-
ously. "You knew about these creatures, didn't you. That's why you
brought me here." It was a statement, not a question.*

*Josea resisted the temptation to mollify the boy's anger. "These
creatures have always been in this land. Once they inhabited the
northern portion of this isle, the barren highlands of raw stone,
where the natives knew them by a score of different names. Lately,
however, they have been moving southward, and some have even
managed to cross into the Isle at the Edge of the World, the place
known as Banba."*

Yeshu'a continued to stare at his uncle, saying nothing.

*Josea looked toward the beach, refusing to make eye contact
with the strange child. "Your mother told me that you have the gift
to cast out demons," he said, lowering his voice. "She says you have
the power to command the Demonkind."*

*"Why would I have that power?" Yeshu'a asked very softly, and
for an instant, Josea saw something else behind the eyes, something ancient and deadly, a creature of awesome power.*

"Your mother claims that you are not the son of your father."

The wind carried the howls of the creatures across the waves.

"And who does she say I am?" the boy asked.

"She says you are the son of God."

"There are many gods."

"But only one true God."

"And who do you think I am?" the boy challenged.

*"I think you are the son of Miriam and Joseph. But your mother
has told me that you have cast out demons, and I believe her." He
gestured toward the beach. "Can you cast these out?"*

*"No," the boy said simply, turning away. "For they are not within
anyone . . . they are of the land and are part of it."*

"Could you not purge them from the land?"

*Yeshu'a leaned on the wooden rails and stared toward the
shore. One by one the Demonkind straightened and looked toward him, serpents' tails hissing on the sand and stones, forked
tongues flickering. One, younger than the rest, suddenly darted
into the water, his talons raised. The boy watched impassively as
the salt water washed over its hooves, the white foam suddenly
frothing bloody, sending it screeching back onto the beach, where
it lay twitching, white bone visible through the smoking skin.*

Several of the Fomor fell upon it, ripping it apart with teeth and claws.

"The natives claim that they mate with human women, and there are tales of half-breed abominations," Josea said quietly. He was watching the boy intently, observing the way his knuckles whitened around the rail and the angry set of his shoulders. He realized abruptly that there was such anger in him, such a terrible rage, kept tightly in control but there, bubbling beneath the surface. "They are creating a new race, an ungodly race."

"I could send them back to their own realm," Yeshu'a said suddenly, "but I would need to remain here, to keep the gates closed. And I cannot stay here, for my work lies elsewhere." He dipped his head, and Josea got the impression that the boy was talking to someone. And when he raised his head, his dark eyes were sparkling. "I could create special keys to keep the door to their world, to the Otherworld, shut." He turned quickly, eyes falling on the bundle of trade objects under the leather tarpaulin: a pan and platter, a knife, a chessboard, a spear, a halter, a horn, a crimson cloak, a whetstone, a sword.

"I could banish them, lock them away behind thirteen keys, hallowed with a power older than this world. . . ."

74

A sharp pain in her leg brought Sarah awake with a yelp.

During her dream, the sword had slipped from her hand and grazed her leg. The skin burned and blistered where the sword touched the bare skin. She jerked the Broken Sword free, aware of the heat radiating from the blade, bath water steaming off of the metal.

Sarah knew instinctively Owen was in grave danger. She jumped out of the bath, jerked open the door, and darted into the room. And suddenly a red demon reared up in front of her, claws raised. Sarah caught a glimpse of leather skin, bulging, slit-pupiled eyes, and a gaping, tooth-filled maw in the instant before the creature launched itself onto her. The sword moved, twitched in her hand, and rose to impale the creature in its chest. Steam hissed, the sound shrill, screaming, before the creature dissolved and flowed into the sword, sparkling rainbow-hued oils curling across the broken metal, scouring off the last flakes of rust, leaving the sword gleaming and elegant.

Naked, she raced across the room. A second creature appeared, another red demon coalescing out of the air directly in front of her. Overlong curled saberlike talons slashed at her, the creature's arm twisting at an unnatural angle. Sarah parried the blow, and the sword shifted in her hand of its own volition, catching the talons, sparks screaming off the blade. The demon drew back its arm for another slashing blow, but Sarah stepped forward and the sword screeched its way along the length of the talons, biting deep into the demon's wrist, exiting through the other side, and continuing into the creature's throat. It winked out of existence, leaving tendrils of blue green fire dancing along the length of the Broken Sword. The sword was pulsating madly, making her grip it in both hands. But when she got to the bed, she felt a wash of relief. Owen was lying still, breathing gently, in the bed.

"Owen . . ."

He murmured incoherently.

"Owen . . . we've got to . . ."

He turned, and a sour iciness flooded her stomach. Owen was gone. In his place was a naked scaled demon. The creature raised its head and opened its eyes. Sulfurous yellow slit-pupiled orbs regarded her impassively, and then the mouth opened and she saw the dirty teeth, ragged, needle-sharp spikes. "Sarah." It stretched, arching its spine, a clawed arm coming out from beneath the covers to reach for her.

"Owen," she tried to say, but her tongue stuck to the roof of her mouth and the sound came out as a muffled grunt. The Broken Sword pulsed in Sarah's hand, and she suddenly knew. . . .

Demonkind.

Spawn of the Night Hag and the Shining One, the Fallen Spirit.

The first inhabitants of this land called them Fomor, savage flesh eaters who despoiled women and made them bring forth monsters.

Most wore the serpent form, but some were hideous beyond all reckoning, having too few—or too many—limbs.

But some—a few, a very few—were beautiful. They appeared as women and men and were sent to entice and ensnare the humankind. Yet Demonkind could only mimic the shapes of man and never fully adopt it, and even the most beautiful of the creatures was never perfect.

GRIPPING THE sword tightly in both hands, Sarah brought it back over her head. She would feed the red demon's soul to the sword.

75

Owen woke to find Sarah standing naked by the side of the bed, the Broken Sword held high in her hands. The look on her face was terrifying. Her skin was devoid of color, her face ashen and her lips bloodless purple lines, drawn back from teeth exposed in a savage snarl. Frothy spittle dribbled from the corner of her mouth.

"Sarah . . . Sarah . . . *Sarah*!" Owen threw himself backward, scrambling off the bed as the sword descended, slicing through the thin cotton sheets, digging deep into the mattress, squealing off the springs. She slashed again, ripping another slice out of the mattress as she lunged across the bed.

"*Sarah!*" Owen tumbled onto the floor, and the descending sword bit deeply into the wall above his head, showering him with plaster and grit. He attempted to crawl away, but her fingers grabbed his ear and twisted savagely, pulling his head back with an unnatural strength, arching his spine, exposing the line of his throat.

The sword appeared before his face, and Owen realized that he was going to die.

And then his flailing hands touched metal, curved and smooth. The Horn of Bran. With the last of his strength, he brought it to his lips and blew.

The sound of the horn.

76

I will hallow these objects," Yeshu'a said, picking through the trade goods piled on the ship's deck. "I will make of them keys and symbols that will bind the Demonkind, barring them entry to this world."

Josea bowed slightly, struggling to keep his face impassive. He knew now that what his sister had said was true—this was no ordinary boy.

Yeshu'a looked over the scattered trade goods on the ship's deck. Stooping, he fingered a curved hunting horn, then lifted it and blew gently into it. The sound was high and pure. "This horn will warn of the Demonkind's approach, and its tongue will scatter them, for is it not written that my father's voice is the sound of the horn, the voice of the trumpet."

Holding it to his thin lips, Yeshu'a blew hard.

And the Fomor on the beach scattered in howling agony.

77

Sarah threw herself backward with a horrified scream. Huddling in the corner, she drew up her knees and wrapped her arms tightly around her naked body. A series of flickering images were seared behind her closed eyes.

Owen's stretched throat . . .

The blade of the Broken Sword pressed against his flesh . . .

A thin line of blood trickling from the wound . . .

"Sarah?"

The young woman moaned.

"Sarah?"

She was going mad—maybe she already was mad. The sights and scenes of the last few days had driven her over the edge. It had gotten to where she couldn't distinguish between hallucinations, waking dreams, and reality. There hadn't been two demons . . . there were no such things as demons . . . and it hadn't been a demon in the bed. It had been Owen, just Owen. But her madness had made her attack Owen, hack at him with the cursed sword, made her—

"Sarah!" A stinging slap across her face rocked her head from side to side. "Sarah! Snap out of it."

Sarah opened her eyes. Owen was kneeling on the floor before her, wild-eyed, pale, and terrified. There was a horizontal scratch on his throat, beads of blood edging it, but he was alive. Alive!

She threw her arms around his shoulders and hugged him close, holding on to him for dear life. And then the tears came, great heaving sobs that racked her body. "I thought . . . I thought . . . I saw a demon . . . and then I thought I'd killed you."

Owen felt tears on his own cheeks and blinked them away. "I'm fine." He pulled back and attempted a smile. "I blew the horn, and that helped."

"I was fighting a red demon. I'd killed two."

Owen came to his feet and hauled Sarah upward. "Maybe I should be insulted."

Sarah looked at him blankly.

"You can't tell the difference between me and a demon."

She looked at him. Really looked at him, taking in his beautiful body, and she realized that despite everything that had happened in the last few days, despite the fact that she was on the verge of losing her mind . . . she was falling for him.

"We have to go," Owen warned as he quickly dressed and gathered their things. "If we hurry, we can still catch the midnight bus. We need to get you to Madoc"—he stopped, gesturing toward the sword and the horn—"so we can . . . I don't know," he finished in a rush. "All I know is that we need to go to Wales. That's where this begins."

And Sarah knew that's where it would end.

78

They never made love. It was always sex.

Raw, unemotional sex that satisfied carnal needs and stirred ancient energies. Just before she climaxed, Vyvienne pulled away, images of the Astral still buzzing in her head. She pressed her hands against her warm breasts, feeling the skin trembling with her pounding heartbeat.

Ahriman sat up in the bed and observed her, fingers steepled before his face as he watched the woman intently. He had seen her come awake from her Astral travels in this fashion on a couple of other occasions and knew that the news was always bad. But surely that couldn't be the case this time. Vyvienne had unleashed three simple dream elementals on Miller.

In her weakened state, Miller would be particularly vulnerable to the primitive intelligences that fed off the shadows of dreams and wishes that percolated into the Astral world. Vyvienne used images plucked from Miller's subconscious; they were designed to terrify the girl. She'd think she was fighting demons. She would hack the demons to pieces . . . and when she awoke from her waking dream, she would discover that she had just stabbed Owen Walker to death.

"I failed," Vyvienne said, pouring a glass of water from the jug on the bedside table. She swallowed it quickly, wishing it were something stronger. "She's strong, master. She doesn't know how strong, she doesn't even understand the nature of the power, but it's coming to her, in fragments."

"Is she of the line?"

"She is . . . but I'm not sure where. I can't follow her lineage."

Ahriman took a few deep breaths, allowing his mind to gain calm control over his body's fury. "What happened?" he asked eventually.

"They're staying in a hotel somewhere in central London. I'm not exactly sure where, the Astral is terribly confused. But the dream shapes found her. She absorbed the first two with the sword. She attacked the boy as we planned. She saw him as a demon, and she very nearly slew him, except that he blew the horn, and that shattered the spell. It also sent ripples through the Astral that spun me away."

"They lead a charmed life, that pair," Ahriman muttered.

"More than charmed."

The Dark Man looked up sharply. "You think they are protected?"

"I would not be at all surprised."

"There are no protectors left these days," he muttered. "The last one passed on over seventy years ago when he had distributed the Hallows to the present Keepers."

"Well, someone is watching over them."

He spun away angrily and crossed to a large wooden chest, tugging it open to pull out a long-bladed knife and a small revolver. "Can you pinpoint their location for me in London? We're running out of time. I'll have to do it myself." He fed five rounds into the cylinder on the revolver, then eased the hammer down on the empty chamber.

"I could," Vyvienne said, and then added with a smile, "but there's no need."

Ahriman looked up.

"I saw a leaflet for the festival on the bed. They're on their way here." She beamed. "They're coming to you."

Ahriman Saurin allowed himself a rare smile. He had always known that his cause was just and that the gods—the old gods, the true gods—were on his side.

And just to prove it, they were shepherding the two outstanding Hallows directly to him.

79

Tony Fowler and Victoria Heath stood in the middle of the devastated bedroom. The young manager hovered nervously in the doorway, watching the two police officers intently, terrified that they might suggest closing down the entire hotel. He hadn't wanted to phone the police, but too many of the guests had heard the screams coming from the room. And now the young man who'd registered for the room had vanished.

Heath and Fowler arrived ten minutes after the incident was finally reported.

Sergeant Heath consulted her notebook. "Several of the guests reported seeing a female who answers to Miller's general description in the hallway. We also have a report of the couple being seen together in the elevator. They got out on this floor and walked in different directions." Closing the notebook with a snap, she shrugged. "Hardly the actions of someone who is a prisoner. Maybe it wasn't them," she added.

"It was." Tony Fowler traced the line in the torn sheet with his pen and then looked at the long, straight gouge in the wall. Metal had struck the wall above head height and scored a deep groove to about chest height. The mark was recent; plaster dust and a long curl of wallpaper lay on the floor beneath it. A tiny tracery of delicate beads of blood was speckled with the white plaster dust.

Closing his hands around an imaginary sword hilt, he raised his arms above his head and simulated slashing downward. If he had been standing too close to the wall, the blade would have struck it . . . which meant that someone was cowering on the floor. But who: Owen or someone else? Miller had been in this room, he was convinced of that, but what had happened, and why had they ended up here in the first place?

The only blood in the room was the few droplets on the floor. There were also traces of semen . . . and the detective had a hard time trying to wrap his head around the possibilities of the petite Miller raping Walker. It seemed completely improbable, yet the mixture of fear and adrenaline did strange things to a person's body. He knew that from personal experience. Tony looked over at his partner, still a rookie compared with him. Perhaps her fresh eyes saw more keenly than his weathered ones.

"Well, Sergeant, what do you make of it?"

Victoria Heath shook her head. "I'm not sure. Assuming Miller was here, was Owen Walker with her? Or was it another man?"

"Descriptions from the witnesses suggest that it was Walker," Tony Fowler said shortly.

"She's running, so why stop here? And it looks like they had sex. Which leads me to believe that it was consensual. Stockholm syndrome, perhaps."

"Where the hostage becomes emotionally attached to their captor. Maybe," Fowler said. "But they've only known one another for a very short period of time. Can it happen so quickly?" he wondered. "Besides, she's never had a proper relationship. As far as we can determine from her background check, there have only been two casual relationships with boys since her late teens. Her mother saw to that."

He looked around the room again. What exactly had happened? Guests in the neighboring rooms had reported hearing terrible grunts and shouts; however, they too had thought it nothing more than wild sex.

Why did no one get involved anymore? When had civilians become so afraid? The world was slowly sinking into quiet apathy.

"I wonder if Walker made a run for it and there had been a struggle. But if so, then how did they get out of the hotel without being seen?"

Sergeant Heath suddenly crouched and lifted the end of a sheet to reveal a printed rectangle of paper. Not touching it, tilting her head, she read, "The First International All Hallows' Eve Celtic Festival of Arts and Culture." Glancing up, she added, "Some sort of music festival, I think. Buses departing from Marble Arch, every hour," she read. "It's being held in Madoc in Wales, starts tomorrow. Maybe it's significant."

"Page could have been there for days," he said shortly.

Still not touching the paper with her fingers, the sergeant ran the end of her pen through a perfectly circular spot of blood. The blood smeared. "What do you say it's the boy's blood?" she asked. "I'll lay money we find his fingerprints on it."

"Could be nothing. On the other hand . . ."

"It's another straw." She smiled.

"And I'll clutch at them all . . . because that's all I've got."

And then there were only three.

Three outstanding Hallows, all of which would be delivered to him within the next few hours.

And then there would be nothing to stop him.

Thirty feet from the iron-studded wooden door, Ahriman could feel the first trickles of power, like insects crawling across his skin, a magnetic energy that raised all the hair on the back of his arms and sent shivers down his spine.

Fifteen feet from the door and he was aware of the force of the power as a tangible presence in the air, swirling and shifting around him, the air itself brackish and tainted with the electric of what the uninformed called magic.

But it was only when he stepped into the tiny windowless cell that the power washed over him completely, laving his naked skin like warm oils or a lover's touch, the power bitter and tart on his tongue.

He found it awe-inspiring to think that this was only a fragment of the energy, leakage from the thirteen handmade lead-lined sealed caskets. The velvet-and-leather boxes had been arranged in a circle, equidistant from one another, around the walls of the cell. Each box sat in the middle of a perfect circle, surrounding a protective pentagram, inscribed with the symbols of the archangels and the thirteen names of God.

Ten of the velvet boxes were locked and secured with wax and lead seals incised with the ancient talisman known as the Seal of Solomon.

He deliberately avoided looking at the three empty boxes; their emptiness mocked him. He turned to look at the monitor, which revealed Vyvienne in the dungeon, where she was taunting Don

Close, Keeper of the Knife of the Horseman. She was tantalizing him with her naked body, using her flesh to drive the man wild, promising him what he would never have in return for the location of the artifact.

Three relics—Dyrnwyn, the Broken Sword; the Knife of the Horseman; and the Horn of Bran—and he would have done what magicians and sorcerers throughout the ages had all failed to do: collect the Thirteen Hallows.

The infamous twelfth-century Scots wizard Michael Scot had managed to collect three of them before his mysterious and untimely death; Francis Bacon had disposed of his, believing that it had brought him nothing but ill luck; Dr. John Dee had lost one of his wives to the Hallows; the notorious Francis Dashwood, founder of the Hellfire Club, acquired two in his long life, both through gambling; and in the late nineteenth century, Samuel Liddell Mathers, one of the founding members of the Golden Dawn, also acquired two of the Hallows, although they mysteriously disappeared when he left London to set up his group in Paris. Mathers had always suspected, incorrectly, that Aleister Crowley had stolen the Hallows.

Sitting on the cold stone floor, altering his metabolism to counter the chill that seeped up through his buttocks, Ahriman looked with pride at the ten ancient artifacts, each at least two thousand years old, though some of them were obviously older and had been ancient even before they were consecrated. He ran his long, thin fingers across the nearest box, which held the Cauldron of the Giant, a tiny three-legged copper bowl. Blue-white sparks leaped off the box, stinging and nipping at his blackened fingertips. Carefully he eased up the wax seal and pushed back the lid, allowing a little of the pent-up energy to spit from the box in a yellow green light and spiral upward toward the ceiling. It hovered just below the blackened stones, a thin thread coiling and uncoiling, then abruptly dissipating in a crackling explosion that sent hair-thin electrical discharges down onto the boxes holding the Hallows. Copper green threads buzzed around the lead boxes, outlining them in emerald before they fizzled out, unable to penetrate the combination of ancient lead and even older magical seals. The Cauldron had been the second Hallow he had collected.

It had been so simple. Once he had discovered the identity of the Keeper, he'd taken the car ferry from Holyhead to Dublin and then driven up to Belfast. In a pub on the Falls Road, he'd met the wizened and crippled Gabriel McMurray, the Keeper of the Hallow. Twenty-four hours later McMurray was dead, and even the RUC, hardened by years of the Troubles, had been horrified by the state of the corpse.

Ten Hallows.

Three to go.

The killings had become progressively easier, and he had become stronger with each death. Ahriman looked around the circle at the Hallows. He knew them all intimately and recalled in exquisite detail the deaths of their Keepers. Here was the Spear of the Dolorous Blow, the Halter of Clyno Eiddyn, the Chariot of Morgan, and the Mantle of Arthur.

Once ordinary everyday objects, they had been imbued with extraordinary power, and when he possessed all thirteen, then he too would have access to that power. He would become godlike.

How long had it taken him to reach this point? he wondered. Ten years, twenty . . . more? He was thirty-five now, and he had first learned of the Hallows when he'd been fifteen, but it took five more years before he had even begun to comprehend their extraordinary history and incredible power.

Twenty years: a lifetime spent pursuing a dream. Those years had taught him much, taken him across the world more than once, usually into the wilder, less hospitable portions of the globe, and his search had given him glimpses into the Otherworld, a place that humankind—petty, blind humankind—could never comprehend.

He replaced the small metal pot and sealed the box, then opened a second box and lifted out the small leather satchel known as the Hamper of Gwyddno. The first Hallow he had acquired. It had happened ten years ago. He had been twenty-five.

Turning the leather purse in his hands, feeling it tremble with energy, he remembered the first time he had seen it.

He had been fifteen.

hriman Saurin always loved staying with his aunt Mildred in Madoc, the tiny village that sat on the border of Wales. Although it had no cinema, few shops, and no amusements, it held a deep fascination for the city-born-and-bred boy. He loved the silence, the clean air, the gentle lyrical accents of the people, and their open friendliness. He was also fond of his wild, eccentric aunt Mildred, his mother's much older sister, and found the differences between her and his uptight mother both shocking and startling.

Ahriman's mother, Eleanor, was short and stout, quite prim, easily shocked, would not allow television on a Sunday, and controlled as much of her son's life as possible. She actively discouraged him from forming friendships with girls and supervised his friendships with boys, frowning on any lad who did not come from a respectable home. She censored his reading, did not allow him to go to the cinema, and directed his entire life toward the narrow path of a college education and the academic degree that she had never had.

His aunt was the complete opposite.

Mildred Bailey was wild, impetuous, a free spirit who had scandalized her family with almost monotonous regularity, culminating with a much publicized affair with a Member of Parliament that had almost brought down the government of the day.

Ahriman had discovered most of this later. All he knew was that the times he spent with Aunt Mildred were among the happiest of his childhood, but it was that last year, the summer that he turned fifteen, that had determined the shape of his future. . . .

Ahriman pulled open the purse strings and peered inside. A hard crust of old bread sat in the bottom of the satchel. Legend had it that if he were to break the crust in two and take out half, and then reach in again and break the remainder of the crust in half again, and again and again, he would be able to feed a multitude. It was a simple spell, common to most of the ancient cultures, though the Christians made much of it, hailing it as a miracle, ignoring the countless times it appeared in the history of many nations.

So many things had happened that year, his fifteenth year.

His father had died, quickly, peacefully, without fuss, the way he had lived his entire life. He had simply gone to sleep one night and his body had elected not to wake up. His parents weren't sleeping together—hadn't for many years—and because it was a Saturday, the one morning in the week when his father slept late, his corpse wasn't discovered until noon. Ahriman found that he could barely remember his father's face now, and his mother's was a shadowy mask; however, his auntie's face was vividly clear.

No man ever forgets the person who takes his virginity.

He had known that summer was going to be different. He was *aware* of his aunt in a way that he had never been before, abruptly conscious of the revealing clothing she wore, the skintight cashmere sweaters, the muslin and cotton blouses that were almost transparent, nipples dark against the flimsy material.

The memory of that fateful morning was still crystal clear. He had awoken early and gone to the window to stare out over the orchard, when he had seen his aunt standing naked among the trees. Wisps of early morning fog twisted and coiled around her deeply tanned flesh, dew beading on her skin, plastering her silver hair close to her skull. She was standing facing the east, arms raised above her head, a black-handled knife and short club in either hand. Around her neck she wore a leather bag on a string. He was turning away from the window, suddenly aware of his own arousal, when Mildred had turned and looked directly at him, eyes bright, her expression almost mocking. And he was abruptly conscious then that his actions in the next few minutes would determine the course of his entire life. He could turn away, return to bed, pull the blankets over his head, and forget everything he'd seen, or he could . . .

Even today, twenty years later, walking barefoot through dew-damp grass aroused him as nothing else could.

He had walked out into the orchard in his light blue paisley-patterned pajamas, the wet ends flapping against his ankles, sticking to his skin. Halfway across the orchard, he had pulled off his clothes and approached the woman naked, stepping into the circle traced on the grass with white chalk. Mildred had opened her arms and drawn him into her heavy breasts, pressing his face against her dark nipples before pulling him down onto the grass.

They had made love as the first rays of the August summer sun had appeared over the horizon, re-creating the act of the goddess giving herself to Lugh, the god of light, the union of human and god, storing up life for the coming winter months. Later, he learned that that day was known as Lughnasagh and was sacred in the Old Religions.

Later, much later that day, she told him she was a follower of the Old Ways, and later still, as the evening drew in, she spoke to him about the Hallow, the leather bag she wore around her neck.

In the months that followed, at weekends, school holidays, and midterm breaks, Ahriman Saurin returned to Madoc, and Mildred initiated the boy's body and spirit into the ways of a religion that had been ancient before the White Christ had been sacrificed on a wooden cross.

Suddenly his studies had direction and purpose, and he earned a scholarship to Oxford. For ten years, he devoted himself to the study of folklore and mythology, religion and metaphysics, and his Ph.D., based on the hidden lore in Frazer's *The Golden Bough*, established his reputation. Yet while the public face of Ahriman Saurin suggested a brilliant young academic, privately his studies were leading him along darker, wilder paths as he researched the artifacts known as the Thirteen Hallows.

And on Lughnasagh, ten years to the day he had first learned about the Hallow that hung around his aunt's neck, he had returned to the village of Madoc and coldly, brutally butchered her, using her heightened emotions to feed energy into the Hallow.

He had then found Vyvienne, a vulnerable teenager, the seventh daughter of a seventh daughter, blessed with the gift of Sight, and begun manipulating her special skills to help him set about finding and bringing together the Thirteen Hallows of Britain.

He needed the thirteen if he was to undo what the boy Yeshu'a had done almost two thousand years earlier. He needed them to open the portal to the Otherworld.

From below, a raw scream echoed faintly through the stones, dying to a rasping, defeated sob. It was silenced abruptly, and then he heard Vyvienne's light footsteps pattering across the bare floor. Moments later the door opened behind him, and Ahriman turned his head.

Vyvienne's naked flesh was spattered with blood, but the look of triumph on her face told him all he needed to know: Don Close had revealed the location.

After replacing the leather bag in its lead box, he lifted an empty casket and drew it closer, in readiness.

And now there were only two.

And they were coming.

82

*B*eyond the limited scope of human senses, there exists a multitude of worlds undreamed by mankind. Creatures and be-
ings that humankind have come to know as myth or legend inhabit
many of these realms, as do the creatures known as demons.

Perhaps they were once of the human race, though the legends
suggest that they were the offspring of the Fallen Angel, Lucifer,
and a daughter of Eve. Condemned by an unforgiving god to suffer
for the sins of their father, they were forever banished to a realm
bordering the human kingdom. They were further tormented by
being able to see in to the World of Men, though their own realm
was hidden from the humankind. And the World of Men had everything that the demon realm lacked: The water was pure and clean,
the air sweet and clear, and there was a profusion of fruits and
foods of every description. But the greatest torment for the Demonkind was the abundance of the humans, with their soft, meaty flesh
and salt blood, delicate inner organs, and that tastiest of morsels,
the myriad human emotions and higher consciousness commonly
known as the soul.

The Demonkind managed to gain access to the World of Men on
numerous occasions, though usually it was but a single creature
who stepped through from the demon landscape and occupied a
weak-minded human. Their life expectancy was always short, for
the raw emotions of the humankind were like a drug to the Demonkind, and soon the demons were forcing the humans into greater
and greater excesses in order to feed their addiction for the drug of
emotion.

The last time they managed to come in force, however, had been
almost two thousand years ago.

For an entire Dark Season, when there was little to do in the

Northern Climes but dream, the Fomor had worked upon a tribe of savage northern shamans, instilling them with dreams of power and limitless wealth and the ultimate prize for those questors driven to search for answers: knowledge, dark, exhilarating knowledge. With sacrifices of blood and fire, flesh and innocence, the shamans had created a rent between the worlds of men and demons and allowed the creatures to walk through. None of the shamans had survived their first encounter with the creatures, though their bodies lived on in a semblance of life, rotting on the bone, until the Demonkind chose a new fleshy host. Without the power of the shamans to fuel the gateway, it had collapsed, but not before it had allowed six hundred and sixty-six of the creatures into this realm, forever confirming the folklore of the number of The Beasts in human consciousness.

In less than thirty days, the beasts had ravaged the countryside, laying waste to all before them. Thousands died to assuage their terrible hunger, and those they did not kill immediately, they herded together in huge feeding pens. Some of the women they took and bred with, and the resultant abominations that crawled and slithered forth created the seeds of the legends that would become the vampire and werewolf.

When the Demonkind, which the humans had come to call Fomor, had devastated the land of Britain, they had sailed west on a captured Irish pirate ship and established a reign of terror on that island that would end only when the De Danann warriors, who were not entirely human themselves, destroyed them in two great pitched battles.

But the remainder of the Fomor never left Britain's shore . . . because they were blocked by a terrifying man-boy who controlled a power of which even he was not fully aware. Using an elemental magic that was older than the human race, he had destroyed the last of the Fomor and sealed the gate between the worlds, locking it with thirteen Hallowed words of power and thirteen Hallowed objects. Only those thirteen words of power and the Thirteen Hallows could unlock the gate.

For two millennia, the Demonkind had gathered behind the gate, waiting in great serried ranks, and plotted their escape.

Many times they had come close to breaching the defenses, and occasionally one or more of the keys had been turned in the lock, *allowing a glimpse of unseen wonders—on both sides—but the Hallows had held.*

The Demonkind knew their time was close.

And they gathered. They could feel the presence of the eleven Hallows . . . and knew that the keys would soon be turned.

And this time they would not be denied. Yeshu'a and his kind were long gone.

This time, there would be no one to stand in their way.

SATURDAY, OCTOBER 31

All Hallows' Eve

83

Owen whimpered in his sleep, jerking Sarah awake.

There was a moment of terrifying disorientation, images from her own disturbed sleep twisting and coiling around her . . . until she remembered she was sitting with her face pressed against the cold, moist window of a stale-smelling bus. Owen was sitting in the aisle seat, his head resting on her shoulder, twitching and shifting, eyeballs dancing behind his eyes.

Sarah straightened carefully, wincing as her stiffened neck and shoulder muscles protested but reluctant to move too much in case she woke Owen. The bag containing the Broken Sword was on the ground between her feet, and she could actually feel the warmth of the sword seeping through the canvas bag. Rubbing a hand down the misted-up window, she squinted out into the darkened countryside, trying to work out where they were. But the coach was moving down a featureless length of motorway, sodium lamps turning the night orange.

There were few cars on the road; a Volvo cruised slowly past the bus, and Sarah caught a glimpse of a woman dozing in the passenger seat, her face green in the light reflected from the dashboard, two overtired children in the backseat, poking each other. She found herself smiling at the scene of normalcy: ordinary people in an ordinary world, unperturbed by swords and artifacts and demons . . . just as her world was a week ago. Almost unconsciously, she reached into the bag and touched the sword, taking solace from the warm metal.

If she accepted the existence of the Hallows and the Demonkind, then she would have to accept that the entire history of the world was wrong. She shook her head, unwilling to pursue that thought . . . down that road lay madness.

"Are we there yet?" Owen looked at her through sleep-dulled eyes.

"Not yet. I'm sorry, I didn't mean to wake you."

Owen returned his head to her shoulder, and it seemed like the most natural thing in the world to place her arm around his shoulders and hold him close. "Where are we?" he mumbled, his voice buzzing against her chest.

"I'm not sure." Tilting her left arm to the light, she read the time. "It's just half past two, so we've been on the road for two and a half hours. We must be more than halfway there."

Owen mumbled a question, but before she could ask him to repeat it, she felt his shoulders slip into the gentle rhythm of sleep.

They had boarded the bus on a side street opposite Marble Arch. It was one of a line of independent tour buses parked along the street with THE FIRST INTERNATIONAL ALL HALLOWS' EVE CELTIC FESTIVAL OF ARTS AND CULTURE stickers in the front window. They had arrived at a quarter to twelve. The place was packed with grungy students, the pavement littered with sleeping bags and knapsacks, and in their dirty and disheveled clothes, the pair blended right in. At exactly ten minutes to twelve, the bus doors hissed open and Owen and Sarah took their place in the line. They found seats three-quarters of the way down on the right-hand side of the bus.

There had been a ragged cheer when the bus had pulled away from the station at one minute past midnight. In the first hour, there had been a halfhearted singsong, a dreary Gaelic whine that set Sarah's teeth on edge, and someone near the front of the bus had played a hauntingly beautiful tune on a tin whistle, but the bus quickly fell quiet as the passengers drifted off to sleep, determined to conserve their energy for the festival.

From inside her bag, Sarah pulled out Judith Walker's notes and tried to read them, looking for clues, for answers. But trying to concentrate on the spidery handwriting in the amber-and-black light made her feel slightly nauseous, and she closed the book and pushed it back into the bag.

There were so many questions and so few answers.

The old lady had been a Hallowed Keeper. Most, if not all, of the Hallowed Keepers had been killed, butchered in a ritualistic manner by someone collecting the objects. It therefore stood to reason that the same person was now after her and Owen, and they could expect to die equally horrific deaths. Or at least Owen would, since he was a Keeper; she was not.

But if she wasn't a Keeper . . . then what was she?

Was her role in this more than just an innocent bystander caught up in something over which she had no control? And what about the dreams? The bizarre dreams of the boy Yeshu'a? Sometimes it seemed as if the boy were speaking directly to her, those dark eyes boring directly into her soul.

And the demons . . . were they real or was she simply losing her mind? Was she even now lying in a hospital bed, and was this nothing more than a drug-induced stupor?

She prayed that she was, because if she wasn't, then the consequences were almost too terrible to contemplate.

yvienne allowed her consciousness to slip out of her body.

Twisting, she looked down at her sleeping body, white flesh startling and vivid against the black sheets Ahriman favored. Her hands lay crossed over her full breasts, right hand to left shoulder, left palm resting against her right shoulder. Her ankles were crossed. Even though she had traveled the Astral plane since she was a child, she still found it eerie to be looking down on herself, knowing that only the faintest of threads—gossamer and golden—connected her body to her spirit.

This was one of the few images the majority of humans carried with them from the Astral world: that of floating above one's own body. Few humans realized that their spirits roamed free in the Astral while they slept, their dreams but fragments of their adventures in the gray Otherworld.

Spinning away from her sleeping body, Vyvienne drifted higher. This, the lowest level of the Astral, was crowded with the spirits of sleeping humans, insubstantial figures moving aimlessly across the sere landscape. Most were naked, their bodies copies of their human forms, complete with imperfections. Only when they had advanced in learning would they discover that in the Astral plane, form was mutable and they could adopt any shape or image they desired. Once they had achieved this understanding, they would delight in assuming a score of forms at night, human, animal, and those in between. Later still, when that novelty had paled, they would revert to their human forms, thought usually enhancing their physical appearances slightly, allowing them to become taller, broader, and always more handsome or beautiful.

Vyvienne rose to a higher Astral level, and immediately the number of forms diminished. She drifted higher still, and the figures became even rarer, though now there were hints of other presences, nonhuman shapes in the Astral: the Ka's. Vyvienne had long since learned to ignore them, understanding that many were simply the shades of the long dead, flickers of powerful consciousness that had left echoes in the fabric of the Astral; a few, however, were truly alien presences and completely incomprehensible.

Once she had tuned out the commonplace shapes and figures, most of the lights and presences in the landscape disappeared. Vyvienne then concentrated on the Hallows' telltale signatures of power, shimmering spirals of intricate knotwork. Even though the Hallows were shielded and locked with lead and ancient magic, there was enough seepage to mark their presence, and directly below her the Astral plane blossomed with the ghostly images of eleven of the Hallows.

And across the undulating gray landscape, two more approached.

Vyvienne raced toward the source of the two Hallows, falling through the layers of the Astral until she was able to see into the physical world—the Incarnate World—below.

She could see Owen Walker and Sarah Miller in a crowded bus, traveling to Madoc. And they were carrying the Broken Sword and the Horn of Bran. The two final Hallowed objects.

As Vyvienne drew back, she realized that the air about her was full of the presences of the Ka's. She glimpsed images of men and women in the costumes of a decade of centuries, of mail-clad warriors and fur-wrapped women. They were gathered in the Astral, watching the couple intently . . . and then as one, they turned and looked at Vyvienne, and the wave of loathing that washed over her sent her spinning back into her own body.

She jerked awake and found herself wondering whom they hated: Owen and Sarah . . . or herself.

"Well?" Ahriman demanded. He was sitting in a high-backed chair set against the wall. With the first threads of dawn silver and mercury in the east, he was a shadowed, sinister shape.

"They're coming on a bus bringing people to the festival. They'll be here within the hour."

"And we'll be waiting."

85

"I had the strangest dream," Sarah mumbled, her voice sticky with sleep.

Owen slid his fingers through hers and squeezed her hand in response. He was staring into the east, watching the dawn break over the distant mountains. He couldn't remember the last time he had seen the dawn. It looked as if it were going to be a glorious day.

"I dreamt I was standing on a platform or stage of some sort. I was naked, and all around me—"

"Were men and women wearing the costumes and dress of a score of different ages."

Sarah stared at him. "You too?"

"And I dreamt that a demon tried to break through the circle of bodies, but they drove it back."

Sarah nodded quickly. She drove the heels of her hands into her eyes, rubbing furiously. "They were the previous Hallowed Keepers," she said decisively.

"How do you know?"

"I know," she said firmly. Suddenly she pointed to a road sign. "Madoc twenty miles." She smiled. "Nearly there."

They continued to hold hands in silence for the rest of the ride.

THE OLD man in the last seat didn't look too much out of place among the shabbily dressed youths. His army surplus coat, trousers, and ragged sneakers were identical to many of theirs, though his was in the decrepit state to which the bohemians could only aspire. Among the smells of unwashed flesh and beer and the sweeter stink of hash, his stale odor went unnoticed.

Ambrose had watched the gathering of the Demonkind in the

Astral above, drawn by the interlocking spirals of power that emanated from the two journeying Hallows.

He had also watched the bright point of blue-black light approach, falling from the rarefied heights of the upper Astral, wrapped around the ghostly image of a black-haired woman. He longed to use a tiny percentage of his immense power to blast the creature but knew that he had to remain shielded. But he would find her; all he had to do was follow the stench of evil, and he would destroy her.

And now he was returning to Madoc.

It would end where it had begun, not seventy years ago, not seven hundred years ago, but nearly two thousand years ago in a tiny village at the edge of the mountains. Ambrose was finally going home.

86

Madoc was a sleepy community of twenty-five hundred people, nestled on the border of England and Wales.

The ancient village was featured in the Domesday Book and had appeared in some of the Arthurian legends. The local museum contained artifacts from the distant Neolithic age, and the meager coal seams of the nearby mountains had yielded fossils from both the Jurassic and Triassic periods. When the mines started closing in the seventies and eighties, many of the young men had left Madoc, seeking work in Cardiff, Liverpool, Manchester, and London. Having sampled the city life, few ever returned to the quiet town.

In the early eighties, Madoc had followed the examples set by some of the French villages in northern Brittany, the crofts in the Scottish Highlands, and some of the smaller towns in the west of Ireland and made a deliberate effort to revitalize their Celtic heritage. A modest interpretative center re-creating Bronze Age village life had proven to be surprisingly successful. Reproductions of Celtic crafts—leatherwork, wood carving, jewelry making—had established the foundations of a series of increasingly successful cottage industries, and now Madoc Celtic silversmithing and leatherwork were exported all over the world.

And when a local schoolteacher and celebrated academic had suggested the all-embracing Celtic-themed festival to the village council, it had been unanimously accepted. It seemed only natural that it should take place on All Hallows' Eve, one of the sacred days in the old Celtic calendar: Samhain, commonly known as Halloween.

The schoolteacher had been instrumental in creating the Celtic revival that had saved the village from the fate of so many others in rural Wales, and the council listened to his suggestions. Not only did he want to create a music festival that would rival Glastonbury, he wanted to create an event. This would be more than a music festival: There would be music, arts, theatrical installations, performances, storytelling, food, and theater. Out of his own pocket, he funded an expensive interactive website that had spread word of the event across the world, and there were inevitable comparisons to Nevada's Burning Man and Vermont's Firefly. The local organizers had been surprised by the response. Within weeks of the initial announcement, the event was a sellout, and now there were estimates that up to one hundred and fifty thousand people would attend.

HAND IN hand, Sarah and Owen wandered through the tiny village of Madoc. Although it was not yet eight in the morning, the small village was crowded, most of the shops were already open, and the main street, which had been designed for horse-drawn carriages and never widened, was jammed solid with cars, minibuses, and coaches.

"I'm guessing this was not the best weekend to come here," Owen shouted to be heard over the noise.

Sarah grinned. "The locals look a bit shell-shocked," she said.

The young couple walked slowly along the crowded streets, enjoying their anonymity, the early morning sun warm on their faces. But the moist country air was already spoiled with the odors of burning food and myriad perfumes. From the far end of town, high-pitched static howled, setting the crows wheeling into the air.

"What do we do now?" Sarah asked. She had managed barely two hours of uncomfortable and troubled sleep on the coach, and she was exhausted, her eyelids gritty. She had a sour taste in her mouth, and there was a constant buzzing in her ears. More than once she had twisted around, eyes wide, thinking she'd heard the sound of a hunting horn.

"We eat," Owen said firmly, feeling his own stomach rumble. "I could do with some breakfast." He stopped outside a cake shop and stared at the bread and confectionery. A short, stout, elderly red-faced woman stood in the doorway, arms folded across her massive bosom. She smiled at the young couple, and Owen nodded in return. "Excuse me?"

"Yes, dear?" The woman's accent was light and lyrical, a little girl's voice in an old woman's body.

"We're here for the festival," Owen said, pitching his voice low, drawing the woman closer to him. It was a trick he often used with older women when he flirted with them. "We are looking for some-place to stay. Have you any recommendations?"

The red-faced woman bellowed a hearty laugh. "If you haven't booked, then it's unlikely you'll find anyplace. The hotel is full and the guesthouses are all booked out. I've heard the tent village is fully booked, too. You might find something in Dunton," she added.

"Oh. Well, thanks anyway," Owen said. "I guess we'll settle for buying some of your bread. It smells fantastic."

"It tastes even better than it smells," the woman said simply.

Owen followed her into the shop, blinking in the gloom. He breathed deeply, savoring the odors of warm bread. "Smells like my aunt's kitchen."

"Your aunt likes to bake?"

Owen nodded, abruptly unable to speak, his throat closing, tears welling in his eyes.

"It's the flour dust," the woman said kindly.

"Our aunt Judith loved to bake," Sarah said quickly. "In fact . . ." She stopped and looked around. "Would this shop have been here years ago, during the war?"

"My grandfather opened it in 1918 when he came back from the war. The first war," she added. "Why do you ask?"

"Our aunt was evacuated to this village during the war; she used to speak about a wonderful bread shop. I wonder if it was this one?"

"This is the only one in the village," the old woman said, beam-ing. "It must have been here. My mother and my aunties ran it then." She leaned her dimpled forearms across the glass-topped counter, pushing aside the DO NOT LEAN ON GLASS sign. She shook her head, smiling at the memory. "I played with the evacuees. What was your aunt's name?"

"Judith Walker," Sarah said softly.

The baker frowned, looking at Sarah's hair. "I don't remember any red-haired girls. . . ."

"My aunt had jet black hair. I get this color from my father's side of the family. He's Welsh," she added.

"Welsh. From where?"

"Cardiff. I'm Sarah. This is my . . . brother, Owen."

"Owen—a good Welsh name, of course. I can see the resemblance," the woman added. She shook her head. "Gosh, I remember those war-time days. I shouldn't say it, of course, but they were amongst the happiest in my life. And Millie Bailey, one of the evacuees, was my best friend." She turned her head and looked out the door at the crowds streaming past, trapped in her memories. "Poor Millie, she would have loved this. She's gone now. And your aunt Judith?"

"Gone too. Recently," Owen said. "That's one of the reasons we're here. Visiting the places that were important to her."

"Memories are important," the old woman said.

Owen and Sarah waited in silence.

"How long would you be staying?" the woman asked suddenly.

"A night. Two at the most," Sarah said quickly.

"Do either of you smoke?"

"No, ma'am," Owen said quickly.

"I have a room, a single room," she suggested. "It's my son Gerald's room, but he's in London, working in the theater. You're welcome to use it."

"We're most grateful," Owen said immediately. "We'll pay, of course. . . ."

"No, you won't," the woman said simply. "Now you wanted some bread."

87

We were expecting ten, maybe twenty thousand people . . . so far we've got about one hundred thousand, with maybe another fifty thousand expected," Sergeant Hamilton said quietly, his Welsh accent lending the words a musical cadence. "It's completely out of control."

He looked from Victoria Heath to Tony Fowler. "I've got officers on loan from constabularies all across Wales, but we're hoping the festival will more or less police itself. There are over fifteen hundred volunteers and they're using the Glastonbury festival as their model." The big man smiled. "I think we're going to be fine. Everyone is here for a good time."

"Not everyone, I'm afraid. I have every reason to believe that Sarah Miller, whom we want to interview in connection with half a dozen murders and the kidnapping of a young American, is here in this village."

Sergeant Hamilton nodded toward the crowd streaming past the window of the small police station. "All my officers are assigned to duty. I've no one to spare. . . ."

"I can see that," Tony said. He reached over and pulled the phone across the desk. "Let me see if I can get some more men."

Victoria Heath turned to look through the diamond-paned windows of the police station into the crowded street below. "If she's here, she could be anywhere."

"Let's wait till everyone settles down for the night," Hamilton said. "We'll check the hotel and the guesthouses, and then I can have the men sweep through the tent village down in the Mere. If she's there, we'll find her."

Tony Fowler slammed down the phone. "Let's just hope we find her before she kills again."

"That'd certainly ruin the festival," Hamilton muttered.

88

idn't Brigid say something about a cave?"

Owen was perched on the window ledge, looking down into the busy street below. Sarah sat on the bed, surrounded by Judith's notes as she leafed through her diary. "Yeah, here it is. Listen to this: 'Ambrose brought us to his cave today. It is at the end of the village, over the bridge and then left along a narrow, almost invisible path. The cave is in the middle of a thick copse, set back into a low mound, almost invisible unless you were looking for it. Ambrose had fitted its stone walls with shelves made from the branches of trees. . . .' "

"They're fairly specific instructions. We should be able to find that," Owen said slowly.

Sarah jumped off the bed and joined Owen by the window, wrapping her arms around his waist. Silently, they looked at the crowds thronging the narrow streets.

"I want to be like them," Sarah said very softly.

"Like them?"

"I want to be ordinary," she said.

"I hear you," he whispered.

He peered at the shop across the road. There was something about the name that rang a faint bell. Bailey's Haberdashery. "Hey, pass me my aunt's address book." Checking the back of the book, he ran his finger down the list of names. "Mildred Bailey," he said triumphantly. "With an address here in Madoc," he added. "That has to be the same Millie."

He thumbed through the diary and scrapbook. "It says here that Bailey died ten years ago, some accident. She was survived by her nephew." Turning to Sarah, he smiled. "Well, we've got two leads now, Ambrose's cave and Mildred Bailey's last known address."

Closing the book with a snap, he said, "We should talk to her nephew, maybe he can help us."

89

There was something moving behind them in the woods.

Sarah could feel the creature's eyes on her, actually feel the newly shorn hairs on the back of her neck rising. Seeing Owen glance over his shoulder more than once, she knew that he felt it, too. She reached into the bag and pulled out the Broken Sword, held it flat against her leg. "We're being tracked," she muttered, falling into step beside him.

"I know."

"Any idea who or what it is?"

"Too many ideas. And I hope and pray it's none of them."

Sarah resisted the temptation to turn around again. "Maybe we've missed the turn," she suggested. They had been wandering through the woods for hours and hadn't found anything resembling a cave.

Owen squinted through the trees. "I don't think so. This is the only path to the left of the bridge, and the track is nearly invisible," he reminded her. "I can make out a mound ahead. Maybe that's the mound my aunt mentions in her diary."

"We're turning in circles," Sarah said in frustration. "It's not here."

"Have faith."

A pigeon whirred through the trees, bringing two magpies into the air, wings snapping. They both jumped.

"This has to be the mound," Owen said. He left the track to cut across through the trees toward the grassy mound, which was covered with hawthorn and holly.

Sarah followed more cautiously, ducking beneath a low-lying branch, using the opportunity to glance quickly behind her. She caught a glimpse of an indistinct shape slipping through the trees.

They had walked past the cave mouth before Owen realized that the shadows were darker behind a particular curtain of leaves and twisted vines. Sarah, who was walking behind him, holding the sword openly now, was horrified when he abruptly disappeared.

"Owen!" Her voice was a hoarse, rasping whisper. A hand appeared through the matted leaves, drawing her in. Ducking her head, she pushed through the curtain of leaves and stepped into a large natural cave. With the leaves covering the opening, the light was green tinged, shifting and dappling the walls with an underwater effect.

The cave was almost exactly as Judith Walker had described. Semicircular, with rough wooden shelving set into the walls and an ornately carved box bed tucked away in one corner. The cave obviously hadn't been used in decades. A solid layer of dust, liberally speckled and scattered with animal tracks and mouse droppings, covered the floor, and thick gauzy cobwebs spread across most of the empty shelves. One shelf at the very back of the cave was piled high with cans of meat, mostly with labels of companies that had gone out of business decades ago. The flaking yellowed remains of a candle were still stuck to a grease-spattered rock alongside the bed.

"I feel as if I've been here before," Owen whispered. "Everything is so familiar."

Sarah nodded; she was thinking exactly the same thing.

Owen spun around to look at her. "You realize what this means, of course."

She stared at him blankly.

"If the cave is real, and the Hallows are real, then we have to accept that everything else that my aunt says in her diary is also real. Ambrose was real."

Leaves rustled, branches creaked, and a shape filled the doorway. "Ambrose is real."

Sarah whirled, bringing up the sword, the broken blade sparkling and crackling with green fire.

"I am Ambrose."

The wild-haired, one-eyed old man who stepped into the cave was shorter than Owen and dressed in ragged army surplus clothing and oversize sneakers. He carried a tattered knapsack. "It's a pleasure to finally make your acquaintance. Owen Walker, I presume, and you . . . you must be Sarah. Sarah Miller. *Enchanté*. Yes," he continued, noting their shock. "I know your names. That . . . and a lot more besides." He dipped his head in a ridiculous bow, then abruptly reached out with his left hand toward the sword.

He touched the artifact with his index finger. Tendrils of emerald light sparked and snapped, curling and twisting around his hand and snaking up his arm. "And you, I know your name as well. Still powerful, still strong, eh, Dyrnwyn?" he murmured. "Still hungry."

"Hungry?" Sarah asked.

"Dyrnwyn is always ravenous. The last time I stood in this place," the old man continued conversationally, moving around the cave, gnarled fingers touching the shelves, hands caressing the smooth stones, "I was presenting thirteen boys and girls with the Hallows of Britain. I thought I had finally seen the end of them."

"You presented the Hallows," Owen began, "but that was . . ."

"A long time ago? It was. But here I am, back again. Good as new. Better than ever. Older than I look, but not as old as I feel." He turned his back to them, brushing twigs and rat droppings from a smooth depression in a large boulder before sitting down. "You have two of the Hallows with you, and the other eleven are perilously close."

He looked up to see Sarah and Owen still standing openmouthed before him and laughed gently. "'Happy are thy men, happy are these thy servants, which stand continually before thee, and that hear thy wisdom,'" he intoned. "From the Book of Kings," he added. "You should make yourselves comfortable. There is so much to tell you, and so little time in which to do it."

"What do you want?" Owen demanded.

"I am asking for your faith."

Ambrose sat back into the stone chair, his head in the shadows, only his shock of white hair and single eye visible in the verdant light. "Some of this you may know, but much of what I tell you will be strange indeed. And I only ask you to consider the events of the last few days and please keep an open mind—"

Owen interrupted, "You said you were the same Ambrose who gave the Hallows to the children all those years ago. But that Ambrose was an old man. . . ."

"Am I not an old man?" He smiled quickly. "I'm older than you think. Much older."

"But . . . ," Owen began, but Sarah reached out and squeezed his arm, silencing him.

"Let's hear what he has to say," she suggested.

Ambrose nodded. "Thank you, Sarah. Now listen. You have in your possession two of the most powerful Hallowed artifacts in the known world. Imbued with an ancient magic, they were created for but a single purpose: to seal the door to the demon realm. . . ."

90

I've lost them." Vyvienne's eyes snapped open.

Ahriman, outlined against the window, turned quickly, sunlight washing his face in bronze, picking up the flecks of silver in his slightly shabby suit. "What do you mean, lost them?"

Vyvienne propped herself up on her elbows, sweat gleaming in tiny golden rivulets on her naked body. "They're here, in the village. It was hard to follow them, because the leakage of power from the other Hallows is making it difficult to distinguish traces of them in the Astral. And the Astral is filled with scores of curious presences, drawn to the power and the approaching time."

Ahriman Saurin nodded slowly. This had always been one of the great dangers in gathering the Hallows together: No one knew who or what they would attract. Crowley had briefly owned one of the Hallows, and it had attracted the creature known as Pan. The magician had spent six months in a mental asylum recovering from the experience.

Vyvienne sat up and folded her arms beneath her breasts. "The Astral is flooded with cold light, making it impossible to see, but I managed to isolate the signature of the sword and the horn. They were at the southern end of the village, close to the river. But then they disappeared. It was as if they simply winked out of existence."

"Something is shielding them," Ahriman said.

"Or someone," Vyvienne suggested.

"No one has that sort of power anymore," Ahriman said confidently. He looked at his watch. "Not for another few hours, anyway," he added with a thin smile.

eshu'a watched impassively as a female demon with the face and breasts of a woman but the skin of a serpent was hacked down by four men. They dismembered her quickly, striking off the head and driving a stake through the center of the chest to pin the body to the ground even as she continued to struggle. The Demonkind were able to absorb terrible punishment, fighting on in spite of appalling wounds.

Another demon appeared, a howling monster who stood twice the height of a normal man and was covered in short, matted gray fur. It had the head of a wolf but the eyes of a man. Scything claws struck down one of the terrified crewmen, slashing through wood and leather armor, cleaving through the rectangular Roman shields the men carried. A raven-haired Greek warrior pushed a barbed spear into the beast's chest, twisted it, then wrenched it out, ripping apart the beast's lungs with the hooked barbs. Two naked woad-striped women fell on the stricken beast, hacking at it with small stone axes, howling delightedly as the beast's thin green blood spattered over the intricate indigo tattoos on their skin.

Yeshu'a stepped forward, and the quartet of Irish warriors who stood guarding him locked shields and moved forward with him, swords and spears ready. But few of the Demonkind had survived the attack, and there was little left for the humans to do.

Thirty days earlier, Yeshu'a had called down a fire from the heavens and washed the Demonkind from the beach in a wall of ivory-colored flames that had fused the sand to white glass. Josea had led his mariners ashore, and the surviving Demonkind had been butchered.

Few of the mariners had wanted to leave the safety of the boats, but promises of reward for the free and freedom for the slaves had spurred them on . . . though their fear of remaining on the boat with the boy had been a greater incentive.

Moving inland, they first freed a handful of tin miners who had been trapped in their mines for days by the creatures. Yeshu'a had called down tongues of fire onto the beasts who occupied the village, and while they had howled in fear and pain, the humans had attacked. Those early victories lent the humans courage and showed them that the creatures could indeed be slain: that they were not invincible. In the days that followed, more and more humans had flocked to the battle, drawn by stories of the boy known as the Demonkiller.

With the boy's powers, the humans were inevitably victorious, though many fell to the beasts' slashing claws and teeth.

On the tenth day of the campaign, Yeshu'a performed his greatest feat of old magic when he resurrected Josea, who had been struck dead by a creature that was neither wolf nor bear. As the human warriors watched, the boy knelt in the bloody ruins of a village the Fomor had occupied, laid his hands on the gaping wounds in his great-uncle's chest, closed his eyes, and turned his face to heaven. Those nearest him saw his lips move, and when he spoke his words were unintelligible. Moments later, Josea opened his eyes and sat up, hands pressed flat to the white scars that bisected his chest.

In the days which followed, many begged Yeshu'a to raise their sons or brothers or loved ones back to life, but he had always refused, and once, when an enormous battle-scarred warrior had threatened him with a dagger, the boy reached out and touched the weapon, melting the iron blade and fusing it into the man's hand. The ship's cook had been forced to take the hand off at the wrist, but the wound putrefied and the warrior had fallen on his own knife ten days later to escape the agony.

Since then most people had left the boy alone, although Josea had insisted that his bodyguards, four savage Irish mercenaries, remain with him at all times. If the boy was killed, then the battle would end prematurely and ultimately the demons would win.

Josea staggered up. There was a long cut slashing across his forehead, arcing down over his left eye. He surveyed the bloody landscape. "Was all of this necessary?" he asked bitterly, spitting the taste of blood and burned meat from his mouth.

Yeshu'a looked around. There were bodies everywhere, human and Fomor . . . and many were children.

This was the last great encampment of the beasts, tucked away in a valley at the edge of the marsh in the shadow of a ragged mountain range. The original human village had been fortified with stakes and a head-high wall. Here the Demonkind had made their last stand, protecting a tiny tear in the fabric between the worlds, which allowed a single demon to slip through, one at a time. The Fomor had brought their prisoners to this place with them—twenty-five hundred men, women, and children, though there were more women and children than men.

The Demonkind knew the inherent power of virginal flesh and souls.

Yet they never had the chance to make the sacrifice. Standing atop a nearby hill, Yeshu'a had rained liquid fire and ragged brimstone down onto the village.

The screams of the children still echoed in the foul air.

"It was necessary," Yeshu'a said softly. "This is the portal where the Demonkind enters our world. On this, the night of the shortest day, when the walls between this and the Otherworld grow thin, the Fomor intended to wrap the humans in wicker baskets and sacrifice them in the old way. The incredible eruption of energy would have ripped apart the opening between the worlds and allowed the Demonkind through in force. Even I would not have been able to contain them."

"There is something you should see," Josea said.

Josea led Yeshu'a and his bodyguards through the smoldering remains of the village, stepping across charred lumps of meat that had once been human. One of the bodyguards noticed that one of the terribly burned figures still moved, pink mouth opening and closing in a blackened crust of a face. He drove his spear through it, not caring if it was human or Demonkind; nothing deserved to suffer like that.

There was a well in the center of the village, a round opening in the ground, the edges of which had been raised with rough-hewn mud-and-straw bricks. Some of the bloodiest fighting had taken place around here, and the ground was slick with the beasts' blood. Josea walked to the edge of the well and pointed down. Leaning over the edge of the opening, the boy peered down, then quickly drew back his head, eyes watering with the stench. "What happened here?" he asked, coughing.

Josea shook his head. "As far as we can tell, the well was stuffed with the bodies of children wrapped tightly in straw. God knows how many were in the well. Maybe the beasts fired the well . . . or maybe some of the fire from heaven brought it alight," he added softly.

Taking a deep breath, Yeshu'a leaned over the well again and peered down. A greasy layer of fat bubbled atop the water, and charred remains of straw were stuck to the sides of the well, along with dangling strips of what looked like burned leather, but which Yeshu'a knew was human flesh.

"This is the place," he whispered. "There is an opening here, a tiny crack, but enough." He staggered back from the well, rubbing the heels of his hands over his eyes. "The well would have been filled with the virginal children, the rest would have been piled up alongside, and then the whole lot set aflame tonight. The pyre would have burnt in this world and the next, tearing apart the fabric of the worlds and allowing the creatures through. . . ." The boy's voice faded away. "We got here just in time."

"Can we seal the opening?" Josea asked.

"Perhaps," Yeshu'a said slowly. He padded to the edge of the well and looked down again.

And a clawed hand shot up, wrapping itself around his throat.

While two of the bodyguards jabbed at the oily water, the other two attacked the arm, hacking it off at the elbow, leaving the fingers wrapped around the boy's neck. Yeshu'a staggered back and flung the limb from him; its fingers scrabbled and twitched on the ground until one of the guards stamped on it, breaking the bones.

"I can sense their frustration," Yeshu'a said grimly, gingerly fingering his throat. "They are close . . . so close, an army the like of which you have never seen. It would wipe mankind off this world forever."

Two Fomor erupted from the water, lank hair matted to their grotesque bodies. The bodyguards cut them down before they climbed out of the well.

"I cannot mend the hole," Yeshu'a said softly, "but I will seal it."

He turned to look solemnly at his uncle. "But someone trustworthy must remain behind to ensure that the seals are never broken."

92

"The well was covered over and the earth blessed with the old magic," Ambrose continued quietly.

The late morning had moved on into early afternoon while he spoke, and the light streaming in through the leafy canopy covering the mouth of the cave painted the interior in emerald. "Then Yeshu'a used thirteen everyday objects his uncle had brought aboard his ship to trade for tin: a knife, a pan and a platter, a whetstone, a red-feathered crimson cloak, a cauldron, a chessboard, a spear, a mantle, a hamper, a chariot, a halter . . . and a horn and a sword," he added with a smile.

Owen lifted the hunting horn, and Sarah felt the sword twitch in her hands.

"Yeshu'a imbued a little of the binding spell into the earth around the well, and the remainder into the objects, which he blessed and hallowed. These were the keys; and only these thirteen keys could open the thirteen seals he placed over the well.

"Then he chose thirteen men and women at random and gave each of them a Hallow and sent them on their way. So long as they kept the Hallow and believed in it, it would bring them great fortune; and it had to be passed from father to son, mother to daughter, in an unbroken line.

"And he made his uncle Josea the Guardian of the Hallows, charging him to watch over the Keepers, but"—Ambrose laughed softly—"dooming him to remain alive forever to ensure the Demonkind never again gained access to this world."

Sarah and Owen looked at the tramp, the unasked question lingering heavily in the air.

He gave them a sad smile before continuing, "In the beginning, of course, Josea was skeptical, but later, much later, when Yeshu'a had been killed by the Romans, the merchant returned to the land of the Britons and accepted the role of the Guardian. He wrote down the first of the Hallow lore. How much of it is true, of course, no one knows. But much of it makes sense. Through the centuries, the Hallows have been at the heart of British folklore. The sword . . ."

"Excalibur," Sarah said quickly, lifting the Broken Sword.

"That is not Excalibur." Ambrose shook his head. "Excalibur came later, much later. Arthur could have been extraordinary, but when he lost his innocence and faith, the Sword in the Stone shattered. He replaced it with the gift from the Lady of the Lake, and she and her kind had no love for the Once King. She gave him the Caliburn blade, and it was cursed by Wayland the Smith from the moment of its first forging. It had been bathed in the blood of babes. It brought only doom and destruction to those who wielded it."

"I thought Excalibur was the Sword in the Stone," Owen said.

Ambrose shook his head. "Two entirely different weapons—one of light, the other of darkness." Stretching out his hand, he pointed at the Broken Sword in Sarah's hands. "Though it has had many names, once upon a time, this was the Sword in the Stone." The sword shimmered briefly, like oil running down the length of the blade.

Ambrose sat back into the stone chair, and when it became obvious that he wasn't going to say any more, Sarah finally spoke. "This is . . . unbelievable."

"Rather an understatement, don't you think?" The old man smiled. "But, then again, how much proof do you need? You are holding the proof in your hands. You have slain those touched by demons, you have seen their true selves."

"And now . . . what's happening now?"

"Eleven of the Hallows have been gathered together here in this village. Bathed in the flesh and blood of the Hallowed Keepers, their ancient power has been heightened." He closed his single eye and threw back his head, breathing deeply. "I can smell the power even now."

"But why are they here?" Owen asked.

"The man who sought them out wishes to use them to reopen the portal between the worlds and allow the Demonkind through. He will do it tonight, on All Hallows' Eve, one of the four times in the year when the fabric between the worlds grows thin. I believe that the Dark Man plans to sacrifice the people gathered for the festival to achieve his ends. Then, when the Demonkind enter this world, the Demonkind will feed on all mankind. They will destroy the world as we know it."

Owen, who had been holding the Horn of Bran in his lap while Ambrose spoke, looked up sharply. "You're him, aren't you?"

"Who?"

"Yeshu'a. You're Yeshu'a!"

Ambrose laughed gently. "No, dear boy, I'm not Yeshu'a."

"I've never heard of Yeshu'a," Sarah said quietly.

"Yes, you have," Ambrose said, "though you would know him better by the Greek form of his Hebrew name: Jesus."

"Jesus! You're saying Jesus came to Britain . . . ," Owen whispered.

"Legend has it that Jesus visited the country while still a child, brought here by his uncle." Sarah stopped suddenly, an ancient Sunday school hymn forming on her lips. " 'And did those feet in ancient time, walk upon England's mountains green, and was the holy Lamb of God, on England's pleasant pastures seen!' "

The old man nodded. "William Blake's poem."

"But if you're not Yeshu'a, then means that you were . . . ," Sarah whispered.

"You're his uncle," Owen said, "Josea."

"Yes. I have had many names down through the years. I am Joseph of Arimathea."

93

Sergeant Hamilton was exhausted.

He didn't think he'd ever worked as hard in his life. Madoc was a small town, with small-town crime—a little drunkenness, minor vandalism, occasional thefts and burglaries—but in the past few hours, he'd filled a month's worth of report sheets: alcohol and drugs, petty vandalism, public order offenses, assaults . . .

He was slumped at his desk when the door opened, the traditional bell jangling. "Mr. Saurin, how may I help you?" he asked, forcing a smile to his lips. As he shook the schoolteacher's hand, he wondered why he disliked the man so much. Perhaps he still had his own sneaking suspicions about Saurin's involvement in the death of his aunt, Mildred Bailey. However, Mr. Saurin was not only the local schoolteacher, he was the individual responsible for bringing the Celtic festival to the village. Responsible for bringing in hundreds of thousands of pounds to the local economy. Speaking out against the schoolteacher would only make him enemies.

Ahriman Saurin looked over Hamilton's shoulder, dark eyes taking in Fowler and lingering on Heath, who were both working at desks in the small station. He suppressed a smile as the woman squirmed visibly in her seat. "I've come to report a burglary," he said smoothly. "One of the youths down for the festival, I'm afraid. Broke into my house this morning and stole a sword and a hunting horn from my collection of antiques."

Tony Fowler immediately appeared at Hamilton's side. "I'm Detective Fowler from London. I heard you mention something about a sword."

Ahriman Saurin gave the detective his most charming smile. "Yes, a young man stole one of my antique swords and an ornate hunting horn."

"Could you give us a description?"

"A double-handed claymore, a *claidheamh mór*," Saurin said, deliberately misunderstanding the question.

"Of the suspect," Fowler said patiently.

Victoria Heath handed Fowler a photograph.

"Oh." Saurin laughed easily. "Yes, I see what you mean. There were actually two of them, a man and a woman. I got a very good look at the man, as it happens. Mid-twenties, tall, hair cut short, green eyes . . ."

Tony Fowler slid a photograph of Sarah Miller across the desk. "Was this woman with him?"

Saurin looked at the photograph and feigned surprised. "Good Lord. Why, yes, but this is remarkable, Officer. This is the young woman all right, though she's done something different with her hair. It's shorter. She was waiting outside for him. She's wearing a pink sweatshirt and tattered jeans."

"Was there anyone else with them?" Victoria asked.

"Not that I could see." He paused, before shaking his head. "No, when they were heading into the woods, they were definitely alone."

"You saw them going into the woods?"

"Yes, just over the bridge."

Tony Fowler grinned savagely. "When was this?"

"Fifteen, twenty minutes ago. I would have got down here sooner, but the traffic was dreadful," he explained.

Fowler turned to Heath, but she was already on the radio.

"If you do find them," Saurin added quickly, "could I ask you to return the two artifacts? . . ."

"They are evidence."

"I just need them for a couple of hours, just to mount an exhibition. It's crucial to the festival. You can have them back directly afterwards."

"I'm sure we can come to some arrangement, Mr. Saurin," Tony Fowler said, stretching out his hand.

Ahriman Saurin shook it warmly, taking care not to crush the detective's fingers.

94

Sarah and Owen stood at the edge of the woods and followed Ambrose's pointing finger toward the solid nineteenth-century farmhouse. "The Hallows are in there. The house is built over the remains of the ancient well."

Owen shivered and rubbed his hands against his arms and across the back of his neck. Sarah found she was clutching the sword in sweat-damp hands, and she kept glancing over her shoulder, almost as if she expected something to come charging out of the trees.

"You're feeling a tiny trickle of the power of the Hallows," Ambrose explained. "They are sealed in lead boxes warded with words of power . . . but they are still incredibly powerful. If he does not use them soon, then the Hallows will break their bonds of lead and magic."

"And then?" Sarah asked.

Ambrose shrugged. "Who knows? They are powerful enough to rip through the fabric of the myriad worlds, opening doorways into uncharted realms."

"What do you want us to do?" Sarah asked tiredly.

"You must stop him, of course." Ambrose said.

"How?" Owen asked.

"Only I can contain all of the Hallows," the old man explained. "We have to get into the house—which is guarded by more than human wards—and then remove the Hallows. The Dark Man and his companion must be slain."

"You make it sound so simple," Sarah said.

"It won't be," Ambrose promised.

THE PLAN had seemed absurdly simple.

Why should Ahriman expend his energy searching for the couple when the police had the resources to do it for him? Discovering that the police had tracked Miller to the village was an added bonus. The gods—his lips twisted bitterly—were smiling on him.

The Dark Man paused at the top of the hill and leaned on the stone wall to look down across the Mere. Stretching into the distance, the fields were ablaze with makeshift tents and colorful stalls. Flags were fluttering everywhere, and thousands of people were dressed in various macabre costumes, celebrating the festival. Some were wearing modern Halloween outfits, others were in dress inspired by movies, others in the robes they thought were traditional. Ahriman smiled; when the Demonkind came through, the humans wouldn't even recognize them.

In the distance, sounding faint and not unpleasant, bagpipe music skirled on the surprisingly balmy October air. There were visitors from all across the world: Many were from the Celtic lands—Welsh, Scots, Irish, Manx, Bretons—with more arriving hourly. Americans, Canadians, Australians. A surprisingly large contingent of Eastern Europeans had arrived during the night. He'd even seen some South African flags. There were at least one hundred and fifty thousand men, women, and children of all ages in the fields before him.

Thirteen enormous pyres were scattered in a seemingly random pattern across the landscape; only he knew that eleven of them contained straw-wrapped portions of the bodies of the Hallowed Keepers and that the fires had been arranged in a very particular order.

And when the fires blazed forth into the beckoning night sky and consumed the flesh, then he would bring the Hallows together and ceremonially shatter them, breaking the seals between the worlds and allowing the Demonkind through. The ancient ritual would bind them to him. He would be their master and they would be his to command. With them he would rule the modern world.

Ahriman looked over the fields again. He wondered if one hundred and fifty thousand souls would be enough to sate the Demonkind's ravenous appetite.

He doubted it.

95

I cannot see any alternative, can you?" Ambrose asked reasonably.

"But hundreds could be killed, thousands injured," Sarah protested.

Ambrose shrugged. "If they remain and the Dark Man activates the Hallows, then they will all die anyway. Millions will die."

"And can you do this?" Owen asked.

"Oh, I can do this . . . and more, much more," the old man promised.

"If you're so powerful, why can't you get the Hallows yourself?" Sarah demanded. "Surely you could march in there and take them?"

"The wards of power the Dark Man has ringed around the Hallows would also weaken my own special powers. I would be helpless." He shook his head quickly. "No, my place is here. I will return to the cave and wait one hour, then I will begin. When you hear my signal, you will make your way into the house, secure the Hallows, and kill the Dark Man and his servant."

"How will we get the Hallows out to you?" Sarah asked.

"Carry them," Ambrose suggested.

"I didn't think we could," Owen said doubtfully.

"Anyone can carry them, but you need to be of the bloodline of the original Keepers to *use* them properly."

"But I'm not related to Judith Walker and yet I used the sword," Sarah said.

"You are not a Hallowed Keeper," Ambrose said simply, his face impassive. "But you fed the sword, and so bonded it to you. And yes, you used it, but only to kill. The great magic of the sword, Sarah, is that it can also heal and create." The old man turned to Owen.

"You have the horn, Owen, but can you control what comes when you call? Brigid Davis could. You can do nothing with the horn, but you could work wonders with the sword, for you're of the blood of Judith Walker, and she was from the line of the original Hallowed Keepers. And let me tell you this, Owen Walker: If you go up against the Dark Man in the house, it is you who must face him with your Hallow, the sword. That is the only chance you will have, for he is a Hallowed Keeper, too."

"But what about Sarah?"

"It would be better if Sarah did not face the Dark Man," Ambrose said softly. He glanced at the young woman. "It would be better if you gave Owen the sword."

Sarah looked at the sword in her hands. Even the thought of handing it over to Owen made her break out in a cold sweat.

Ambrose shook his head in amusement and then, without warning, reached out and snatched the sword from Sarah's grasp. Blue green flames danced along the length of the blade, hissing and spitting like an angry cat. He thrust the sword into Owen's hands. "If the circumstances were different, I would tell you its history and powers. . . ."

Sarah suffered as if she'd just lost someone very close to her. She felt chilled and shaken. However, the constant pressure that had been sitting behind her temples for the past few days was suddenly gone, leaving her light-headed and dizzy.

In contrast, Owen felt himself shivering with the raw power that trickled through the sword, tingling along the length of his arms, settling into his chest and down into the pit of his belly. It seemed almost natural to hold the sword aloft in both hands, broken blade pointing through the green canopy toward the sun. Bruises faded, cuts healed, his curly hair suddenly grew back, blossomed around him in a mantle, sparkling and crackling softly.

Ambrose picked up the horn where Owen had dropped it. White light coiled around the rim of the horn's mouth. "I'll take this with me. It will help."

Owen lowered the sword, and when he looked at Ambrose, his green eyes were hard and unforgiving. "I cannot agree with what you want to do."

"Give me an alternative," Ambrose suggested.

Owen chose to ignore the question. "Tell me how you intend to panic the people into leaving."

"No," Ambrose said simply.

"People will die," Sarah protested.

"Sooner or later we all die."

96

Ahriman was putting the key in the lock when Vyvienne pulled the door open and almost dragged him inside. He was disappointed to see that she was still wearing her loose robe and hadn't bothered to get undressed.

"They're close," she whispered, face ashen with excitement.

"Who?" he asked.

"Miller and the boy. They're close, so close. I've felt them—flashes, vague impressions, nothing more—but each time they were closer to the house. I think they're coming here."

Ahriman rubbed his hands together briskly as he followed the woman up the stairs to the bedroom. Usually, he would have admired the sway of her buttocks beneath the thin cloth and fondled her as a token of his appreciation, but not today. Today, he needed all his energy for the ritual.

"Do you want me to contact the police?" Vyvienne asked.

Ahriman barked a laugh. "No. I had hoped they would capture Miller, but this is even better."

Vyvienne stood in the doorway and watched her master pull off his clothing, buttons popping in his eagerness. "I think there's a third person with them," she said quietly.

He stopped and turned to look at her. "A third person?"

"I'm not sure. It's just the way they wink in and out of the Astral, and the way the Astral itself is opaque and twisted, making it impossible to travel through, impossible to see anything in it."

Ahriman sat on the bed as he pulled off his trousers. There couldn't be anyone with them; they were strangers in a foreign land. There was no one to help them. "They are both carrying Hallows. Perhaps the combination of artifacts is shielding them from us."

"Perhaps," Vyvienne said doubtfully.

Naked, Ahriman stood and spread his arms wide, muscles creaking as he stretched, then he smiled at Vyvienne and allowed her to step into his arms. He kissed the top of her head in a rare gesture of affection. "Do you know what day this is?" he murmured.

"October thirty-first, All Hallows' Eve."

Ahriman Saurin shook his head. "This is the last day of the modern age. Soon this world will belong to me."

97

Ambrose lifted the horn to his lips.

He knew all the Hallows by heart—their names had changed through the years, but he had handled them all . . . indeed, he supposed he had chosen them all. In a more innocent time, for a more innocent reason. Quirky pieces for mercenary gain. Innocent objects, now imbued with a terrible power.

They had been created to do good, but through the ages they had always ended up touched and tainted by evil. The Sword of Dyrnwyn had been used to kill, the Knife of the Horseman used to wound, the Spear of the Dolorous Blow used to maim, the Crimson Cloak used by butchers and torturers to terrify.

It was not that the objects themselves were evil: They were merely powerful, and the powerful attracted the curious, and so many of those who set out on this path of discovery were ultimately seduced by the attractions of evil. He turned the horn over in his gnarled hands.

He would use the Horn of Bran to call the five elements. Once it would have been used in ceremonies to welcome the coming of spring or to drive off a particularly harsh winter.

He was going to use it to kill.

Many lives were about to be lost. Hundreds, possibly thousands. He could rationalize it by pretending that they had given their lives to save so many others.

The old man bent his head. If he had tears, he would have wept them, but he'd long ago forgotten how to weep. Instead, he looked at the Horn of Bran as he turned it in his hands, relishing these last few moments of the—his lips twisted at the thought—the calm before the storm.

Once, the horn had had another name, but he couldn't remember what it was. He'd bought it from an Egyptian . . . or Greek . . . No, he'd bought it from the Nubian trader who specialized in carved bones. Ambrose smiled as he remembered: That would have been two thousand years ago, and the memory of that day was as fresh as if it had just happened. He could still smell the sweat from the man, the peculiar odor of exotic spices that clung to his skin, the distinctive stink of camel that clung to his ornate robe.

Ambrose had simply admired the hunting horn for itself, a unique and beautiful piece of craftsmanship, unusual enough for him to be able to ask a good price for it. There was a Greek merchant in Tyre who had a passion for bone carvings; he would buy it, especially when Josea had spun him a suitably exotic yarn. He had intended to introduce Yeshu'a to the Greek on the return voyage from the Tin Lands, though he would have to watch the merchant, for he preferred the company of boys . . . though on reflection, he remembered that the Greek preferred his boys beautiful, and Yeshu'a could never be called that.

But Yeshu'a had taken the horn, along with all his other trade goods, and imbued them with an ancient magic. He had made them into what they were now: the Thirteen Hallows.

And now Yeshu'a was worshipped as a God, or the Son of God.

Josea wasn't sure if Yeshu'a was a god; certainly he was more than a man. Yet there was a magic in the world at that time, elder magic, powerful magic.

It had been a time of wonder.

There was little wonder left in the world in these modern times. Perhaps that was a good thing.

Lifting the horn to his lips, Ambrose drew a deep breath and blew.

98

One newspaper would later call it a freak storm.

Another claimed it was the storm of the century.

But those who were there, those who survived it, would claim that it was unnatural, as the dusky landscape radiating beautiful golds and reds changed dramatically in a matter of seconds.

Unlike the usual rumble of thunder that generally precedes a storm, there was a low, dull sound . . . almost like a trumpet or a tuba.

Or a horn.

The clouds rolled in quickly, boiling up from the south and west, flowing over the mountains in a tumbling sheet. Shadows raced across the ground, chilling everything they touched, huge drops of icy rain spattering onto the dry earth, popping off the leather tents and cloth awnings over stalls and stands. Almost as one, the festival-goers groaned aloud; it had looked as if it were going to be such a nice evening.

PADRAIG CARROLL of the Irish folk group Dandelion was climbing onstage when the sun vanished behind tumbling gray black clouds. He swore silently. This was just his luck: His first big break—he knew there were at least two record scouts in the crowd, and the BBC was recording it—and right now the concert was going to be a washout. He glanced at Shea Mason, the drummer, and raised his eyebrows in a silent question: Do we go on?

Mason nodded and grinned. He was sitting at the back of the stage under the awning. If it rained, Padraig and Maura, the lead singer, would be soaked. He would be safe.

The crowd was shifting impatiently, turning to watch the gathering storm clouds as Padraig picked up the guitar. Static howled, drowning out Maura's greeting in Irish. The guitarist stepped up to the mike and repeated the greeting in carefully rehearsed Welsh. There were whistles and cheers, and in the distance a dog howled.

"We'd like to welcome—," he began, and the lightning bolt struck him through the top of the head.

The incredible surge of power shredded his body, boiling flesh exploding, spraying slivers of cooked meat onto the front row, the guitar bursting into molten metal. The electrical charge rippled through the power lines, and the speakers erupted in balls of flames, red-hot cinders spinning out into the audience. All over the stage, power cables started to burn.

Those nearest the stage screamed, but their cries were misinterpreted by those at the back, unable to see clearly, who started to shout appreciatively and cheer for the pyrotechnics.

A second lightning strike danced over the drummer's metal kit and landed on Mason's studded leather belt, fusing it to his body. He tumbled backward into the heavy black curtain decorated with the Celtic festival logo. It wrapped itself around his body and immediately started to burn. Mason was still alive, but his screams were lost as a series of rattling lightning detonations rippled across the field, destroying people at random, blue white balls of light dancing from metal chairs and tables.

In the sudden gloom, the lightning flashes were incredibly white and intense, blinding everyone in the vicinity. The crowd panicked and ran. Then the heavens opened, and a solid deluge of rain—some of it electrically charged—immediately turned the field into a quagmire.

A three-hundred-year-old oak split down the middle, burying twenty people beneath its branches. A silver jewelry stall exploded, shards of red-hot metal hissing out into the crowd. A falafel stand took a direct hit, the gas cylinder detonating in a solid ball of flame, spraying long streamers of grease and hot fat in every direction.

Those who fell were crushed underfoot.

And above the screams of pain and terror, the lightning cracks and the rolling continuous thunder, no one heard the sound of a hunting horn and the triumphant howling of savage beasts.

TONY FOWLER watched lightning dance down Madoc's main street, skipping from metal to metal, reducing cars to blackened ruin, wrapping ancient lampposts in writhing fiery worms. A manhole melted to smoldering slag, and Fowler turned away as a young man ran straight into the seething mess.

"Everything's dead," Victoria Heath said numbly. "Phones, radio, power."

The detective turned back to the window. "Dear God, what's happening?" he whispered. The street was a heaving mass of humanity. He saw two men kick open the door of a house opposite and push their way past the old woman who appeared in the hallway. A score of people ran into the hall, trampling the woman underfoot in a desperate attempt to escape the lightning. Thunder boomed directly overhead, shaking the entire building, lead tiles sliding off the roof to shatter in the street. A young woman went down, a rectangular tile protruding from her throat; the youth who tried to help her collapsed as another dozen tiles rained down on top of him.

In his long career in the police force, Tony Fowler had known fear on many occasions: his first night on the beat, the first time he had faced an armed assailant, the first time he had stood at a murder scene, the first time he had stared into the pitiless eyes of a killer. But time had dulled that emotion, and lately he had been feeling only the terrible anger of the victims. That anger had driven him to hunt down evil people like Miller who could kill and maim without compunction. In the last few years, Fowler had found he had been able to strike back at these people without reservation, treating them as they had treated their victims.

But Tony Fowler felt fear now, the cold, empty fear the rational mind experiences when faced by the unnatural. He was turning away from the window to face Victoria Heath when light blossomed in the street directly outside the window. The glass exploded inward. There was no pain, only an incredible noise and heat, followed by complete silence. He caught a brief glimpse of a tiny red-speckled pattern appearing on Victoria Heath's white blouse . . . funny, he couldn't remember a pattern. The pattern appeared on her face . . . bloodred slivers of torn flesh. He watched her fall . . . and then the pain and the noise came.

99

Vyvienne jerked and twitched with every peal of thunder, every lightning flash. The room was in almost total darkness, but the white light silhouetted Ahriman Saurin against the window, naked flesh white and stark. In the distance they could hear screams and explosions, and the fields below the house were speckled with fires.

"What time is it?" Ahriman asked numbly.

"Five, six . . . I'm not sure." She was standing close enough to feel the chill radiating from his body.

"Looks like twilight," he said absently. "It can't be natural."

"I don't know. I can feel the Hallows buzzing below us, flooding the Astral with light. I'm blind there."

Ahriman watched as one of the carefully prepared pyres in the distance burst into flame, long streamers of light flowing up off the oil-soaked wood. Burning figures whirled away from it. Spinning away from the window, he caught Vyvienne by the arm. "We can't wait any longer. We've got to use the Hallows now!"

"But the missing two—"

"We don't have a choice," he said savagely. "We have eleven of the thirteen. If we break enough of the locks, then the Demonkind may be able to force their way through."

"It's too risky," Vyvienne said. "The storm isn't natural. Someone—someone powerful—has called it. And that sort of magic, elemental magic, is one of the oldest in the world. Something's out there, something old."

"I've waited too long for this." Lightning washed his face bone white and shadow. "The bonfires will burn, taking the last of the Hallowed Keepers, while the people—the sacrifices—are fleeing. We will never have this chance again. I'm using the Hallows now!"

Vyvienne bowed her head. And because she loved him, she put her hand in Ahriman Saurin's and allowed him to lead her down the stairs.

She allowed him to lay her down on the pentagram in the middle of the sacred Hallows.

And she allowed herself to enjoy one last kiss before he sliced her body open and peeled back her skin.

100

"What the fuck does he think he's doing?" Sarah's voice was high and shrill. "It sounds like a war zone."

Owen ignored her. His eyes were fixed on the farmhouse directly in front of them. With the sword clutched in both hands, he felt so confident, so assured. He was aware of the thunder and lightning booming and crashing over the village—and only over the village. The fields below were awash beneath a torrential downpour, but the effect was particularly localized, and although they were less than two hundred yards away, there was no rain here.

Moving stealthily forward, Owen could actually feel the presence of the Hallows buzzing in the air around him. There were whispers that were almost words, snatches of what might have been song, but faint, indistinct, ethereal. But he could tell that they were calling, calling, calling. The Hallows were alive: They were trapped and in pain.

"They're here," he said simply. "Belowground."

Sarah didn't ask how he knew; she was feeling the loss of the sword like a missing limb. While she'd held it, she'd felt so confident, so assured . . . but now . . . now she wasn't sure what she felt anymore.

The farmhouse was in darkness, no lights showing within. The couple crept across a cobbled courtyard, keeping to the shadows, looking for an open window, but the house was locked up tight, and heavy drapes covered the lower windows. They completed a circuit around the house and returned to the kitchen door.

The thunder and lightning had stopped booming and crashing over the village, and now the screams of the injured echoed across the still air. Car and house alarms were ringing everywhere, and the stench of bitter smoke was replacing the acrid ozone in the air. The air smelled of burned meat.

Owen reached out and touched the door handle. Green fire spat, and he snatched his hand back with a hiss of pain. In the gloom, they could see the blisters forming on his fingertips.

"Ambrose said that the place would be guarded by more than human wards," Sarah reminded him. "Some sort of magical protection."

Holding the sword in his left hand, Owen stretched out and pressed the broken end against the door. Green fire danced over the blade, which came alive with cold white light. Then the light flowed out of the sword and raced across the door, outlining it in a tracery of white. Glass exploded inward, and the handle started bubbling, the metal running liquid down the scarred wood. Sarah caught Owen's arm and dragged him away as the door went crashing inward, liquid metal from the hinges puddling on the tiled kitchen floor.

"I have a feeling they know we're here."

SITTING NAKED in the center of the perfect circle, Ahriman gradually opened himself up to the power of the Hallows, first absorbing the trickle of power, allowing it to seep into his flesh, settle into his bones. Images flickered and twisted behind his closed eyes. Power from the burning bonfires flowed into him, the last tendrils of life of the original Hallowed Keepers floating through the air in billows of smoke. Touching him.

He was unaware of the couple upstairs. He was conscious only of the ritual he had practiced every day for ten years, only this time he was doing it for real.

Ahriman Saurin's hands worked on the floor, brushing back the light dusting of earth to reveal a metal door set into the ground. The door was circular, of old metal, studded with great square-headed rivets set into a frame of massive rough stone blocks. The rust-stained doorway was inset with thirteen huge keyholes. Shapes flickered behind the keyholes. Two thousand years previously, Yeshu'a had banished the Demonkind and sealed their doorway. Yeshu'a and his world were long gone, but the demons remained.

Ahriman Saurin reached for the first lead box.

A solid beam of cold white light lanced upward, blinding him, flooding the room with the scents of a thousand Thoroughbred horses. He reached in and lifted out the Halter of Clyno Eiddyn, allowing the leather to fold open, the rich skin hissing and whispering softly. He picked up the first Hallow—in the Astral, the darkness folded over the light—and began to rip apart the ancient material, destroying it.

A gossamer key appeared in the topmost lock—and turned with a rasping click.

IN HIS green cave, Ambrose staggered, pressing his hand to the center of his chest. He felt as if he'd been stabbed. One of the Hallows had just been destroyed. But there was nothing he could do except wait . . . and listen to the screams of the dying and injured.

"Hurry," he whispered in the lost language of his youth. "Hurry."

SARAH STOOD at the bottom of the stairs and looked up into the gloom. She was freezing—the building radiated a greasy chill—and she wanted to turn and run but knew that she could not. The house was silent and empty. Arcane symbols had been carved into the wood above the doorways, and the windowsills were also incised with the curious designs.

She had felt an almost overpowering desire to stretch out and trace one of the twisting patterns, and she had actually been reaching for it when Owen had touched the flesh of her hand with the flat of the sword. The snap of cold metal brought her alert again, and she realized that she'd been mesmerized by the twisting Celtic spiral, tracing it to a nonexistent center.

"More of the Dark Man's wards," Owen said, "designed to ensnare."

He had changed since he'd taken the sword, subtle, almost imperceptible changes in both posture and attitude. He looked taller, the skin on his cheeks was tighter, emphasizing the bones, and he acted with absolute confidence. Remembering how she had felt, Sarah found herself envying him. She wanted the sword—*her* sword. "Down here," he said, reaching out to touch the handle of the cellar door with the tip of the Broken Sword. The door frame came alive with a tracery of fire, scorching the wood, searing away the symbols.

"I don't think we should—" Sarah began.

"They're down there," Owen said simply. The sword was trembling in his hands, vibrating softly as he pushed at the door. It fell off its hinges and clattered down the steps.

AHRIMAN WAS deaf to the world.

He was deeply engrossed in the ritual, transferring the energy from the Hallows, now augmented by the burning flesh of the Hallowed Keepers, into the locks of the metal door.

His hands reached blindly for a second box and opened it.

Again the white light flowed up but was almost immediately extinguished as Ahriman's large hands closed over it. The Pan of Rhygenydd, perpetually filled with dark blood, crumpled beneath his powerful grip, spraying his naked flesh with crimson. He folded its companion piece, the Platter of Rhygenydd, over and over in his fingers, finally snapping it into four quarters.

Another key formed and turned in the lock. Something hit the metal door, a single blow from below, the sound deep and booming, echoing around the small chamber.

THE SMELL at the bottom of the stairs was indescribable. Old and long dead, the ripe foulness hung in the air in a solid miasma. Sarah and Owen knew it was a body—or bodies—and both were suddenly glad that the light didn't work. With Sarah's hand on his shoulder, Owen walked forward. He felt as if he were leaning into an unfelt breeze; he could feel the Hallows' power washing over him, his clothes heavy and irritating where they rested against his flesh. The air itself had become thick, soupy, making every breath an effort, drying the moisture in his eyes, mouth, and throat until he felt as if he were breathing sand.

And then the Broken Sword flashed alight, burning away the stale air, blue white light bathing the corridor in harsh shadows, illuminating the iron-studded wooden door directly ahead.

Owen darted forward, his grin feral.

FIVE LOCKS were broken now.

Ahriman concentrated on opening the sixth seal, but the pounding of the demons on the far side was incredible, the noise deafening as they hammered on the metal, howling and screeching, rocking the door on its hinges, disturbing his concentration. Hooked claws kept appearing in the openings, and the door was visibly straining upward, metal bulging where the locks had been turned.

The Dark Man was tiring.

The incredible effort of will was draining him, leeching the energy from his body, and the arcane occult formula that he needed to keep crisp and clear was beginning to shift and blur in his head. He was aware that the Demonkind were trying frantically to push open the door and that the ancient metal was shivering in its stone frame . . . but he knew that he should be aware of nothing. Any lapse of concentration would be worse than fatal, for Ahriman knew that death was not the end, and this close to the demon realm there was every possibility that his spirit would be sucked into that place, to suffer an eternity of suffering.

Holding the sixth Hallow—The Whetstone of Tudwal Tudglyd—in his hands, he squeezed it. The ancient granite stone should have snapped and burst, but nothing happened. Leaning forward, he pressed his left hand, palm down, on the shivering metal door. "Give me strength," he prayed. "Give me strength."

Noise and movement on the other side of the door ceased . . . and then the answer flowed up his arm.

AMBROSE WAS dying; he knew that now. With every Hallow the Dark Man destroyed, he killed a little more of the one-eyed old man. There was blood on his lips, a tracery of veins visible in his eye. He had felt the destruction of the five Hallows as physical blows, had seen the shadows swallow the light, and for the first time in two thousand years he felt the terrible despair of the truly lost. So it had all been for nothing, all those deaths he had caused, and now Sarah and Owen were probably dead, too.

He had a sudden flash of the whetstone crumbling in Ahriman's fingers, turning to powder and grit, and saw the key turn in the sixth lock.

They had waited so long for this.

The legends of their own kind spoke to them of a time when they had walked in the World of Men and feasted off the delicacy known as flesh. There were stories too of those who had escaped through other hidden or temporary doors, bridges, and portals.

But now the time of waiting was over.

Six of the burning locks that sealed the door between the planes of existence had been turned.

Odors, rich and meat and salt and full of possibilities and opportunities, flooded through the tiny cracks, driving those nearest the opening into a frenzy.

tanding before the iron-studded wooden door, Owen gripped the Broken Sword in both hands and squared his shoulders.

"What's the plan?" Sarah whispered.

"There is no plan," Owen said. He reached forward and touched the end of the Broken Sword against the door. The metal studs hissed and bubbled, and then the wood dissolved into fine dust.

As Sarah followed Owen through the opening, she could have sworn that his skin shimmered with metallic highlights.

The tiny room was an abattoir.

A dark naked man crouched in the center of the room, straddling a butchered body. Much of the face was missing, the teeth marks on the chin and edges of the jaw, where flesh remained, looked like human bites. The Dark Man's face, neck, and chest were covered in thick blood.

Vyvienne's torso had been opened from throat to crotch, the skin pulled back to reveal the curve of ribs and internal organs. The remaining Hallows were lying on the woman's body, thick with gore.

Ahriman Saurin twisted his head to look at the pair in the doorway. His savage smile was appalling, fresh with the meaty blood from Vyvienne's carcass.

"Good of you to bring me the sword," he hissed, and plunged the Hallow—a tiny intricate carving of the Chariot of Morgan—into the gaping wound in the body below him, bathing it in blood and fluids. When he lifted it out, he crumpled it in his hands to a shapeless mass.

Owen and Sarah both heard the click and snap of a lock, and then the butchered body shifted upward slightly. They saw now that she had been laid across a metal manhole that was black with blood. The metal doorway jerked, straining upward, and a gnarled black tongue slithered in the opening, lapping at the blood.

"Too late," Ahriman Saurin hissed.

Owen felt the sword move, twist of its own accord, and suddenly he was moving forward, the weapon gripped in both hands, keeping the sword low and to the left, bringing it up—

Ahriman jerked up the closest Hallow and shook it out. Owen caught a glimpse of fur, a stag's head complete with antlers, in the instant before the sword struck it, sparks in the air. "Behold the Mantle of Arthur!" The Dark Man straightened and spun the cloak about his shoulders, settling the antlered hood onto his head. Saurin's left hand shot out and caught the sword blade in an explosion of green white fire.

Owen tried to pull it back, but it was caught fast.

The hammering beneath the round metal cover was deafening, demanding.

"My subjects hunger," Ahriman whispered. He tugged at the sword, and Owen felt it slide from his grasp. "The sword is the most powerful of all the keys. If I open its lock, I won't need to use the others." He tugged at the sword again, almost wrenching it from Owen's hands. "You should be honored: The beasts will feast on you first."

"No . . ." Owen tried to pull back.

"Yes." Ahriman jerked him forward.

He was going to lose the sword, Sarah realized. And once the Dark Man had the sword, then the world would end. . . .

And from the darkness, Sarah flung herself at Owen, hitting him high on the shoulders, pushing him forward, and driving him *into* Ahriman's arms. Owen was still clutching the sword, and the sudden blow sent it slamming forward, the metal blade scoring down Ahriman's hands, the broken point of the weapon plunging into his chest, sliding off his ribs as it simultaneously ruptured his lungs and heart.

Ahriman looked at the sword, and then his eyes widened as the sword began to glow and burn, and Owen stepped forward and turned the blade full circle before jerking it free. Cold white light blossomed in Ahriman's eyes. His mouth widened and he tried to speak but could form no words. His chest heaved and then he vomited white fire.

The sudden explosion of light threw Owen and Sarah back into the hall, out of the circular room, which now throbbed with the fire lancing from Ahriman's body. He stood, arms outstretched, crucified by the light. Cold fire washed over the lead boxes, melting them, exposing the artifacts within. Flames spat and hissed, and then one by one the Hallows came to brief, incandescent life, flooding the room with rainbow colors.

For a moment, the two magics—dark and light—warred.

It lasted less than a heartbeat, and then the room was plunged into total darkness.

In the long silence that followed, the crack and snap of the settling foundations was deafening. Stones grated, earth rumbled, and then a shaft of light appeared in the blackened room, a solid beam, circling slowly over the ancient well, the gateway to the Otherworld.

Owen and Sarah crawled to the doorway and peered inside, blinking in the light. The bodies of Ahriman Saurin and Vyvienne had vanished; nothing remained to mark their presence. The Broken Sword, its blade now shining silver and complete, lay on the floor atop the Mantle of Arthur.

The ancient door in the floor had been fused into the stone, the keyholes sealed with white glass.

103

It took them a moment to realize that the tiny wizened creature lying slumped in the stone chair was Ambrose.

Sarah and Owen knelt before him and spread the remaining Hallows next to the Horn of Bran: the Mantle of Arthur, the Chessboard of Gwenddolau, the Knife of the Horseman, the Crimson Cloak of Feathers, and Dyrnwyn, the Sword That Is Broken.

"These were all we could save." Owen brushed strands of hair off the old man's forehead. His skin was so fragile and translucent that the bones and ridges of wasted muscle could be seen clearly beneath it.

Ambrose straightened with effort and touched each in turn with trembling fingers, seeing them for what they were, remembering what they had once been. "It is enough," he whispered.

"We've won," Sarah said encouragingly.

"For now."

"What about the Hallows?" Owen asked. "What do we do with them?"

"You must travel to the New World to find new Keepers."

"The New World?" Owen questioned.

"America," the old man answered.

"Me?" he asked.

"No . . ." Ambrose's lips curled back from his yellowed teeth in a parody a smile. "You," he said, looking at Sarah. "You are of the line of Joseph of Arimathea." Brittle, dry fingers touched her flesh. "You are my descendant, Sarah, and you will take up my mantle."

"I cannot."

"I uttered the same words. You have no choice. Take the remaining Hallows and return them to their rightful owners. You will know them when you find them."

"But I don't know what to do!" she protested.

"There is only one rule: The Hallows must never be brought together. Everything else will come in time." With his last breath, he added, "Go to America. It is your responsibility now."

It took them several moments before they realized that Ambrose was dead.

FREAK STORM KILLS HUNDREDS

The freak storm that struck the west coast yesterday has now claimed 622 lives. Most of the victims were visitors to The First International All Hallows' Eve Celtic Festival of Arts and Culture, which was being held in Madoc, in Wales. Meteorologists are still puzzled why the massive depression didn't appear on their radars. The 9,000 injured are being cared for in a number of hospitals, including . . .

SUSPECT BELIEVED KILLED

Police believe a woman they wanted to interview in connection with a series of brutal murders in the capital was one of the victims of the Madoc disaster. Although the body in question is too badly burned to make a proper identification, it is hoped that forensics will provide the answers.

POLICE MOURN OFFICER

One of the victims of the Madoc catastrophe, Detective Anthony Fowler, was laid to rest today. His partner, Sergeant Victoria Heath, is undergoing surgery at St. Francis Hospital, where she is expected to make a full recovery. No other details were immediately available.

Epilogue

The young couple with the oversize backpacks standing in the immigration line in LAX looked similar to most twenty-somethings coming home after a European tour. They could easily be mistaken for students returning, exhausted and grungy, from a European vacation.

Yet unlike the students from Stanford to their left whose suitcases were filled with first-edition poetry from the Cotswolds or the goth couple to their right whose bags were overloaded with tchotchkes like little black taxicabs and miniature statues of the Tower of London, this pair carried luggage that contained far more precious cargo. According to their passports they were recently married, Sarah and Owen Walker, returning from their honeymoon in England. The blue customs form listed the items they were bringing into the country: a horn, a red-feathered cloak, a dark leather cloak, a knife, a chess-board, and a sword.

All of the items were listed as "curios" and were "of no commercial value."

AUTHOR'S NOTE

Most of the Hallows mentioned in this novel still exist, as do the group of people known as the Hallowed Keepers.

In the Otherworld, behind a door of glass and wood and stone, the legion waited.

Patiently.

They had many allies in the New World, and the couple had none.